Frederick Metcalfe

The Oxonian in Iceland

With Glances at Icelandic Folk-Lore and sagas

SALZWASSER
VERLAG

Frederick Metcalfe

The Oxonian in Iceland

With Glances at Icelandic Folk-Lore and sagas

1st Edition | ISBN: 978-3-75253-407-8

Place of Publication: Frankfurt am Main, Germany

Year of Publication: 2021

Salzwasser Verlag GmbH, Germany.

Reprint of the original, first published in 1867.

THE

OXONIAN IN ICELAND.

THE OXONIAN

IN

ICELAND.

WITH GLANCES AT

ICELANDIC FOLK-LORE AND SAGAS.

BY THE

REV. FREDERICK METCALFE, M.A.,

AUTHOR OF

"THE OXONIAN IN NORWAY," &c.

CHEAP EDITION.

LONDON:

JOHN CAMDEN HOTTEN, PICCADILLY.

1867.

PREFACE.

"GOOD wine needs no bush" is an old and true proverb. What a bush is to a wine-shop, a Preface often is to a book—a mere puff preliminary touting for readers, or an apology for shortcomings on the part of the purveyor for the public. This being the author's view of the matter, he will eschew a long preamble. He will neither magnify what is good, nor extenuate what is bad in the volume. If the excellent public take a look in, they will soon discern whether the article offered to them is on the whole worthy of their patronage. The thing must tell its own tale.

The Sportsman, the Member of the Alpine Club, the Botanist, the Geologist, the Ethnologist, the Historian, will be able to judge for themselves, by inspection, whether there is aught here likely to gratify their individual tastes. One thing must be said which does not appear in the body of the work. The interior of Iceland has not been penetrated since 1815, when Henderson, who travelled for the British and Foreign Bible Society, besides taking a circuit of the island, crossed and recrossed it more than once. The author, however, visited some parts which even he did not see. Of other British travellers, all have confined themselves to the South-West and West, with Thingvalla and the Geysers.

One reason for this neglect of a very interesting corner of Europe by the most gadding nation in the world, is doubtless, that, until recently, it was a region difficult of access. To brave the North Atlantic in a yacht, a man required more than a usual supply of *æs triplex circum pectus*. And when a traveller did at length set foot in the country, the prospect was, and is even at the present day, by no means cheering. A people speaking a language unknown to the rest of Europe; abiding for the most part in dark caverns of dwellings, anything but attractive to a Briton, and so sparse in number that you must traverse three square miles on an average to find a couple of them. While, as if to mock the foreigner for his infatuation, his way is beset, not only by dangerous rivers, appalling lava streams, hidden pits of fire, and chasms of ice, but his imagination is tortured by chimeras dire, phantom gorillas, or by whatever name he may please to call the shapes in stone and slag, that grin and frown at him on his solitary journey.

It only remains to say, that the legends in the following pages were partly collected by the author from the mouths of the natives; partly are taken from a little work called 'Islenzk Æfintyri,' by Messrs. Grimsen and Arnasen, published at Reykjavik; partly are due to Professor Maurer's valuable work 'Isländische Volkssagen der Gegenwart,' Leipzig, 1860.

OXFORD, *July*, 1861.

CONTENTS.

CHAPTER I.

CHAPTER II.

CHAPTER III.

CHAPTER IV.

CHAPTER V.

CHAPTER VI.

CHAPTER VII.

CHAPTER VIII.

CHAPTER IX.

CHAPTER X.

CHAPTER XI.

CHAPTER XII.

CHAPTER XIII.

CHAPTER XIV.

CHAPTER XV.

CHAPTER XVI.

CHAPTER XVII.

CHAPTER XVIII.

CHAPTER XIX.

CHAPTER XX.

CHAPTER XXI.

CHAPTER XXII.

CHAPTER XXIII.

CHAPTER XXIV.

CHAPTER XXV.

CONCLUDING CHAPTER.

THE OXONIAN IN ICELAND.

CHAPTER I.

A Times' Advertisement—The Edda reader—Appliances for Icelandic Travel—Scenes of the Sagas—The two wives—Why Iceland is so interesting to an Englishman—The learned Professor—The doctors disagree—Surturbrand—The Clyde-built screw—Spanish Waves—"She went down man and mouse"—Dining on the narrow gauge—The Faroëse judge—The Fauna of the Faroes—Pied Ravens—How to subsist in a famine.

"The screw-steamer Arcturus with the royal mails will sail for Iceland, from Grangemouth, on Saturday the 16th of July." Such was the advertisement which I read out from the Times' newspaper to the party assembled at the breakfast-table, about a week before that date. "The very thing! How fortunate! Now you must go!" exclaimed *A.*: "Perhaps you will never have so good an opportunity again of visiting a country, which, I know, you are longing to see."

"Well, if you do go," interposed the fair *B.*, who had of late been deep in the grandly grotesque legends of the deities of the Northern Olympus, "you ought to have a temporary loan of that horse Hofvarpnir; who could ride alike through air and water; for you will never be able to make your way through the bogs and lava, and ice and snow; not to mention those furious bridgeless rivers, which, you know, the Copenhagen people affirm are bigger than ordinary this year in consequence of the severe winter and late spring."

"Or, perhaps, Sleipnir, with his six legs, would do as well," I put in maliciously: "With Hermod the Nimble, you remember, on his back, he sprang over the gates of Hel. And, if I must walk over those horrible conglomerates of palagonite and pitch-stone, tufa and trachyte, it would not be amiss to have the refusal of those heavy shoes of Vidar, son of Odin."

"Granted that you can get over the ground, how are you to exist? Starvation will stare you in the face, till you will reflect her image in every bone, and the very ravens will despise you. I have it. You must procure some of the flesh of Saerímnir, the wild boar of Valhalla; you remember, what was cut off for food in the day, renewed itself during the night."

"To be sure! but you have forgotten Thor's goats, which were first flayed and then done to a turn, and rose Phœnix-like from their ashes, or rather bare bones, in the morning."

"Goat's flesh forsooth! as if an Englishman can

travel on goat's flesh; No, No. How stupid of me to forget. What you really ought to have is that wonder-working tablecloth in the Norse story. Have you forgotten, 'Cloth, spread yourself, and serve up all manner of good things'?"

"A truce to these fancies," rejoined *A.* "I shall pack you up a nice box of ham and tongue and cheese and biscuit; and your rod and gun will supply the rest. Coffee, we have heard, is to be had everywhere in Iceland; very good too, with sugar-candy and ewe-milk cream, and those delectable skier—Mind you bring me back a recipe for making that dish—I am sure it must be quite equal to anything that Devonshire dairies can produce. What I want you to visit Iceland for, is, to see with your own eyes the spots we have been reading of in the Sagas. You must visit Hlidarendë, where that peerless, noble hearted, Gunnar lived, and Bergthorshvoll, where wise old Niál was burnt, house and family and all, by those stern incendiaries. It made me shudder when you read the tale."

"Ay! and what a contrast between the characters of their two wives! Bergthora, you remember, had the offer made her of being allowed to come forth scatheless from the flames, if she would; but she preferred to die with Niál. Yet she was a Christian, and no superstitious Hindoo; while the proud Halgerda, with her thief's eyes, who might have saved the princely Gunnar, if she would have woven him a fresh bowstring from her hair, she would not; and so his enemies stormed his dwelling, and overpowered him with numbers."

"Yes," continued *A.*, "and you must see Drangö, the island-fastness of that Wallace Wight of Iceland, Gretti the strong, and the place where Olaf the Peacock lived in such state, and Patricksfiord, called after the Hebridean bishop of that name, by a disciple of his, who landed with book and bell long before the heathen Norskmen came and colonized the country."

"Norskmen!" ejaculated I, "do you know I have great doubts of the accuracy of that romantic tale about the first colonizers of Iceland; which makes Harald the Fairhaired conquer the petty kings of Norway at Hafursfiord, upon which they take ship, the Mayflower of the day, and bolt straight to Iceland, the prototypes of the pilgrim fathers. Such is the generally received account of the Scandinavian Exodus. Recent research, however, shews that the above can only be true to a certain extent; but while it, in some degree, spoils the romance, it gives Iceland a fresh and peculiar interest in the eyes of an Englishman. You are quite right about the missionaries. There is sufficient evidence to prove that Ireland and the British Isles did send Papar to Shetland, and the Faroes and Iceland, before Harald the Fairhaired was born or thought of; but what if Britain supplied a large portion of the *second* wave of colonists also. We find from Landnamabok,—the Icelandic Domesday Book,—that of the settlers who divided the whole island among them, the greatest and most powerful sailed from the Western Islands and Ireland. Why, that very Niál you mentioned was of Gaelic extraction. His name betokens it. While Halgerda's slave Maelkolfr,—the namesake of a Scotch king of that time—was nothing but Malcolm an Irish captive. Yes! I verily believe that these people of Iceland are many of them bone of our bone and flesh of our flesh: and if you wish for an authority for the surmise, let me quote you the words of the most learned Norwegian of the present day, Prof. Munk*: 'to the Icelanders, therefore, the Western Islands of Scotland—as in a certain degree the chief cradle of their race, even more than the mother country, Norway, itself—ought to be of peculiar interest, and are even to be looked upon by them with a sort of filial piety: and therefore, of course, unless we have a surplus of the stepmother in our composition, Iceland must be regarded by Britons with a sort of parental affection.'"

"But you are losing sight of the most interest-

* Since the above was written, Mr. Dasent, in the Preface to his admirable version of 'Burnt Nial,' has shewn, that a good half of the settlers started for Iceland from the British isles; a country which was made the stepping-stone, in fact, between Norway and Iceland.

ing subject connected with that country," broke in a distinguished member of the British Association, then holding court at Oxford, and shaken through all its strata, primary, secondary, and tertiary, by the disputes of the believers in Darwin and Moses respectively: the one party—with an energy only second to that of those inhabitants of Ombos—luxuriating in the idea of being nothing but atoms, and the descendants of crocodiles—I mean apes; the other, with the fury of a Tentyrite, indignantly repudiating the atomic theory, and triumphantly pointing to Adam and the animals filing past him, as completely demolishing the 'Natural Selection' theory. "If," continued Professor Megatherion, "you do imitate that worthy friar of Oxford, Nicholas de Lyn, and go to Iceland; pray try and obtain some fresh light on that vexed question, whether the upheaval of the trap, one of those doleritic formations, which pass into the most diversified amygdaloids, marks the third or fourth period of Iceland's volcanic activity. Then again, you know, (I'm. sure, I didn't,) Bunsen thinks that palagonite is the foundation of the whole island, while, according to Sartorius von Waltershausen, the palagonite consists entirely of submarine lavas, or of ashes modified by the influence of water. Then, you see, with regard to the Surturbrand, Steenstrup says it is composed of driftwood, while another great authority, I think Professor Silliman, says it is not drift-wood, but stratified forests, buried by submarine volcanic eruptions of ashes. For my part, I am inclined to think that those Icelandic eruptions, generally, proceed from the oxidation of the metallic bases in vast subterranean laboratories rather than from the general fusion of the earth's nucleus." After taking breath, he returned to the charge—"Then, again, the boiling springs, where does the hot water come from, from the earth's inside—its intestines I might say, or from its surface—skin, so to speak?"

"And don't forget," interrupted the Edda reader impatiently, when you get to the Geysirs, to ascertain whether it is true that the Great Geysir is gradually choking up its windpipe — excuse me, water-pipe — with silicious sinter, and is in a fair way of perishing by diptheria."

July the 14th found me at Grangemouth in the Frith of Forth, and on board the Arcturus, a Clyde-built screw, of only 230 tons register, and 60 horse power. I was a day too soon, after all, in spite of the agent's asservations about the boat's punctuality in coming from Copenhagen. The captain and crew are Danes: the engineers Scotchmen. I am glad to find that she behaves very well in a heavy sea, for she looks a mere cockleshell to venture over the North Atlantic's 'Spanish waves.' These heavy swells begin north of Shetland, and take their name from their Spanish gravity, or because it was over this sea that the Spaniards first went to America. Or perhaps, the reader will supply a better etymology. The boat belongs chiefly to a Scotch gentleman, the owner of a mercantile establishment in the North of Iceland. The Danish government guarantee him 6000 dollars yearly for six years, (two of which are expired,) besides having advanced 30,000 dollars for her purchase, taking interest for the outlay at 4 per cent. She makes six voyages a-year, the first in March, the last in October. It was high time that a steamer should be put on this terrible vovage. Ship after ship had been wrecked, and many a valuable scientific collection of natural curiosities for the Danish government had been swallowed up by the ravenous ocean. Take the case of the packet before this, Sea-Lion, Sölöven, she put to sea from Reykiavik one stormy autumn-day. That night shrieks were heard by some peasants on the shores of the Faxe Fiord; a horse came on shore still warm, and that was all with an approach to life in it, that ever was found. "She went down, Sir, man and mouse," said an Icelandic Candidatus Juris, on his way home to his native volcanoes and cinder heaps; which he infinitely prefers, he tells me, to the smoke of Copenhagen or even the green flats of Denmark. In short, he is a bird of the same feather as all his countrymen; they must after a time wing their way back to Iceland, "hinn besta land sem solinn skinnar uppâ" (the best land upon which the sun shines). One of their most popular poets has given expression in some good verse to this *heimveh*, which attacks them after a time.

But, bless me! we hove the anchor half an hour ago, and I was already in imagination *en route* for a new country—a new pleasure!—and here we are still hugging the muddy flats about Grangemouth. Hard aground, and a falling tide. A hawser, and the engine reversed with full steam on, get us out of our difficulty. Arthur's seat, Berrick Law *, and the Bass rock are soon behind, in spite of 80 tons of coal on deck for Captain Allen Young of the 'Fox,' who is expected shortly at Reykjavik on the North Atlantic Telegraph expedition.

Fair Isle, whilome the winter quarters of the Ducal Armada Captain, raises itself from the placidly gleaming sea, in the afternoon of the next day, and at 9 P. M. Foula's stately headland is 12 miles to starboard, and the vessel lunging about in a nasty swell, the lees of a N. W. gale. But, at all events, that is better than the gale itself. Our plates and dishes are henceforward confined in a straitwaistcoat. In other words, three narrow-gauge lines of rails traverse the table. The motion of the

* It is a mistake to suppose that the local term, 'Law' in Scotland is to be referred to the Lögberg (law hill) of Iceland. This word 'Law' comes from the A. S. 'hleo,' or 'hleaw,' and means merely 'hill.' In English it has gone into 'low,' as a termination, as Bas*low*, Brink*low*, &c.

vessel reminds me vividly of the swing at the village fair I had once when a boy the hardihood to enter into. The bell sounds to meals as loud as ever, but few seem to hear it. That young Scotch philosopher is nowhere to be seen, and no wonder; he is constantly devouring lollipops, and before the end of the voyage he tells me in confidence that he has eaten 5 lbs. avoirdupois of sugar stuff. The Sörenskriver, or chief judge, of the Faroes is on board in uniform. The poor man has lost his young wife, and is returning to his desolate home at Thorshaven, with his mother. "My family happiness is all over now," said he, "I must get back to Denmark as soon as possible."

I obtain from him some information about the Fauna of the Faroes, which will serve us perhaps to beguile the monotony of the voyage. Its lingclad hills are without ptarmigan, although apparently well suited to the habits of that bird. A few pairs were brought from Iceland by the steamer, but they did not survive the second day of the voyage. The attempt to naturalize hares has succeeded better. A few were brought and turned out in Stromö, the island on which the capital stands, and they have now become so plentiful, that last winter they were sold for five pence a-piece. One that I saw was nearly the colour of a rabbit. In winter they are white. They will now be introduced into the other islands. In summer, they keep to the mountain heaths, but in winter approach the farms near the sea. On the Sörenskriver's official farm are some lakes into which he is going to introduce perch and carp from Denmark. There are fine trout in several of the lakes; some of which are of considerable size; one in Sandö is four miles long. Snowy owls are not uncommon in the islands, and pied ravens (Corvus Leucophoeus), which are supposed to be a variety and not a distinct species, are frequent. At Laxen, two black ravens had among their progeny some which were dappled largely with white. White, as the Northmen will tell you, was the original colour of these birds; they were turned black for babbling.

On the Sörenskriver's property there is a Giov, or narrow creek, into which a whale once took it into his head to insinuate itself. All went on swimmingly with the monster, till he arrived at the terminus; where not being able to 'back astarn,' and not having elbow room, to turn himself, he was fairly trapped, and met with the fate of a whale who was involved in similar difficulties in the holes of Skraedda on the mainland of Shetland. In the Faroes, the flesh of the whale often does duty for beef, being like it in taste, and has many a time proved an antidote to famine: while dried holibut supplies the place of bread. It is indeed well that the sea does such great things for these poor people, for if they looked to the land it would often be perplexity, as far as satisfying hunger goes. This year, for instance, the winter has been compared to that of 1816 for severity; and the consequence is that numbers of sheep have perished. Most of them, I believe, by dropsy and colic from ravenously devouring, in their skeleton state, the fresh spring-grass. A similar disease is well known in Iceland.

CHAPTER II.

Tell in the North Atlantic—Storied rocks—A gorgeous vision—The unfortunate Olë—The murder of Bresteson, prince of the Faroës—Needle's-eye cave—Thorshaven Roads—A gang of convicts—Absence of female beauty—Description of Thorshaven—Popery at a discount—Excursion across the mountains—Contents of the game-bag—The ruins of Kirkubö church—A fragment of the true Cross—Ribbaldi—Zeolites and Opals—The governor's garden—No Pharos in the Faros.

ANOTHER of our voyagers is a young Faroëse student, returning home after a six years' absence, having finished his studies at the University of Copenhagen. He tells me, the peasants understand the Icelandic Sagas, when they are read slowly to them. Although the Icelandic and Faroëse are like in words and structure, they sound, in the mouths of the latter people, as different as Danish and Norsk. The official language, including that used in the school and the church, is Danish.

But, besides this, they have a ballad literature of their own, which has been partly published at Copenhagen, by Mr. Hammershaimb, who lives at Quivik in Stromö, and is one of the seven native clergy. To the sound of one of these Kaempeviser, chaunted slowly by themselves, without an instrumental accompaniment, these people will dance in a ring for hours, and a most monotonous and heavy affair, I understand, it is; at least to the ear and eye of the bystander. One of their favourite dancing chaunts is "Oluva-Kvædi," about king Pippin and his daughter Oluva. And then comes the refrain, with an abortive attempt at livelinesss:

> "Stride we fast along the floor,
> Never spare your shoon,
> Yule is come, so drink your fill:
> Guide us God aboon!"

One piece of information I obtained about these islands will doubtless interest those who are not ready to join in Hotspur's reprobation of ballad-mongering. It is now known, (see Dasent's Norse Tales, Preface,) that Tell made his appearance in the North hundreds of years before his exploits were localized on the shores of the lake of Lucerne. The tale of Tell first appeared in Switzerland in 1499. But as early as the end of the 11th century the tale had been told of the Scandinavian hero Palnatoki, by that picker-up of all sorts of quaint information, Saxo Grammaticus. In the 13th century, it was told of Egil, Volunder's younger brother. It was also told of St. Olaf and Eindridi, and of king Harald Sigurdson and Hemingr; both of whom lived in the 11th century. Well, to make a long story short, the legend also occurs in Faro. The ballad goes by the name of *Geyti Aslaksson.* Many of the features and incidents are the same as in the Swiss story, the names are different of course. King Harald (alias

Gessler) asks his men if they know of any one who is his match in strength. "Yes," they reply, "there is a peasant's son in Upland"—so that, strictly speaking, the legend belongs to the Scandinavian Main—"Geyti (Gaute), son of Aslak, who is the strongest of men." Forth goes the king, and at last rides up to the house of Aslak. "And where is your youngest son?" "Woe worth the day! he is buried in Kolrin kirk-yard." "Come and shew me his corpse then, that I may see whether he was as strong as men say." The father puts off the king with the excuse, that it would be difficult to find his son's remains among the many that lie buried there. The king rides over the heath, and meets a man in scarlet*, coming home from hunting, bow on shoulder. "And who art thou, my friend?" "Gaute, son of Aslak." The dead man, in short, alive and well. The king tells him he has heard of his prowess, and is come to try his strength with him. Gaute is quite ready, he says, be it in hurling the javelin, or 'putting the stone,' shooting with the bow, Rarey-fying horses, or swimming. His majesty fixes on the last. He swims right well, but Gaute swims better; and he ends by giving the monarch such a ducking, that he is borne to his castle devoid of sense and motion. Harald swallows his anger, as he had done the water; at least he dissembles, and

* Skarlat, a fine cloth of any colour, opposed to the coarse wadmaal. See *Liber Albus*.

bids Gaute shoot a walnut from his brother's head. Aslaksson assents, and invites the king to come to the forest, and witness his dexterity. He prays to God and St. Olaf to direct his arrow-head, (ráða for örvaroddum.)

"Geyti legði örv á strong,
Gud var honum hollur,
So skeyt hann ta litlu nötu;
Ikki rördist kollur."

"On the string the shaft he laid,
Jesu hath heard his prayer,
He shot away the little nut,
Nor hurt the lad a hair."

Next day the king sends for the skilful bowman.

"List thee, Geyti Aslaksson,
Truly tell to me,
Why you had the arrows twain,
In the wood yestreen with thee."

Aslaksson—

"Therefore I had the arrows twain,
Yestreen in the wood with me,
My brother dear had I but slain,
The second were aim'd at thee."

Above is a specimen of the Faroëse tongue, as given by Hammershaimb; but it is proper to say, that the natives, on seeing his book, observed, "That is not our talk."

Coupling, then, this early diffusion of a story—the leading trait of which is this wondrous feat of marksmanship—throughout the Scandinavian North, with the fact that it is also current among the

Samoyeds and Mongolians, do we not seem to arrive at the conclusion that the incident dates from a period when the Arian migration from the plains of Asia had not yet taken place?

With talk like this, I whiled away the afternoon of July 17; the heavy roll had prostrated some of our companions, and acted like fern-seed on others, rendering them invisible: while the fog has had a similar effect on Syderö, the most important island among the Faroes for agriculture; which we have been skirting some time without being aware of it.

Most people, who know any thing about trap (stair) rocks, know that the Faroes are trap from top to bottom; and that the sea-cliffs present an admirable instance of the perfect terrace or tier-like regularity of this formation. Regarded by geologists generally as the product of submarine volcanoes, their tabular structure is explained on the principle that the pressure of the ocean above would spread out the volcanic matter like a layer of mortar, and, by preventing the escape of the enclosed vapour, would preserve its fluidity for a long time, and thus contribute to the perfect horizontality of the beds. Time after time did the earth's centre belch forth its contents, and each time with the same result, the formation of a new stratum, which was of darker or brighter hue, according as the erupted matter was lava or sand. At last comes some great igneous commotion, and, like Venus Anadyomene, but with a little more splashing perhaps, uprises from the sea the gorgeous vision.

I know of nothing that more captivates and excites the fancy, than the first sight of a country from the sea, especially a country like this of wild fantastic magnificence, with its stupendous sea-cliffs, its towers masoned up to heaven; where at one time story on story alternately seen framed of ebon and vermilion,—compared by the Scalds to the labours of the giants—as they dominate over the deep. At another time the fiords, those long drawn aisles of rushing mighty waters, are flanked by sheaves of huge perpendicular basaltic columns *—organ-pipes, if you will—hundreds of feet high, their angles sharp as if cut by the chisel. Now the channel broadens, and is bounded by green slopes, and, anon, before passing forth into the vast bright ocean beyond, it narrows dangerously, and is wrapt in mysterious threatening gloom, like that strait and narrow way that leadeth to the blessed eternity.

Yonder, abreast of us in the mist, are those singular islands, the Great and the Little Dimon; the precipitous sides of the former being among the best

* These were originally pine-forests, which king Olaf turned into stone. He desired to acquire the Islands, but a Faroëse told him that it was a poor country, where no wood grew. "So let it be," said the king; and the trees underwent the fate of the children of Niobe.

spots for birdcatching in the Faroes. The Danish government owns a good deal of the old Church land, as likewise the escheated farms of felons and others. The Great Dimon belongs to them, and one Ole Jensen was their lessee. He was one of the most adventurous cragsmen in these Isles; and my informant told me that he had seen him, when depending by a rope in mid-air over the precipice, sway himself several fathoms out of the perpendicular, in order that, on the rebound, he might get a footing on a shelf hollowed out of the trap, the nesting-place of birds innumerable. Only the other day, one of Ole's men was lowering a sack of meal from the pier of the island, being in fact the sea-lashed precipice; the weight proving too great for him, he let go the rope; a bight of it caught the unfortunate Ole, and he was hurled beyond redemption into the abyss below.

Skuö, yonder, peering darkly from under its fog-cowl, is dear to the Faroëse for its old-world recollections. On it was the residence, in life, and now is the narrow house, in death, of Sigmund Bresteson, prince of the Faroes; who, having been Christianized by that most zealous of preachers, king Olaf Trygveson, determined, like his master, to make Christians of his subjects, by fair means or foul. To Thrond, his chief adversary, he proposed the alternative of the font or the axe, and Thrond chose the former. But Heathenesse again lifted up her head alike in Norway and Faro; and Thrond, who had bided his time, attacked and made himself master of Sigmund's stronghold, who narrowly escaped death by swimming over to Hvalvik in Suderö, yonder—then called Sandvik—a distance of four miles. Thorgrim the Bad, at whose cottage he sought refuge, saw and coveted a thick gold ring upon his arm, and the proverbial root of all evil led him to murder his princely guest (A. D. 1002): thus fulfilling the prophecy of king Olaf, who, regarding the circlet as an heathen amulet—for it was in fact taken from a temple in Norway—urged Sigmund to cast it from him; and on his refusing to do so, foretold that it would be his death.

And now we are skirting Sandö, the verdant pastures of which are so favourable for sheep, that some forty thousand of these animals are said to be fattened there yearly.

Yonder is Skaalhoved, rising a thousand feet aloft, and under its shadow some modest looking ant-hills, scattered upon a green declivity, which however my glass exalts into some grass-roofed houses, with a church close by. Before long, we are passing between Stromö and Naalsö (Needle Island); not that it bears any resemblance to our Needles, but from the Needle's-eye-like cave piercing its southern extremity; through which we can see the daylight, and under whose arches, frosted with delicate zeolites, in still weather, a boat may pass.

But see, the judge has got his effects upon deck, his basket-work from Elsineur, his Danish rocking-horse for the motherless boy, and his two long-legged Cochins, which seem waking from a melancholy dream. Hark! the anchor-chain suddenly stops its rush, and here we are at 10½ P.M. in the roadstead of Thorshaven, the capital of the Isles; defended by that fort whose cannon are only terrible to its garrison, and the one unfortunate prisoner who is lodged there, for want of a jail. Did I say one prisoner? Surely, those too must be convicts, who are rowing the boat to the ship with more than usual convict energy. All are clad alike in a rusty-iron coloured jacket, with stand-up collar, and dark knee-breeches. All have a dejected look, and sallow faces, as if they fed on prison diet; and all have their hair cropped short; while the coxswain, whose countenance is really very like the traditional ones of Jack Sheppard, with his straight dark hair, at least what there is of it, flattened on his crown, looks what he is, the leader of the gang. His rust-coloured tunic is of finer and newer cloth than the rest, and he keeps regarding his well-formed calf with evident satisfaction, and arranging his cap with the air of a dandy: while the rest of his crew persist in touching their caps to the judge at every word they utter. These, reader, are not convicts, but citizens of the city of Thorshaven, which has 900 inhabitants, while the chief place on Naalsö has only 150*. That rust-colour is called 'moret †,' the native hue of many of their sheep. It is mentioned in the Sagas, and is the national colour of their cloth.

That other gentleman, who has just come on board, dressed in ditto, ditto, with calf-skin sandals, tied with white thongs round his ankles, after the fashion of the old Norsk kings, is Mr. M., M. P. for the Faroes, a most intelligent and agreeable person. As for the plain physiognomies, you never do see a good-looking woman in the country; like mother like son. With respect to the universal pallor of their countenances, it must be owing to the fogs, and the want of sufficient sun-light, to bring out the colour. With the flowers it is just the same; at least with the garden ones. The governor tells me that the shrubs he introduced from Denmark flower, it is true, but the bloom is of a pale and washed-out appearance.

Next morning, July 18, a boat which I hail, as it rows past, takes us ashore. The peasant-crew are from Sandö, and all in brown collarless jackets. They have hen's eggs for sale, 20 for 4½*d.*, and a patient for the doctor with a swollen eye. Possibly,

* The population of the Faroes is fast increasing. Not so that of Iceland.

† The name and colour are also common in Shetland.

if the doctor demands a fee, he will give him eggs. A score of them, I find, are equivalent in value to one hen; while geese fetch 1*s.* 3*d.*

The houses of Thorshaven are all of wood, imported from Norway, in the absence of native timber; the framework resting on low walls of unhewn stones. They are mostly painted black with white window-sills. From the sea, the little spot, jammed down between the rocky hills behind, and the waters of the bay in front, looks picturesque enough; but it certainly does not improve on closer inspection. Such a labyrinth of crooked, narrow, steep lanes, paved with stones of fearful slipperiness, each at an obtuse angle to its neighbour; not to mention the foul fishy smells that wanton in the air. "Which is the way out of this?" I demand, in Danish, of a hulking fisherman, with blue eyes and curly fair locks. "What were ye speering, Sir?" replies the man, in a tongue very like Scotch. Who but a Briton could have looked like he did! He is from Papa Stour in Shetland, and has come for the summer to catch cod. "And do they dance the sword-dance yet in Papa Stour?" asked I, coupling the question in my mind with the information I had recently obtained about the national dances still existing in the Faroes. "To be sure; there's Gideon Fraser, and John Fraser, and Magnus Fraser, and another Fraser, can dance it well enough." So having got this piece of interesting information, we steer off for the country, not unpursued by small beggars, a thing I saw nowhere in Iceland; where Ulfliot's stern code seems to have extinguished the breed. Our object is to go over the mountain, and pay a visit to the remarkable ruins of the church of Kirkubö, about five miles off.

Simon Lindskö is our guide, of course dressed in convict colours, and munching what looks like a Bologna sausage, but which is in reality a barley-cake. The only remuneration he asks is two marks Danish=9*d.* A most intelligent fellow he is, verifying so far the observation of old Grabe, that he would "sooner talk with a Faroese peasant all day, than with a German boor for half an hour."

"But what building is that?" inquired I, as we left the town, on seeing a neat edifice surmounted by a gilt cross. "That is the Romish chapel. There are two priests here, a Bavarian, and a Belgian." "And how many laity of that persuasion?" "Why, there is one old fisherman, and a family of four besides; but most of these are the priests' servants; and people do say they receive very high wages. I find that Mons. J., the identical vicar-general of his holiness the pope, whom I heard of in Lapland, has likewise visited the Faroes, with his coadjutor, Mr. B., who is now in Iceland.

On we trudge up the hills, and for a short space have the benefit of a road; meeting several people bearing peats on their shoulders from the mountain to town: a sight reminding one of the vicinity of Lerwick. The load is carried in a lovë, or kind of crate, made of laths, which is supported by a strap going across the forehead, after the manner of the Newhaven fishwives. In a mile or two the high-road comes to an end. "We have to work at this road two days a year gratis," explained the guide. At this rate, the only road in the islands will be long before it is completed. Simon is a great shooter; in proof of which he exhibits his right hand maimed by the passage of a ramrod through it. As we descend the other side of the mountain, and pass a dreary lake half hidden in the mist, I shoot some oyster-catchers (Tjalder), whimbrels (spou), and golden-plovers (brachfugl). That shaggy apparition, bounding up the cliffs, recalling to my mind that crux of infantine tongues, "along the rugged rocks the ragged rascal ran," is one of the native sheep. That topknot of fluttering wool, floating from his brow, reminds me that here, as in Shetland, the fleece is not clipped, but 'rooed.' If any part of the wool is not loose at the time of the operation, it is left on the animal, till nature loosens it, and makes a present of it to the birds or beasts.

The ruined church of Kirkubö, which lies in one of the prettiest spots in Faro, at the bottom of a richly grassed slope, well repaid us for our visit. It was intended for the metropolitan church, and was commenced by Bishop Hilarius, in the 12th century, but was never finished. The last bishop of the isles, being much annoyed by French pirates, fled to Stavanger in Norway, and became bishop there in 1556. At present the country belongs ecclesiastically to Sealand's-Stift in Denmark.

The walls are of a native stone of exceeding hardness, and four feet thick. The mortar, which is of pounded mussel shells, shews little signs of decay; and reads a useful lesson to the present generation of masons, both in Iceland and Faro; but, like the 'sermons in stones,' it is but little regarded. At all events, the mortar now used here is fetched at great expense from Denmark. The style is Gothic, and of the simplest character. The interior is about 72 feet long by 22 broad, and the roofless walls some 35 feet high. To the north of the chancel is a square apartment with a groined roof, most likely the vestiarium, communicating with the chancel by a door. The corbels of the nave, from which the roof arches were intended to spring, exhibit human heads rather well carved. The plain flat walls within are relieved at regular intervals by square pieces of a red stone let in and carved with crosses and other devices. There is a row of Gothic windows in the southern wall, overlooking the sea, but none in the north wall. Outside, at the eastern end, just north of the great east window, is a representation in stone of our Saviour on the Cross, between the two thieves. Behind this slab, according to tradition, is a fragment of the Cross, and if any one attempt to remove the plate, he will not go unpunished. Twice did some sacrilegious wretches make the attempt, and each time to their grievous bodily harm. Round the sculpture runs an almost erased legend, said to be in Latin, and giving the date of the church; the peasant living near assured me it was Greek: it certainly was so to him.

Close by the ruins are the remains of an ancient cemetery; and, nearer the sea, a still older church of stone, which has outlived its more ambitious sister, and is still used for public worship. At the ends of the sittings on either side of the aisle are curious panelled carvings, representing the Apostles with their respective symbols. To the north of the very plain altar is a canopied chair of carved Gothic woodwork. Close by the door great plants of Angelica were thriving wonderfully in the fat soil. Here, as in Iceland, it is a regular article of food. A hole in the cliffs above is pointed out as the hiding-place of the infant Sverrer, after having escaped from Norway with his mother, who was a sister of the bishop of Kirkubö. It was this Sverrer, whom king John of England aided with a hundred men in his struggles for the Norwegian crown. "They were called (Ribbaldi *) ribalds,"

* This word in old Norse means a violent fellow.

says the old Chronicle, "and could run like deer and fight like demons."

We returned to Thorshaven through thick mist, which seems to cling as tenaciously to the flanks of its mountains as does the sea-louse to the sides of the fish in its sounds. On the road I picked up some London Pride, kidney-leaved sorrel, two or three saxifrages, the common butterwort, wild thyme, heather, thrift, and orchis maculata. The Scotchmen who were of the party hammered away vigorously at the rocks, and the result was some tiny bits of zeolite, and stones impregnated with copper, but nothing like an opal or a specimen of importance. The best zeolites are obtained in the sea-caves; but approach to them is not always easy, and the time occupied on such an expedition so much depends on the wind and tide, that it is not advisable to attempt it with so little time as is generally at the passenger's disposal. One of the party had to take a crew of eight men to ensure his timely return from a visit to a sea-cave opposite Thorshaven.

Those who had not ventured beyond the town were loud in their praises of the governor's garden, with its columbine, its primroses, its budding roses, its gooseberries and currants, and strawberries nearly ripe. At one hospitable mansion, we take some Madeira; at another, some very good hock; and down we flounder through the uneven narrow alleys to catch the steamer, whose time is up. The natives who met us seemed generally very well behaved, in spite of the premium on drunkenness which the very low price of spirits offers. The best cognac (as it is called) sells at one shilling a bottle.

Our hopes of being off this evening are doomed to disappointment. Fog is pleaded; but the real cause of detention is, I suspect, an anchor lost in the bay last voyage. I recommend a herring telescope to assist in the search for it. The only one procurable renders objects discernible at eight fathoms; but the water is fifteen fathoms deep: so our skipper returns at last anchorless, and too late for him to risk groping his way through the dark and dangerous passages of the isles, unillumined as they are by anything like a light-house. "Faros, because they have no Pharos, I suppose," burst out an indignant passenger, illustrating his wit by that most original quotation, 'lucus a non lucendo.' Be it here remarked, that with a westerly wind Thorshaven is not a good harbour. In bad weather the steamer takes refuge in Kongehaven, in Osterö, which is an excellent haven.

CHAPTER III.

We weigh anchor—Lost in a fog—Rescued by a creature in yellow—The fowlers of the Faroes—The terrors of their trade—Over the cliffs—Birds innumerable as the sand on the sea-shore—A school of whales at play—British fishing vessels—Exchange no robbery—We dine off a holy fish—Shaving the ladies—Puzzles and paradoxes—First sight of Iceland—The Westmann isles—How they originated—After the black death days how the whole land was repeopled—Magnificent needles—The 'Fire islands'—Where to find the great auk—Legend of the Geirfuglasker — The amphitheatre of Faxe-Fiord — Cast anchor in Reykjavik Bay.

July 19.—The mountain walk had weighed down my eyelids heavily; for, though we lifted anchor at 5 A. M., it was not till 8 that I was roused by the steam-whistle piping harrowingly. Arrived up on deck I see, or rather do not see, how matters stand, for a fog of the thickest had blindfolded every thing. This much was plain, that we were still involved among the islands. The current is hurrying us along pretty much where it pleases, and if we do go stem on to the precipices, the screw, unlike paddles, will help us but little. Well then may the skipper whistle for help, and whistling he has been in perfect desperation for some time past. At this juncture an object is discerned moving on the sea astern of us. Aiblins, it was a seal, or a porpoise! as the Scotch minister suggested when discoursing upon Jonah. No, by the sea god Neptune,—Niord, I should say, it is a boat rowing towards us, its only occupant something like the yellow dwarf, at least in point of colour; for he is yellow from head to foot, being encased in a garment of new sheep-skin. In his skiff is what at first looked like a trident, but which eventuates in what we should call a landing-net equipped with a very long shaft. This is not, however, designed for catching fish, but birds. Beside him are two marvellous-looking guns and several dead auks and guillemots. It is a real native occupied in earning his daily bread. "Are you for Thorshaven?" "No! to sea, to the northward. Will you shew us the way? You shall be paid." "I am all alone, and the tide is running furiously in Skaapenfiord. Put her head to the north-east, and you'll strike the Sound between Trollhoved and Hestö. That's Sandö yonder to the westward."

But, without a pilot, getting out of our difficulties unscathed was very problematical. And in spite of the man's protestations that he is all alone, and cannot row home again against the tide, he is hoisted on board. He tells me he has been out fowling. With his net he catches the langweh or guillemot (Uria Troila), either flying close to the cliffs or whilst sitting on the shelves. Sandö now becomes visible looming through the mist to larboard. The water around is smooth as oil, evidently boding mischief—placidi pellacia ponti—while, only a few yards off, are seen white-headed toppling billows. Up jumps the man in yellow, his mouth full of bread, with him a rare delicacy: a coin in one hand and a screw of tobacco in the other. In a twinkling a rope lowers him into his boat, and he disappears in the mist rowing for dear life. Well he may; for if he gets into this fearful current, with its boiling, spinning eddies, he will not reach home to-night, perhaps never.

But we ought to say something more about that fowling, that dreadful trade in which the Faroese engage. In the first place, why do they catch these birds at all? Is it for their feathers? Surely they ought not to weigh in the scale with human life. Or is it for their flesh? An Englishman, with his beeves, and his hogs, and his feast of fat things, scornfully rejects the idea. But it is not so with the poor Faroese. Salted Puffins, dried guillemots and auks, rashers of smoked whale, are the first necessaries of his existence. Never were there spots better suited for birds, than the stupendous sea-cliffs of these islands. The red layers of sandstone or burnt clay, which alternate with the layers of trap, looking something like the walls of Balliol College Chapel, being of a more perishable material, are eaten out by the weather; and in this way cloisters, hundreds of yards long, are hollowed at different heights in the cliff, admirably suited for ornithological comfort and sociality. For 1500 feet from the top to the bottom of the precipice, birds may be seen sitting in serried rows, each species of bird, be it gull, guillemot, puffin, or cormorant, having its distinct *locus in quo*. The rules of precedence are most accurately adjusted and observed.

It is a sight funny beyond measure to view the white breasts of these birds jammed closely together, with scarcely room for a pin between; while their wise heads go everlastingly bobbing, bobbing, nidding, nodding, with vast solemnity, for all the world like the courtiers of the Great Mogul, before the Great Mogul ceased to be. A shot fired would kill a hundred, while the rest would take to the water, or the air, not without a discordant chorus of sounds indicative of grief, alarm, and anger. The fowler pots the game, and bags them by wholesale; but as to his own safety, of this he seems to make little account.

One method of fowling is this. Two men agree to ascend a cliff. One of these commences climbing to the first shelf, being pushed up from behind by the pole of his comrade below. Having landed safely on the shelf, he pulls up the other, who is attached to him by a rope fastened to his girdle. And so they climb, shelf after shelf, till they arrive at the best preserves. Of course if one overbalances himself, and falls, the other goes down with him They are partners in life and in death.

If the nature of the rock prevents this method being pursued, another scarcely less perilous one is resorted to. A man is let down by a long rope from the top of the cliff. We won't speculate how often the rope is rotten. It is an expensive article to replace, and the people are poor, and the rest may be guessed at. Well! above stands a man on the watch. Down goes the fowler with the rope fastened to his body, and a small string in his hand for giving signals to the watcher above, and for hauling up the booty. Arrived at a shelf, he must often make a pendulum of himself, oscillating till he swings into the alcove. He then disengages himself from the rope, and with his pole and net attached to it, bonnets the simple birds by hundreds as they sit in the plenitude of self-satisfaction and sapient stupidity. While others, more mobile in their disposition, he nets as they fly past him. The spoil is either showered into a boat below, or hauled up by the string aforementioned.

In the worst places, for instance on the stacks and needles (drangur, in Shetland drongs), thick ropes are left from year to year, to be of use on future occasions. Chains are now getting used for this purpose, or very strong cables of horsehair. Mr. M., M.P., told me he saw an old man fall upon the turf fainting, while his son was descending in this way the fearful precipice of Myling, which sinks sheer into the sea a height of two thousand feet. Nor was it to be wondered at; for he was the first that had ventured down for thirty years. On the last occasion a fragment of rock having become displaced had overwhelmed the luckless climbers. The Faroese used to have a notion that if a man fell from those lofty precipices, he burst in mid-air; and if it chanced to be a horse, his shoes came off, all the nails becoming straight!

This very year a fowler had walked along one of the cliff-terraces, and had sat down to rest. The roof fell in, and all that his yokefellow could find of him was a shred of his garter. Well may these poor fellows—in some respects resembling the doomed gladiators with their 'Ave, Cæsar, morituri de salutamus,' and yet how unlike them—as they go day after day on their death's errand sing a Psalm and mutter a prayer for God's protection. The people in fact are generally of a strongly religious turn. Danger is their schoolmaster. Before crossing a perilous fiord the rowers are said to rest on their oars, and do the same.

Yonder, to our right, Vaagö is dimly visible, a name also to be found in the Luffodens, from which islands, judging from the similarity of local names, the original population of the Faroes are conjectured to have come in Harald Harfager's days. The waterfall, which makes a clear jump of two hundred feet into the sea, is invisible. The "witch-finger" sticking out of the brine to the height of some thousand feet, is clouded in haze; while Tindholm's Gothic spires, whereon an Eagle once lodged an infant, are equally undemonstrative.

Mogenaes, the westernmost of the whole group,—the little holm attached to which is said to be the only breeding place of the Solan goose in Faro—with its beautiful basaltic pillars, comes more out of the obscurity. Before long we are out of the fog, and the Faroes become a dark patch spread out upon the shining ocean. So befogged in fact are these poor people, the heavens being clear upon an average only one-twelfth of the year, that they have become quite connoisseurs of fog. A white belt upon the Fjeld has one name; and a fog grouped in grey masses has another; while if it wraps land, sea, and sky in one clammy curtain, it is pronounced to be mjorki (darkness), and there is an end of it.

"There they be's, a jolly lot of 'em," sung out the mate, as we entered a thick school of whales. What a sight to be sure! a thousand black monsters all round us, some so close that the vessel actually seems to graze them, as they twist, roll, and spout indignantly, some running butt into each other, Malay fashion. One fellow, in the fulness of his fury or folly, jumps a clear twenty feet into the air.

These are the famous 'Ca'ing whales' of Orkney and Shetland, called by the Faroese 'grind'*; and

* From their tendency, perhaps, to enter narrow places. Grind = gate.

which they have the sense to eat; while the Shetlanders, to whom Providence sends a similar boon at times, will only use the oil, even though they may happen to be reduced to starvation-point by a failure in the herring fishery, or a hard winter. If Claud Halcro were still in the flesh, and had grown wiser with age, he would doubtless say with Glorious John, "'Take the goods the Gods provide thee,' and don't starve in the midst of plenty." These whales (Delphinus Melas) are making straight for the Islands; they always do in fact, when they get anywhere near them, impelled by some strange curiosity or fatality or something. The moment they are espied from the cliffs of Faro, the fiery cross (grindabot) will be sent abroad; and all that's available of boats or men will hurry to the locality, and, with many-tongued noise and inconceivable tumult, drive them, fatuously following their unwise leader to some narrow creek, where once on shore they are despatched with knife and spear, and the sea is incarnadined with their blood *. For thirty years down to 1857 the average annual number thus slaughtered is said to have been twelve hundred, while in 1843 as many as three thousand were killed.

Mogenaes is now twelve miles astern, when we come upon some sixteen sail of English fishing vessels. Their mainsails are half-furled, and to prevent

* Two hundred of this school were secured, a comparatively small number.

them from drifting too fast before the wind (some motion is necessary), a three-cornered sail is immersed in the water astern with a rope fastened to each corner. One of these goes under the bottom of the vessel, the others to the bulwarks, and so the sail is kept distended, and acts as a drag, while the crew pursue their hook-fishing at leisure. Their favourite bait are large white snails. When short of these, they come into port, let down a score or two of cods' heads, strung together like onions, into the sea; and which in the morning are dragged up covered with snails. These fishing yachts often muster two hundred strong; one only of which belongs to Faro; the rest are Dutch, French, and English.

We hail one vessel which sends a boat aboard with fish. She is from London, the property of a tobacconist; has been out ten weeks, and has only taken six hundred cod, having been much hindered by fog. What they catch now, they salt and stow away; when they return home, in about six weeks from this time, they will take with them a lot of live cod in the well; a tittle in one day's fish-total of all-absorbing Billingsgate. The journals and contributions to the "Arctic letter-bag," are at once laid aside, and a sixpenny subscription entered into by the passengers to buy the fish. But it is not money that the fishermen want. A great stone bottle which they hold up implies a desire for grog; and the bottle is filled by the 'Restaurateur,' as he calls himself. A dozen cod-fish of large size are soon on deck, and last, not least, a monstrous halibut, "spatium admirabile rhombi," seven feet in length, and requiring three men to haul him upon deck, by a strong rope fastened round the tail. He was caught yesterday by a hook on which was placed a slice of a cousin of his, and is still breathing; while his parasites are holding on with grim tenacity, faithful to the last. Well does he deserve his name Helleflynder, "Holy flounder;" an etymology which is nearly lost sight of in our English equivalent 'halibut.'

What visions of fish-dinners diversify the oppressive line of dire salted viands—sausages, tongue, hung-beef, and anchovies, which have been our lot and our horror ever since bidding adieu to the "roast beef of old England!"

> "genialis agatur
> Iste dies, propera stomachum laxare saginis."

To the consternation of all, after sharpening our appetites for the fresh halibut-cutlets, news is brought us that the *chef de cuisine* declines dressing them to-day, his line of action having been already chalked out; besides which, in his opinion, halibut ought to be salted before being eaten. "Ruin seize thee, ruthless cook!" is the absurd apostrophe of one of the party, who has been reading Gray, the most Scandinavian of our poets, to bring his mental pulsations, as he says, into unison with his first visit to the land of the Old Gods. A deputation is at once sent to the kitchen; soft sawder and a profusion of bows divert the functionary from his fell purpose, and fresh halibut-cutlets, which one of the passengers pronounces 'exquizzit,' appear on our bill of fare.

The fine weather had elicited from her retirement a pretty little Icelandic girl, hitherto invisible. Her fair face is marked with a recent gash. She has brought with her a razor from Copenhagen for papa's beard, and in her delightful simplicity had been endeavouring to explain the use of this wonderful instrument, by applying it to her own chin! "I suppose she intends the razor as a surprise for her father," observed I to the captain. "Oh! no. I knew that he was expecting one." So that this order for a razor was a matter of public notoriety all the way from Reykiavik to Copenhagen. So it is in thinly peopled districts. Nothing can be done in a corner. But how is this? the barometer has fallen, and still fair weather.

The student of Gray has changed his ground, and is now reading up the 'Tempest,' doubtless in order "to bring his mental pulsations into unison" with the impending storm. But he is destined to be disappointed in spite of the barometer.

The quicksilver, I find, will sometimes entirely disappear, like the water in the pipe of the Great Geysir, and even then the weather will be tolerable. So that it is as it should be, and quite in keeping with the regions of paradox which we are approaching: where the magnet forgets its affection for the pole; where as many as nine suns have been seen in winter without affording the warmth of one; where the favourite time for thunder and lightning is mid-winter; where a river of to-day becomes a mere fountain to-morrow, and *vice versâ*; where islands rise out of the ocean, and sink down again, as if nothing had happened; where tiny clouds, according to the testimony of veracious travellers, at times swoop down like falcons on the head of the wayfarer and disorder his brains.—A land out of whose bowels is dug that mysterious surturbrand which geologists have been addling their brains to explain the origin of, but in vain—a land where people get their wood from the ocean—and where ocean-cod are taken in inland lakes;—where, if you find a stalactite, it is due to fire instead of water: where dark ducks with white rings round their eyes swim in the boiling Hvers—and where ice and fire are often on the best terms with each other. So that fine weather and a low glass are really quite the correct thing.

Whales again ahead! the same sort as we saw before, their spokey back-fins revolving close after each in regular succession like the wheel of the Great Eastern, if it has one. But, look, they are mere minnows to that Triton seventy feet long if he is an inch, swimming very near the surface of the water, and clearly shewing by the interval between his back-fin and his steam-hole what a leviathan he is.

It was at 2 A.M. on the morning of Saturday, July 21st, that I awoke, stifling, as I fancied, in volcanic smoke; but in reality with the close vapours of the cabin. There lies the cause of my asphyxia, that Danish waiter snoring heavily on the sofa; who, before betaking himself to rest, had battened down everything. Mounting on deck to inflate my lungs with oxygen, I find that I have stolen a march on all the rest of the voyagers, and get my first view of Iceland. Yonder, above the fog-bank which blocks out the lower landscape, rises the highest mountain of the country, Oraefa Iökul, 6241 Danish feet above the sea; its white crown of unsullied snow contrasting startlingly with the grey shadows of the morning. Underneath it, and close by the shore, but invisible, rise the cliffs of Ingolfshöfdi; famous as the spot where Ingolf the Norwegian landed, when he came to establish himself in the country in the year 874. A little East of this lies Breidamark's Iökul, whose glaciers advancing and descending towards the sea have covered up the spot where once dwelt Hrollaug, nephew of Rollo, that 'gangrel carle.' But see! further to the West is another high mountain, Myrdals Iökul, usually as white with ice and snow as its huge adjoining sister Eyafialla Iökul. But now its garment of brightness has been torn from it, and exchanged for a covering of sackcloth and ashes. The cause of this phenomenon is the terrific explosion of Kötlugiá, which began in May of this year, and lasted for eight weeks, and which will be described hereafter.

The glorious sight of this new country, this utgard, or outlying world, where fire and frost have striven for the mastery, with its long line of majestic snow mountains, so absorbed my mind, filling it at the same time with all the grand associations of the olden days, that I did not at first perceive that a wind had sprung up dead against us, with a big head-sea, making progression difficult. It was not till 5 P.M. that we near the Westmann Islands, so called from those Irish slaves who fled thither after murdering their master, Hiorleif. To our left rises a fine arch, piercing right through an island, in whose vaulted halls the Atlantic must now be sounding terribly, boiling in the fierceness of his anger. Just facing the roads is the mighty block of Bjarnarey, with its twisted layers of trap, exactly parallel to each other. In one spot the sea-face of the cliff exhibits what look like the butt-ends of a row of horizontal logs, cut off flush with the precipice, reminding one of the corner of a Norwegian timber house. I point it out to a passenger, who mumbles something about the rocks having got to loggerheads. It looks as if the basaltic pillars, for it can be nothing else, have been first knocked down, and then dame Nature, in Neronic mood, seems to have treated them as if they had only one neck, and decapitated them all at one fell stroke. Over all, the isle is covered with a carpet of emerald, dotted with silver; or to speak according to the ledger, the green grass has several hundred white sea-birds upon it.

At the factory opposite, which is the abode of three merchants, a flag is flying in reply to our signal for a boat to come and fetch off the mails, but no boat will venture out; so we hold on our course, and it may be weeks before the advices from Europe come to hand. The little church, situated like the houses on a small green plain, is hedged in to the North West by the lofty serrated peaks of an ancient volcano.

Popular superstition, instead of attributing all these bizarreries to Nature's own handiwork, ascribes the whole affair to a Troll, who in a fit of spleen flung the half dozen islands hither from the Hellisheide on the mainland nearly opposite.

But here is a genuine Icelandic legend, which, with all succeeding ones, I beg such of my readers as take no interest in such matters to skip at once; "überhüpfe den Teufel" (hop over the Devil), as the German schoolmaster advised his pupils to do a passage in the construe which he could not understand.

In the days when the black death was raging

through the land, (1402–4,) eighteen wizards retired to the Westmann Islands, to be out of the danger of contagion. After some time they became curious for news from the mainland, and despatched thither one of their body, who was fairly up in the Black art, for that purpose; he being expressly told, that he must be back before Yule, or they would send him a message that would be the death of him. The man wandered through the land, but did not meet with a living soul in the deserted houses. At last he came to a cottage, and rapped, when the door was opened by a beautiful young damsel. Of course she was highly delighted, for she fancied before that she was left alone in the world, and begged him to stay, and keep her company for a time. His comrades, said she, would never be so particular to a day, especially when there was a forlorn lady in the case. Her soft oratory prevailed, and stop he did, and that till Christmas eve. And now he sprang to his feet, and insisted upon it that go he must. "But you cannot possibly get over to the Islands to-night; so won't it be just the same to die here as on the road?" He at once saw that he had put off going till it was too late, and resolved to abide his doom where he was.

As night approached, he grew silent and reserved; the damsel however was quite the reverse. "Well, and what are they doing on the Islands?" she inquired. "They are just sending off the message."

Presently his eyes became heavy with sleep; a sure sign that the envoy was at hand;—yea, even at the door; for he is now fast asleep. At this moment she perceives a reddish brown vapour piercing into the dwelling, which by degrees assumes the form of a man. "And what's *your* pleasure, Sir?" she boldly exclaimed, "To kill that fellow; but you're in my way—leave his side." "To be sure I will; but first do me a favour." "And what's that?" "Let me see how big you can make yourself." "At your service, Ma'am!" And immediately the apparition makes itself so big, that it fills the whole house. "And now, pray, let me see how little you can make yourself." "With pleasure, Ma'am:" and in a moment the messenger transforms himself into a fly, which tries to crawl through the damsel's fingers to the sleeper. She puts a hollow sheep-bone just in its way; into this the fly crawls; she at once puts a stopper into it, and pockets the bone, fly, and all.

The sleeper awakens, "Where is the messenger now?" she asks. He confesses to total ignorance on the matter......And so they pass the merry days of Yule most agreeably together. About New Year, however, the man again becomes very taciturn and thoughtful; and informs his mistress that they are just going to send another message, which must be fatal. The damsel speaks to him words of comfort, and fairly shames him out of his fears.

On New Years' eve, he says, "The message has got to land, and is coming hither very very fast; for this time the spell is fearfully strong." "Come along with me," says the girl: they set off, and at last stop in a thicket, where pulling aside a bush, she shews him a flag of stone, and bids him raise it—

> "It was by dint of passing strength
> He moved the massy stone at length"—

and sees the entrance to a gloomy subterranean chamber. Through this they grope their way, and at last see a candle of human fat burning dimly in a human skull. Beside it on the ground lies an aged man of fearful aspect, who at once exclaims, "How now, foster daughter! there must be something very extraordinary in the wind to bring you here. It's many a long day since I had the pleasure of beholding your face." She tells him breathlessly the threatened danger, and at his request shews him the sheep's-bone. The moment he sees it, a great change seems to pass over him; he rolls the bone about in all directions, and strokes it on the outside. "Help, help, Father!" shrieks the damsel; "the man is getting sleepy, the messenger must be just at hand." Straightway the old man draws out the stopper, out comes the fly, which he strokes gently, saying, "Now off with you, and swallow all the messengers that come from the Islands." A fearful sound was heard; off buzzed the disengaged bottle-imp, or rather bone-imp, without delay, and became at once so big, that the upper part of its jaw reached to the sky, while the lower jaw touched the earth; and thus received all the messengers, and gave a very good account of them. And so the wizard was saved. He at once left the cave with his preserver, and went to her cottage, where they married and had children, and of them the whole land was re-peopled.

Singularly enough, and to my no small comfort—for it is ill conning over Icelandic lore in a storm—as soon as we have cleared the Westmann Islands, the wind and sea moderate considerably, and our rate of going doubles. I suppose there are wizards still lurking about those isles, who can, like Prospero, blow up a tempest or the semblance of one at will. Out to sea on our left are three magnificent perpendicular columns bolting out of the deep like great Bauta stones over the grave of some Icelandic demigod. See! that mass of white darting up like lightning from their bases, and half veiling their gaunt forms; it is the white rage of the ocean expending itself upon their everlasting strength, and falling back in baffled impotence. Further out still is another monumental giant, before whom the old man of Hoy would dwarf into a ninepin. You would think that a few winters' storms would level such seemingly tall and slender shafts with the sea. But no: some of those Icelandic needles are mentioned as having existed a thousand years ago.

Early on the morning of July the 22nd, we are in that vast bay called Faxe-Fiord, one horn of which is Snæfel Iökul, in the north-west, whilst the other end of the bow is the promontory, at whose tip is Reykianes, the dread of mariners. And no wonder; for behind that odd squat-looking isle, the Meal-sack, as it is called,—its top white with guano,—stretch out the 'Fire-islands' for two score of miles: one of them named Geirfugla-sker, from being the abode in former days of that rare bird the great Auk. Naturalists have at times rowed out thither to get the eggs, but they have gone back without them, the surf rendering landing on the skerries impossible. Nay, I am credibly informed, that the bird is extinct here, as large sums have been offered for the bird or its eggs in Reykjavik, and neither the one nor the other are forthcoming. On the east coast there is another island of the same name, alias "the Whalesback," where this rare bird may perhaps still be met with.

If the great auks, however, are extinct, there are other creatures in these islands such as naturalists do not generally include in the sphere of their researches.

Once on a time, on one of the few days in the year when the islands are approachable, a man named Thorsteinn set out with several others for the Geirfugla-sker, from Hvalsnes. There being symptoms of a coming storm, the boat's company, after being but a short time on the skerries, set off again for the mainland; nor were they aware in their hurry that Thorsteinn was left behind. Return was impossible; and as there was neither shelter nor food on the rocks, they gave him up for lost. Next year on their visiting the spot, who should make his appearance but their lost companion. He looked remarkably fat and well, but would not give any account of himself during their absence.

Some months later, one Sunday morning, a cradle stood by the door of Hvalsnes church. In it was a new-born child, over which was spread a gorgeous cloth of gold embroidery. On the priest getting sight of the cradle, he inquired with a loud voice for the father; this he did three times. Nobody answering, he baptized it on his own responsibility. Scarcely was the service over, when a woman wondrous fair to look at, and richly clad, entered the church in great haste and anger. She tore the babe from the cradle, gave the golden christening mantle to the priest as a baptismal fee, and imprecated this curse on Thorsteinn, that he should become a great fish, and continue so till he had sunk nineteen vessels. Since that time the mantle has been used as the altar-cloth. Thorsteinn rushed towards the cliff of Leirufel, let himself down into the sea by a rope, and swam in the shape of a whale to Hvalfiordr.

Here he anchored himself clean athwart the bay, and succeeded in wrecking eighteen vessels. In the eighteenth boat were the sons of a priest, a noted necromancer. By the power of his art he drove the monster ashore, and its bones may still be seen.

The only introit to the bay is between the Naze and the Meal-sack; and so difficult is the passage at times, that the steamer has been off here for a week, without being able to get inside. At breakfast time, the land about Reykjavik is distinctly visible.

On the flat coast to our right, low conical mountains rise at intervals in the background: on the larboard bow stands the mighty bluff of Esian, at whose foot Orlygr Stapson, the disciple of Bishop Patrick, built a church dedicated to St. Columba, the Apostle of the Picts, in the place of the heathen temple which was the oldest in the country. Behind it we see the tall Akrafial, and then, circling round to the north-west, peak purples after peak, between whose portals enter the deep-bosomed fiords, darkly cradled in the mountain-shadows; till the eye, after sating itself in their mysterious gloom—which may shroud, for aught that appears to the contrary, the approach to Hel, or to Valhalla—roams along the dim outline of the coast; here and there resting on the sail of a fishing yacht, miles away, but caught and rendered visible by the morning sun: till at last our vision is entranced by the sight of the glistening snow-fields, half hid in haze, which reach their climax and their western boundary, in the noble peak of Snaefel, distant full seventy miles as the bird flies.

Some object to this view, on the ground that the bay is too widely extended, and the features lose distinctness aud impressiveness from lack of concentration. But in an atmosphere so clear generally as that of Iceland, space is annihilated; and nobody can look on a vision like the one before us without a swelling bosom.

At ten o'clock A.M. we cast anchor in the harbour of Reykjavik, after putting to the right about hundreds of sea-birds, lying sleeping, like the fabled halcyons, on the calm sea-mirror; and running a dead heat with a huge whale, who only tailed off when we were close in shore. The bright sun-light gives the place a cheerful appearance; while the little Icelandic Miss, her dimpled smiles hiding the envious wound made by the razor, rushes to me exclaiming, "That is the Domkirk; is it not handsome? and that is the Latin School; and yonder is the residence of the Governor, Grev Trampe."

Meanwhile, the French brig of war, *Agile*, sends a boat's crew aboard for letters; and from the coxswain I learn that the weather has been very bad up here during the last few days; true to the saw, or rather seesaw, 'Good weather in Iceland, bad weather South, and *vice versâ*.'

CHAPTER IV.

Jorgensen's hotel—Buying and selling in a church—Sick of civilisation—Horsedealing—The Pope in Iceland—A champagne supper—Start for the Interior—Oriental cavalcade—The beauties of the Arctic Flora—Wild swans.

MR. JORGENSEN'S hotel and its discomforts are soon well known to me. Some of the French sailors are there trying to look happy, with their *petit verre* of so called cognac and their cup of coffee; but it is evidently a failure with them. I find that matters are in a provisional state here as far as the accommodation for travellers is concerned. Mr. Jorgensen rented a very large building, which was also the Club-house; but the rent becoming excessive, he gave it up, and took these his present confined premises; where he is building a couple of bed-rooms; which are, however, not yet finished. To make matters worse, his wife, a Dame Quickly in her way, and an excellent manager, is dead, so that everything is out of joint. Well might an intelligent Icelander, in reference to the loss of the hotel, observe to me, "It is a bad job, sir; we really cannot afford to lose anything in Reykjavik." Matters do indeed look most unpromising; and the only other Englishman on board, who is going to see the Geysers and returns with the same vessel, wears a most lugubrious aspect, on hearing that the only sleeping places for us are some very hard short sofas in the eating and drinking room; which apartment will perhaps not be empty of spitting visitors till after midnight.

But some tolerable roast mutton, golden plovers, and sweet omelet, washed down by some fair claret, reconcile him and myself to the situation. This done, we promenade the town, the streets of which are Macadamized, and flanked by open drains on either side. They all run at right angles, and the houses, which are of wood, are painted white, green, or red. The aspect of the place is anything but picturesque, and is inferior even to a second-rate Norwegian town. The Latin School, however, is really a very respectable building, and of considerable size; and as it stands upon an eminence looking down on the town it forms quite a commanding feature in the metropolis of Iceland.

The church, too, is a goodly edifice, and though not belonging to any particular style of architecture, looks solid and substantial without and within. In the vestry there are some ancient embroidered robes. But the object most worth seeing in the building is the font by Albert Thorwaldsen, a present to the land of his forefathers.

The next day I went to the bookseller's to purchase a map of the country; who said he would take me to the Icelandic Society's Book *dépôt*, and I might choose for myself. So saying he led the way towards the church; but, as he was the conductor of the choir, I fancied he wished me in passing to visit the scene of his orchestral triumphs. "This way, Sir," said the disciple of Caxton and Handel, advancing up the belfry stairs, which seemed to obtain additional light from his fiery red nose and huge mop of flaxen hair. "Ah! to be sure, thought I, Quasimodo, proud of his bells. They are no doubt worth seeing." Arrived at a door, he entered a chamber just over the nave of the church. This was the Icelandic Society's *dépôt*, and here the place where they sold their books.

Some other society seemed likewise to be installed here; for there was a model salmon net, and some agricultural implements in the apartment. In the evening I called upon the Rector of the High School, an enlightened and agreeable man; who presents me to his family, and with two of the School Programmes, containing translations in excellent English by himself from Snorri Sturleson; from whom I find he is the twenty-first in direct descent. On the table was Lord Dufferin's 'Letters from High Latitudes.' The Icelanders, who cannot see the fun of that exceedingly amusing book, pronounce it grotesque and exaggerated, and think it the book of a man who, in his two days' journey along the beaten path to the Geysers, and other two days' residence at the very Danish capital, Reykjavik, had no opportunity of gaining any real insight into the manners and customs of modern Iceland. One thing, however, is certain, that he made a wonderfully good use of his limited opportunities.

"And what brings you to Iceland, may I ask?" said the Dominie. "You know it is the most difficult and expensive country in the world to travel in. No inns, no roads, no carriages, no anything for the convenience of the traveller. Nothing but bogs, rocks, precipices; precipices, rocks, bogs; ice, snow, lava; lava, snow, ice; rivers and torrents; torrents and rivers. For my part I never think of venturing into the country. And alone, too! Are you not afraid of the Utilegumenn?" (the Robin Hoods of the interior.) "You must be a Geologist; somebody come to see after the Sulphur mines; or a Botanist perhaps—or have you come for the same purpose as those two Englishmen in a yacht, to find a country where they really could rough it and rejoice therein; a place in Europe and still out of it, to all intents and purposes?"

"Well, Rector, you are partly right. I do like getting out of the regions of respectability—pardon me—once in a way. Hard fare too for a time is a fine alterative. 'Persicos odi apparatus.' But besides that, your country has an interest for me apart from questions of physical science. I want to see with my own eyes some of the places where the scenes of your Sagas and legends are laid. I belong to a nation arrived at a very high state of civilisation, artificial in the extreme; in short, we live and move and have our being in a state of machinery from beginning to end. And somehow this very modernism begets a desire for reverting now and then to old things, old people, old ballads, old customs—something fresh, and rare, and vigorous. I want to look for a bit at the rock from whence we were hewn, and the hole of the pit whence we were digged." "Ay, ay! Sir, rocks and pits you'll find in plenty . . . ."

The next day put my love of enduring to a severe test; and it required all my stock of fortitude to imitate the bright example of Mark Tapley, and be jolly under difficulties. While still aching in all my bones from trying to sleep on the so-called sofa, a tap came at the door; and a man, who described himself as a merchant, entering, asked me if I wanted change for English sovereigns; modestly offering to relieve me of my gold on the very equitable terms of my making him a present of 5 per cent. beyond the rate of exchange as noted in the last Copenhagen paper, which I shewed him. No sooner was he gone, than another moneychanger succeeded, offering still less. What! another? will the line stretch out to the crack of doom?

> Uno avulso non deficit alter
> Aureus (i. e. golden offer).

"Avaunt, Sirrah! Take a homely man's advice . . ." The kites had snuffed out their prey; and it was only by taking refuge in the street that I escaped the eternal rat-a-tat-tat of these respectable people. Sooth to say, I afterwards discover that my tormentors were only of the lowest class of traffickers. No sooner there, than I am offered a horse for sale. A nice looking animal really, a dun with a black cross down his back and shoulders, and only eight years old. "Well, here you are, I'll buy it." The money, something under five pounds sterling, had scarcely changed hands, when the pony's age grew from eight to fifteen. Visions of spavin, broken wind, curbs, sprung sinews, and other equine disorders, rushed upon me. But I consoled myself with the thought that the superadded years was an invention of the enemy, to wit, another dealer, whose horse I had rejected. Such a generation of horsedealers I never beheld. Every one had a splendid beast to sell. Oh! for the lantern of Diogenes to discover an honest man!

"Here comes the jolly Rector. Hurrah!" "Ha! ha! ha! Precisely. Conturbabantur Constantinopolitani innumeris difficultatibus." At last, I succeed in buying another really good horse, a cream-coloured one, and I hire two more; and also engage a guide, one Olaver, with his two horses. The want of a saddle is supplied by a greasy looking individual, looking very like a shoemaker, but in reality a functionary of some importance, who lets me one for a small sum.

Suffice it to say, that a keen tendency to bargain cropped out everywhere, and I was already longing to be off into the interior, where Iceland, by the universal consent of all travellers, appears to much greater advantage than in Reykjavik.

Meantime, my good humour is quite restored by the courteous salutation of a pleasant-humoured gentleman, the French consul, who invites me to come and see him. I find this is a delicate acknowledgment of the slight attention I had been able to render his daughter on board the steamer; who turns out to be no other than the fair little demonstrator of the uses of a razor. Her cheek is healing fast. The mother, who speaks very good French, has an opportunity of practising the language with that handsome, dark, French priest, whose downcast lids only half conceal the two gleaming fires beneath them. He is one of two foreign ecclesiastics who have been despatched here by his holiness, "to recall the lost children to the fold."

One cannot always command one's thoughts; and I cannot help confessing, that as I thought of the approaching extinction of the power of the papacy in her focus, and this flicker at the poles, I could not forbear recalling instances I have seen, of no matter what sort of animal, where the heart had all but ceased to beat, and yet the extremities were kicking most vigorously.

They have purchased a large plot of ground for some six thousand dollars, and have built a house upon it, and were proceeding to build a chapel for their own use and that of the foreigners, i. e. French fishermen, and men-of-war's men, who congregate here in the summer: but the works have been stopped, and a fine of 40 dollars imposed upon them. It now comes out, that, unlike Faro, where the Danish law of freedom of religion is in force, Iceland still preserves the ancient law, forbidding the popish religion to be openly exercised, or the maintenance of any places of worship but those for the Lutheran confession. Why were not the Frenchmen told this before making the purchase?—Ahem!

"And have they any converts?" I asked of my hospitable host, as he pledged me in a glass of champagne, his easy-going manner and sleek appearance betokening a head and stomach in capital order, and himself to be a person not the least likely to become a proselyte. "Oh no," he replied, sotto voce. "They are most agreeable people, and a very nice accession to our limited society; and we are very glad of talking French with them; but there is no danger of our being converted. We are too material a people for that," he added, settling his portly figure comfortably in his chair, after doing ample justice to a most capital supper. He was quite right about Monsieur and his confrère. They quaffed the champagne with much gusto, and were so amiable and chatty, that I accepted their invitation to visit them before leaving Iceland.

A pamphlet was subsequently put into my hands written by S. Melsted, one of the Professors of the Theological School here, wherein he sets forth plainly, as a warning to his countrymen, the difference between the creed of Luther and that of Rome. There is no chance, anyhow, of the clergy going over. Even in the olden days, before the Reformation, they were never very submissive to Rome.—'Its a long cry to Lochawe.'—And so, in spite of the thunders of the Vatican, which dwindled down into something very faint in sound before they reached Iceland, they reserved to themselves, among other rights, one which they contended for from the earliest times, that of a Christian priest being allowed to marry at pleasure.

Before setting out on my travels, be it said, I got much more than a crumb of comfort in the assurance of people who had lately been up the country, that the rivers are not a whit bigger this year than usual; and that instead of being too late for such an excursion, this is the best time, both because the snow has already melted a good deal and reached the sea, and also because the horses are now at their fattest and strongest.

It was not till noon on July the 26th that my caravan was ready for starting. First rode the guide, leading in his right hand the front baggage horse, fastened by a rope tied tightly round his lower jaw. To his tail was fastened the next horse in the same manner, and so on. Before morning, the guide cried loudly, "Hah! haw! Hah! haw!" a signal to the horses to be on the move; but, in spite of the premonition, one beast stood stock still, and the continuity was broken; whereupon down got the guide to splice the fracture. This event occurred again in the course of the day, when looking back, by the meerest chance in the world, I saw that half the convoy was a long way astern in the midst of a stony moor. The Arab, who travels just in the same way, fixes a bell to the last horse; if this ceases tingling, he knows that the line is broken.

I may here say for the edification of those who turn up their noses at anything but Oriental travel, that there is much here to remind one of the East. The Icelandic tent is uncommonly like that of the Bedouin. The *skier* (curds) again, the be-all and end-all of Icelandic eating, is also *the* dish of the Eastern Nomad tribes. Except a Nomad, nobody but an Icelander would stick so tenaciously to the saddle, and evince such a hatred of walking; while the passion for storytelling and recounting the deeds of their ancestry is shared alike by the Icelander and the rhapsodists of Asia.

About four miles from the town we cross a small river near its junction with the sea. There is a salmon-fishery here rented by a merchant of Peterhead, who has a similar establishment at Borgarfiord. The fish are cooked and packed in hermetically sealed boxes on the spot. Sandy tells me that they have only caught 5000lb. this year.

The aspect of the country is wild and savage enough. Mountains in every direction; those on the right having the peculiar abrupt outlines, and some of them the conical shape, that bespeak volcanic action. The road, tolerable at first, becomes in time a mere row of deeply cut ruts full of muddy holes, charged with water by the recent rains. Still there was something delightful in the very thought of turning one's back for a time on towns and the inhabitants thereof; in feeling that human nature really did not require so much pampering, and dressing, and shaping, after all: that if I wanted shelter, there was the tent to cover me; or if food, my baggage contained it, or the means of getting it. The rain too has ceased; although my skin-overhauls and mackintosh made me quite independent of rain. The sun was out, and the Arctic Flora glistened cheerfully, and spread abroad ambrosial odours. On the dry stony spots grew the beautiful *Dryas octopetala*, or mountain avens, in thick white patches. The *Statice armeria* with its rose-coloured heads and downy stalks, as well as wild-thyme and the different galiums, seemed equally anxious to avoid the boggy ground, leaving it in the undisturbed possession of the saxifrages, the butter-wort and lilac-coloured cuckooflower; while here and there a space of short grass spangled with dandelions and buttercups, and green with the multifarious delicate plants of the far North, shewed that the short summer was now near its full.

I had seen the *Maître d'hôtel* of the French man-of-war with some golden plovers in his basket this morning; so that I was prepared for the bird's melancholy cry. Three ravens, tame as barn-door fowls, sit by the wayside begging, or scolding, or something; a couple of wild swans flap heavily from the dark rush-fringed tarn, where I can descry red-throated divers, and some small kind of duck intently watching our procession. Anon, two falcons are heard screaming aloft, while another, large and of a light colour, sits perfectly motionless on the rocks, with a tameness quite 'shocking;' but I am balked of a shot by the guide's mongrel cur, which I had already discovered to be a pest and a nuisance, chasing up all the birds he can snuff or see, in spite of all my remonstrances to his master.

This fellow I soon found to be as great a nuisance as his dog. Strangely enough, we find in the way a full bottle of brandy; this he takes possession of; and the result of the find was soon evident in the way in which his brother, who was accompanying us for some miles—the guide seemed to be a more seasoned vessel—rolled in his saddle, as he came galloping his unfortunate beast with fury over the stones, after having stopped behind to gossip with a great caravan of men and ponies resting in the moor. After five hours' riding, I mount my second horse; my guide does the same, taking leave of his inebriated brother with a smothering kiss, and a cloud of dislodged snuff.

"What do you call that?" asked I, pointing to a deep perpendicular-sided ravine through which a brook was dashing. "Gill" was the answer, the very word used for such a spot in the North of England. The road was desolate enough. Here and there was a small "bei" or "cote" (=cottage), looking much more, however, like a potato-pie overgrown with grass.

It is nearly 8 P.M. when the rain recommences, and we are still in the midst of a horrible stony waste bordered by lofty mountains, while to the right lies a lake out of which project cones of volcanic material. "Whenever are we to get to that Almannagiá?" I kept inwardly asking myself: 9 P.M. and no signs of it.

CHAPTER V.

The Almannagiá—A crack in the lava—What was the cause of it —The Oxerá—The blue pool of doom—The old parliament days —Camping in a churchyard—Icelandic version of the ballad of Leonora—The Lögberg—Flosi leaps for his life—The old versus the new religion—The missionary Thangbrand—Christianity gains the day—Baptism in hot water—The Raven-chasm—Icelandic ptarmigan.

BEFORE I was aware of it the road began descending by a cleft a few yards wide, and slanting down a precipice some two hundred feet high. The surprise was complete; although I had heard that the dip was very sudden. The descent itself is steep no doubt, as Englishmen count steepness; but it is a mere exaggeration of travellers to call it a "frightful dangerous chasm." There is nothing dangerous or breakneck about it in the least; the incline being less than that of a very easy drawing room staircase, where an Icelandic pony, which can "clim like a caat," as Sandy said to me to-day, cannot possibly be at fault. Besides which, there is no risk of the traveller becoming giddy, as the disrupted trap through which he passes is a wall unto him on his right and on his left.

This is the famous Almannagiá down which so many a free-born peasant-legislator of Iceland used to journey to the parliament; the kindred of those

S. G. ADA MARGETTS.

THE LÖGBERG & ALMANNAGIÁ.

fine fellows, so unlike the slave-born founders of old Rome, whose names made the kings of Europe tremble, and whose descendants sat on the mightiest of their thrones. Arrived at the bottom of the descent, we find ourselves in a broad alley of perfectly level sward, running right and left past the bottom of the narrow staircase we have descended.

This alley, or by whatever name it may be called, has been caused by the vast field of lava, which covers the country, having split to the perpendicular depth of about one hundred and eighty feet sheer down. The fissure is three miles long and in a perfectly straight line. When the fracture occurred, one side of the fissure, that to our left, remained immovable, while the other staggered asunder for several yards, and then threw its head backwards, as if in astonishment at what had happened; so that the right side of the chasm is about eighty feet lower than the left one. This is owing to the lava plain behind it having sunk downwards; perhaps from its weight pressing on the soft ground, which must have formed the bed of the north end of the Tingvalla lake; before the mighty Skjaldbreid vomiting forth its entrails, the lake fled and its waters were driven back into their present more contracted space. At a distance of six or eight miles across the lava-basin, a similar process has taken place. The mass of lava is, there as here, rent in a perfectly straight line, and one wall of the rent is much higher than the other. Moreover, this plain between is exactly of the same width as the head of the lake; another proof of the correctness of the theory on which we have endeavoured to explain the above stupendous phenomenon.

Suppose, by way of further illustration, that, in place of a huge mass of lava, there had been some vast building; the two ends of which rested on secure foundations, while the centre part had no foundation at all; the result would be, that, while the ends stood firm, the middle would part away from the extremities and collapse, sinking lowest where the substratum was softest. But to return to the Almannagiá. We trot along its green bottom, now the joy of wild looking sheep, fantastic shapes of stone glowring down upon us from the rugged ramparts, that from the

> 'level meadow of deep grass
> Suddenly scale the light.'

Anon, there is a sally-port through the right or lower wall, through which we see the river at our feet, and, further on, the little church standing near the lake; while in front of us, just across the river, is the site of the old open parliament of Tingvalla, and if the eye passes over, it, and traverses the outspread lava basin, a dark straight streak may be seen by daylight, which is the other fissure above mentioned, and which goes by the name of the Ravnegiá (or Ravenrent): and runs exactly parallel to the Almannagiá.

Before descending, however, to ford the river, we keep along the level sward of the Almannagiá, which is for all the world like the dry moat of some mighty fenced city; the inner wall of which exhibits a variety of embrasures and machicolations.

Further on we descry, wonderful to relate, a river, bursting by a lofty fall over this, the left rampart; and into the very fissure in which we stand. Surely some new thing has taken place; it is rushing towards us, and we shall be overwhelmed by the resistless flood. But no; after bounding fiercely towards us between the walls for a few hundred yards, it is suddenly brought up in a deep pool; and then making a sharp turn to its left, it explodes in a cataract through another sally-port, and expands into a broad river, which sweeps swiftly past the church and into the lake. This is the famous Oxerá, a stream of much eccentricity. Sometimes it will disappear bodily, nobody knows where. Thus in the year 1740, when the Deputies were assembled, it vanished, reappearing however a few days after, and leaping over the precipice with a sudden prodigious crash. The blue pool, where the river joins the plain, played a tragic part in the old parliament days. It must have often been conscious of the screams of poor sack-packed wretched females, who had been condemned for child murder, and were engulphed here without having the luck of the Count of Monte Christo. Be it remembered, that the Spartan code of the country, at one time, sanctioned the destruction of sickly infants. At the present day, too, it seems allowed. At least this much is certain, that hundreds of infants are lost from being weaned on the day after birth. Of other malefactors, murderers were beheaded, while witches, as being the blackest of sinners, underwent a more cruel death, being burnt by the river side. On the banks of the Oxerá, opposite the church, may still be seen the stone foundations of the booths, where dwelt all the rank and beauty and talent of Iceland at the yearly meeting of the assembly. The astute and worldly, but withal learned and polished, Snorri Sturluson, the sage Niál, the impetuous Kiartan—all the great names, in short, of that Scandinavian breed, to which, and not to the Saxon, England owes her pluck, her dash, and her freedom. The beautiful Odny, and the other fair daughters of the land, would make a point of being here; and of course the pedlars, the Bryce Snailfoots of those times, with silver ornaments, and cloths fine and coarse (skarlat, and vadmál), would not be here the day after the fair.

After fording the river, and unpacking the baggage, I prepare for my first bivouack; while the guide drives the horses into a moor beyond the precincts of the *tún*, or cultivated enclosure, this being one of the first things to be seen to in Icelandic travel. As there is no other sufficiently dry and level spot to be found near for the purpose of encamping, I avail myself of the dark-complexioned priest's permission to pitch my tent in a *particular* spot in the churchyard, which he points out, saying, "*There*;" not however without sundry misgivings on my part. King John, when he gave utterance to his speech, "If this same were a churchyard where we stand," &c., seemed to associate the place with every thing that is uncanny and melancholic; and I must own that my flesh did creep somewhat at the thought of camping alone in one.

Can this be that weird spot I have read of in some Icelandic churchyard, "whereof the ewe not bites," though it will crop the herbage all around. Once an inquisitive fellow dug into it, and found a man's body all fresh, as if he was alive, and clothed in red. He shovelled in the earth might-and-main, and from that time to this nobody has ever been buried in that spot. Certainly, my repose was none of the soundest that night. A churchyard is, really, not the proper place for a night's rest. The blood gets thick and heavy, or excited, or something.

Another strange story of this strange country, very like Bürger's *Leonora*, but with features in it altogether Icelandic, rose to my mind. "A young fellow had promised to call for his sweetheart on Christmas-Eve, and accompany her to the Midnight Mass,—a custom now obsolete, which prevailed late into Protestant times in this country. On his way to her, he had to cross a swollen torrent. His horse stumbled among the floating ice, and an unlucky pull at the rein causing it to lose its footing, he was thrown into the water, apparently killed by a blow on the neck from a sharp ice-block. Alas! when he promised to fetch his bride, he neglected to add, 'if God will.' Long waits the maiden for her lover. At last, near midnight, he comes; and lifting her silently up behind him, rides off to the church. Once, on the road, he turns round to her, and says—

'The moon glides, the dead man rides,
Do you see the mark on my neck
Garun, Garun?'

The maiden is alarmed, but by a strong effort she keeps her seat, and on they ride to church. Here they stop, close to an open grave.

'Bide ye here, Garun, Garun,
While I flit Faxa, Faxa*,
Eastward from the *tún*†.'

On hearing these words, Gudrun,—that was the maiden's name, but the spectre could not frame to pronounce it right, because *Gud*=God in Icelandic—falls fainting towards the ground, but, luckily, in her descent clutches at the bell-rope of the Lych-gate‡,

* I. e. the horse. Taxa is the Icelandic for a horse's mane.

† I. e. the churchyard enclosure.

‡ *Sáluhlid*, the soul-gate: a roofed portal, generally opposite the western entrance of the church; and which is often the only belfry.

where the horse had halted; the bell tolls, the ghost vanishes, and she is saved.

A dash into the fresh waters of the Oxerá next morning acted as a fine tonic to the nervous system. I question whether any of the present generation of Icelanders ever thinks of such a thing as taking a bath. In the olden times, swimming was a common accomplishment; and to judge from Snorri's bath at Reykholt, and others that are mentioned in the old sagas, ablution must have been in fashion.

The little church of Tingvalla is new, and of wood; two properties belonging to almost every church in Iceland; they don't look like churches. They might be so many wooden warehouses, with their square-headed windows, and utter want of architecture. Here and there one sees a sorry remnant of better tastes; a chandelier, or a chip of wood-carving, belonging to the old church now razed. Here, for instance, is a pulpit, dating from 1683, and an old altar-picture of no merit, and for which the clergyman thinks it necessary to apologize, saying that they have not sufficient funds to purchase a new one. The first church at Tingvalla was built of timber, a present from Harald Sigurdson of Norway. It was destroyed by a storm on the death-day of Bishop Gissur, when the Thing was in full conclave.

Near the church-door is a large unhewn stone of oblong shape, on which is scored the exact ell-measure of Iceland. It formerly stood in the church-wall of the ancient church, and has doubtless been witness to many a shrewd bargain at the national meeting; when piles of cloth would exchange hands, and in case of dispute about the quality, it would be made use of as an impartial referee.

A rough walk of a few score yards brings us to the justly celebrated Lögberg (Law-hill), the site for 1000 years of the open air parliament. The religio loci is well calculated to work strongly on the mind of the spectator. But its natural features are such as to make an impression never to be obliterated. Fancy yourself on a tolerably even, grass-grown, *plateau*, on the edge of a plain of dark, rugged, moss-dappled lava; and then fancy that all along the edges of this *plateau*, which is in the shape of a rude irregular lozenge, yawning grooves open out, perpendicular and very many fathoms deep. And then again, below this, came as many more fathoms of sapphire-tinted water, which has flowed down from the mountains by concealed channels, and again speedily disappears, and escapes by subterranean ducts into the adjoining lake of Tingvalla.

At one spot, the sides of this giddy cleft contract to within nine ells of each other; and over this yawning chasm once sprang for his life like Morton, in *Old Mortality*, over the Black Linn of Linkwater, a criminal named Flosi! If he could have got to the south end of the irregular lozenge, he need not have leapt at all, for there it is that the otherwise complete isolation is cut off;—the *défaut de cuirasse*—the chasm narrowing there to a mere crack: and it is by that spot that we ourselves got into this wonderful fastness. But Flosi well knew that on either side of that entrance armed men kept watch and ward to prevent ingress and egress, like to those cherubims of the flaming swords that turned every way to keep the way of the tree of life. About the centre of the enclosure is the place where the president sat in a booth (the ruins of which were visible forty years ago); and around him, on banks of earth, which are still to be traced, the forty-eight dömmer or doomsmen. A few paces to the north of this, is an eminence, from which another functionary recited the old laws and promulgated new ones. Without, were the people of the country crowding round to the edge of the abyss, and barred by it from entering the sacred precincts.

About the year 1261, Iceland ceased to be a free Republic, and was ceded to Hacon king of Norway; while in 1387 it passed under the crown of Denmark. Its shadow of a parliament, however, lasted till 1800, when it was finally abolished. But in the palmy days of Icelandic liberty, i.e. from 927 to the beginning of the 13th century, scenes of great historical interest used to occur here during the sixteen days' sitting of the assembly.

Let us transport ourselves to this spot eight hundred and sixty years ago. Iceland was then ill at ease. She was groaning and travailing in earnest expectation of a new faith, which people said was going to cast out the old one. The sanguinary rites of Thor and Odin were not to be any longer; a new God, likest to the White Baldur, of all the Scandinavian Pantheon, was about to cast down the national Dagons.

These twenty years the agitation had been going on. Doubtless, the more enlightened among the people were beginning to think that their Gods were no Gods; and the Godi, or Prince-Pontiffs, would be inclined, like the Roman augurs, to laugh in each other's faces when they met. As in the days of our own Reformation, the people would not know what to believe. So true it is, that events and situations reproduce themselves. First, came one Frederick, a Saxon Bishop, from beyond the seas, in company of Kodran, a native Icelander, and preached the new doctrines in the north, and Thorward, the son of Spakbodwar, had actually set up a temple to the new God in Hialtadal.

Then came one Stefner, exiled by king Olaf from Norway in the days of Pope Gregory the Vth; but he utterly failed in his mission; for only the next year, 997, a law was passed at this very place, interdicting any one from giving fire or water to the adherents of this pestilent sect.

A man of another stamp takes his place, also sent by king Olaf to teach the doctrines of Christianity. This was Thangbrand, the son of Vilbald, Count of Bremen. On one occasion, being entertained at a banquet by Hubert, the Papal legate in the province of Canterbury, he was presented by his host with a shield, bearing upon it the device of the Holy Rood. This he sold to king Olaf Trygveson, and with the price of it bought a beautiful Irish damsel—an odd purchase for an ordained priest. Killing a man in a duel, who tried to seduce his mistress, he fled to Norway, and became priest of Mostur.

His extravagance however getting him into pecuniary difficulties, he turned pirate, and by this means repaired his impoverished exchequer; and not long after, by way of punishment, he was sent by king Olaf to Iceland as a Christian missionary! Here he is attacked by Berserkers; lampoons—a favourite weapon of the Icelanders—are levelled at him; and magicians—after the manner of those of Egypt, who withstood the Prophet of the Lord—play their devilish pranks in defiance of him. But Thangbrand is not to be daunted. The Berserkers he fights and slays; the lampoon-makers fare no better; and so convincingly does he discourse of the glory of the angels of God, that many of the natives, and, among others, a great man of the south, Hallr of Sida, believe, and are baptized by him. At last, the authorities take up the matter, and our missionary is arraigned for homicide at the General Assembly. The sentence is, that nobody shall feed or harbour him. Being thus starved out, he is forced to beat a retreat. His ship is wrecked, but he escapes, and again setting sail arrives safely in Norway, leaving behind him the reputation of being a most cruel and violent man. And doubtless he had more of the spirit of Saul than Moses in his composition.

Such then was the posture of affairs. There were some open proselytes to the new faith, and no doubt more secret ones. At last, the Christians determine to go boldly to the parliament, and preach the religion of Jesus, come what may.

The leading men in the movement are Thormod, and Hialt an Icelandic magnate, both emissaries of king Olaf of Norway; and lastly, Gissur, also a noble Icelander, who had been baptized by Thangbrand, and now returned from the court of king Olaf. These three then, with others, clad in full canonicals, seven in all, and carrying two crosses, boldly advance to the outer edge of the precipice surrounding the Lawhill, and while their incense-pans shed abroad fragrant odours, they boldly expound their doctrines in the face of the assembly. Nobody ventures to gainsay them, for all are astounded at their understanding and eloquence.

Thorgeir, the President, a heathen, is fairly puzzled,

and adjourns the meeting. On reaching his tent, he casts himself on his couch, and rolling his head up in a sheepskin (breiddi felld a höfut ser) so lay all the rest of that day, all that night, and the day after till the same hour.

Meantime the two parties prepare to sacrifice. It is the Prophet of Israel and the Priests of Baal over again. The heathen victims are a couple of malefactors from every province in the land, while the Christians propose to sacrifice to their God with the best people that they have. At this juncture, Thorgeir, the President, having taken counsel of himself, rises from his couch, and sends round a herald to convoke the Assembly. After setting before them the disastrous effects of a civil war, which seemed imminent, he suggests a compromise; and so adroitly and plausibly put are his arguments, that both parties agree to abide by his decision in the matter. Upon which, he passes judgment to this effect, that all Iceland should be baptized, and believe in one God, (aller menn skylldo verda skirdir a Islande, oc trua a einn Gud†.) The exposure of infants, and eating of horseflesh were still to be allowed; pet observances, which it was deemed politic to concede for the present. Nay, more; if any one had a fancy for sacrificing to Thor and Freya, he might do so; but it must be done privately on pain of banishment. Any man might keep a Teraphim, but publicity must be avoided.

† Kristnisaga, cap. 11.

One very amusing feature in this most momentous transaction is related by the old Chronicler, verifying with a witness the truth of the proverb about the proximity of the sublime to the ridiculous. Another thing the heathens stickled for. They were ready to be baptized, but on one condition. The water must be warm; cold they positively declined. This little prejudice was of course humoured, and at a very cheap rate, considering the scarcity of fuel; for the country has always an unlimited supply of hot water in her natural boilers. The East country folks were baptized at the hot-springs of Laugardal, which I pass to day: while the West country heathens resorted on their way home to the numerous hot springs of Reykiardal.

Modern optimism may be disposed to criticise the above terms of compromise, and pronounce the whole an insensate jumble: but let us depend upon it, that as Rome was not built in a day, so neither has any change of religion been made in a country all at once, pure and simple. The gods of Egypt were long objects of adoration, side by side with the Deity who spake from Sinai. Long after S. Augustine, pious Britons were imbued with the old Pagan spirit; a spirit which without spectacles may really be discerned, even at the present hour, only under another name, strongly saturating what is called Christianity.

While I stand looking at the upper fall of the

Oxerá, the priest points out to me the exact spot where witches used to be burned, viz. just where one of the numerous small giás, which rend the lava around, opens out on the flat shore of the river.

The packing has been completed on our return to the churchyard, and the guide is ready to start: his bloodshot eyes and husky voice connect themselves in my mind with the stray brandy bottle, on which we happened yesterday, which is lying empty on the grass; having cracked, he says, and let out the liquor!

For two hours our way wound across the great lava-basin, occupying what I believe to have been once the north end of the lake. The twists and turns of its surface are here and there as sharp and fresh, as if it was only yesterday that the hell-broth had stiffened into stone, in the very act of waving and winding its tortuous eddies, and sucking up all in its hot embrace. Were it not for the bathos, I should liken parts of it to rolls of twisted tobacco; while the bits of igneous rock which bestrew the whole country in various places are exactly like fragments of Bologna sausage, specked with white lard. In the crevices of the rocks a grove of stunted birch-trees have insinuated themselves, while Grass of Parnassus, dwarf heather, and other plants, seem bent on softening the rigour of the scene. We have above advanced a theory to explain the subsidence of the basin over which we are now travelling. A further cause may be, that the bowels of the earth under our feet may have contributed a portion of the mighty stream of burning materials, which finding a vent in the mountain of Skialdbreid, north of this, poured down hither; and under the weight of this superincumbent mass, which is perhaps one hundred fathoms in thickness, the earth below, already hollowed, would naturally collapse and subside.

After floundering along over a ridge and furrow path, made by the horses always placing their feet in the same spot, we rise by degrees, and cross the Ravnegiá by the narrow bridge which some fallen masses of mossgrown rock have reared over its startling depths. Looking back for a moment to the dark parallel belt of the Almannagiá, I see it crossed in one place by a bit of bright silver. That is the fall of the Oxerá.

Presently some stray whimbrels approach with that soft fluid jug of theirs, which is not unlike the cry of the nightingale, their wings flickering like the uncertain play of the electric light: while a lot of ptarmigans are stealthily creeping out of harm's way, among the grey-coated lava, which would effectually conceal their similarly coloured plumage, but that their speech bewrayeth them. A suicidal act on their part, which all who know the nature of these birds are aware they cannot abstain from.

It may be here as well to say a few words on the Icelandic ptarmigan. As the traveller in Norway is aware, there are two sorts of ptarmigan in that country: the mountain ptarmigan, (lagopus vulgaris,) which is identical with that which is to be found in the North of Britain; in summer its predominating colour is grey, speckled with black; in winter it is white. The other, which the Norwegians call the *skov*, or *dal-rype*, (wood, or dale ptarmigan,) is a much larger bird; attaining to the length of seventeen inches. Like the smaller variety, it is white in winter, while in summer it is of a reddish yellow plumage, much resembling our Red Grouse. Are both these species to be found in Iceland? The natives affirm that they have only one kind. The specimens which I shot differed in colour from those I had bagged in Norway. They were neither so grey as the mountain ptarmigan, nor so red-brown as the wood-ptarmigan; while in size they more nearly approached the former. So that I was led to think—and I find since that Faber, as quoted by Mr. Yarrell, had already come to the same conclusion—that the ptarmigan of Iceland is a distinct species.

On the other hand, the two birds have perfectly different notes. The wood-rype utters a very loud cluck, like our grouse, which I have heard a good mile off on the hill-sides near the sea in Norway; while the note of the lesser bird is totally different. By some it is likened to the harsh cry of the missel-thrush, by others to the croak of a frog; while on the grey rocks of the Luffodens I have taken it for the cough of a sheep. Now in Iceland I have heard both these notes, (the cluck-note however somewhat modified,) which would indicate that in Iceland, as in Norway, there are two distinct species.

S.G. — Ada Margett.

CHAPTER VI.

Icelandic passion for snuff—Laugardal—The Bridge-river—Where are the forests?—The Geysers—The Strokr growls—We bait him—Boiled alive!—The great Geyser makes no sign—Aids to devotion—The tempest demon abroad—An inundation—Ari Frodi—Mode of travelling on the Fjeld—Camp under Blue-fell near the source of the White River.

On the road, I hang behind to explore a curious cave under the lava, not however *the* cave, as I subsequently found; which the guide makes no mention of. As I ride on to overtake him, to my consternation I see he is throwing his head back, taking in great gulps of what I conjecture to be brandy. On nearing him, however, I discover that it is his nose and not his mouth which he is dosing out of a horn; from whence he imbibes whole ounces of snuff at a time. Some Icelanders, in order to husband the precious powder, insert a peg of tobacco, I am told, in either nostril! Twelve pounds of snuff a year is no uncommon allowance. The price is not less than three dollars per lb.

At length the path winds round a mountain of bare black dust and cinders, with pinnacles of yellow tufa protruding from the summit: having been most likely denuded by the tempests of ages, which have failed, however, to eradicate the pretty white *Silene Maritima*, *Cerastium Latifolium*, and *Cerastium Alpi-*

num, which flecked the slope. From the top I see what I fancy must be the sea.

Further on, we double some magnificent jagged cliffs to our left, the Eastern boundary of a grassy plain. But what on earth means that hubbub among those golden plovers? See, that one is wounded; it has fallen in that horseshoe-shaped spot surrounded by the swollen brook. He is only malingering. It is the bird's object to cover the retreat of that young one, who can run fast enough, but cannot fly, and is pounded by the brook. I was recalled from this amusing scene by the neighing of my horse, and looking round I found the guide was out of sight. Off I set, and at last descried him and the cavalcade creeping along like flies at some distance. The stupendous objects around dwarf everything in a surprising manner in this country.

We have now entered the plain of Laugardal, fertilized by the descent of numerous streams dashing from the mountains, to join the neighbouring lakes. Several grass-roofed cottages crouch on the slopes. Were it not for the smoke, curling from these abodes of man, one might pass them sometimes without being aware of their existence. The back-premises, especially, are generally a continuation of the adjoining declivity; with no window or door visible, these being for the most part in the front. A traveller relates that in the dusk he rode up a grassy slope, and came butt against some object. It was the chimney of a house! At the end of a lake, far away to the front, I perceive smoke driving in large volumes before the keen northerly wind. "It must be some people burning turf," said my trustworthy companion. Will it be believed that these are hot springs of great celebrity—the very springs, I believe, whence the water was obtained for the fastidious Christian converts mentioned above.

Fortunately, the Bruará (bridge river) is moderate in volume to-day, so that we can wade safely to the middle of it, and then ride over the few planks—alias bridge—which span the depths of the narrow cleft in the precipice, over which the river here makes a fine fall—a bridge in the midst of a river! But so it is. Better late than never. And I believe it is universally allowed that half a loaf is better than no bread.

In a stunted birch copse, further on, I see the *Orchis Maculata.* Elsewhere I pick up the Frog Orchis (*Satyrium viride?*) a plant, if I remember rightly, not known in Great Britain. Many causes have contributed to destroy these woods. Chiefly, perhaps, the improvidence of the natives. In the early days a chieftain used to take possession of as much of the wild land as he could encompass by fires lit in sight of each other between sunrise and sunset. And no doubt a little burning of the bush was resorted to, to facilitate matters. At a later period, when there were many workers in iron in the country, the woods were cut up root and branch to make charcoal; and behold the result: not a tree, properly so called, in the island. The first human being we have seen on our road to-day here meets us, to wit, a strapping damsel sitting astride of a prodigiously fat pony.

I stop for a few minutes at the farm of Austerhlid, and gain from the farmer, to whom I have a letter of introduction, some useful hints about my further route. A Reaumur thermometer, which hangs outside his dwelling, marks only eight above zero; while he is engaged in the summer occupation of hay-making. It was about nine, P.M., when we reached the Geysers, about which every traveller has so much to say, that I must endeavour to say as little as possible. The shadows of evening, and dense volumes of steam spouting out in all directions, at first hid from my sight a large bell-tent. The occupants of it are some German naturalists, who have come from the north by the desert of Sprengisandr, and have collected several specimens of natural history.

From them I learn that my guide's statement, of the Sprengisandr route to the north abounding with dangerous bogs, is a pure fiction. On the contrary, as the very name imports, the way is singularly dry; so dry, in short, that for two days the horses must travel for sixteen hours before reaching grass. My guide has travelled that road twice or thrice before, and the only real impediment are the rivers Hvitá and Thiorsá, of both of which however he must know the fording-places. The Germans arrived here yesterday, just too late to witness an eruption of the Great Geyser. My tent was pitched within twenty yards of the lair of this monster.

Many times in the course of the night I was disturbed by his roaring and rumblings; but nothing came of it. The water in the basin boiled over, and I could hear it rushing down that mound of stone cauliflowers with which the fountain has in the course of ages surrounded itself. At one time the thunderings and subterranean voices waxed so loud that I sprang up. Things, as far as the dim light permitted me to see, looked very promising.

> Magna et præclara minantis
> Vultus erat—

Dense volumes of steam partially hid the rising dome of boiling water; but again matters stopped here.

There were many false alarms the next day, and the Germans, whose fifteen horses were all ready for starting, are in despair. "You must be content with the Strokr, Gentlemen." So we proceed to this spring, which is one hundred paces south of the Great Geyser; and, although it has no cone, but rises from the flat, is the more picturesque of the two. Forthwith, we collect handfulls of turf and stones, and throw them into the Strokr's pipe. But nothing seemed to move him. The waters below grunted and snarled like a baited badger, but were not to be drawn. "In the sulks," said I laughingly, as I stood with my back to the orifice. "Here he comes," shrieked one of the party, as I heard a hiss like a rocket disengaging itself from its stick. "Rush for your life!" And rush I did, but my foot catching, down I fell. "Boiled alive" was my instantaneous thought; "The seething waters will descend and overwhelm me." And so they would have done, had not the wind been from my side of the spout, and carried the waters in the other direction. What a sight! A column of turbid water never ending, still beginning, darts into the air at least one hundred feet, bearing along with it all the unwholesome food with which we had been loading the creature's maw. The physical reason for the discharge, which is a feature common to several of the Icelandic hot springs, is pretty well understood. The pipe, which is forty-eight feet deep, diminishes from six feet, its breadth at the top, to eleven inches at bottom. The injected mass of stones and other material acts like the shutting of a safety valve; the steam has not a proper vent, it collects rapidly in the subterranean chambers that arch over the fountains of the great deep until they are charged to bursting, and suddenly driving back the continually encroaching waters, they lift off the obstruction, and rush into mid-air with the velocity of a missile from the chamber of an Armstrong gun; and are often illuminated, as on the present occasion, by a beautiful iris.

And where does all the water come from? That, too, is easy of explanation. It is the drainage of the hills around, which meeting heated surfaces gets to the boil, and explodes when it has a chance. As for the decomposition of the palagonite-tuff by the hot water, the precipitation of silicious sinter, the pranks played by the sulphuric acid and sulphuretted hydrogen, and all that sort of thing, as most readers would be choked off by it, we shall go for a change of air to the neighbouring farm-house, to see about the repairing of one of my packsaddles, as I have learnt that Thordar the proprietor is, like most Icelanders, a cunning artificer in iron*. It was quite impossible, said Thordar, to attend to my little matter now. Bad weather was coming on, and the hay not in. Upon this I seize his rake, and set to work might and main, to help the women in getting the hay together, astonishing them all by my wonderful vigour. Looking at me for a moment or two, Thordar observed, "Han er hamhleipa† til

* 'A smith,' in Icelandic, is one who works either in iron or wood. 'To smithy' is to build or form. The word occurs in the Edda.

† The word contains an allusion to the Werewolf superstition prevalent in Iceland.

at rakë" (Anglicè, 'He is the very ——— at raking);' and then went off to his smithy.

That night closed in with storm and rain. I slept in the tent alone; my guide preferring the shelter of the farm-house. In my dreams, I fancied the Great Geyser had erupted and set fire to my tent, making my effects crackle like burning thorns. I awoke, and found that it was a storm of hail pattering against the canvass; which by the sparse light of the morning I saw was all taut and right. Anon, comes a smart rap at the tent-door; while a surly guttural voice exclaimed, "More! more!" It was a raven, who had come thus early for the bones—not mine, Reader—but the mutton bones, which after breakfast he got accordingly. The ravens in the neighbourhood of the brook Cherith were much better behaved. An adjoining hole, full of sapphire-coloured water, always on the simmer, boils my coffee excellently, superseding the spirit lamp. Close to this lucid fountain is another, the colour of red ochre.

It rains heavily all this day (Sunday, July 29). The Strokr makes several erruptions, but the Great Geyser is not up to the mark at all. Is he in his dotage? Fifty years ago he is said to have exploded every six hours. Summers and winters one thousand and thirty-six,—for that is his age according to the latest census,—have doubtless abated his natural powers, and he will before long become superannuated, and give way to the pushing youngsters around. But we must not jump too quickly at conclusions. The peasants say that it is quite as it should be. The Strokr, like the stormy petrel, exults in the tempest*, while the Great Geyser, like a Parisian, shews only in fine weather.

It was no small satisfaction to me, in my strange solitude, to read the services of the day. I question whether in the noblest cathedral, with the solemn organ pealing, the devotional spirit could be more stirred within one, than here in the midst of God's wonders, with the earth shaking and thundering, and the smoke ascending like the smoke of a furnace, while "He who maketh the clouds his chariot" is heard approaching among the valleys. Burns says the tempest is the best time for devotion. What would he have said to a tempest in this vale of Siddim? In such a place and time, if ever, sound in one's ears those

> "Airy tongues that syllable men's names
> On sands and shores and desert wildernesses."

Thoughts of home cannot but rush vividly into the mind: joys, and hopes, and fears, with which another intermeddleth not; visions of one who bid the traveller God speed over the deep and over the wilderness. A few rapid weeks, and that delightful vision again assumed the shape of a beautiful reality, welcoming home the wayfarer, and radiant in smiling

* Nordurhver in Laxadal, in the north east of Iceland, is said to have the same peculiarity.

joy:—a few more rapid weeks, and the reality melts again into a vision, a vision of the past, never again to be seen in this world; a sweet, hallowed, entrancing memory.

That night the tempest-demon was fairly loose. Sweeping fiercely down the mountains, the wind threatened to uproot the tent, wailing the while, as the Icelanders would say, like the spirit of an exposed infant ("að hljoða eins og útburðr"). Some old Greek dramatist dilates on the secret feeling of satisfaction with which one hears, when safely housed, the storm-drops rattling without; and the canvass did its work bravely. To my horror, however, next morning, I find that a hole in the sward at the head of my bed had collected the deluge, which was overflowing the whole tent. In this dilemma, decision was everything; and I place sundry bottles and kettles under the edges of my waterproof carpet, and by this device I defy the puddle in my place of refuge; to which certain huge spiders had also resorted, whom, if my incarceration lasts much longer, I shall be disposed to make pets of after the manner of Robert Bruce. Geyser's 'pipe is out:' only false alarms, and abortive explosions, although this is Monday, and the last eruption was Thursday at midday.

The guide appears, and informs me that the storm will have swollen the rivers and covered the mountains with snow, so as to render travelling impossible, and suggests—turning back! As for the Sprengisandr route, this, although he has travelled it more than once, he flatly refuses to attempt; although Mr. Austerhlid, who has kindly come to see after me, offers to procure us a guide over the ford of the Hvitá (white river). There was no help for it, but to take an additional guide—a guide to guide my guide—and proceed to the source of the Hvitá, and thence northwards by the Kiolvegr, as it is called, which is a considerable *détour*, as compared with the directer way by Sprengisandr, to my ultimate destination—Myvatn.

The weather clearing up, we start at 1 P.M. with the Hreppstiori, Sigurðr Haukadalr, as our guide. Haukadalr is known to Icelandic fame as the place where Ari Frodi, the first historiographer of the north, received his education. Born in 1068 he came hither in the year 1075, and is the author of the Landnâma Book, at least of a part of it, it having been continued by learned men after his death. This and the work called Schedae, likewise on the early history of his country, is all that remains of his writings.

Our extra guide is provided with materials for caulking a hypothetical boat, which is reported to be lying on the Hvitá near its source. In a couple of hours we are fairly launched upon the Fjeld. A curious scene! Bare sandy wastes from which the wind has breast-ploughed the turf, and then blown away the earth for two or three feet deep, leaving at intervals only a few pillars (shaped like those cones one sees in the ballast holes by the side of a railway); where the earth, being pleached together by the roots of dwarf willows and grass, has defied the pelting storm. These little cones are emulating those sugar-loaved mountains to the left, black as ink, nearly a score in number, clustering in front of a huge Iökul, which is white with snow or blue with everlasting ice*. All our ponies are now loose, and driven before us, trotting away from one bunch of flowers to another to gobble it up before we overtake them. *Silene Maritima* is most common; *Saxifraga Hirculus* (Yellow Marsh Saxifrage), with its bright golden blooms, is frequent in the wet spots; and on the sandy banks of rivulets the *Epilobium Angustifolium*, called by the natives 'Eyre-rose,' spreads out a pink coloured carpet. This way of driving the horses is called *að reka hestar,* the usual procedure on the Fjeld. On the lower levels, where farm-enclosures occur, or near home, they are, as we have seen, led in a string (*að tomme hestar*).

After fording one or two rivers, we come in about five hours to a little oasis of grass; and the horses are suffered to graze, while the men consume their dried fish and bread. How favourably these Icelanders contrast with the Norwegians, who are per-

* The Jarlhettur and Langejökul.

petually guzzling enormous quantities of porridge and flad-brod. These people, on the contrary, will frequently go a whole day without eating a morsel.

We are now skirting the right bank of the impetuous Hvitá, ploughing itself a deep channel through hideous banks of mud. The path lies over the descending slopes of the extinct volcano Bláfell, scored with deep gullies and rapid torrents; add to which, dangerous quicksands and dreadful bogs baffle the fagged horses. At length, about 10 o'clock P. M., we arrive at our camping place close by the river and under the Bláfell, whose snowy top shews clear and sharp above the belt of fog which envelopes lower objects. In the midst of depressing rain the tent-pegs are driven into the earth; dwarf birch taking, for the most part, the place of grass as food for the poor horses. A camp-fire is out of the question, and after a light supper we are soon all three fast asleep in the tent.

CHAPTER VII.

A frail ferry-boat.—The guide at fault.—Utilegumenn—A tale of the outlaws.—Sigurd Palm.—Dead-man's knoll.—The abomination of desolation.—Sunset in the wilderness.—Hveravellir—Icelandic packhorses.—I catch a young swan.—Mountain pastures.—Crossing the Blanda river.—Abundance of white flowers.—The horses lost and found.—First view of the Northern sea.—The worthy pastor of Maelifell.—Icelandic hospitality.

JULY 31.—At 6 A.M. the wind is too fresh for us to venture over the rapid torrent in the frail bark, which Sigurdr has found and caulked, and pronounces seaworthy. The gale subsiding about 11 A.M., I cross over in it with a part of the baggage. The horses are then driven down to the bank, and after much stone-throwing and shouting, off they start towards me. The stream is very strong, and one old packhorse, who swims very low in the water, narrowly escapes drowning. But, though carried down some distance, they all come safe to land. A general yawning ensues, then a universal roll in the black sand, and before they have time to run off they are caught and loaded.

The Hreppstiori, after giving careful directions about the route, here leaves us. Fortunately the day is fine, and I have a compass. I remember that it was on this very route some ninety years ago that Eggert Olafson, who has published an account of his travels, lost his way in a storm, and for three days neither horses nor men had anything to eat. Down to our left is the source of the Hvitá, viz. a lake full of icebergs, into which a glacier is descending. In spite of the coldness of the waters, it is said that there are here plenty of excellent trout. Some wild swans are basking near the lake, and I am strongly tempted to ride off and try to intercept them, as they most probably are moulting and cannot fly. But the guide is evidently all abroad, neither do the copious drinks of snuff he gives his nose seem to enlighten him; and a snow fog may come on; and so we proceed without stopping in a north-easterly direction, as pointed out by the Hreppstiori.

On either side of our path rise Iökuls covered with a lambs-wool layer of cloud, almost like a very well-dressed and very well-powdered wig. Above them, the sky has that dark tint as far as the eye can reach, betokening snowfields beneath. The sun is bright, but the air keen, and my hands can hardly hold the reins for the cold.

Once or twice the guide looked anxiously at my compass, uncertain about our route; when suddenly, on issuing from the bed of a torrent, I espied an odd-shaped tent with some horses grazing near it. The very people I am in quest of, said I to myself; no doubt they are some of those utilegumenn (Angl. Sax. Utlah=outlaw), those mysterious moss-troopers who exist in certain spots of the howling wilderness in the interior. Felons they are, unwhipped of justice, who have fled from the abodes of men, say some, but whatever their origin or history, tales are afloat about them all through the country, till they have become people of romance; invested with supernatural powers and attributes akin to those of elves and demons. Who is it but these people that carries off the 40,000 sheep that annually disappear, nobody knows when or whither? Sometimes, strangers of peculiar dress and appearance and mounted on strong-built horses, shod with horn and not with iron, make their appearance in the towns; and people have a shrewd guess what they are. Gatherers of Icelandic moss in the mountains in the early summer, and shepherds in search of stray sheep, know more perhaps about these matters than they choose to reveal.

Perhaps the following tale may serve to throw light upon their peculiar habits of life.—Down in Skagafiord (whither I am travelling), there lived some years ago one Svein, who had two children, twins, a boy and a girl, Biarni and Salvör, who were devotedly attached to each other. One summer's day, when they were about twenty years old, the two set off together with many others to the mountains to gather moss. While there, Salvör fell sick, to the great grief of her brother; and to make matters worse, they were left alone, for the rest of the party were forced to go home. While sunk in melancholy dejection, Biarni hears the tramp of horses, and sees two men riding towards him, the one dressed in black, the other in red. After some talk, the stranger in red asks him for the hand of his sister; but Biarni very properly declines having anything to do with a person totally unknown to him. That night his sister disappears while Biarni is asleep; and though search is made for her in every direction, she was nowhere to be found, and her disconsolate brother returned home without her.

Ten years had elapsed since this untoward occurrence. Biarni was now married, and a man of some substance. One day in autumn all his sheep strayed away; Biarni started off in search of them in spite of the tears and entreaties of his wife. After wandering about in the mountains for three days, he suddenly came upon a beautiful valley with a fine farm-house in it. It being evening, he went up to some women, who were haymaking near, and asked for a night's lodging, which he readily obtained. Among them was a damsel, the very image of his lost sister.

Next morning, she comes to his bedside with a change of clothes, which he must put on, says she, as it was Sunday, and they were to have the church service to-day. After breakfast, he goes to what appeared to be the church. As he entered, Biarni, happening to look around, recognises among the congregation the very man in red, who had asked him for his sister's hand; while the clergyman officiating is no other than his companion in black. Presently, he perceives among the rest a female handsomely dressed. Can it be? yes, it is his long-lost sister: and directly the service is over he rushes into her arms. At the same moment, up comes Red-mantle and says, "Biarni, forgive me; I it was who carried off your sister, and gave her to Black-mantle to wife. He is my son, and our parson here in the valley. It was I who drove away your cattle, that you might come after them into the mountains and see your twin-sister again. That little girl who showed you to your chamber is her daughter. You must stop here another night, and have a long talk with your sister."

Next day, he takes leave of Salvör with many tears; promising however to visit her again next spring, and make a long stay. His host and the parson show him the road out of the valley, and he arrives safely at home. One morning, some months after, three men with baggage-horses arrive at Biarni's dwelling; and he and his family pack up bag and baggage, and go off to the valley, where they lived happily for many years. When he grew old, Biarni returned to dwell at his native Skagafiord, and before his death narrated the above history. Which, all things considered, is a very singular one indeed, and reveals a state of things going on in the interior of Iceland peculiar in the extreme.

"Sæl vær-tu!" cries out a man by the tent-side as we approach; and we respond in the approved manner, "Vær-tu sæl." Eheu! my hopes of an adventure are doomed to be disappointed. These are not outlaws, nothing so romantic. A frightful pest, the scab, has been ravaging the flocks in the south, and these three men are stationed here to watch and capture any stray sheep that may come wandering northwards from the infected districts. For, improbable as it may appear, these animals, moved by some strange impulse, will swim over rivers and wander across the deserts of the interior, going from one end of the land to the other. To the east and west are nothing but hideous snow and ice-mountains; so that if they make for Skagafiord, they must come this route, and within the ken of the three watchers.

Sigurd Palm, a fellow as swart as an Italian, and with small twinkling black eyes and intelligent face, is the chief of the gang: evidently a character. He opens a box and pulls out (imagine it!) a German and Danish dictionary, and a German work on physical science. He is engaged on the study of that language. What English peasant would occupy his spare time thus? An Icelandic psalm-book, a hundred years old, and a Bible, are also among his library catalogue. While I am looking at the books, Palm overwhelms me with questions about England, swinging his body backwards and forwards all the while with an absorbed air. This trick is observed by an ancient traveller in Iceland as a common occurrence; and he derives it from the custom here prevalent of fulling cloth; every man being his own fulling-mill. A cup of capital coffee is now prepared, for which Palm declines payment, but in vain. Among his effects, I see a piece of obsidian, or Icelandic agate, which he says "old people, only old people, have superstitions about." But doubtless, he is himself using it as an amulet against all sorts of evil. Twenty-four virtues, I believe, used to be ascribed to this stone. In the tent are two full-grown swans which Palm ran down yesterday, despatching them with a stick. The poor victims were moulting their large quill-feathers.

Our way now lies over lava worked into beautiful arabesques of varied forms; which might have served as models for the flowing patterns of Norwegian wood-carving. An art which, though once at home in Iceland, seems now almost to have disappeaerd. Here and there I see the *Silene Acaulis* (Moss Campion) in large round patches of freshest green, strewn with a mass of pink blossoms; a couch fit for the repose of cherubs. For the last few days the whole landscape has been white with snow, which however the sun has managed to chase away to its impregnable strongholds on the surrounding Iökuls. Yonder is a gerfalcon which has apparently winded some cowering ptarmigan; while a raven is looking on in a state of sleepy abstraction from an upheaved boulder.

What is that white glistering object yonder? A flight of wild swans surely. I must have my gun ready. "Ay! Ay! it is all right," said the guide, as we crossed at the moment a tearing torrent, and entered upon a fearful scene of desolation. This is the mark I was looking for: "Dead man's knoll." So the swans turns out to be human remains:

> "The bones of men
> In some forgotten battle slain,
> Bleached by the drifting wind and rain."

What a truly Icelandic finger-post! It was in battle certainly, but not with men, that the owners of these bones were slain. On the 1st October, 1850, three peasants, who were returning to the north with three hundred sheep and twenty-two horses, left the last human habitation on the route which we have been tracking. They were never seen again alive. People knew pretty well how it was. "Han ward uti," is a common saying in Iceland, "He was lost on the field." Such was the case here. In the following spring, a traveller came upon numbers of bones of sheep and horses about the spot, which have since been gathered and heaped together upon that sand-hillock. According to my guide, it was not till seven years later that the bones of the men and the mouldering remains of their tent were found*. The party was overtaken by early snow, which would blind their vision, and paralyze body and mind.

We now enter upon the Hraun. It was ruin indeed, the abomination of desolation; as if the elements of some earlier world had melted with fervent heat; and as they cooled had burst asunder, and been hurled by the Demons of Misrule and Upside-downism into a disjointed maze of confusion worse confounded. Quagmires of melted glue—so sticky were they—on the one hand; bristling, bare, wrecks of fractured lava, on the other; the one threatening to engulph man and horse, the other to maim and mutilate us. Then, again, yawning caverns and cracks gluttonous for our mangled remains; angular barricades—

> "The nodding horror of whose shady brows,
> Threats the forlorn and wandering passenger."

while, as if in bitter mockery, cairns of stones are piled up at intervals to shew the road, which is 'no man's road' at all, whatever a chamois or reindeer might have thought of it. The whole scene around was one to make the flesh creep, and mine crept accordingly, while my teeth or tongue chattered within me saying—'This *is* desolation.' Those peo-

* In spite of the name "Dead man's knoll," of course there are in reality no human bones here; as these would be transported to the nearest church.

ple whose religion consists in the worship of fire need only come and see what I see; and their veneration would cease.

What a relief to me at this moment, as I scrambled with bones unbroken to the highest point of our route, and beheld a scene of transcendent pomp and splendour! The dark cloud-curtain over the Iökuls to the south-west was terminated abruptly by zigzag streaks of ruddy gold shooting athwart the dappled flecks of opaline pink, which dot and drape the sky upwards to the zenith. And, see, yonder appear four violet-edged eye-shaped sky-rents, gold-centered; and away to the north-west, horizontal layers of salmon-colour, maize, and magenta. And then the heavens are bathed, in front of us, with one delicate uniform glow, and we can descry in that direction the lilac-coloured mountains of the distant Skagafiord, while to the east are pale snowfields tipped with the reflected light of the sinking luminary.

But see, yonder, a few miles off to our left, heavy volumes of white vapour are rolling along; and sure enough, by referring to my map, I find that this must be the hot springs of Hveravellir, which, according to Eggert Olafsen, were in his time the most extraordinary work of nature in Iceland, but the chief one of which I believe is now effete: with my glass I can detect several caldrons at work. It was now evening, night, I may say; and after descending rapidly over inclines of sand, we encamp in a peninsula, formed by the river Blanda (Blanda-krok), where there is only a scanty supply of herbage for the horses. The spirit-lamp soon procures a cup of hot coffee; and I bivouac in tolerable comfort.

These Icelanders seem to have lost their ingenuity when they left the old country; or, which is more probable, it got knocked out of them later by famine and Danish neglect. A Norwegian guide has always a net of birch-twigs, in which he first fastens the traveller's packages, and then suspends them on either side of the straddle, the whole operation being performed with great celerity. Not so the Icelander. Next to the packhorse's back, he puts under the straddle, instead of a sack or skin, two oblong mats of a peculiar soft turf, cut just under the grass in the moors, after first paring off the sward. These are continually getting out of place, and have to be set right. Then, again, instead of birchen net-work, he binds the packages together with ropes, which, naturally give with the jolting, and have to be tightened; and stoppages without limit are the consequence.

Our course lies along the left bank of the great river Blanda. A few snow buntings sit piping among the grey stones, and wild swans are feeding on the swampy edges of the stream, which here splits into numerous channels separated from each other by banks of black lava sand, capable of swallowing horse and rider in their treacherous abysses.

Suddenly, as we turn a rock, a small tarn comes in view. Away rushes the dog, and a family of swans scuttle into the water, he after them, overlooking in his ardour one of the cygnets which rolls over neck and crop, and, before it can recover itself, is fast in my clutches. He reaches from my hip to my heel; and as he utters his complaints, the parents—the male in the air—hoop in reply. It would have been easy to have sent a cartridge through them. Mercy however prevails, in the spirit of the Levitical code; and after watching these and some other broods on the water, we proceed on our journey, first letting the captive go.

The wretched dog pursues everything. Sheep, which now reappear, he pursues to their ruin: one or two falling into ravines, and no doubt breaking their limbs. But here are two noble rams,—the very fellows one sees in the old English picture-books,—who stand gravely surveying us. Like a true cur, he takes refuge behind us, having a wholesome dread of those crumpled horns. These animals are of great use to the farmer, from their courage and sagacity. In case of a sudden snow-storm, in early spring, when the sheep are some distance from home, the ram leads the terrified flock to a place of safety. At present all the sheep are on the mountain pastures (afrettur). On a certain day in June they were driven up in thousands from the dales by numerous men and dogs. On a certain day in September these will return, and rendezvous at a spot on the mountains. The animals, which are all marked—these marks are hereditary—will be driven home again; the fat ones will be slaughtered, and the flesh dried, the others housed for their winter's starvation.

The river-bed must be half a mile broad here; the guide is uncertain about the fording place, and flatly refuses to do what is the rule of the road and the sacred duty of a guide in Iceland, go in advance across the surging channels, and probe the depth. "Dog of an *Icelander!*" I was tempted to exclaim in the words of the younger Philipson in Anne of Geierstein, "thou deservest to have thy bones broken for undertaking a charge which thou art as incapable to perform as thou art to guide me to heaven!" The man had clearly mistaken his profession, and would have been much more at home following the unmistakable route of the treadmill.

But it was no use to imitate the water before us and storm. I felt I was entirely at the man's mercy. There was not a house or a human being for miles. So I let him follow his own devices. Upon this he dragged the horses in, without attempting to gird the packages as high as possible on the baggage animals. The water rose at once on a heap, and for a few moments it was an even chance whether the smaller horses should not be swept away by the stream. Luckily, the beginning was the worst: after this, the water gradually shoaled; the other arms of the river were less hazardous, and so at last we got safe to land; but with some of my effects drenched and spoiled.

Our road lies to the eastward over black sandy hills quite bare of grass, thickly sprinkled, however, with the white flowers of *Cerastiums*, the *Cochlearia officinalis*, the *Saxifragus hypnoides*, and of course the *Silene maritima;* imparting to the scene, otherwise so dreary, a pleasant bright look. Just at dusk the path forks. Which line shall we take? The map and compass are consulted. The guide is in doubt: so I determine to encamp for the night, a flat space offering a chance, not always to be met with, for so doing. The pattering of the rain, which had come on, and the gurgling of the adjoining stream, soon sent me to sleep.

August 2.—At an early hour, I was awakened by my companion, who makes the following cheerful communication: "The horses are gone; I have been looking for them these two hours. I traced them to the marsh, and then lost the spoor. I hoppled them last night too. Some men, who were going to the north haymaking, lost theirs on this route, and they were not found all the summer." "Thou Job's comforter! Here, take my glass and mount those lava hills, and look if you can see them." In an hour he returns having seen nothing of the horses. "Well! go back to the Blanda; they have surely gone that way. Take some food with you."

Meantime, as the sun has come out, bestrewing the marsh with millions of diamonds, there being no fear of interruption, I have a duck in the stream. Nothing like that for raising one's mental barometer: and forthwith the son of Kish's good luck occurs to me, and I bless the augury, and continue the journal. Sure enough, the man returns at last not unaccompanied. The truants had strayed into a secluded swamp, a very Goshen of verdure; and their bellies are almost too big for the girths.

By the map, I find that one of the paths must lead to Akreyri; but upon the whole I consider to take the northern one, which will bring us to Skagafiord. By degrees we get into a grassy, uninhabited valley, pent in by tall cliffs where grow many wild flowers; numbers of ponies, chiefly piebald, pasturing on the slopes. At last the end of the vale opens, and before me in the distance lies the noble Skagafiord, with the precipitous Drangö, rising like a fortress from its mid-waters.

Rounding the bold Maelifels-hnukr, 3476 Danish feet high, and crossing a bog, bored with deep hollow runnels of water, we are speedily at the door of the worthy pastor of Maelifel. "Enter, stranger, and rest thee; thou art welcome to my best; my spare bed is at thy service. It is too late to proceed further to night." The deeds of the venerable pastor kept pace with his words. Coffee and conversation pave the way to something still more substantial. The intellectuals, too, are cared for; my host producing several Icelandic works from his library: among which is a complete copy of Finn Johnson's Historia Ecclesiastica Islandiae; a book not easy procurable, as the stock in hand of the third volume was consumed in the great fire of Copenhagen. The Landnâma tells us of a curious *ruse* resorted to by an early colonist in these parts, one Önundr. He ascertained that a rival colonist, Eirekr, was going to ride round the bounds of a new territory on a certain day, carrying fire with him in the usual way. Upon which he shot a burning arrow in the same direction, and thus acquired the land for himself, as the legal title to waste land was to carry fire round it.

A runic stone is next shewn me of prismatic shape, which was recently dug up in the churchyard. "Here lies Olaver," is all of the inscription that is decipherable. One thing is certain, that it does not refer to my guide, of that name, who is lounging about the premises, allowing the pastor's wife and servants to attend to my baggage.

After a substantial repast, washed down by cherry brandy, I survey complacently that Prodigal Son on the wall, dressed in a red coat and yellow knee-breeches, whom his father in a full-bottomed wig is hastening to embrace, backed up by domestics bearing a crown and robe; while behind them stands the fatted calf. The pastor had no calf, so he killed a fatted lamb for me instead. In due time I was ensconced in the berth-shaped bed; from which I was prevented from falling by an ancient carved board, which was put along the bed-stock. This is the land of dreams. The pastor had been telling me of the Troll who haunts the neighbouring mountain. And before long I was flying before him, and took refuge in a cave, secure, I fondly imagined, from the monster. But alas! no. He stamped violently with his foot over head; which went into the earth; quietly observing, "Sit tibi terra levis;" and down fell the roof of the cave upon me. Heavens! I suffocate, and with a prodigious effort I burst asunder my living tomb, and—off flies the great heavy eiderdown quilt into the floor.

What eating and drinking went on the next morning! (August 3,) and such a parcel of roast lamb is placed by the kind lady in my baggage! "Long may your amiable spouse and yourself live, Séra Sigurdr!" The reader will please to note that in Iceland the clergy are still addressed as Shakespear's Welsh parson was, by a title now monopolized in England by Knights and Baronets.

CHAPTER VIII.

How the peasants are lodged—A country church—We cross the Herredsvatn—Thorwaldsen's birthplace—The legend of Silfrastadir—A breakneck ride—The peasant Deputy—Gretti the Strong—Arrival at Akreyri—Oddr Thorarensen—A tempest—I get rid of a nuisance.

THE great river Herredsvatn not being fordable here, we descend to the North. A bitter cold wind makes the hotsprings near the church of Reykir smoke their best. The turf walls of the old house close by are a fathom in thickness. Biarni, who dwelt there, pats me on the cheek most lovingly, and bids me enter the house. I never saw anything like it. Saw! I did not see, for, once over the threshhold, I was in darkness. Bowing my head for fear of accidents, I came at last into a long dimly lighted room, in which I counted seven beds in a row along the walls. Coffee and brandy were offered me, but the atmosphere was too strong for my lungs; and after groping about into a sort of smithy, and then into a larder, both lighted from the roof, I regain the outer air, and visit the little church. The chancel was separated from the nave by lattice work. A number of bonnets were hanging from one of the beams. The explanation given me of this unusual sight was, that the country folks came to church from their distant homes in their national black nightcaps which are more convenient for travelling, but which during the service they exchange for their bonnets. The bells were according to the common custom suspended in the roof of what in England would be called the lych-gate.

Passing a not inconsiderable waterfall in the 'Black river,' we cross some meadows, and find ourselves on the banks of the Herredsvatn. One Anders, an unkempt giant, who dwelt in a potato-pie (alias cottage) close by, catches his horse, and assays to guide us across. The spray dashed up by the northwind from the long cavalcade was chilling enough, and when the water rose to near my knees, I might as well have been bodily in the water. First we took a line at an acute angle to the shore, and landing on a tolerably firm bank doubled back in the other direction, and by this crab-like movement managed to land safely in a morass.

In the turf-built parsonage of Miklebaer close by, the grandfather of Thorwaldsen the sculptor formerly dwelt, being the priest of the place. That great genius was born neither in Iceland nor in Denmark, but on the high seas, between the two countries.

At Silfrarstaðir the entrance of Nordrárdalr we pass a curious legendary stone of oblong shape with three holes drilled in it. It is called the Skeljúngr stone. The tale runs thus. It reminds me of the binding of Fenriswolf in the Edda to the mickle stone hight Þviti. The shepherd of Silfrastaðir was killed in a wrestling match. After a time it was discovered that his spirit walked. Two shepherds who succeeded him were found throttled in the mountain: and nobody will take the place for some time. Late in the autumn, a Herculean fellow, who says his name is Grimr, applies for the situation. He is advertised of the danger but, nothing daunted, takes the place. All goes well till Christmas-Eve: when Grimr lies down to sleep on an oxhide, next to the door of the great common sleeping room. At midnight a loud rattling is heard, and Skeljúngr appears. Seizing the oxhide, on which Grimr lay, he tries to drag it out Grimr and all. Grimr plants his foot against the wall, but the woodwork gives way, and he is dragged out by the spectre. He now jumps up and closes with his ghostly adversary. He is the weaker of the two; but after a tremendous struggle, by a dextrous shift he throws his opponent. In a twinkling he whips out his knife, cuts a thong from the hide and binds the strong man to it, while he runs for fire wherewith to consume him. On his return, stone and spectre are gone. Ultimately, he finds them on the spot where the stone now stands close by the river, into which Grimr, after burning the monster, threw his ashes. Skeljúngr has not 'walked' from that day to this.

Owing to a series of unnecessary delays, although

it is now evening, we have still the Oxendals-heide to cross; there being no tolerable sleeping quarters on this side the mountain, and a severe cold which I have taken rendering it unadvisable for me to camp out to-night. This arrangement does not at all jump with the guide's humour; so, by way of shewing his displeasure, he dashes furiously among the horses, and lashes them into a gallop. Our first obstacle was a mountain torrent, which swept away one of the animals, although he fortunately managed to recover his legs again in time. What a pace we went! the path winding on the face of precipices, when a stumble would have sent horse and man to perdition. I modestly ventured to suggest that such speed was hazardous; but the man only cracked his whip, and screamed madly, "Hoho! hoho!" and held on in his breakneck career. Providentially, we arrived safely at the top of the pass. Here stands a great boulder stone, called the Lurkar-steinn, in memory of some Icelandic hero; but the horses are vanishing in the misty vapours of an Arctic midnight, and dangerous bogs are beginning; so a lengthened inspection of the stone was impracticable. In another hour I see farm buildings standing in the midst of a spacious newly mown *tún*; and before long, to my no small comfort, I am under the roof of Stefan of Steinstadir.

My host, the peasant deputy, a man of rugged but good-natured frank aspect, reminding me of

Scott's Swiss Landamman, stood by my bedside in the morning with kind inquiries as to how I had slept. Behind him followed his wife, with coffee and cream and sugarcandy. A most intelligent fellow is Stefan. Besides being a member of the Althing, he is administrator of the royal domains, which are very extensive in this country, comprehending all the property of the extinct religious houses. He tells me that those lofty sharp-pointed peaks yonder, which rise so suddenly from the fresh fallen snow on the mountain on the other side of the valley, are called Drángr. The national hero, Gretti Asmundson, once clomb up them, and in proof of his feat left there his knife and belt. In the sitting-room below hangs a printed paper framed and glazed. It commemorates one of my host's family and his many virtues, with the date of his birth and death.

As we journey down the valley, I see on the other side of the river the church of Bægisa, where Ion Thorlakson, the Icelandic translator of Milton, formerly officiated. In the stream are some likely looking holes, which must hold fish if there are any in the river. In one spot the rocks, which encase the waters, contract, and two buttresses of solid masonry jut out; the foundations, one would think, of a destroyed bridge. This is a not uncommon phenomenon exhibited by the trap dykes in Iceland.

Early in the afternoon we reach Akreyri, the

horses racing with each other as soon as they get sight of the promising quarters. They are indeed wonderful creatures. The ride of last night, rivalling that of the wild huntsman—dashing as we did over stock and stone, tramp tramp through thick and thin—has lamed only one of them.

The warmest welcome possible awaited me at Mr. Oddr Thorarensen's, which was all the more valued that the evening closed with a tremendous storm from the north-east. The heavens had been growing black with clouds and wind, and there was now an abundance of rain. On the mountains the fresh snow was a foot deep, as a gentleman who came in half blinded and frozen had found to his cost.

In front of the windows a crowd are collected; a yacht is driving ashore in the gale. The suspense however is terminated by the vagabond anchor catching hold of that of a brig, which luckily is strong enough to hold both vessels. The first thing to be done was to get rid of my so-called guide. So having secured the services of another man, I inform him, evidently to his no small surprise, that he is at liberty to return home; I paying him the expenses of his journey thither, in addition to his wages.

CHAPTER IX.

The Vadlaheide—Origin of the Christmas tree—Iceland the home of German legends—The parsonage of Hals—The gerfalcon and the ptarmigan—Music at a premium—The fiery ordeal—The quaking river—The water-sprite—Gnats—Golden eyes—Stolen property recovered—"Metaque fervidis evitata rotis."—Reykjahlid—Myvatn.

August 6, I start for Myvatn, wading the river at its junction with the fiord. From the top of Vadlaheide is a view of Eyafiord, opening out to the North, while, to the South, up the blue gorge of the valley, is Modruvellir, the site of the ancient leper hospital. Near it grows still, for aught I know, a large rowan tree. A tale is told of it as follows:—

Two persons, a brother and sister, were accused of some crime and condemned to death, though they protested that they were innocent. Before their death they prayed that God would hereafter raise up some testimony of their innocency. Before long, a rowan tree shot up from the spot where they were executed. This tree in process of time came to be called the holy tree, and people assert, that on Christmas Eve all the branches have been seen hung with burning lights, which could not be extinguished, however strongly the wind blew—The origin here, then, of the German Christmas tree—The wood of this tree must never be used for any ordinary purpose. If it is used as fuel, those who sit round the fire are sure to quarrel; if any part of it is employed in building a house, the curse of barrenness will rest upon all the females in it, whether of the human or animal creation; and if a portion of it should be built into a boat, the boat will be lost with all on board.

For an hour or two we are splashing through fresh snow, and then descend and cross the Fnjoskadal's river, a very clear stream of no great depth, on the further bank of which is the chief wood in the country. It hangs on a sunny height facing the South; and, ninety years ago, Eggert Olafsen saw trees growing here with stems more than forty feet in the clear; he also found near the remains of an ancient iron-work. Everything deserving the name of a tree has disappeared. At present none of the stems exceed ten feet in length. What the locust left was destroyed by the hailstones. What man's improvidence spared, the ruthless storm cleared. Thus at Modruvellir, the place mentioned above, a whole forest was annihilated by a storm one wintry day in the year 1607. In the thicket, I flush several ptarmigan, but see nothing of the terrible bull of the dale; who at times meets the belated traveller, dragging his hide after him with a hideous din; and sometimes, at dead of night, penetrates among the farm-buildings, making the inhabitants thereof to quake in their beds, reminding one of the Viehschelm of Suabia. The German legend of Schneewitch is likewise known in the neighbouring Eya-fiord; while Cinderella exists in an Icelandic dress, not omitting the slipper. It must not be supposed, however, that Iceland is indebted to Germany for these interesting fictions: on the contrary, it seems now pretty well agreed, among those learned in comparative mythology, that Germany's legends are only second-rate translations and imitations of the great Scandinavian originals; which floated hitherward from the east on the crest of the northern people-wave. The student of Shakspeare will be interested to hear, that *Amlodi* in Icelandic means a daft person, who can do nothing well; a person, in short, with some of the leading features of the character of the Prince of Denmark. A play, which Shakspeare based on the Danish tale of Amlethus, recorded in Saxo Grammaticus, Lib. III. sub finem. Romeo and Juliet have also counterparts in an Icelandic tale. Herne, the hunter, it is needless to remind many of our readers, is a localised version of the wild huntsman, who, in his turn, is a transformation of the majestic Odin; shorn of much of his wild grandeur under the influences of Christianity.

Thorstein Paulson, the priest of Hals, gives me a hospitable reception; being well seconded by his fair daughters. Sigrida brings me mutton chops; Holmfrida, pancakes and coffee; while Haldora and Valgerda prepare the bed. All these creature-comforts were destined for a much worthier individual, whose mantle however descended upon me: I mean the archdeacon of this immense district; who lives at Langanes, far out in the north eastern horn of the Island. 'First come, first served,' is a proverb acted upon here: and when that rosy-cheeked functionary, in his shining yellow wig, arrives at a later hour, he is bestowed elsewhere. Sera Paulson practises homœopathy. He is in consequence the *bête noir* of the allopathic apothecary, my excellent host of Akreyri; who brimming with kindness to all, discharges the single drop of gall in his constitution upon the new-fangled leech of Hals. The parson is also a sportsman, and presents me with a trophy of his prowess, a large gerfalcon; which, in hot pursuit of some ptarmigan, had dashed among the buildings, and fallen to the pastor's gun. In his opinion, there is only one kind of ptarmigan in Iceland; a question however which, as we have seen, admits of some doubt. A curious superstition is current in this country, that when the falcon has killed the ptarmigan, and ripped a hole into the heart, he begins to scream for sorrow, because he then discovers that the victim is his sister. The reindeer, which were introduced into this country nearly a century ago, have all become wild. Their sharp hoofs are said to have been found to damage the grass, and the peasants gave up the idea of keeping them. Indeed, none but the Mongolian race seem to have an aptitude for managing these animals. The Norwegians have likewise tried it, but failed. When the pastor was stationed at Axarfiord, to the North East, he shot eleven of these animals in one winter, when they came to within a mile or so of the farm-house. Wild geese flock in immense numbers to that part of the island, and do great damage to the hay-crop. Swans, he tells me, do not lay till they are two years' old. The birds of one year moult their wing-feathers in July; while the birds with broods do not begin this operation till the middle of August; and in two weeks they are again able to fly. During moulting, these birds retire to the most hidden recesses of the Fjeld.

A guitar, hung against the wall, indicates the presence of musical accomplishments in the family; a great resource in this thinly peopled rugged land; where the harp and the viol are not at their feasts, and Nature's fiercer minstrelsy takes the place of softer music: the scream of the bird of prey; the din of the waterfall; the hissing of the boiling springs; the howl of the storm spectre, or those still more mysterious accents, ascribed by popular superstition to the spirits of deserted infants, which often at midnight-hour are borne upon the ears of the trembling inmates of the farmsteads.

As I stood in the doorway, next morning, inhaling its delicious breath, my inquisitive eye settled upon the most ponderous hammer I had ever seen;

its use was not to be divined, till an ancient dame solved the enigma, by lifting it up by both hands, and beginning to beat some dried fish. Afterwards, I perceived that it was as invariable a chattel of every dwelling, as the great stone with a hole in it, frequently a column of basalt, which stood before the door for the traveller to bind his horse to.

A ride through a wide fertile valley—where grew the bog cotton (fifa), used by the natives for candle-wicks—brought us to the Liosvatn, a large lake whose surface is dimpled by rippling rings of every size, symptomatic of hungry trout. Formerly, but with no reason, it was imagined that the waters of this lake ebbed and flowed at intervals. "That is called Brunni graes, there is a superstition about it," said the guide, as I asked the name of a blue flower. "If a lad puts a bit of this under a lassie's pillow at night, and she sleeps till morning without detecting it, she falls in love with him; if she finds it sooner, they become sworn foes." After dodging about among cinder heaps and scoriæ, we pass over a moor seamed with ruts so deep and narrow, formed by the stamping of ponies for centuries, that it was only by platting my legs well under the horse's belly, I escaped getting my knees or ankles dislocated. The natives, to avoid such concussions, hoist up first one leg and then the other. This is only one danger of Icelandic travelling, which requires as much circumspection as passing through a fiery ordeal. The sprouts of lava, often protruding athwart the path, as sharp as quills of fretful porcupine, if they do catch horse or man, will rend and tear them as a gerfalcon does a ptarmigan. Not to mention, that amid the lava there are often small holes, the entrance to fearful caverns. The guide tells me that not long ago, when he was travelling, a horse slipped his leg into one of these holes, and in his struggles to get free, the limb was cut clean off above the hock; so razor-like are the edges of the lava.

Another danger, *the* danger in fact of the country, is crossing the rivers. Here, for instance is the great Skialfandi-fliot; so called by one of the early settlers, Gardar, who dwelt for a winter at its mouth, from its rapid quaking motion. Big it is indeed, for it has come all the way from the middle of the island. Between those mighty ice-laboratories, the Klofa and Arnafell Jökuls, it and its giant sister the Thiorsá were cradled; and parting at the moment of their birth to meet no more, except in the eternal ocean, the one rushed southward, snatching a kiss at the fire demons of Hekla; the other, hurtling past that ruin of ruins the Odáda Hraun, swept straight into the embrace of the Frost-giants, who beset the Greenland sea.

Here must be the ford, to judge from those few horse-tracks. Off I jump and tighten the girths; and recommend the guide to do likewise; but an

Icelander being a very centaur, and part and parcel of his steed, he does no such thing. "Follow my horse exactly," says he; which I take care to do, my knees bent and legs thrown back almost on to my nag's tail, to avoid contact with the snow-water. Looking at the stream won't do. It induces giddiness; and, after a time, the wayfarer will fancy that he is being carried down by the current; and is not quite clear whether his heels and his head have not changed places. Mind, and keep a tight hold of the rein; for, if your poor nag stumbles over a huge hidden stone, and splashes and crashes about in his efforts to recover himself—as mine does at this moment—nothing can save you from being thrown and pommelled to death by the stones and water, but a dexterous handling of the bridle. I should like to have seen Asheton Smith, or the author of "The Horse and his Rider," in similar circumstances.

But I was like to forget another danger, from which no lightness of bridlehand will deliver you. Who hath not heard of the water sprite? In the Rhine it is a beautiful maiden, who Siren-like sings men down to their watery doom. In Iceland, she at times takes the shape of a steed. Its colour is mostly grey, seldom black. When the ice splits in winter with portentous sound, it is the neigh of the Nykr. His chief delight is to haunt dangerous fords, assuming the shape of the traveller's own horse; who mounts him and does not detect his error, till the animal draws him below the surface in the centre of the stream. Sometimes, one meets with a cross between this monster and the horses of the country; and then the rider has a poor chance indeed. *Apropos*, the mouse-coloured horse which I am riding is crossed—not in blood, but across his shoulders, and down his back—with black streaks; and therefore I need not be alarmed; for as the peasant who sold him me said, "Look at this, Sir; he will never drown." Anyhow, we got over without mischance, in spite of dangers natural and supernatural. The water-sprite was biding his time. He preferred, as his victim, that fine young fellow Oddr Jonason, who two days after this, though he knew the ford well, was drowned in attempting it, leaving his poor young widow to fight through the world by herself.

At the cottage just above the ford, a pretty fair young mother with dark wavy hair, her sleeveless black vest adorned with dark red braid, like a hussar's jacket, and dotted with a number of little metal ornaments, offers us milk; which, as she has only one cow, I decline. Arrived on the steep ascent, we discern the river, winding, serpent-like, over the flats, till it joins the sea; while above, that column of mist, which we have seen rising geyser-like before us for miles, marks the locality of Godafoss, one of the greatest waterfalls in Iceland. More of it hereafter.

From the top of Fliotsheidi we have a fine view of a row of snow-covered mountains to the eastward, foremost among which is Bláfell, and are soon descending rapidly into one of the numerous Reykjardals (smoking valleys) of the country, deriving its name of course from its aggregation of hot springs. Lower down the valley is Grenjardarstaðr, one of five parishes in the patronage of the crown of Denmark, and abounding, I am told, with runic remains. A little north of this place is the Uxahver, another geyser of great propelling power; said to derive its name from an ox, which falling in was at once rejected; or more probably so called from its bellowing noise. While the horses are being shifted, I shoot some golden plover and ptarmigan; but as it is almost impossible to get game cooked, and other food is generally procurable, not to mention the contents of my saddlebags; I resolved subsequently to spare the poor birds, which were as tame as barndoor fowls.

At Thverá in Laxádal, into which I now descend, flushing numbers of ptarmigan, abides one Jon Joachimson, a rich farmer, who shews me a very clean room, and prevails on me to taste what he calls cognac, i. e. rum. The dark lava spots in the bed of this river are favourite haunts of salmon; but hereabouts there are only trout, a fall below preventing the course upwards of the salmon. At the mouth of the Laxá is a salmon fishery rented by a Scotchman, the chief owner of the Arcturus. An Icelander gave me a graphic account of a scene he witnessed at this spot. An eagle seized a salmon lying close to the shore. The stream being strong, the bird not being able to rise at once with his prey, to prevent himself being carried away, clutched the bank with one foot while with the other he held the fish. The salmon pulled so hard to release itself, that it caused the eagle's legs to stretch asunder almost to rending—nearly a yard apart, said my informant. At last the foot of the bird on shore relaxed its hold, and off rushed the fish, plunging with his adversary into the foaming depths of the pool. In due time the couple came to the surface, when the eagle dug his other talon into the luckless fish, and extending his mighty wings, flapped upwards with his prey, which, unlike the serpent in Shelley, was powerless out of his native element. I heard that a Briton toiled all day on this stream with his rod, and did not hook a single fish. In short, the Icelandic proverb, said of an unsuccessful piscator, fitted him exactly, 'Ham kom aptur med aungulinn i rassinum,' ('He came back with the hook in his behind.' He was doubtless a bungler; and a clever flyfisher would meet with splendid sport in this country. *The* great difficulty would be lodging-accommodation. Numerous gnats took advantage of our being entangled in the ford—

> "This unrelenting beast
> Marking his hour did bear us company,
> And tweaked a memorandum on my nose."

At Myvatn, which actually takes its name from these creatures—while its waters originated *a micturitione Diaboli*—I was not plagued in the least by them. The season for them seemed to be over. An old traveller relates that they have sometimes attacked horses in such numbers as to kill them outright.

The banks of the Laxá present one of the most extraordinary natural phenomena in Iceland. Huge breastworks of lava and slag rise up to the height of several feet on either side the river, as if nature had been carting thither, only yesterday, a quantity of the refuse of her subterranean laboratories, and making embankments to prevent the encroachment of the stream. It is in fact the work of Krablë, the fire-stream from which poured right down this valley to the sea. Near the landing-place I shoot one of several ducks; which proves to be a golden-eye, but only a female. On Myvatn's Sands, a tract of herbless black lava dust, we cross the horse-path leading to Husavik*.

* High up in the tufaceous cliff, between Husavik and Hallbjarnarstadr Kambr, is a huge semi-petrified whale, the ribs of which are uncovered. Besides which, at a height of about 200 feet, in what appears to be palagonitic tuff, are whole beds of *Venus Islandica*, containing millions of individuals belonging to a former creation.

This may have been, for aught I know to the contrary, the scene before now of such gramarye as the following:—Formerly, on new year's night, if any one had lost some property, he would plant himself at a place where four ways met, the hide of a grey ox thrown over him, the horns being well fitted to his brows, after the manner of friend Bottom and the ass's ears. In his hand he held an axe, the edge front-ways; and there he stood, like a statue, turning neither to the right hand nor to the left. Before long, the Troll-crew would beset him with devilish antics, asking him all sorts of odd questions. Woe betide him if he answered. Madness was the penalty. While, if he could only hold his peace till the morning-light, he would learn the whereabouts of his lost property.

At length we come to a fresh-looking stream of lava, over which the horses stagger, and slip, and clatter; and one of them, rather than face its terrors, takes to the small lake on our left. This Steiná (stone stream), otherwise Thurá (dry stream), as it is called in the language of the country, was vomited forth in 1725 by Leirnukr, a volcano near this; which, with its neighbour Krablë, divides the infamy of turning many a smiling green acre into a black frowning horror. Destroying a neighbouring farm, with every green herb upon it, it swept towards the little church of Reykjahlid, whose turn, everybody thought, was to come next. But the ark of God was spared, as if by a miracle; the fire-chariot shaving within a foot or two of its walls—"Metaque fervidis evitata rotis—."

The waves of the stupendous torrent, which we are now crossing, are more deeply channelled than any I have yet seen. An eyewitness of this eruption states, that in the day a blue sulphureous flame hung over the stream. At night it was all of a red glow, dyeing the heavens the same colour. At times, owing to the weariness, mayhap, of the subterranean stokers, the torrent relaxed; when its surface became covered with a solidified rind some two feet in thickness. Anon, the fiery tide flowed again, and pressing on the hardening mass, split the epidermis—just as I have seen the water-flood burst the ice encasing the bosom of the mighty Danube;—and the masses of stone were swept along by it, just like the lumps of disrupted ice on the water. Vapour-swollen caverns and deep crevasses yawn around; the latter hedged here and there by vast slabs of dusky lava, of various degrees of thickness—very boiler-plates to look upon; while black statuesque figures, and morsels of goblin tracery and sculpture, as if from the halls of Eblis, are grouped together in the wildest and most wonderful confusion.

F.M. J.V. Richardson.

CHAPTER X.

Krablë and the Sulphur mountains—Streams of black lava—A bottomless pit—A mountain of black agate—All the colours of the rainbow—A disaster—The Godafoss—A weird scene—Touting for practice—A people living in tents—Talk about Icelandic and English clergy—Ash-Wednesday custom—Fredricksgave—Introduction of reindeer into Iceland—Scab-sheep—An unprotected female—'Time was'—Free-trade—Talk about the weather—An ancient Icelandic fiddle.

ON a green slope, miserable remnant of the fertile meadow which once gladdened all eyes, stands the farm-house of Reykjahlid. It is close to the shores of the second largest piece of water in the country—Myvatn, said to be 40 miles in circumference; but whose broad expanse is so broken up by countless reefs and islands of lava, that it looks like a bunch of small lakes close to each other. The water is said not to be more than four fathoms at the deepest; and there are hot springs in it, the vicinity of which is as congenial apparently to the fat trouts, as Carlsbad and Teplitz are to the over-stuffed German professors. On the islands Angelica grows in abundance; while every imaginable kind of duck lays eggs there without limit. The most prominent feature in this astonishing landscape is the tall conical mountain, Windbelgiar-fiall (Wind-bellows-fell), rising to all appearance sheer out of the north-west end of the water.

Mr. Peter Reykjahlid's bed is any thing but comfortable; but his coffee and char from the lake reconcile me to the other drawbacks; and the wild fowl's eggs, hard-boiled and eaten cold in Icelandic fashion, were appetizing beyond measure. Neither were the dried trout, an article of exportation to the other parts of Iceland, to be despised.

It was a drizzly dull morning (Aug. 8) when I started for Kreblë and the Sulphur mountains, through a country compared by some travellers to that in the vicinity of the Dead sea. Our guide was a white-haired boy with a wide-awake hat slouched over a hideous wide-mouthed face—a physiognomy in strict keeping with the scenery—himself gummed to a piebald pony. Our road is first over cinder heaps, and then over black lava saffroned with yellow moss, now starting up into jagged points, now grottoed, or, in places, mouthing with low-browed arch, as if here was the entrance to some vast wine-cellar. A two miles' ride brings us to a sandy plain, with numerous gamboge-coloured pustules, steaming lazily, as though the earth had recently been in conflagration. It was only necessary to remove the fevered skin of these excrescences to secure specimens of native sulphur.

Winding up a tortuous defile, cut through the chain of red and yellow hills that gird the plain,—with here and there strips of *arundo arenaria* growing upon the dried surface,—we descry before us, on arriving at the summit, another vast plain of black lava, diversified at intervals by conical hills, and bounded to the north-east by tall black mountains. Close under us, between the black lava plain and the heights on which we stand, is another small level sandy tract, where a dozen steaming caldrons are at work, and poisoning the air with sulphuric gases.

Leaving our horses, which are alarmed, we descend on foot to see this great sight, over the leprous crust that caked the flat. A cry from the cavern-mouthed boy is too late to stop me, and in goes my foot through the crust, disclosing a festering hole gaping under my very eyes, from which I am saved by the clutch of my attendants. One cannot be too cautious here; to the 'ignes suppositi' the descent is extremely facile. The hot earth is sloughed all about underneath. We approach with cautious tread, half blinded by steam and suffocated by sublimated sulphur, the closely packed caldrons all boiling with a thick lead-coloured mixture. One of these evidently rises at times several feet; for it has surrounded itself with a blue round slimy breastwork disgusting to look upon. In another of these boilers the pasty soup is so thick and slab, that its attempt to boil is a signal failure, degenerating into a futile sluggish simmer. We pelt these monsters with stones and other missiles, and the others snarl spitefully; but this last we fail to rouse from his sulky apathy.

These sulphur fields are more extensive than those at Krisuvik, in the south-western corner of the island; but the mineral is said not to be so pure. In ancient times as much as 220 cwts. per annum used to be taken hence on horseback to the manufactory at Husavik. At present, the seemingly inexhaustible stores are unworked; but the same English gentleman, who has a lease of the Krisuvik mines, is reported to have secured the refusal of these*. If so, it will be a question whether it might not be shipped on barges on the neighbouring lake, and, by dint of a little blasting of the rocks in parts of the Salmon-river, be thus conveyed by water to Husavik. But, like everything else in Iceland, the light is under a bushel. If it be really true that Icelandic sulphur may be obtained at the half the price of Sicilian, it only shews that British capitalists have been hitherto sadly devoid of enterprise in this field.

Rejoining the ponies, we ride northward along a narrow path wedged in between the tract of black lava on one side and a chain of mountains on the other; whose sides are feathered with willow, birch, alchemilla, and wild geranium. From the latter plant, the natives used to make a blue dye, Odin's colour. Presently, a fresh stream of black lava descends to our left. It is coeval with the stream we crossed last night. Ascending steep hills blotched with

* I did hear, however, that he has hitherto found sulphur-mining in Iceland only a poor speculation.

steaming patches of all the colours of the rainbow, we come upon a circular tarn, lying hundreds of feet below us in the precipitous-sided crater of an extinct volcano. This bottomless pit is the traditional hell of these regions—the retreat of wicked spirits. At times, the prisoners are partially released from their thraldom; when they may be seen hovering over the gulf in the shape of birds; like the poor flutterers over the Folgefond in Norway. Between this dread spot and the distant fumaroles on the flanks of Leinukr, is a plain, on the scant herbage of which the sheep are said to wax fat speedily; and where the guide tells me he has seen reindeer in hard winters. Another round pool of icy cold snow-water lies north of this; half a dozen yards beyond which are some small spitting kettles full of a slate-coloured mixture boiling energetically; the soil round which is as brittle, and little to be depended upon, as proverbial piecrust.

Escaping unscathed from all this malignity, I was setting my face to Kranblë, from whose top I had counted on seeing a magnificent panorama. But an envious mist has settled upon him, with the evident intention of sticking there all day, as closely as a salmon fisher does to a good pool on a subscription river in Galway. Doubling, therefore, round the mountain, and passing over snow new and old, we enter a defile with Krablë on one side and a tall mountain on the other. This is the Hrafnetinnefiall, (the obsidian mountain,) the steep sides of which are strewn with blocks, some of immense size, of this beautiful vitrified stone; which varies in colour from jet black to a smoke grey, and exhibits different degrees of fineness. When the sun shines, the sides of the mountain glitter like that in the Arabian tale; but the fog has obscured its radiance. In securing some specimens, I have the ill luck to cut my thumb to the bone, owing to a razor-edged fragment slipping from my grasp. My bridle hand too! Heavens! what a misfortune! But it is not my right; and that is a consolation; and it must be yours too, gentle reader; for in that case you could not have had a faithful account of my impressions of Iceland jotted down fresh as I received them.

Having rounded Krablë, we re-descend the furrowed sandy slopes by which it is shored up, and get another view—rendered still more startling by the phantasmagoric power of the mist—of the sulphur and brimstone ridge which we had crossed early in the day. To compare its tints with those of the cliffs of Alum Bay in the Isle of Wight, would be to give a very washed-out idea of its kaleidoscopic look. Imagine a low long mountain combining all that is most glaring of yellow or brickdust in one of Turner's later extravagances. Imagine heavy masses of the whitest vapour rolling over this, and athwart a field of inky black lava close by its side. Dante, even, might have thrown into scenes of his Inferno a fresh touch or two, if he could only have seen what it was given to me to-day to witness. And Breughel—not 'Velvet,' but 'Hell'—Breughel, as the Germans irreverently call him—could not but have profited by a peep at this Tartarean region.

Topping this ridge again, we have a fine view of Myvatn. But alas! all my fond hopes of shooting the wild fowl, and catching the many varieties of trout and char, that disport themselves above and below its surface, have been severed together with my thumb by the hateful black agate; and I must be content ignominiously to devour fish and fowl without a particle of the relish with which Auceps and Piscator sit down complacently to discuss the victims of their art.

Next morning I reluctantly return towards Akreyri; diverging however up the right bank of the Skialfandifliot, to visit the Godafoss. The broad river contracts by degrees, and issues from a rugged defile of singular grotesqueness. The torrent has in some places scooped out caves in the trap-rock, faced with skew-arches, which would have done honour to any railway contractor. The rocks seem determined not to be outdone by the doings of the water. "If you can roar, I can scowl. If you can cut capers, I can cut faces." Unsightly shapes were there, glouring among those rifted chasms: *Omnium gatherum* monsters, writhing over the surging abyss; sheaves of basaltiform trap, some butt-end towards the water; some inclined; some perpendicular, or gathering to a point like fan-tracery. The cause of all this chaos is, that the water-sprite, or the river if you will, has been bridled by a curb of stone; which provokes him into leaping bodily into a circular pool, over which two Trolls keep watch and ward.

In the centre of the semicircular barrier is a grassy rock. On its right, one vast stream makes a swoop clean over a dimly seen cavern; while, on its left, the water is scattered in a continuous chain of beautiful perpendicular falls. One of these, as if impatient of control, and averse to waiting for its turn, has actually tunnelled for itself a slantindicular passage from the upper river bed, and through the dam, from a hole in the face of which it bursts forth instead of over it: and two other bodies of water, resolved by hook or by crook not to be left behind in the race, have mined a short cut deeper still, and are seen leaping out in furious frolic by posterns still lower down the wall:—'postica falle clientem'—a weird scene; rendered perhaps more supernatural by the absence of all trees to soften and veil its ghastly features: add to which, the mountains in front, in reality of no great height, look dimly huge, quite sky high, through the fog, which has suddenly enwreathed them, rolling up from the northern sea. Gretti the Strong came off victor in a terrible encounter with the powers who haunt this spot. In Scotland any work of great labour and antiquity is ascribed to Auld Michael, Wallace, or the Devil; in Iceland, Saemund the Learned, and Gretti the Strong, take the place of the two first-named functionaries.

Unwilling to trespass again on the hospitality of the good priest of Hals—for which diffidence on my part he rated me soundly afterwards—I stop at the farm of Liosvatn, and meet with but sorry quarters; I am bored moreover by a man from Reykjavik, who, possessed of a small stock of English, is desirous of improving it, and turning it to account as interpreter to the North Atlantic Telegraph people; whose present visit to survey the island seems to be exciting much attention. To while away the time, I take up the Akreyri newspaper. In a corner of it I read how that a peasant, who has been cured by a doctor of a long-standing complaint, "thinks it a duty he owes to his country to advertise the name of the man who, under Providence, was his preserver." The classic unction of this advertisement was quite diverting.

Aug. 10. A morning of thick drizzle cleared up into a lovely sun-shiny day, which brought us merrily to Hals. As my wounded hand was becoming very painful, it being almost impossible to dispense with it in riding, the surgeon-priest dresses it for me. Some gunpowder and copper-caps was all that I could possibly get him to take in acknowledgment of his many kindnesses. Haymaking has begun on the islands at the head of Eyafiord; from which it derives its name. Upon these, tents are pitched, where the haymakers will domicile during the nights, in preference to fording the river and sleeping in the neighbouring town. This is one of the many Orientalisms that crop out in this land. Feeding cattle with dried fish is a custom common to this and the East, while the use of dried cowdung for fuel will remind the reader of a similar custom prevailing among Asiatics, and mentioned by Livy, "fimo bubulo pro lignis utuntur." In crossing the river, we have to take the tide "at its height," and achieve not a fraction of glory. Far from it. My baggage gets another ducking; and had not the bottom been a flat sand, we might have got something worse than our wetting.

My excellent host, Mr. Thorarensen, and his amiable lady, receive me again most warmly under their hospitable roof; and I obtain from them some valuable hints for prosecuting my journey along the coasts of the northern fiords. At supper I make the acquaintance of my host's younger son, a fine lad; who is studying at the Latin school at Reykjavik, and is now home for his two months' vacation. It is usual for the students from a distance to hire horses at Reykjavik for the trip; which they keep till they return in September. Many parents exclaim loudly against the length of the journey, and the expense of living and immorality of Reykjavik; and an agitation is going on for the reestablishment of another school in the North. Formerly, a seminary for young men did exist at Holar; but this, with the bishoprick, has long since been abolished. Unless something is done, it is said that there will speedily be a want of clergy.

"Something of the kind," said I, "has been feared in England: at any rate her church clergy are reported to be gradually becoming of a lower intellectual grade than formerly." "And what is the reason of that?" inquired one of the party. "Various reasons are assigned. But perhaps the true one is, that the clergy of the present day, what with dissenters and vestries, have so many difficulties to contend with, and receive so little thanks for all their pains—being too often regarded in the light of the town common of which all may take advantage gratis—that young men hesitate to embrace the clerical calling." "How do they pay the clergy in England?" asked a merchant. "Their income is derived from various sources, partly from land, partly from fees, partly from offerings, as they are called, made at Easter." "Ay! I understand. Our clergy receive offerings too, but it is at New year. And do the parishioners pay these offerings regularly?" "Some of them do, but others do not; although in reality they are obliged by law to pay a fixed sum. But they know the clergyman will never sue them, so they take a mean advantage of his forbearance." "Ay! Ay! I see. They think the priest can live upon his religion. Very starving food, Sir. He cannot wax fat upon that."

On Ash-Wednesday I now learnt that a curious custom prevails in this country. The girls get some ashes from the grate, and put them in the tiniest possible bag, which they attempt furtively to pin about the dress of one of the male sex; pretty much as a kitchen-maid would pin a dish-clout to the tail of a male intruder into the culinary regions. If they can succeed in the attempt, and the victim carry the bag ever so short a time without detecting it, he has to pay a fine: he may, if he like, retaliate; which he does by pinning a small bag containing a stone to the dress of his fair persecutor.

Aug. 12.—There being no church at Akreyri; I resolved to start early, in order to reach Fredriksgave in time for mid-day Sunday service. Instead of 9 A.M. it was 3 P.M. before the guide made his appearance, and then he was evidently the worse for drink. We had not got far on our road, when the horses, no doubt aware of the state of things, started off in all directions, one back to the town. After chasing and catching the truants, his next task was to chase his own hat, which flew off in another direction. The animals were now tied together, and we assayed to start afresh, but Jon being oblivious forgot to give the word of command, and half the horses stood stock still; while the other half were *en route*. I was in despair. Olaver had been dismissed, but surely I had got a Roland instead. Patience is an article of which the traveller in Iceland must have good store. Otherwise he had far better stay at home. From all I can learn, the African traveller does not meet with more trials.

After five hours' ride, the ordinary time required being two, we came to the banks of the Horgadal river, which though not broad came tearing out of the valley with a highly rabid look. At all events my man did not lack courage, for he dashed in recklessly to try the depth, in spite of my cautions. Presently he returned, saying it would do; and in we went; but the poor horses groaned in agony, as the water rose up to their shoulders, and threatened to do more. I afterwards found this was not the ford at all, but a very dangerous spot: and when we got to the other shore, we had the greatest difficulty in getting up the steep bank; the horses falling back several times into the stream. We now get involved in an impassable bog, and it was not till late that we reached the Amtman's.

Of these officers there are four in Iceland, one for each province. To become an Amtman it is necessary to have studied at the University of Copenhagen, and to have obtained the rank of *laudabilis* in the professional examination. The next lower functionary, the Sysselman, must also have studied at Copenhagen, and come out not less than *haud illaudabilis*. Of these government officers, who are judges, collectors of taxes, &c., there are nearly two hundred in all in this country. The clergy are not required to go to Copenhagen. They must first study at the Latin School at Reykjavik for about eight years, and then at the Theological Seminary for two more. Formerly, the clergy were what is called home-taught: several whom I met with had received their education in this manner under the paternal roof.

The Amtman, who is reputed to be one of the most able public servants in the country, received me most courteously. The official residence is quite a palace for Iceland, standing on the site of the monastery of Modruvellir, which was founded in the year 1295. Since the visit of the present king of Denmark hither, when he was crown prince, it has been called Fredriksgave in memory of that event. Of the ancient monastic buildings, nothing now remains. The church is as usual a mere wooden room. In a gallery just under the roof, which must be as hot as an oven in summer, is the pew of his majesty's representative. The rest of the congregation sit below.

I learn from my host that the wild reindeer frequent mostly the north-eastern parts of the island, as well as the district between Thingvalla and Reykjavik. Henderson the missionary encountered a flock of them, which he describes as wonderfully tame, in 1815. But I had not the fortune to see any. Before long, our conversation gets upon sheep. In fact '*Nous revenous à nos moutons*,' may be said of every second Icelander just now. The scab! how it comes? how it goes? can it be cured? how many sheep it has destroyed? Such are the main topics of talk everywhere. Olavius in his travels in Iceland, about the year 1770, mentions that the same plague was then, as now, ravaging the flocks. Then, as now, there was a prodigious dispute about the origin of the evil, and what was to be done. To cut the matter short, all the infected sheep were sentenced to death; and thousands upon thousands were slaughtered. The slaughtering theory finds a host of advocates at the present day. The intelligent Amtman, even, is for this step. He attributes the spread of the disease to foreign (English) sheep imported into the country; while the people in the south, with much more reason, attribute the disease to the close packing of the poor animals in winter, about a *square foot* being the space allotted to each. A newspaper war between the north and the south is now raging on the subject. I meet here with a gentleman who has lately been appointed Sysselman in Rangavalla Syssel, where the pest is the worst. But as most of his emoluments are derived from the peasants, and they, in consequence of their losses, have nothing to pay, he has thrown up the appointment.

Another visitor is an unprotected female, a young lady from Reykjavik. She started in company with the north-country students, and will go back with them, spending the intermediate time in visiting her kinsfolk and acquaintance (almost everybody is every other body's kith and kin in Iceland), with the stray chance of an escort betwixt and between.

In winter, the people make much use of snow shoes; a pair are shewn me about 80 inches long, and 4½ inches broad, fluted underneath. The art of using these had become entirely lost, when, in 1775, one Buch of Husavik was employed by the Danish government to teach the inhabitants the use of them. In short, from various causes—some say owing to Danish oppression, and the interdict against English and other traders — this country had in the last century sunk to the very lowest ebb. The people had forgotten everything. Even beer-brewing had become extinct. Millstones were no longer known, all the bread being made of meal imported from Denmark. It was about 1770 that by order of the Danish monarch some patterns were reintroduced from Norway, and the people taught to hew millstones for themselves, the material for which abounds in the country. Other efforts were made by the Danish government to rouse the population from their apathy, and ameliorate their condition. Thus salt-works were established in various places, and the numerous hot-water springs near the sea were sought to be made available for the manufacture of that material. But the manufacture languished. The salt had lost its savour. Fir-trees were sown, but grew not. The forests, once exterminated, were not to be restored. The sulphur mines were worked, but this too ended in nothing.

Again, Christian the Vth sought to remove that eyesore from the face of the country, which converts all the meadow land into the appearance of a churchyard, or aggregation of ant-hills: I mean the grass-grown tussocks; which some travellers have supposed were thrown up by the peasants themselves under the idea that by increasing the superficial surface of the ground, a larger crop of grass might be produced in proportion; but which in reality are caused by the melting snows of spring. But still these grassy humps have maintained their ground, increasing ten fold the labours of the mower; and it is only in the last year or two that serious attempts have been made by some of the more spirited agriculturists to get rid of them. In short, the country had become so completely impoverished by Danish exactions, bad seasons, and the extinction of national spirit, that *fuit Ilion* might be said of it in every respect; and it now only remains to be seen whether the recent establishment of free-trade will not have come too late. One thing is certain, that while the Danes kept the trade in their own hands, all chance of raising the material condition of Iceland was out of the question. What they did with one hand they were only undoing with the other.

The winter in the north of Iceland, as might naturally be supposed, is much keener than in the south. The summer, on the contrary, is generally finer and clearer here than down south. Much, however, depends on the wind. Even in summer, a north wind brings snow and sleet in the north; while in the south the same wind brings fine weather. Again; while a southerly wind is almost invariably attended by rain in the south, in the north it brings with it fine clear weather. Curiously enough, a north-east wind is called a 'land-north' wind; the word *land* applying, we presume, to Norway, *the* land or continent *par excellence.*

While here, I was disappointed in not seeing a relic of antiquity belonging to the Amtman's clerk. This was a fiddle of the old Icelandic pattern 'fidla.' It was described to me to be a hollow oblong case, as thick as a man's arm, and of the same width throughout. In place of this obsolete instrument, the Icelanders now use what is called the Langspiel; which, unlike the fidla, tapers, being narrower at one end than the other. It has three strings.

CHAPTER XI.

My guide becomes a teetotaller—"Priest B. of A. was suspended for drinking"—The effects of drink—Gallopping along the edge of a precipice—The empty saddle—The possessed of Gadara—"He is killed"—A clerical library—Ride along the Eyafiord—Fresh water cod—An Icelandic clergyman's fees—A clerical Lazarus unknown in Iceland—Shark-fishing—An old heathen temple—Heljadalsheidi—A stone-flood—Holar—A monster funeral—Episcopal portraits and visitations—"Gudbrand was a man albeit a bishop"—Ecclesiastical art—Churchyard musings—The church-loft—A whole churchyard rises at once.

BUT the day is wearing (August 5), and I have far to ride; so I must take leave of my kind host and his lady. In my hurry to be off, I stumble over the threshold, and fall. "Never mind," said the Amtman, "it is a good omen. We have a proverb, 'Fall er farar heill úr gardi, en ekki í,' (A fall out of the house is lucky, into it, unlucky.") My guide is a sobered and an altered man. The big-wig had been wigging him severely; and I am bound to declare that the man, though not as sharp as Icelandic agate, was most faithful, civil, and obliging; and religiously abstained from all fellowship with his enemy throughout the journey. In the course of our travels, I took up my parable more than once against dram-drinking. I smote Ion friendly, however, and did not reprove him harshly. It is my belief that many of these poor fellows drink for want of a fixed occupation, and to relieve the tedium of idleness. "I know it is a very bad habit," said he, "very bad; but there are many of the clergy that drink hard, and they have more understanding than us. If the old fox swallows the poison, it is no wonder if the cubs do the same. There was Priest B. of A. He is dead now: he was suspended for drinking. They say he used to bob down when he was on the preaching-stool and swallow a dram."

I can, alas! corroborate as an eyewitness the truth of Ion's assertion, that some of the clergy—but I think not many now—drink, as the following will shew. Late one evening, when I had still some distance to ride to the end of my day's journey, I entered a lone house to make inquiries about the road. Drinking brandy here was a tall middle-aged man wrapped in a travelling cloak which was girded tightly round his waist; while what German students would call kanonenstiefeln swallowed up his legs. His countenance, which bore a certain air of good humour about it, was a good deal lined, more however I thought with the hot fingers of the rosy god than with the claws of care, or the furrowings of profound thought. A leer in his restless humid eye, and a degree of uncertainty in his gait, seemed to corroborate my suspicion. He was the priest of the district, returning from a christening, the very man at whose house I purposed stopping the night.

"Ah! you are an Englishman; I salute you:" it

was only by a strenuous resistance on my part that his embrace stopped short of a kiss. "The Icelandic horses are good horses. You'll come to my house. Good! good! but you need not start yet. You don't know the way! Ha! ha! ha! you must wait. I can ride it in the dark."—"But, Séra, it is seven o'clock, and the road is long. It must be two or three hours off—we had better be moving." "It's all right. The Icelandic horses are good horses. You are an Englishman, I am an Icelander. I am a priest. You are a priest. Við erum bádir vígðir prestar. (We are both consecrated priests.) Præst — præst— præstus sumpsimus ambobus. I have forgotten my Latin; Præsti sumus ambobus consecratus. To be sure! begge to inviede prester. I can talk Danish a little, you see; but Latin I have forgotten. I can only talk a lille smule Latinsk."

In despair of getting him off, I mount and ride away with my train. The wind is high, and the obscure path lies along the edge of the sea-cliff; at other times losing itself in morasses more inland. Our pace was necessarily slow. Presently, I hear shouts behind me, and lo! the parson at full gallop after me on his long-tailed horse: his cape flapping in the wind like the wings of an obscene bird, and his hand pressing his glazed hat upon his brows. He dashed frantically against me, so as almost to dislodge me from the saddle, with a loud "Ha! ha! ha!;" and it was only by a dexterous movement that

I escaped being thrown over the cliffs. His reverence continues his mad career among the horses, who squander right and left in alarm, as if a bomb had burst in their midst; to the great peril of themselves and my effects. I beg him to go on in front, and shew us the way. Off he darts along the very verge of the precipice, screaming frantically, "This way! this way!" Presently he drops behind, and I take advantage of the lull in the tempest to forge ahead. Looking behind I see his horse trotting after us, the saddle empty. "For Heaven's sake, stop! Jon: he has fallen over the rocks." But no: here he comes, rolling heavily in his cannon boots. His hat had blown off, and he had dismounted to catch it. Seizing his horse, I descend to help him on to it.

"Do you wish to get to my house to night?" "Yes." "Well then, let go my horse, and leave me alone." After half a dozen ineffectual attempts, he is again mounted. "Your fylgimadr (guide) is a stupid fellow. Stupidus hom—hum—hom—Stupidus hominibus quibus non potest—I've forgotten my Latin. Hominus qui nequit sequi viam debuit—debet:—hominus quibus nequit directus ire vapulabatur! Yes!" "Vapulabatur" he bawled, shaking his whip savagely at the guide, who seemed overwhelmed with shame and dismay; "Vapulabatur!"

On a sudden the demon of drink was again upon him, and he plunged violently down a steep ravine like the possessed of Gadara, screaming hoarsely, "Come along, English priest. This is the way. Follow me, I say. Ha! you dare'nt." And then I caught floating on the blast, "Hominus!—vapulatus!—Ha! ha! Præstus sumpsimus ambobus!" Jon groaned out, "Dreadful! He is worse than priest B. of A. who is now dead, and was suspended for drink." "You see, Jon, what drink does." "I do, indeed. I'll never be drunk again. But when the priest drinks, or the sysselman drinks, all drink. But we must follow him."

And so we did, but with much caution. The ravine ploughed down into a roaring stream, and I could just see this wild huntsman, flashing in the dusk through the moonlit spray, and then clambering cat-like up the opposite cliff. By good rights he has forfeited his neck long ago, but the poor patient steed, a very fine animal, knows what he is about and if left to himself will bring him safe to his own door yet.

"Come along, English priest! It is a Satan's longa via. Skratten! (Old Scratch!) Citatis equis advolant Romam. Ha! ha! I've not forgotten my Latin, you see. You can't quote Latin like me. Try now." "What author?" "Virgilius; No: I mean Erasmus; Desiderius Erasmus. I have you there. Ha! ha!" "Well, sir priest, do you remember what Erasmus replied to the monks when they lampooned him?" "No!" "Well then I'll tell you:—

> 'O monachi quorum stomachi sunt amphora Bacchi,
> Vos estis, Deus est testis, teterrima pestis.'"

"Skratten!" ejaculated the priest, starting as if an adder had stung him, and again he tore away in a gallop along a mere rut over a moor full of impediments. "Citatis equis!" I could hear him shout, and then a kind of Procumbit humi bos sound, bump, thump, and then—dead silence.

"He has been thrown. Dreadful!" groaned Jon. "He is worse, much worse, than priest B. of A. now dead, who was suspended for drink; I will never drink again. He is killed!" We dismount in a twinkling to render assistance. One leg was still in the stirrup. His sagacious beast has not moved an inch, and thereby saved his life. We extricate him: and he turns out to be very little the worse: but the shock had sobered him. At this moment a rider joins us, who tells me that we have now only another half-hour's ride to the parsonage, and that the path grows smoother. "Is he often in this way?" I whispered. "Why yes, sometimes;" replied the peasant, who was a parishioner, "he does drink somewhat, but he is a very friendly, good sort of a man." His reverence, who was perfectly mute, starts off at a brisk pace; we close upon his heels, following the wave of his cloak through the gloom; and before long the bark of the watch dogs tells us that we have reached our destination. Groping through a long passage, we at last reach his sanctum sanctorum.

On the book-shelves I saw a Virgil, Ciceronis de Officiis, a Handbook of Mythology, a Greek Lexicon, and several volumes of sermons; while under the table, upon the table, and in various parts of the room, were bottles, mostly empty.

But it is time to draw a veil over the scene. Hannah More said of the Welsh clergy in the last century that they made cider and dug potatoes to improve their income, and drank hard when they could get it; and indwellers in the principality and its environs in the year 1861 can say whether the present mountain clergy are Nazarites or not. So that one must not judge too hardly of a class of men with so few advantages as the Icelandic clergy, or imagine that there are many among them like the above priest.

The shortest way from Fredricksgave to Holar, the seat of the ancient bishoprick, which I purpose visiting, is over Hialtadals-heidi; but it is so impracticable—indeed dangerous to life and limb—that, as an Icelandic distich relates, the Father of Evil himself on one occasion refused to take that route, when he was bound on a pressing errand to that venerable seat of learning. As far as the scenery is concerned, our ride along the Eyafiord was most delectable. The profuse rain of the early morning had ceased, and the sun shone brightly, bringing out the snow-tipped mountains on the other side of the blue fiord, in all their rugged majesty.

In one place we ride along one of those beaches of shingle, thrown right across a bay, making a lake of it; where I pick up several pieces of cornelian and chalcedony. Half up the fiord is Hrisey, once covered, as its name imports, with wood; and on this side of it Staerriarskogar, whose name also betokens ancient forests, now nowhere to be seen. The clergyman of this place is the son of Iceland's best historian, Jon Espolin. He keeps his library in the church: only following the example of his betters at Reykjavik. On a cross-beam are a row of new books; a Commentary, I find, on the Revelations of St. John by Espolin, which the son has had printed at his own expense at Akreyri. At the mouth of Svarfadal we pass another lake, divided by a narrow bank of shingle from the sea, which is said to abound with fresh-water cod. Their piscine forefathers were no doubt as fond of salt-water as codfish are generally, but their descendants finding themselves in a lake, which gradually became less and less salt, made a virtue of necessity, and acquiesced in the novel order of things.

The priest of Vellir, Séra Paul Jonsen, is my host for the night. He throws some more light upon the loaves and fishes that fall to the lot of an Icelandic clergyman, which will perhaps prove not uninteresting to those of the cloth at home. His living is worth about 300 dollars annually in money, in addition to his farm, which, like most of the Icelandic clergy, he cultivates himself. He was presented to his benefice by the Bishop, to whom all the Church patronage belongs, with the exception of the following five livings. Reykjavik, which is worth about 1200 dollars, Breidabolstadr in the South, Stadirstadir in the district of Snaefell, Hitardal in Myrassyssel, and Greniadarstadr, which I have already mentioned.

His fees are as follows, as fixed by law:

Burial, 1 to 2 dollars.

If he pronounces a funeral oration, 2 or 3 dollars extra.

Marriage, 1 to 2 dollars.

But lately he received 6 dollars for performing this ceremony.

Baptism, ½ dollar.

Churching (ad leida i kirkja), 2 marks.

The amount of New Year offerings is fixed by the law of 1782 according to the tithable value of the farm in the occupation of a parishioner. Thus, if in the ancient valuations it is rated at twenty thousand, he pays 8 marks, and so in proportion. The parishioners, as far as I could ascertain, are very openhanded in those matters, paying custom to whom custom is due with much cheerfulness. Live and let live is, as between them and their minister, not a mere dead letter, but a rule to be acted upon. One peasant had last New Year's day made an offering to my host of 4 dollars, while his wife, with a delicate generosity, had added an ancient silver beaker (*staup*). If I were asked to compare the temporals of an Icelandic and an English clergyman, I should say that, taken as a body, the former are the better off of the two. In the first place, their education is gratis. Again, their income may be small; but their wants are small in proportion; while their farm supplies them with most of the necessaries of daily life, and they have horses to ride in abundance. Séra Paul has 10 horses, 7 cows, and 60 sheep. Their world does not require of them, as in England, much attention to dress; for they do not pay much attention to it themselves. A shabby exterior is not in their eyes a cardinal vice. And, as a consequence of this state of things, the Amos Bartons of England are unknown in Iceland: there are no societies for supplying her clergy with the left off clothes of the laity. Whatever other mantle may have descended upon them, at all events no eleemosynary vestments cover their shoulders. In Iceland, in short, a country at which an English tradesman would turn up his nose, and pronounce it an uncivilized wilderness, a clergyman, with his £30 a year and his farm, is better off than the clergyman in England with no house and a hundred per annum. And as a lay-beggar is a thing not to be met with here, so is a clerical Lazarus equally unknown.

In the course of the evening another guest arrives, a fine young fellow engaged in the shark-fishery off the coast. These fish are to be found in great abundance a few miles from the land. The fishing lasts from April to the beginning of September. The hook is frequently baited with seal-fat. Horse-flesh is also bought up all over the country for the purpose; a food, however, which is not so cheap as may be supposed, for if not eaten by the peasants themselves, it is not unfrequently used, when dried, to sustain the life of their starving horses during the winter. The abundant oil of the liver is boiled out at little establishments along the coast—one of which I scented plainly enough to-day—and then exported to Denmark. These fish run to the length of 21 feet; but I could not hear of any being caught in Iceland so large as a monster of this species taken in the autumn of 1860 at Whalsey in Shetland, which was 27½ feet long; while the oil from its liver sold for £16 10s. On the wall hangs a langspiel, an oblong instrument of three strings, the intermediate step between the ancient fidla, described above, and the fiddle proper.

The next day my host rides with me to a very interesting spot, higher up the valley, the site of an ancient heathen temple (Hof), the proportions of which are still plainly to be made out*. Round the spot runs a circular mound of earth, now grass-grown, about 56 paces in circumference. Apparently, within this enclosure was a square building, being the temple itself. Almost in the centre of the circle is a pit about 4 paces square, the receptacle into which the blood of the victim flowed. In the middle of this pit is an eminence on which stood the sacrificial stone. On the north side of this place of sacrifice is an elevation, the platform (stadir), on which were the statues of Thor, Odin and Freya. Opposite them, across the blood-pit, was a partition wall, over which the people beheld the ceremonies from the outer court of the building. The priest entered the enclosure by a door to the south east, passing along the eastern wall, in which were two entrances. But the iron spell which bound the hearts of the people is dissolved; the grim gods have been driven from their mystic shrine; and the pontiff's place is supplied by the Lutheran priest, who is my obliging cicerone; while, very likely, the pontiff's blood runs in the veins of the well-to-do peasant living hard by, who offers me schnaps and coffee.

His son undertakes to guide us over the river, which is dangerous to the uninitiated. It was only

* The above description is derived from my own inspection, and the observations of my companion. Great uncertainty, I believe, prevails as to the actual dimensions and shape of these buildings. See Dasent's 'Burnt Nial,' Introduction.

this spring that it was the death of a luckless peasant. The mountains which wall in the valley are very fine, exhibiting the succession of horizontal stories, with *entresols* of red, so frequent in this country. The torrents which burst out of the gorges to join the main stream give evidence, by the zeolites and crystals strewed about, of the mineral riches stored within their hidden recesses. Our path lies to the south-west, over slopes embroidered with blue and white varieties of *Gentiana Campestris;* and *Erigeron Alpinum* is frequent. At Kot, the last inhabited spot in the valley, we hear that there is deep snow on the mountains; so, instead of making straight across to Hofsös, on the Skagafiord, as I had meditated, I deem it safer to take the direct track to Holar, by way of Heljadalsheidi. Before long, crowning a steep ascent, we are on deep snow, in the vicinity of which I gather some *Ranunculus Glacialis* in full bloom. Our descent had begun on the other side the pass, when a distant bark recalls my attention from two eagles wheeling overhead in graceful eddies; and looking up the almost perpendicular cliff, I see a number of sheep rushing down it before a dog, which at a beck from his master below had gone in pursuit of them.

The shades of evening were lengthening after a beautiful day, when our laborious course over the pass terminated in Kolbeinsdal. The mountains lining this valley have a trick of becoming surcharged with water like a sponge, after heavy rains; when a part peels off, and descends below, annihilating all before it. We pass the site of a once thriving farm now overrun with one of these stone-floods. Some bottomless morasses, and a river and a tongue of land are crossed, and we are in Hialtadal. Yon white building standing on the solitary moor, with one or two cottages near, is the church of Holar (Holum is the oblique case), the seat for seven hundred years of Iceland's northern bishoprick.

Aug. 15, as I lay abed, I received a visit from my host's father, the venerable priest Séra Benedict, who is the seventh in direct descent from Bishop Gudbrand, and the eleventh from Bishop Arneson. These people are very fond of "endless genealogies." He tells me that one Einar Biarneson, a peasant in the neighbourhood, and withal an accomplished genealogist, once told him he knew of two Icelanders whose relationship to Queen Victoria he could trace. He is now deceased, but his son, who has a similar talent with his father, and is possessed of an Icelandic memory, lives near Holanaes, where I hope to meet him. The site of the ancient heathen temple is now covered by a farm-house. Close to it was buried Hialt, who gave his name to the valley. According to the Landnama Book, his funeral was celebrated with great pomp, and 1200 people were invited to the Grave-ale, the greatest number that ever came to such a ceremony in Iceland. Hialt was, in fact, a man of great consequence, and his sons were fond of display. Having some dispute about the inheritance, they went to the Thing of Thorskafiordr, (of which hereafter;) and so magnificently were they apparelled, that the sensation among the people was tremendous, and they cried out, "Here come gods!"

The see of Holar was founded in 1106 by Gissur Isleifsen, the most celebrated bishop of Skalholt, and endowed with lands by the monk Hilarius. But it is now all over with the place. With its bishops; its printing-press, its school, and its other glories have ceased. Of its long line of Romish and Reformed bishops, the portraits of a few hang upon the mildewed walls of the church, under whose damp and decrepit pavement some of them repose. The altar piece of carved wood representing the Crucifixion was the gift of a pope. An angel floats over each thief as well as by the side of our Lord. To the north of it is Bishop Gissur kneeling opposite to his wife, on whose head is placed a very broad-brimmed high-crowned Tyrolese-looking hat, only not quite so conical. Between them is the Holy Rood. The legend round this oil-painting runs thus—

Praesulis externum Gissuri perspice vultum,
Aurea sed clarae mentis imago deest,
Ad latus effigies speciosae conjugis astat,
Interior cujus promicat axe poli.

Next to this picture comes a portrait of old Gudbrand, the 2nd evangelical bishop, who established the printing-press and translated the Bible. He died 1620 aged 78. He has a fine thoughtful face, terminating in a forked beard, and wears a black cloak lined with fur. He has a book in his hand. The custom of holding visitations has fallen much into disuse of late among the members of the Icelandic episcopal bench, who naturally shrink from the terrors of the bridgeless river, the dizzy profound of the precipice, and the hardships of camp life in general. Not so bishop Gudbrand. On one of his rounds a peasant girl visited his tent. Gudbrand was a man, albeit a bishop, and an erring man too. A daughter not born in wedlock (londatter) was the result. "But you know," said my companion, "that was not long after the Reformation, and the Church was still infected by the Popish leaven: besides which, people were not particular then, and did not think much of a bishop going astray; and so he remained a bishop." Nay, more; that daughter married a peasant named Skula, and became the mother of two bishops, Thordar, bishop of Skalholt, and Thorlak, 3rd bishop of Holar, whose portraits hang yonder. She was also grandmother of Thorlakson, 4th bishop of this see, whose portrait and those of his three wives are to the south of the altar. There he is sure enough, a coarse looking ecclesiastic, bearded, and of a beefy countenance, with his three helpmates by his side, wearing close caps, steeple crowned broad-brimmed hats, fringed and banded, and large stiffly starched frills round their necks; while their long stiff black cloaks are decorated with clasps all down the edges in front, and being only fastened by big clasps on the bosom, reveal the splendours of their petticoats of yellow and red figured brocade.

The curtains hanging on poles on either side of the altar are of yellow silk, embroidered in squares by the nuns of old, but now mere rags. It is interesting to know that, according to tradition, an English lady was brought hither to teach the art of embroidery; and the ruins of her house were formerly pointed out. Attached to the chancel-screen are a set of scenes from the life of John the Baptist, sculptured in high relief, in white alabaster, picked out with divers colours. Marvellous to relate, this curious work of ancient art did not go the way of all Icelandic monuments, viz. to Copenhagen.

"Tread carefully there," cried the priest, as I moved forward to examine the stone font, many centuries old, the master-work of an Icelandic sculptor. "Tread carefully! that bishop's vault in the floor has sunk in, and has not yet been repaired." Alas! so it is with the most cherished mementos of humanity. Deceased friends and relatives consigned so carefully to what is called the long home, in consecrated earth. A few short years elapse; and in spite of bishops' Faculties, the new generation want, and must have, the ground to make improvements, or build railway stations; and that dust—once again, as the Christian firmly believes, about to mould itself into a body, new, but still the same—is scattered—whether it be the dust of great Cæsar or of Yorick—to the four winds of heaven. Those pagan Northmen, who would crawl up into the mountain when their eye was dimmed with coming death, and their natural force wellnigh exhausted, and hide them from the face of man; or get some faithful friend to bury them, with none but the silent stars as witnesses, were not so wrong after all.—"So Moses the servant of the Lord died, and He buried him in a valley in the land of Moab, over against Beth-peor: but no man knoweth of his sepulchre to this day."

"And whose portrait is that?" asked I, pointing to one framed and glazed, and hanging in the nave. "That is Gaimard the Frenchman who travelled in Iceland; I believe he is no longer living. You see we have canonized him!" The great bell of Holar, called Likabaung, the gift of the first evangelical bishop, Olaf Hialtason, was, according to an old rhyme, cast at Hamburg. It is now rent in twain. After bishop Jon Arason's murder, or execution, his corpse was brought hither for interment, when the great Likabaung began tolling of itself. The loft above the church presented the usual mixture of old curiosity-shop and storeroom. Bishop Gudbrand's Bible lay in a chest with some curious old clasped books, bound in parchment; while scythes and skins, hair-ropes and registers, meal and mutton, fish-hooks and frocks, were scattered thickly about amid mouldering memorials of episcopalian grandeur and nothingness.

I must wind up my stock-taking in the cathedral of Holar with a tale of one of its dignitaries. The see was ruled from 1498 to 1520 by bishop Gudiskalkr, surnamed Grimmi, on account of his skill in the black art. A pupil of Holar school had a great desire to get hold of his book on magic, (Raudskinna,) so called doubtless from its red-skin binding. But, like that wondrous tome of Michael Scott's, it had been placed in his grave with him, and it would cost the life of whoever attempted to get it, if he did not succeed. The scholar, no mean adept himself in the art, caused the whole churchyard to rise by his spells, the bishop among the rest of the wakers, in his full episcopal robes, and with the coveted book in his hand. Dean Ramsay, or somebody, tells a tale of a cool-headed Scotchman, who on encountering a ghost phlegmatically inquired, 'Are you alone, or is it a general rising?' and there is no reason to believe that even in the latter event he would have been taken aback. Not so our student:

> "His breath came thick, his head swam round,
> When the strange scene of death he saw."

Bewildered and unnerved, he clutches at the book,

but in his hurry lets it slip; when a fellow-student spoils the whole thing. His instructions were to ring the bell directly his friend had got the book fast, when all the sprites would vanish on the instant. Being in too much of a hurry, however, he rang a moment too soon; the dead disappear, and along with them the bishop and his book. The student knew full well that by a certain day he was doomed to die. He goes to a good clergyman in the west, and seeks by prayer and meditation to avert his fate, or at least to prepare himself for it. All goes well till the day, when he went out rowing in the priest's boat, and never returned.

CHAPTER XII.

An Icelandic patriot—Hospitalities—Reykjavik a Danish town—A stirrup-cup—Hofsös—A gerfalcon on the wing—Slaughter of forty-six whales—A leaf from the book of the thane of Fife—A description of Skagafiord—Drangö—The Troll and his wife—The murder of the Icelandic Wallace—The avenger of blood—Grettisaga — Auceps — The Fleke — Wild strawberries — Trout fishing—A magic scene—A man with a prodigious memory—His library—I acquire an ancient MS.—Departure from Hofsös—Beds of roses—The ferry over Herredsvatn—A legend about seals—The Troll-Metropolis.

The worthy pastor is a most patriotic Icelander, jealous of the honour of his country, and mindful of the days when his forefathers, sooner than bow their proud neck to the tyrant, left smiling valleys and a milder climate, to pluck up liberty from the North Atlantic wave. While we were regaling ourselves upon the fatted lamb and Madeira, he unburdened himself respecting the advantages of Danish leading-strings. He could not away with the idea of their fostering care. It had ruined the country. 'Odi Danaos et dona ferentes.' "You English are a great nation," he continued; "you remind one of the old Romans. But remember that we had our upper and lower houses of parliament before you: alas! that's all over now." "But you have an Althing at your capital Reykjavik." "Reykjavik quotha? Reykjavik is a Danish town. What can be expected from a parliament sitting there? It is a mere shadow of a parliament. What we wish for is a legislative assembly, with a veto reserved to the king; not as now, a mere consulting and advising body. What the people would like would be to be joined to Norway. The ancient Iceland I am proud of, the modern I almost pity." "But," interposed I, "liberty is one thing, licence is another. I have heard that there is a great deal of rabid radicalism abroad—freethinking too in religious matters; is it not so?" "I fear it is too true. We have to thank the French Revolution for that. It was not, however, till about 1810 that the effects of it reached our distant Iceland."

"Let us take a Heste-skar (stirrup-cup) before parting," said my host. "In ancient times, glasses full to the brim were placed upon that flat stone outside the house, and each guest stooped down from his saddle and took one."

Our course lies along the right bank of the Hialtadalsá, passing As, a place of no little celebrity; for here was erected, 985 A.D., the first Christian church in Iceland, by Thorwald Spakbödvarsen. Recrossing the Kolbeinsdal river, we find ourselves on the eastern shore of the Skagafiord, and reach Hofsös, where a rapid stream joins the sea. There are two mercantile establishments here, one conducted by Mr. Paulson, for a Copenhagen house, the other the property of an Icelander, Mr. Holm. And right good fellows they were. The N.W. wind, which has as usual brought cold bad weather, makes me thoroughly appreciate their hospitalities. Two Danish vessels are lying in the offing, about to carry home the train-oil, dried fish, wool, swan-skins and quills, furs, and knitted socks, &c.; which form the staple of Icelandic merchandise. N.B. For shooting or fishing, Icelandic socks surpass, in durability, warmth, and cheapness, anything I ever saw. Those of a brown or moret colour are said to be the warmest. I manage to secure some white fox-skins at less than half the price asked in Reykjavik. The white and brown varieties of the fox (Icelandicè 'toa'=our 'tod') are the same animal, only in different states of colour, as is shewn by the dark hairs to be found on some of the white specimens. The brown skins cost here from six dollars upwards; the white ones are less than one dollar. The supercargo of one of the vessels insists on my accepting the skin of a great northern diver, which was caught the other day in a net set along shore for salmon; the skin of a gerfalcon, very white, and therefore very old, is also placed at my disposal. An intelligent youth, one Snorri Biarnason, the son of my host at Vellir, who lives here, tells me, he has seen these birds swoop down upon an unfortunate ptarmigan, and take off its head with its wing, as if with a razor! In the old hawking days, some three thousand dollars a year accrued to this country from the sale of these birds. Last winter Snorri saw a number of whales in the fiord, in some holes in the ice. A seal-net, twenty fathoms long, three feet deep, one foot in the mesh, was at once procured: a boat was dragged over the ice, and launched; the monsters were encircled in the net, and forty-six stabbed and bagged.

In Roman Catholic times there was a brisk traffic between this country and Great Britain. This being prohibited in the time of Henry VIIIth by the Danish authorities, the English sailors committed many acts of violence. At last, the peasants having determined to take vengeance on the marauders, adopted an expedient similar to that of Macduff, thane of Fife. Being themselves unprovided with fire-arms, of which the English had no lack, they advanced under the cover of birch-boughs, which they held in their hands, so that their assailants could not take aim at them, and coming to close quarters they overpowered the foreigners by force of numbers. Eighty English were slain; others fled to Holar, where they took sanctuary at the Bishop's, Jon Williamson.

Aug. 16. The waters of the Fiord are basking lazily in the morning sun, no longer dashing their white heads frantically, as they did last night, against the wall of regularly sculptured basaltic pillars; which though not lofty are of great width. Straight across the Fiord, distant about nine miles, is Tindastol, the famed mountain of onyx and chalcedony, with the precipitous coast of Hegrenaes, stretching northward as far as the eye can reach. Out yonder, about half-way over the Fiord, is Drangö, rising like a fortress, and by its side, the Kelling (carline), sharp as the column of Luxor, which Mr. Holm tells me is 95 fathoms high, with a base of some thirty fathoms. Near it once stood another column, the Karl, which sank into the green waves many years ago, probably during the earthquake, which presaged the eruption of the Kötlugiá volcano in 1755, when the sandstone rocks of Drangö and Malmö fell in vast masses, evicting the numerous feathered squatters without mercy. The Icelandic peasant will tell you that those twin columns were that veritable Troll and his wife, who one night lifted a cow, and were crossing over the fiord with her, the wife leading the animal, the husband driving behind, when they were overtaken, not by the owner of the cow, but by the rising sun, and turned into pillars of stone; the animal becoming neither more nor less than the island Drangö.

But to the reader of Icelandic lore yon island is particularly interesting, as the abode and death-place of Gretti Asmundsen, the hero of the *Gretti-saga*, a composition of the 13th century. Of a chivalrous and noble disposition, but withal of a fiery temper, and endowed with Herculean strength, he was not the man to submit tamely to insult or injury; taking the law without scruple into his own hands, till at last his hand was against everybody, and everybody's hand against him. His enemies having procured a writ of outlawry against him, a price was set upon his head, and he had to hide in caves and deserts for many years. At last he fixed upon this island fastness as his place of retreat, with only his younger brother Illugi and a thrall to bear him company. The period of his outlawry was nigh expiring, according to the Icelandic statute of limitations, when his enemies, fearful of losing their revenge, prevailed on one Thorbiorn Aungul to murder him. One stormy night this caitiff sailed to the island. The thrall, whose duty it was to draw up the ladder every evening, by which access was gained to Gretti's abode, had neglected this precaution, so that the murderers had no difficulty in scaling the cliff. As ill luck would have it, the outlaw was confined to his bed, having wounded his foot with an axe while hewing driftwood, so that the assassin made short work of it. Illugi might have escaped, if he would have promised not to try to avenge his brother, but he nobly refused to do so, and was also murdered.

Aungul bore off Gretti's head to the Althing; but he was looked upon by the assembly as a base Niddering for slaying a disabled man, and instead of receiving the wages of blood, he was driven into banishment. He went to Norway, and from thence to Miklegaard (Constantinople), pursued, however, with the steadiness of a sleuth hound, by another brother of Gretti's, Dromund. Michael Katlak was at this time emperor. One day, the murderer was shewing off Gretti's sword, at a tourney, to an admiring crowd of Varangians.

> Some one might shew it at a joust of arms,
> Saying, 'King Arthur's sword excalibur.'

"I slew him with his own sword," said the boaster. "Look at this dint here; it was made by his brain-pan, which was exceedingly hard, I assure you." "Astonishing!" exclaimed a person in the crowd. "Just let me look at the blade. Well to be sure, that *is* a dint!" he added, getting the weapon into his hand; and down it descended upon Aungul's head, cleaving it through and through. Dromund (for it was he) was immediately cast into a dungeon, where, to while away his solitude, he sings some of the songs of his native north. A female passing overhears him, and is so captivated by the music, that she makes inquiries about him, and ransoms him. As a matter of course, his benefactress falls in love with him. Her husband naturally became suspicious of the stranger, who was thus suddenly installed in his wife's good graces, and endeavoured to surprise the pair. Various were the shifts employed to baffle the injured husband's vigilance. At one time the lover is hidden in a chest; he next disappears through a trapdoor; and another time, like Falstaff, is hidden under a heap of foul linen. This story of the love-affair is evidently taken from the tale of Prince Tristan, an Icelandic translation of which, together with many other French romances, was made by order of king Hacon of Norway in 1226. The main parts of Gretti's history, however, as given in the Saga, must be true, as they are corroborated by the Landnama and Snorri Sturlesen.

But, apart from its legendary and historical reminiscences, Drangö is interesting in a material point of view. For its size, it is said to be the most useful plot of ground in Iceland, giving food to many families. At at early period it came into the possession of the see of Holar. It was not the scanty grass that grew upon its top, which a few sheep are boated over to nibble in the summer, but the birds that rested in its cliffs, that gave the island its value; and the bishops were perfectly alive to its importance. In the inventory of the episcopal goods, the leathern rope for letting the fowlers down the cliffs is mentioned. A good one was valued at 5 species dollars,—the price of a good horse in those days. It was made of the thickest ox-hide, and consisted of seven pieces, each piece being eighty fathoms long, and requiring sixteen ox-hides for its construction. The length of the whole therefore would be 560 fathoms.* Six men stood above to hold it, while another stood by on the watch for any signal from the man below, who was engaged in securing the birds. *Uria Troila* is the species in greatest numbers; in Icelandic, svartbag.

* E. Olafsson.

The chief method of taking the birds at the present day is by the fleke, which I saw. It is an oblong piece of board, or rather two or three boards fastened together, thirty-two inches long by twenty-eight broad. In this, above a hundred holes are drilled at intervals in straight lines, to each of which is fastened a strong snare of twisted horsehair, (black preferred.) At the end of May, hundreds of men repair to the island in boats, with thirty of these flekes to a boat. These instruments are then anchored off the island with a heavy stone and rope: and on each of them is fastened a bird as a decoy. The men then row to their huts ashore, or out to sea, to fish for isa (coal-fish); visiting the flekes twice a-day. Sometimes the board is found covered with the simple victims caught in the snares. The uncleansed feathers sell for 28 skillings per lb. The flesh is eaten fresh or dried.

But it is time I should be off to the lake, which lies about four English miles north of this, and try my luck with the trout there; as the char and sea-trout, which are caught all along the shore in stationary nets, do not seem inclined to take my fly at the mouth of the river. Snorri guides me along the shore, which is propped up by more basaltic pillars. That island yonder is Malmey, while that magnificent precipice rising triumphantly out of the sea is Thordarshöfde. It derives its name from Thordar, who was fifth in direct descent from Ragnar Lodbrok, and his wife granddaughter on the mother's side of the

Irish king Kiarval.* On the sides of this noble headland is one of the few spots in Iceland where wild strawberries grow and ripen. Behind it lies the lake I am going to, the two ends of it separated from the ocean by a beach of shingle; so that what is now fresh water must have been at one time salt sea, and Thordarhöfde an island. Between this lake and the sea there is no stream (ös); so the salmon and sea-trout have no access to it, which they have to Micklevatn, another lake about twelve miles north of this, which consequently abounds with both those kinds of fish. Wild-swan feathers strewed the beach, and ducks and great-northern divers were sailing away out of gun-shot. Two eagles were equally circumspect, soaring aloft at the back of Thordarhöfde, intent though they were on finishing up their fish-dinner with a dish of ptarmigan.

Before long I secure some very fine trout, brilliantly spotted, and above three lb. in weight, amid cries of "Sei! sei!" the Icelandic exclamation of astonishment. Numbers of fish kept rising at my grilse flies, but generally half in play; the breeze having died away, and left the water too smooth for sport. So, drawing the boat, in which Snorri had been rowing me, ashore, we remount the horses, which had been tethered in the deep trough of a wave of shingle, filled with the greenest grass. Two masses of roseate mist hung about the tall mountains

* Landnama, P. III. C. X.

to the eastward, one diademing their tops, the other girdling their waist; while a splash of purple, thrown by the fast-setting sun, tinged the dark interval of cliff which lay between these fleecy appendages—one of those magic scenes which haunt one's mind for a lifetime. Wild thyme (blodberg), buttercups (brennisolei), and hawkweed (fifel), grew on the meadow; and, close to a cottage, some cumin, which the natives dry, using the seeds as a condiment.

In this humble abode dwelt one of those men who are to be found only in Iceland. Thorsten Thorstensen, a tall, gaunt, grey-haired, man, his cheeks arabesqued by the cares and hardships of three score winters, was mending a fishing-net outside his dwelling. Upon being informed by Snorri, that the English priest had come to see his library, he conducted us with great readiness into a narrow chamber; the receptacle of much learning and—more dirt. Here were piled in utter confusion several printed books and manuscripts. Thorsten is the son of a student, and grandson of a clergyman, and himself a great reader, book-collector, and transcriber. Wherever a leaf was missing from a printed volume, I found its place supplied by a pen and ink copy of what was gone, in a hand almost like copperplate. Here is a book published without date, by N. Fischer of Amsterdam, being a collection of verses in Dutch, French, English, German, and Latin, descriptive of the most remarkable events in the Bible, with many good engravings. Taking up a very musty fusty tome, I find it is the life and acts of Dr. Faustus. A woman enters the cell at this moment most opportunely with a bowl of fresh milk, which helps to wash down the dust that had escaped from its leaves into my throat.

Here, again, is an old manuscript containing ballads, lullabies, and charades. Here is a copy of a saga, never printed: entitled Barði Birtu og Skarfi Skinu, relating the doings of some of the ancient dwellers in these parts, before Thangbrand came to drub them into Christianity. How that a mystic light was seen hovering over Gravarös three nights running; and how a man, gifted with second sight, upon being consulted thereon, said it portended a coming change of religion; and how all the bonders round soon became Christians, save and except the functionary of the heathen temple. Whereupon the converts tumbled the temple about his ears, and shewed him how his gods were no gods, but mere idols of wood and stone. By the bye, I cannot hear that any such mysterious light has been seen, since the Romish priests have come to convert the country. So the portents are not encouraging for them. Meantime, Thorsten has rummaged out of the dust and cobwebs a beautifully written copy of the Jonsbok, the book of laws, sent by King Magnus Lagabeter of Norway to Iceland. As is often the case with Icelandic manuscripts, the paper was very brown. This is due, I am told, to the ink, which was a decoction of willow sprigs, &c.; which, though black and bright at first, dried very slowly, and in process of time gave the above tint to the paper. This prize, which I acquire for a small consideration, was sold to the bibliomanist by one Magnus, who assured him that it was 'eldgammel,' at least three hundred years old. A beautifully illustrated example of this book may be seen at the Museum in Copenhagen.

"And now Thorsten," said Snorri, coaxingly, "just recite to us a bit out of one of the sagas; the stranger wishes to satisfy himself, whether your memory really is so good as he has heard it is." Thorsten seemed to have become quite a different being, all life and animation, the moment he got among his books, like that giant of the classic mythology, who acquired a fresh lease of vital energy the moment he touched his mother earth. His wrinkled face was flushed, and his eye lit up with a new lustre, and he gave a strange look of conscious pride and humility mixed—if that is a bull it must be taken by the horns and removed in the second edition—"What is it to be then?" he asked. "From Grettisaga," replied I, "there, where he is murdered," holding the book in my hand to verify his accuracy. Off the old fellow started, reciting the very words of the saga with extreme volubility. Snorri then tried him in the Eyrbyggia saga, the Laxdaela saga, and the Svarfadalsaga, with the same result. "And now a bit of Niála," said I; and away went the reciter at the same rapid pace. In short, he was not to be posed. The Landnama was the only saga he did not profess to remember: and no wonder, for it contains some three thousand names of persons, and fourteen hundred names of places, and is often merely a dry catalogue. This was all very remarkable; but Snorri informed me that he is not the only man in the neighbourhood gifted with these extraordinary powers of memory.

August 17.—I take leave in the afternoon of my kind friends. Another beautiful day, which the shoals of eider-ducks under the cliffs seem to be making the most of; while the great northern divers are twisting themselves round and round, like weathercocks in gusty weather, watching my movements with suspicion, and preparing for one of those tremendous dives, from which one thinks they never will rise again. The banks of the river at the head of the fiord are carpeted with thick beds of dwarf willow-herb, half-a-foot high (*epilobium frigidum* or *latifolium*), which are now in full bloom, and look at a distance like beds of roses. After an hour's ride along the shore, I encounter my old adversary, the mighty Herredsvand river, which has become dual, and split into two arms which are too deep to ford. In the ferryman's cottage I see bunches of *millefolium* hanging up to dry, from which the natives prepare a tea, said to be good for purifying the blood. Dried and powdered, it is sprinkled on wounds. The tide being out, we trot over the wave-marked bed of black sand to a hillock, which at high water is an island Here lies our frail boat among a lot of *arundo arenaria*, the wild corn of the country. Our luggage is transported at twice; the same with the horses; the ferryman rowing his very hardest to prevent his cockleshell being carried out to sea, or being upset by the plunging horses, which the guide kneeling over the stern is holding by their halters. Much circumspection is necessary. It is only last week that the ferryboat above this was upset by mismanagement, and three men drowned.

Numerous seals, with their usual inquisitiveness, approach to have a look at us. Every Icelander knows quite well that they are in reality king Pharaoh's people (Faraóslidar), who were drowned in the Red Sea. And indeed they still form a human community at the bottom of the ocean, only that their outer man is disguised in those wrap-rascal seal-skins. Once a year, on St. John's eve, they come ashore, cast their skin, and dance and sing and frisk and romp about, like sailors after a long voyage. 'Catch a weasel asleep, shave his eyebrow:' if you can only manage to carry off a skin while the uncloaked ones are at their games, the owner of it remains a man or a woman for the term of his or her natural life.

Once on a time, a peasant in these parts saw a lot

of them at their revels, and securing the slough of a charming young lady, whose beauty was clearly deeper than her cuticle, he made her his wife. They had two children, and lived very happily and contentedly together. The skin he kept in his strong box, the key of which he always had with him in his breeches pocket. It happened that on the Christmas Eve of the third year of their married life, the wife was indisposed, and stopped at home; while her husband and the rest of the family went to church. In putting on his best clothes he forgot the key, which he left in the pocket of his every-day suit. When he returned from church the chest was wide open, and the skin gone, and his wife gone too. When the children used to walk on the sea-shore, a beautiful seal used to swim near, and bring them pretty shells and stones, and sometimes fishes.

Two marks (ninepence) satisfies Gissur, the ferryman, who helps to resaddle the dripping horses. "What is your name?" "Frederick." "Indeed! well, to be sure! he knows a man too called Frederick. So they have the same names in England and Iceland. How funny!" The island between the two arms of the river was a place much heard of in the ancient days, and is often mentioned in the Landnama. It is likewise a sort of metropolis of the Trolls. A Troll diocesan abides in the cliff; the lay element is also well represented in the person of a Troll-Amtman.

CHAPTER XIII.

Nursery rhymes—A dangerous morass in the dark—Peter of Siöborg An eider duck preserve—A *rara avis*—A baptismal basin—The master of Ravenswood's fate—The talismanic pebbles of Iceland—Entertaining angels unawares—An old Icelandic female costume —Hvamm—Agate-cove—Tindastol—A judgment of heaven—Kissing the parson—The virtues of Caltha palustris—Icelandic worship—A national vice—Hunafloi—A magnificent pageant.

WHILE Halgrim, the next ferryman, is sent for, his wife, the amiable Sigrida, whose weak point seemed to be snuff, which clave to her nose in rich profusion, entertained me with the recital of some gaffers and gammers, accumulative stories, jingles, lullabies, riddles, &c.; in which Icelandic mothers are very great. One of her budget was a Grylukvaedi, i. e. a ditty describing the doings of Gryla, a fearful old hag, with as many heads as Hydra, who, from Christmas to Twelfth-night, moves about to take the naughty children; while her grim spouse Leppa Ludi carries the sack to put them in, eating them one by one at discretion, like a hungry Frenchman does bread at the two franc dining-shops in the Palais Royal. So much for the *naughty* children. Whether there is an Icelandic St. Nicholas to descend the chimney and reward the *good* children, Sigrida could not inform me, in spite of the quantities of mental emery-powder (snuff), which she applied to her nose in order to sharpen her apprehension.

But here comes Halgrim, and off we go to the ferry, and another hour is spent in the loading and unloading and swimming and rowing. Our road lies along the sandy sea-shore strewn with skeletons of birds, drift wood, broken oars, mussel-shells and the beautiful pink-coloured *pecten Islandicus*. Dusk finds us on a dangerous morass so full of pools and quagmires, that, in the thick fog in which approaching night came wrapt, what was earth and what water did not admit of a ready solution. The guide thought he saw a track, but track there was none: and every now and then the sagacious ponies, like Shagram in the *Monastery*, aware of dangers which were invisible to us, would start from our course, and try a line of their own along the quaking moor. At last, looming strangely over the flats, I descried what looked like a fortress in the fog. We made towards it, and found a rocky precipice, vague in vapour, rising without any previous notice out of the level swamp, like a sea-cliff out of the waves. In fact, I subsequently found that this rock was an island anciently off the mouth of the river. The vast quantity of decomposed rock brought down from the interior of the country, not finding a ready outlet, gradually silted up, forming the choice landscape through which we have been labouring.

"That's Siöborg" (the sea-castle), said Jon. "Peter

lives here." And winding under the wall of rock, we rose by a sloping path to the table-land above, on which was a church and a house, with a quantity of great drift-logs leaning against it. Peter gave us as warm a welcome as the absence of window-panes in his newly built strangers'-room would admit of. He is the son of my old friend, the clergyman of Maelifell, and owns thirteen horses, sixty milking ewes, and five cows. The latter account for the beautiful cream to my coffee; while the milking ewes are responsible for the fresh butter, which though of a pale colour was by no means unpalatable. In the lake close by, there are plenty of trout. Peter is getting up an eider-duck preserve upon it; so that he permits no gun to be fired, and only takes a few score of eggs.

One morning last March, when the ground was covered with snow, and the fiord with thick-ribbed ice, he found, on opening the door in the morning, two strange birds, such as he had never seen before, pecking about near the house. Setting the door of the church open, he enticed the birds into it with some grain. The poor captives ate corn voraciously; but he forgot to give them water, and kept them in the suffocating atmosphere of the common sleeping apartment (Badstovë). If he could have understood 'What does little birdie say?' he would no doubt have given them water and air. As it was, one of them died in twenty-four hours, the other in forty-eight. It was his belief that they had been carried hither from Greenland by the drift-ice. It was, I found, our blackbird (*turdus merula*), a bird unknown in Iceland; and which must have been driven hither by a southerly gale.

In the church is a brazen baptismal basin (Döbe-fad), the legend on which had hitherto puzzled all the antiquaries, local and peripatetic. I found it to be a sentence in old German, five times repeated, and in very quaint characters:

ICH BART GELUK ALZEIT,

'I bear luck always.'

August 18. A lovely morning, Peter obligingly offers to guide me through the bog. He is mounted on his favorite cream-coloured pony, a dray-horse in miniature, of whose powers he vaunts as much as if he himself were one of the old heathen Northmen, and the horse dedicated to Freya. But this son of Nimshi may find, if he does not take care, that a horse is but a vain thing to save a man after all. It was only yesterday that he was within an ace of the master of Ravenswood's fate. He was riding across the Herredsvand—a venturesome undertaking—and landed on one of the many sandbanks that divide the river into several arms, when down sank the steed into a quicksand. The water and sand rose above the mane, and its very head was under for a moment. "Had it been water," said Peter, "I should not have cared, but in such a mixture as that no horse could swim." At this perilous moment he struck the animal with all his might on his prodigiously strong crest, at the same time clinging to the mane. The gallant beast made a marvellous spring, and in the effort both girths snapped, and one of the stirrup leathers. He is riding to day with only one stirrup. Peter gave himself up for lost; but still he managed to stick on; and the animal, almost by a miracle, saved himself and his rider, having got foot-hold on firmer ground.

Our path soon leaves the shore, which is varied with pebbles of many colours, and ascends the inland shoulder of the Tindastol. In the bed of one of the many torrents that drip down from among his spurs, I saw lying a very geometrical piece of basalt; opening to my mind's eye visions of caves, columned as if by the aid of the chisel and the mallet; their roofs resplendent with dropping crystals, and floors tesselated with pearly chalcedony and black agate. The eve of St. John is the time to explore these magic spots. Who has not heard of that spring of golden water, begirt by mural rocks, in the heart of the Tindastol, where the Wishing-stone and all the other talismanic stones of Iceland lie enshrined? To be sure, the place is rather difficult of access, being cut off from the rest of the world by the Trollabotna (Troll-bottom); the haunt of those mischievous genii; and a ride through the air (gandreid) is a part of the programme. And where is the horse to come from? 'First catch your hare, and then dress it.' Here however the order of things is reversed. The bit and bridle are the first thing; of which the grave-yard will supply the chief materials. Having procured this, cast it over the first object you set eyes on, and forthwith your steed stands before you; mount him, and away you go, 'the celestial courser pawing the unyielding air' with all the imponderability of a witch's broom-stick.

At Skidarstadir, the first and only house on our route, the farmer, Gunnar Gunnarson, begs us to turn in and take refreshment. The last and only time he entertained a stranger from my part of the world, he almost realized the possibility of entertaining an angel advanced by the apostle. This was forty-five years ago, and the stranger was Henderson, the missionary of the Bible Society. While I sip a glass of curaçoa (!) Gunnar's wife, Ingibiorg, a delightful old lady, with fair-complexioned cheeks, shining with motherly good humour, exhibits her ancient Icelandic costume. To gratify my curiosity she puts it on. First comes the horn-like nodding falldr, sixteen inches high, as white as snow, fastened to her head by a silk kerchief covering her hair. Then comes the petticoat of green brocade. Her vest is fastened across the bosom by a silver chain, passing like a stay-lace through the eyelet-holes; the silver bodkin for threading it being fast to the end of the chain. Diving into a roomy chest, she brings up a velvet belt, studded with silver hemispherical buttons. Over all comes a very long black cloak, of the Noah's ark cut, which is adorned at its salient points by strips of black velvet. Thus arrayed, she hands us skier in a lordly dish.

Meanwhile, one of the lads produces some long transparent six-sided crystals, which he picked up on the mountain above. My host is well to do. A hundred sheep, fifteen horses, and seven cows are grazing themselves fat on his verdant meadows. Another hour's riding brings us to the house of the clergyman at Hvamm*. He is away haymaking. The grass has been cut for three weeks; but bad weather has prevented it drying. The proximity of Tindastol must have something to do with this, as, with us, the weather has been generally fine. On his arrival he rides down with me to Laxavik, a little bay, into which the river has burst its way, strewed with drift wood. The scenery is very striking. To the left, a white waterfall jumps at one bound over the cliffs, never touching ground, as the Irishman would say, till it reaches the sea. To the right, under Tindastol, bristle up some of those dark lofty needles that portal the coast. It is my purpose to take boat and row round to the famed Glerhaller-vik (Agate cove), a very hotbed of cornélians, onyxes, and chalcedony. But the crew of a fishing-boat,

* A combe or recess surrounded by hills; like our Ilfracombe.

which comes in laden with halibut and skate, informs us that the surf outside is running too high for our purpose. So I content myself with picking up several pebbles on the shingly beach. Now there was once a road under the cliffs, which would have made me independent of wind and weather; and the reader shall hear what has become of it.

Once on a time, a great whale drove ashore at the foot of the Tindastol. Hearing the good news, the people of Reykastrand, on the other side of the point, started off for the spot. They of Laxadal were not a whit behind them, and claimed the jettsam, on the plea that the ground belonged to their parish. "No such thing," said the rival claimants:—"however, if you will take your oath that the ground you are treading upon belongs to you, the whale shall be be yours." The Laxadal folks swore accordingly that it was. And, strictly speaking, this was true: for, before leaving home in the morning, they put some slips of green-sward into their shoes; and so, the earth they trod upon did belong to Laxadal. The other party, true to their promise, forewent all claim to the spoil, although in reality the ground belonged to Reykastrand. The Laxadalers commenced cutting up the whale, but, while so engaged, a mass of rock became loosened from the impending cliff, and overwhelmed them all; at the same time blocking up for ever the road round the promontory. Some say, a great white figure was seen high above upon the mountain who struck the rock with his staff, and the cliff at once rent asunder.

On our return to the parsonage, one of the pastor's flock, who has called, before taking leave kisses him, and tries to do the same by me; but I manage to keep him off. His wits are clearly obfuscated with drink; presently he returns, and gives the parson another hug. A third and a fourth time he enters, and does likewise. And still the good clergyman, exhibits very little impatience at his osculatory obtrusiveness. My hand being still unhealed, and very painful, he recommends frequent applications of the cool leaves of the marsh marigold (*Caltha Palustris:* in Icelandic, Hofbladka). His own son had lately the misfortune to be thrown from his pony, inflicting a terrible gash on his forehead, which defied all plaisters; and was only cured at last by the above recipe. I tried it and the wound healed in a few days. "I do remember an apothecary, and hereabout he dwells," is a sentiment beyond the experience of most Icelanders. So each man is his own herbalist, and many diseases are cured by nothing else than the native plants.

August 19. When I entered the church, his reverence was already at the altar, on which two candles were burning. He kept alternately facing the congregation and chaunting a solo, or turning his back upon them while they chaunted. Over his surplice he wore a scarlet cope, with a silver cross embroidered upon it, whose dimensions were coextensive with the breadth and length of his back. In a pew near the pulpit, fenced off by a lattice from the rest of the church, sat my friend Ingibiorg in her national costume, which is assumed in special compliment to me; as otherwise she only wears it when she receives the Holy Communion. Inside the chancel screen are the elders of the parish. Foremost among them sits Gunnar Gunnarson, with an expression of becoming gravity, as Hreppstiori (Rape-steerer), or representative of the absent majesty of Denmark. A cynic might peradventure look with an eye of ridicule upon this simple scene, with its modest accessories. The drawling chaunt—the low-pitched edifice, the ceiling of which nearly touches the head of the priest as he stands on high among the people—the grotesque old font-cover, with those six funny little men carved at its six corners; the small wooden images peering down from the cross-beams, remnants of the ancient church; the quality-pew; the broad stare at the stranger of the juniors, and the more furtive and subdued glances at me which the solemn seniors dovetail into their expression of earnest worship! But this worship has nevertheless its good fruits in real kindliness of word and deed, and in disinterested hospitality towards the stranger. Acts of violence are all but unknown, as may be inferred from the fact that a recent attack with the knife by a drunken person is the talk of all Iceland. While, as for prisons, they are never heard of.

One drawback of unbought hospitality among strangers is, that the traveller feels bound to be on his journey again as soon as he has rested. And so it was on this occasion, that feeling a delicacy in trespassing any longer on my host, I ride this afternoon [the Sunday ends at 6 P.M.] across the mountains due west to the Hunaflói. On the heath, we put up several broods of young ptarmigan basking in the sun. At the first house we come to in a grassy valley, after crossing the pass, we receive urgent invitations to stop and take coffee. If you should ever travel in Iceland, reader, beware of the coffee-drinking. You have a point to make by nightfall, and ask the road at a lone farm. The response is, "Wont you take some coffee?" You are riding to be in time for the church-service; a peasant standing at his door hails your guide. Muttered talk ensues, and thereupon comes the guide, his countenance pregnant with meaning. Surely he has some news of importance to communicate. But it is the old tale, Monsieur Tonson come again. Coffee! "Sigurdr wishes to know if you wont take some coffee." This involves roasting, grinding, and boiling; and nothing will make the people understand that you are much obliged, but must decline.

The sun was just setting over the broad expanse of the Hunaflói. A mirage (Uphyllíngar), acting like the patent derrick, lifts two fishing-yachts high out of the dreamy sea. This great bay runs inland some forty miles, while its width is above thirty. And yet, opposite to us, we distinctly see the glorious blue mountains that overshadow its western shores, with patches of snow upon their sides. In very clear weather, Cape Horn, the north west point of the Island, distant ninety English miles, is said to be visible from hence. The view of the long line of peaks, of many varied shapes, reaching away towards Cape Horn, reminds me of a similar pageant I have witnessed in the West fiord in Norway; with the Loffodens stretching their serrated peaks far away to seaward in the subtle colouring of eventide.

CHAPTER XIV.

Skagaströnd—An Icelandic archdeacon—"God save the Queen"—The visitor in white—Höskulstad—Séra Bjorn and his budget of legends—The changeling—A beautiful melody—We recross the Blandá—A sick bed—"'Tis sport to see the engineer hoised with his own petard"—Hjaltabakki—A country doctor—There are more things in heaven and earth than we dream of—Typhus—Leprosy—Parish guardians—The Classic Vasdal—The raven's warning—The biter bit.

Tidings of my possible arrival had preceded me, and I meet with a hearty welcome from the party assembled at Mr. Knutsen's, the merchant at Skagaströnd. Had I arrived yesterday, I was to have assisted at a pic-nic to the top of the Spákonufell (Spaewifes-fell), a curious flat-topped mountain near, which, though not above 2300 feet high, from its isolated position, like the Righi in Switzerland, commands a view hardly to be matched, including Grimsö, nearly a hundred miles off, and Snaefell, which is thirty miles further. The archdeacon of the district has been introducing a new clergyman to the parishioners to-day: ascending the pulpit, and first descanting on the many virtues of the late priest, and then recommending the new one to their consideration. Punch and cigars move merrily round, and the notes of an accordion, played by my old friend Mr. Holm, of Hofsös, serve to promote the festivities of the evening. Long after I had retired, "God save the queen" ascended from below; voices and instrument resounding in honour of my country.

August 20. The archdeacon, who was secretary to the late Bishop Steingrim, before his departure, invites me to visit him. I see him now before me: that Icelandic archdeacon, mounted on his sturdy pony; a frieze cap, tightly fixed upon his head; a belt confining the folds of his ample dreadnought round his spare figure; while over his two pair of trowsers and seal-skin boots were drawn an all-engrossing pair of stockings. Nor must his capacious saddle-bags be omitted, containing, I should think, something besides his sermons. Icelandic archdeacons, I perceived, don't go clad in gossamer. "A summerly day for you," said my host; "You ought to be here in winter. It is impossible then to get out of the doors for the snow and wind. Ugh! dreadful weather!" he added, as a shudder passed over his burly frame, and his physiognomy became convulsed at the very thought of the ghastly visitor in white, soon to be at the threshhold again with his attendant satellites.

At Höskulstad, the excellent Séra Björn Thorlakson makes me rest a while, and refresh me. He is well versed in the popular legends and superstitions of his country. The spirits of 'utburdir' (exposed infants) still haunt the neighbourhood. Sometimes at nightfall, when the doors are shut, a strange piercing cry, as of loud wailing and lamenting, is borne upon the ear of those assembled within—náhljód, death-screech it is called—and they say, 'Hear you not the utburdr gol?' It may be that this sound is the first moan of the coming tempest, the herald of a storm. Séra Björn, however, says he has often heard it in the south, and that it is nothing but the screech of a white and yellow owl. But how does he account for those strange forms which have been seen accompanying the cry, limping along sideways, with one foot and one arm foremost? Woe betide the belated traveller, if the goblin manage to shuffle round him three times: he will lose his senses for ever.

Once on a time, a girl, who had exposed her infant, was milking her ewes in the sheepfold. "Alas!" she said to another damsel similarly employed, "What shall I do? I am invited to a party to-night, and I haven't a proper dress to go in." "Oh! yes, you have though," muttered a voice from the top of the sheepfold wall. Be easy on that score. I will lend you my swaddling-clothes to dance in." It was the voice of the girl's own child, which she had deserted. At the same moment, an arm darted down from the wall, and stabbed the mother dead.

In these parts it is the rule never to leave an infant in the cradle alone, for fear of a changeling being put there instead. Once on a time, two Troll-wives came into a cottage, where there was only a two-year-old child tending the cradle. The one said, "Taki má," (Let's take it). "Ekki takki má," (We must not take it), was the other's reply. "Why so?" "Because there is a cross under and over the child." A precaution of the mother's.

Another mother, who had been less vigilant, had a changeling mothered upon her. So what did she do, but take it cradle and all into the kitchen, put some firing in the grate, set on it a very small pot to boil, with a stir-about stick in it, so long that it reached up to the top of the chimney. Upon this, the creature in the cradle stretched itself out in a strange manner, and turned into a wrinkled old man. "I am now so old, so old," said the transformation, "as one may see by my grey hairs, and I am father to eighteen bairns in Alfheim, but I never yet did see such a long porridge-stick as that in such a little pot." The Christian mother, who had hidden herself near, jumped into the room at these words, and began threshing the ancient abortion, till the Troll-mother came with the abstracted child, saying, "You and I don't do alike, I dandle your baby, but you beat mine." (Eg dilla þinu, en þu fleingjer mitt.)

Many were the legends and lullabies which Séra Björn had to tell me. The most famous Icelandic lullaby is the Ljuflingsmál; and hereby hangs a tale. Once upon a time, a bonder's daughter became a mother by an elf. Her tale was of course not believed at home. One evening, when she was trying to quiet her baby, she and the infant were so rudely remarked on, that she began to greet bitterly. At this moment, a strangely beautiful melody was heard at the window, which soon lulled the child to sleep. That is the Ljuflingsmál, and it is supposed that the minstrel was the baby's father.

But it is time to be going, as evening is approaching, and I have the Blandá to cross at the Hrafneyri ford. "It is not so small just now," exclaimed the prudent Marin, the clergyman's wife. "If you do feel giddy, mind you don't look at the water, but across to the bank. You had better stop the night." "I am sorry I cannot set you on the way," put in her husband, "but the archdeacon is expected immediately, and I must be at home to receive him. Good bye; thanks for the honour of your company." It was nearly dusk when we got to the ford. The river was full four hundred yards wide, and Johannes, the man who shewed the way across, half seas over, to begin with. His first question is of course, my name? and second, whether there are not many Johns in England? No Icelander ever thinks of omitting to ask that. My guide made a point of indulging in moral reflections upon the sin of drunkenness. "I never take a drop now," he said mournfully; "I have refused drink several times since we started. People drink here a great deal too much. But when the clergy drink, what can we do?" and then he went on, "I once knew a clergyman, &c." But, as the reader is already well acquainted with Ion's tale, I will introduce another "Scene of Clerical life," instead.

There was once an Icelandic parson, who was very hard upon his parishioners, and threatened them with the pit for the smallest sin. In his parish lived an old woman, who was a very bad church-goer, in spite of all his threats. At last she fell sick, and sent for the clergyman to visit her. He went to her with all speed, and began to offer her ghostly advice and consolation. But she stopped him short, saying that she had something weighing heavily on her mind, which she wished to tell him of. "By all means," replied the priest. "Well, you know," said she, "I dreamt the other night that I had come to heaven; I tapped at the door, for I was cold and wanted shelter. And a man came to it with a heavy bunch of keys in his hand. I asked him his name, and he said it was Peter; so I begged him to let me in. 'Impossible,' he replied, 'this is not your place.' 'Oh! do let me in, I am so starved; if it is only just behind the door.' 'It cannot be.' At this moment I spied, just near by, a huge store-room, and I besought him to let me in there; this he consented to, and opened the door of the store-chamber, into which I hurried; and well pleased I was to do so. Inside, I saw a heap of sacks of all sizes, big and little, with something in each of them, and the mouths of the sacks fastened. There were also some gloves there, some of which were quite full, while others had only something in the fingers. I asked Peter what was in these sacks. 'Oh! these are the sins of men.' Then I said, 'Might I just see our parson's sack? it can't be large.' 'To be sure,' said Peter, 'lo! here it is;' and he showed me the biggest sack of them all. 'What a monster!' said I; 'and where is mine now? it must be no trifle.' On this he shewed me a glove with only a very little in its fingers. Thereupon I went out in great amazement, and Peter closed the store-room door after me. It is this," said the crone, "that weighed so heavy on my mind; and I sent for you, Séra, to tell you of it." His reverence, however, seemed to have had quite sufficient; for he bolted at once, without administering any more ghostly advice. The old lady had fairly turned the tables upon him.

My quarters this night were such as to make me regret not accepting Marin's invitation. "You may go further and fare worse" is a proverb as well as a fact in Iceland. I had a fine opportunity, as a student of natural history, of testing the propensities of the pulex irritans. 'Fiet experimentum in corpore vili.' A heap of codfish and haddock lay before the parsonage of Hjaltabakki, indicating the source of a part of the pastoral income: net-fishing being an employment which the priests of this country practise in common with the earliest teachers of the Gospel. For leads, horse-bones are used; for cork, pieces of driftwood. Salmon are also caught in the neighbouring stream; and I meet a man riding across the moor with a net, which he is going to set. If it were not for the fish, the people here, south of the Blandá, would starve. The sheep have been destroyed for the scab. The priest has slaughtered one hundred.

August 21. A leisurely ride, under a warm sun, brought me at noon to-day to Hnausum, the residence of Mr. Skapteson, one of Iceland's half dozen doctors. "Passages from the diary" of such a physician would be worth reading. Many a tale, doubtless, could this stalwart disciple of Æsculapius tell of his lonely rides during twenty-one years' practice at all hours, and at all seasons, over the fells, across the roaring streams of spring and the hidden ambuscades of the winter ice. These long rides, face to face with Gorgon Nature's countenance glaring out of the mist, would, methought, intensify a man's fancy, and make him see more things in heaven and earth than one generally dreams of. Our conversation fell upon second sight, "Well, what's your opinion about it?" said the doctor. "That it depends a good deal on the state of the stomach." "That may be, but not always. What do you say to this? I saw a man, Magnus by name, starting with his crew by boat up the Fiord. I don't know why, but, just when he gave the word to hoist the sail, I saw he was feigr (Scoticè, fey). It was fine weather, but I felt convinced that he would never get home alive, and sure enough, half way up the fiord the boat upset, and he was drowned."

Typhus, he tells me, is often very virulent. Of leprosy* he has seen about twenty cases. A rich bonder, in the neighbourhood, the bone of whose leg was wasting away with this dreadful disease, went to Copenhagen, in spite of his advice to the contrary, to have the limb amputated. Not long after his return, the other leg was attacked in a similar way. The doctor tells me that he met with one clear case where the husband caught the disease from his wife. The poor lepers have a bad time of it. Formerly, there were hospitals for their shelter; but now they are pushed about from pillar to post, and nobody likes to give them shelter. By the law of Iceland, anybody who has resided ten years in a parish has a claim upon it for support in case of need, so the parish authorities adopt an expedient worthy of being studied by an English guardian of the poor, viz. of forcing labourers and others, who have no fixed abode of their own, to shift their quarters before the decade has elapsed. About ten years ago, there was a terrible disease among the children of these parts. The symptoms were cough and difficulty of breathing, and a thick skin of white slime was found in the throat. The doctor called the disease *Angina polyposa*, or *Angina membranacea*.

* In Icelandic, likþra, a living death.

For the Border chieftain,

> Thirty steeds, both fleet and wight,
> Stood saddled in stall day and night.

The Icelandic doctor has no less a number for the purposes of his farm and his practice, which lies far and wide, and is as broad as it is long. Encasing himself in over-trousers, buttoning all down the leg, and belting the biggest cloak I ever saw around him, while a woollen comforter just leaves room for the smoke of a very good cigar to curl round his nose, the doctor starts with me, after our midday refection, up the classical Vasdal, the scene of one of the most interesting Sagas of the country.

But that slope just facing his residence has a legend of its own. Upon it, two hundred years agone, stood the farm of Skidarstadir. The owner of it was a son of Belial, who had no fear of God before his eyes, and took a special pleasure in making his people work on Sundays. Like master like man: and so the whole household, excepting one young girl, joined hand to hand in iniquity. She, for her part, was the best and gentlest of creatures, never thinking of herself, but always striving to do good to others. Even the poor dumb animals came in for a share of her kindness, and among the rest a raven, who had its nest close at hand, was fed by her morning and evening. At last it became so tame that it would hop about, and take food from her hand. One Sunday the peasant and his men were at work. In vain

"The beams of God's own hallowed day
Had painted yonder spire with gold,
And calling sinful man to pray,
Loud, long, and deep, the bell had toll'd."

Just then the raven came as usual, but would not take his food as at other times from the girl's hands. When she tried to approach it, it hopped a couple of paces from her, and so on, till she had followed it a good bit from the house. At this moment down thundered a vast portion of the mountain yonder—the scar is visible—and overwhelmed the cottage and its godless inhabitants; all but the girl, whom the raven had saved; so that the destruction did not come nigh her.

To our right is a lake, abounding with salmon and trout; and in autumn the haunt of many wild swans, which 'sing,' said the Doctor, 'beautifully in still, frosty weather.' To our left rises a precipice of black basalt, nearly columnar; while high up, amid the deep and compact *débris* of its falling walls, grows a single rowan tree, which the people around seem to regard as little short of a miracle. A waterfall bounds from the cliffs, which an iris has dressed in holiday attire, to greet us as we pass; and soon we get another greeting, or rather *charivari*, from a pack of noisy dogs, which rush out, in all their foxiness and fury, from among a crowd of haymakers, provoking an observation from the doctor about the geese in the Capitol. In sooth, they are very vulpine in look, so that the medico's thoughts would naturally, as in the fable, put the fox and the goose together. Outside the door of the farm-house of Hvamm, to which its mistress, one of the haymakers, welcomes us, stands a tall piece of basalt, with a hole drilled in it, to which I fasten my horse. This stone was originally a walkingstick, the cudgel of a troll-wife, who, irate at the bells for calling the peasants to midnight mass on Christmas Eve, threw it at the church tower. She missed her mark, however; and, forgetting to note the clock, was overtaken by daybreak, and became petrified up the cliff yonder.

While drinking coffee, and smoking one of the bundle of fragrant weeds which the doctor's good-nature has forced upon me, I regard with curiosity the grim-looking family portraits, the work of a native artist, who is capable of much better things. "Ah! I have lost *him*," said the widow mournfully. Only a week ago, a boat, which had accompanied for a short distance an outward-bound ship in Isar Fiord, disappeared. Was it the skipper's rum that *spirited* it away? Howsoever it was, the son of Mrs. B. was one of the crew of six, none of whom survived to explain.

F. M. ADA MARGETTS.

CHAPTER XV.

Undirfell—Scene of the Vasdal Saga—Ingemund the lord and pontiff of the valley—His murder—An Icelandic Adonis—The heathen temple—*Menyanthes trifoliata*—Its various uses—The philosopher of Thorormstunga—Icelandic computation of time—A menagerie of sea-monsters—Amulets—Just in time—The Troll-mother—A Grettistak—The hills of Vasdal are a cluster of volcanoes—Steinnes—An Icelandic proverb—Bishop Steingrim's secretary—The monastery of Thingeyri—The Icelandic translator of the Bible—A hymn to the Virgin—A strange tale—Runes and occult philosophy—Icelandic passion for reading old books—A windmill.

AUGUST 22.—To-day the clergyman of Undirfell, where I slept, rides with me to visit the site of the old abode of Ingemund, the patriarch and priest of the valley, and chief character in the Vasdal Saga. It lies on the right bank of the river which we cross. A causeway conducts from the stream to the present farm-house, and the intelligent owner, one Benedict, shews us the remains of the heathen temple just behind it. It stood on an eminence, and must have been one hundred feet long and forty broad, judging by the traces of the turf-grown foundations of the walls.

A spaewife once told the noble Ingemund of Norway, that he would end his days in Iceland, and as a sign of the truth of her prophecy, alleged that a little silver image of Freyr, which his friend Harald Harfager had given him, and which he had lost, would be found there. The truth of this prediction was further verified by some necromancers, who, in the spirit, paid a flying visit to Iceland. So finding it useless to resist his destiny, he left his smiling patrimony for this country, and became the lord and pontiff of Vasdal. With characteristic generosity, he had once assisted in need a wretch called Hrolleif, the son of a villanous old hag, who dwelt in the vicinity. One day, interfering in a quarrel between his own sons and this fellow, he was mortally wounded by his precious protégé, who cast a spear at him across the stream. The fine old fellow, knowing that his sons were sure to kill the murderer, if they became aware of the wound, but unwilling to cause the death of one who had eaten of his salt, concealed it, till the caitiff got clear off. So beloved was he, that two of his friends killed themselves on the news of his death. Eventually Ingemund's sons avenged their father's murder. The eldest of them, Thorstein, seems to have been a man in advance of his heathen age. His brother Thorer was afflicted with that remarkable disease, shall we call it, the Berserkergang, which would come upon him unawares, and throw him into a frenzy of ungovernable strength. Distressed for his brother, Thorstein vowed a vow to the God whom he thought mightiest, even Him that made the sun, that, if he would deliver his brother from his malady, he would bring up a poor foundling, which had been exposed by its unnatural mother. His grandson,

Ingolf, was so handsome, that, as a ditty of the day commemorated, all the damsels liked to dance with him, and the old women too, with only two teeth left in their head. Having received a mortal wound from a wild boar of a brigand, this Icelandic Adonis begged that he might be buried on a hill near the pathway, that the maidens of Vasdal might think of him as they passed.

The whole scene hereabout is described with such minuteness by the saga—which, witchcraft apart, must be genuine, as much of it is quoted by the Landnama and other sagas—that the actual localities can easily be identified. Such, for instance, are not only the temple and dwelling of Ingemund, but also Liotstadir, which lay behind some hills of loose stone, where dwelt the hag who owned Hrolleif for a son; while higher up the valley, Jokulstadir, the abode of the fighting Jokul, the third of Ingemund's sons, can likewise be identified. Near it lives, at Thororms-tunga, a character whom I set off to visit.

The morasses are deep, but fortunately they are covered with the grass called by the Icelanders Reidingrgras, or Hor-bladka, (*Menyanthes trifoliata*), the power of which, to prevent the horse and rider from sinking in, is truly wonderful. Wherever you spy the bog-cotton (Fifa), beware; but wherever the thickly-matted felt of the Menyanthes is to be seen, you may advance boldly. The water beneath may ooze through the grass, and the matting may bend under your weight for several square feet around; but if the horse is clever, and can step lightly—and Icelandic horses, when they like, can step very lightly indeed—its tenacity is proof against his hoofs. This grass is used for other purposes. From its velvety texture, devoid of sand and dirt, it forms when cut into strips an admirable substitute for sacking or other material to defend the backs of the poor horses from the cutting of the straddle. In ancient days, culprits were condemned to pass under a yoke made of strips of it, by way of punishment. Again, when two men swore to each other foster-brothership, three long strips of this turf were fastened at their ends to the earth, and supported in the middle by spears, and under this the two men passed.

But I am quite forgetting Jon Biarneson of Thorormstunga. An old man, of some three score and ten years, was outside the door sharpening a scythe. This was he. A peasant by birth and calling, this man, besides cultivating his paternal acres, labours in other fields with even greater zest and perseverance. Thirsting for knowledge of all sorts, he has especially devoted himself to mathematics! He is the almanack-maker of the valley, and I succeeded in obtaining the one for the year 1861, which he has drawn out and calculated.* This self-

* Bishop Jon Arneson wrote a little work for the use of the Icelanders, entitled, 'Dactylismus Ecclesiasticus, or Finger Rhymes

taught genius, corresponds with Gunnlaugsson, the geographer of Iceland, and author of that splendid map of the country, which is not inferior even to our Ordnance maps. Among his papers I see a calculation of the eclipse, which occurs this summer, with neatly drawn diagrams. Another manuscript is devoted to calculations of the path of comets. Nothing in physical science seems to come amiss to him. Treatises on botany, chemistry, and mineralogy, mixed up with notes on the tides, on storms, and the weight of the planets, occupied the manuscript quartos which I hastily inspected.

Like the middle age philosophers, his science seems blended with a very fair allowance of superstition. Several pages of one of his books are devoted to coloured pictures by himself of sea-monsters, mermen, mermaids, marmenils, the margygr, the nykr, the kumbr, and all those strange creatures that haunt the lone fiords and seas of Iceland. Out of

for calculating time.' By means of the plan of technical memory here laid down, the peasants could calculate beforehand the day on which Easter fell in any year on their fingers: with other useful methods of computation. The number of days in any particular month, an Icelander thus ascertains, if he is in doubt. Shut the fist, and let the first knuckle represent January with its 31 days, and the depression between that and the next knuckle February, with its less number of days. And thus every month that corresponds to a knuckle will be found to contain 31 days; and every month that corresponds to a depression, a less number of days. The little finger knuckle will represent July, and beginning again with the fore-finger knuckle, it stands for August.

various leathern bags the philosopher next produced specimens of curious Icelandic stones, which he had picked up in his wanderings. Petrified wood from the cliffs in the valley, zeolites, Ebenezer stone, swim-stones—hollow, and capable of floating in the water,—the Lausnarsteinn,* good in female labour, and the no less potent Oskasteinn, or wishing-stone. Of course he has his budget of supernatural stories, some of them told him by one Dadi Nielsen, an eccentric person, who used to tramp about the country in all weathers, telling stories, and at last died a regular Icelandic death, being lost in a snow-fog, near Höskuldstad, and not found till the following spring. Here is one of Biarneson's tales which he told me with air of the most perfect faith in its truth.

A peasant woman, Margaret by name, went one Christmas day to the church of Ripr, at the head of Skaga Fiord. After receiving the sacrament, she felt an uncontrollable desire to ride on home before the rest of her people. Finding she was gone, they proceeded homewards a short time afterwards, following her horse-track in the snow. Directly after passing the ford, they found to their surprise, that, instead of going on straight homewards, she had taken a sudden bend to the eastward, right away from the proper direction. Two of the most active

* This is nothing but a horse-chestnut, not a bean, brought to the shores of Iceland by the Gulf-stream. I believe a similar superstition concerning it formerly prevailed in Cornwall.

of the party followed her trail, and at last overtook her riding at a round pace through the twilight. "Margaret! Margaret! whither away?" "Away! why following my husband; and sure he must know the path. But I don't see him now, though he was here a moment ago." They had saved her just in time, it was evidently one of the infernal crew misleading her to her destruction.

"Now Biarnesen," said I, after the old man had told me several stories of gramarye with a wrapt air, "do you believe in the existence of these supernatural beings? Did you ever encounter one yourself?" "Well, do you know, when I was a boy, I and several other children were at play near the house. We were throwing stones for fun at a large stone, standing by itself, when, suddenly, we all heard a horrid scream come from it. We ran away in a terrible fright. Now, what was that? It could not be a trick, for there was no place for any one to hide."

Taking leave of Biarnesen, I started back down the valley. Below Underfell, we pass a stone, several tons in weight, poised upon its edge and resting on two other stones, which lay on the slope of a mountain. It is called a Gretti's Tak. These stones, which abound in Iceland, and resemble the rocking-stones of other countries, are universally supposed to have been thus reared up by Gretti. Of course one stronger than Gretti must have been here: but, whether these mighty boulders are due to the ice of the glacial period, which melting, deposited them in their present ticklish position; or whether storms and rain, having denuded the earth around, have lodged them where they are; or whether the volcanoes have in their eruptions thrown off their ice-covering, and with them the embedded boulders, and hurled the mass forward to great distances, till the current, being able to go no farther, stopped, leaving the stones lying at haphazard; must be a question, and a very interesting one, for Geologists.

On the left of the lake, at the mouth of the valley, is a still stranger phenomenon, the Vatnsdalholar (the hills of Vasdal). According to an Icelandic proverb, there are three things which you cannot number in Iceland; the islands in Breidifiord, the lakes on Tvidaegra heath, and the Vasdal hills. Being an especial admirer of proverbs, I did not for a moment think of carping at the veracity of this. Hills, some perfectly conical, others truncated cones, some the size of a haycock, others, mountains—warts and Ossas—are congregated thickly together over about the space of a square mile. Where the plot is thickest, they are generally bare of vegetation, their sandy sides converging to a top, on which lie a quantity of igneous stones. Of course they must have each been the seat of a volcano, which, after the usual fashion of volcanoes, would naturally assume the shape of a cone; and as the explosive power died out, their mouths would become chokefull. Storms would soon blow the sand and lighter portions away, leaving the great jagged stones which they could not remove bristling about the apex and sides.

It was night when we roused the dogs of Steinnes, and the Archdeacon Jon Jonson was already abed. But up he got, with his whole household; a good supper was provided, and withal a downy couch, wherein sleep bound me fast till the sun must have well frighted away all the Trolls that play at hide-and-seek among those fantastic hills of Vasdal. The parish church is four miles off, at Thingeyri, once the seat of one of the chief monasteries in the Island. Between it and us is an impassable bog. So the good pastor takes me round by a long and devious path to this interesting spot, of which, however, hardly a vestige remains, except grass-grown hillocks. The present place of worship is of wood, and roofed as usual with turf. It was restored and ornamented in 1695 by Larus Gottrup, Lögmadr of Iceland. Passing through the Saluhlid (Lych-gate), we tread on an old stone, with the date 1596, in memory of Jon Jonson, another Lögmadr. The altarpiece is of alabaster, illuminated with gold and colours. It represents in three compartments the Scourging, the Crucifixion, and the Resurrection, with the angel Gabriel and the archangel Michael interposed. Above the Crucifixion is God the Father; while over all is a

Gothic canopy. Near this is the portrait of a venerable, fork-bearded, aquiline-nosed bishop; his cloak lined with fur, and in his hand a volume bound in vellum. I recognise at once the lineaments of Bishop Gudbrand of Holar, the translator of the Bible. It represents him at the age of seventy. The faded silken and velvet vestments were once beautiful. On one chasuble are embroidered figures of the Saints. On a transverse beam are little carved wooden figures of Christ and the Apostles, seemingly of great age. From the great thickness of the walls, the daylight in winter-time must, even at midday, be administered in homœopathic doses through the small square windows. To disperse the gloom, there are ten brass reflectors against the walls, giving the utmost effect to the light of the corresponding number of candlesticks. Outside the churchyard is a twin grass-grown mound. According to tradition, it is the burial-place of two monks (Munkrleidi), who were notorious evil-livers, and who, having come to their end in a violent manner, were denied sepulture in the consecrated precincts.

In the adjoining farm-house are some curious MS. books; one of which contains a collection of sagas and ballads, most likely made on the spot. The following verses in it to the Virgin were evidently taught the mariners by the monks, to be said by them in peril:

Domine Cœlorum,
Medela reorum,
Salus anxiorum,
Preces famulorum
Deum deprecare,
Vales impetrare:
Severum pulsat mare.

Another, a Macaronic, sings the praises of the Virgin, who was worshipped in Iceland with a fanatical worship:

Gaudes gratiosa af Gudi fructuosa,
Og dyrmaet Drottins rosa,
Deus castitatis, hortus voluptatis,
Hortus aromatum dulcis charismatum,
Gemma polorum, &c.

The good monks, like the Icelandic clergy now, used to prescribe for the ailments of the people, bodily as well as ghostly, but in a different way. The following charm for the hickup is to be found in Icelandic as well as Latin. We give the latter version: "Christus mihi in pectore! Apage singultus! Prior eram in mente Dei quam singultus. Deus propitius esto animæ ejus qui mortuus est singultu." This prayer repeated nine times *without drawing breath* is a certain cure for the hickup. The above will serve to remind us of our more simple charms:

"Hickup, hickup, go away,
Come again another day," &c.

And

"Hickup, Snickup,
Rise up, right up," &c.

From another MS. book I extracted the following

curious anecdote: "On October 1st, 1786, Sera Oddr Gislason preached at Silfrastad. On his return homewards to his parsonage he called at the farm of Vidivellir. He was not intoxicated (odrukkin). From thence he set off, in the twilight, to his house at Miklibaer, and was never seen afterwards, although great search was made for him. Moreover, the road is good and level, and the distance between the two houses is not greater than from a farm-house to the Stekkjarvegr (the sheepfold in spring, i.e. about six hundred yards). His horse with its reins hanging down was found next morning in the paddock. So it was supposed that he left the animal, and wandered in a confusion of mind, which had come over him, to the river, and was lost. People said, that eight years before, a woman who was on the point of death by her own act, sent for him, and begged him to bury her in consecrated ground; but he said, 'No.' Then she said, 'You shall not come to lie in a churchyard yourself.' This priest was son of bishop Gisle Magnussen of Holar. His daughter Ingibiorg married the priest of Audkulla, who, in the winter of 1817, mounted his horse, a capital animal, to accompany a friend over the ice of Svinevatn (a lake near this). They were never seen again, horse or man. Their traces were followed to a Vök (hole in the ice), at which the marks of the great nails of the horseshoes were visible. Here they disappeared."

Another beautiful MS. volume, written by Paul

Vidalin, chief magistrate of Iceland, contained extracts from Albertus Magnus, a treatise on Steganographia, or cypher writing, and another tractate still more interesting on Runes and Occult Philosophy. This book, if it ever were sold, was promised to Mr. John Arnesen, librarian at Reykiavik, who is a great collector of Icelandic lore. It belonged to a woman in the south, who had lent it to the lady of the house for her winter's reading. What a fine opening here for a book-hawking society! The people thirsting to read, no matter what it is; and so few printed books to satisfy their desire. My hostess is the widow of Mr. Olsen, late administrator of crown property. A windmill close by, a sight rarely seen in Iceland, is due to his enterprise. This farm, formerly the property of the monastery, is said to possess great capabilities. A few deep drains carried across the bogs into the river or the sea would repay the outlay a hundredfold.

CHAPTER XVI.

Icelandic taxation—I part from the archdeacon—A singular castle—Snipe-moor—The pirate Skegge—Midfiord—Robbing a tomb—"A bird in the hand worth two in the bush"—Murdered in her arms—The ancient Icelander at home and abroad—The ferocity of the gull—The schoolmaster abroad—Hrutadalshals—The birth-place of Gretti—Hrutafiord—Lemon-coloured poppy—"Am I not a bird and a brother?"—The Troll turned navvie.

Leaving Thingeyri, we are soon on the shore of a great inland sea, the Hóp, whose white-maned waves are galloping pell-mell to the beach, under the lash of a north-westerly gale; bringing along with them crisp foam-flakes, 'torn from the fringe of spray,' to mix with the no less white swans' feathers scattered on the margin of the water. Bitterly cold it was, and not easy to sit on horseback for the wind; but the good archdeacon insisted on piloting us through the ins and outs of the morasses. Southward we looked straight up Vasdal, behind whose terminal mountains rose another, blue with distance. "That," said my companion, "is Krákr, or Lyklafell; it lies close by the snow-fields you skirted in the middle of the island."

By way of beguiling the tedium of the path, I talk upon the taxation of the country. Taxes are computed in ells, which was formerly the unit of value in Iceland, as a slave is now in Africa. The origin of this singular payment is doubtless due to the fact, that in ancient times, when coin was not always at hand, the state-burdens were paid in homespun cloth. At present, other articles may be paid in lieu of cloth, according to a fixed tariff. Thus, an ell is considered = 1lb. of butter, or 1lb. of tallow, or 1lb. of wool, or 2 fishes of 2 lbs. weight each, or ½ a pot of train oil. Again, 6 milking ewes in spring are computed = 100 ells; a wether, over a year old, = 20 ells; a cow = 120 ells; a horse = 100 ells. The chief state tax is the Scat. The amount of this depends upon the number of hundreds at which a farm is set down in the old census: a hundred probably representing as much land as will support a cow. But another element enters into the calculation; viz. the number of persons in the household. If the household contains as many persons as, or a less number than, the farm is set down hundreds, the owner pays scat; but if the number of persons on it exceed the number of hundreds at which it is set down, the owner escapes scot-free. Thus, if the farm is set down at ten hundreds, and has ten persons on it, the owner pays 20 ells; but if there are eleven persons on it, he pays nothing. All priests and government officers are exempt from this payment by law. So that very large proprietors can always escape the impost, by taking care that the number of persons in their household exceeds the number of hundreds at which the property is set down in the books. Moreover, if I mistake not, the impost never exceeds 20 ells, so that the poorest and the richest proprietors pay exactly the same amount. The incidence of the tax is manifestly unjust; and loud complaints have been made against it. But the reader will perhaps not wish to labour further through these dry statistics, so we will now take leave of the archdeacon, before crossing the Vididals river, which comes tumbling down the valley of that name, to swell the waters of the Hóp.

"Ago tibi gratias Domine reverendissime," I apostrophized his reverence, who had dismounted to take farewell. "Incolumis redeas ad uxorem et familiam tuam," was the heartfelt reply. And so we parted. It really gives one quite a pang to take leave of these warmhearted people, whom one will probably never see again in this world. Nor did I feel this the less, now that a chilling mist was rolling up from the sea; and beyond the river, on whose brink we stood, nothing but desolate rocks were to be seen.

But stay! Yon ancient castle looks frowningly enough, perched on the top of the isle-like rock; mayhap, however, within it lives some descendant of those ancient Vikings, who, whatever their faults, prided themselves on their hospitality to the stranger. Half an hour's ride up the steep ascent shewed me that cold comfort only is to be got in the ruined Borg. What a singular place! Fancy to yourself a circular rock, (? an extinct volcano), perpendicular externally, except on one side, where you scramble up a steep slope, barred at its summit by a wall of loose flat basaltic slabs, evidently built up by the hand of man. Arrived on the top, you have a fine view of the distant ocean, with the mountains that look down into its waves. Gazing over the outside edge of this platform, I perceived that the rock is split into perpendicular columns; while taking a step or two backward, and looking inwards, I see, sheer down beneath me in the heart of the mountain, a natural courtyard, about one hundred and thirty feet in diameter. The entrance to this amphitheatre is from the South-east, where a perpendicular slice, about forty-two feet wide, has been cut out of the crater's wall. It is blocked up by an artificial fence of basaltic slabs, laid upon one another. The portals of living rock on either side this wall are some fifty feet high. The whole mountain is basaltic, and a fortress by nature. Finboge the Strong, a noted Viking, who is the traditional fortifier of the works, would at once see its importance as a place of refuge and defence in his frequent broils with his neighbours. The spring inside the area, of which Eggert Olafson makes mention, was nowhere visible.

Working in a south-westerly direction from this, we pass the head of another lake, Westrhóp. The peasant at the farm of Little Borg tells me he nets salmon in it. Had time permitted, I should have thrown a fly on the promising looking stream that flows into this fine sheet of water. The clergyman of Breidabolstad was not less kind to me than his brethren. He apologized for giving me a sofa to sleep on, but sooth to say, for reasons which students of entomology will not fail to appreciate, this sort of couch is generally to be preferred to the rúm or berth-like bed carpentered into the walls of the room.

AUGUST 24.—After a hearty breakfast on fresh fish, my host seduces me into a second glass of brandy with the proverb which he cites, "A fish ought always to swim twice, once when he is alive, and once when he is dead." Séra Olav formerly held the living of Helgafell to the westward, but finding its duties too onerous for his threescore years and ten, he moved to this place. His wife is blind and sickly. How they compassed the journey hither is a marvel. Imagine all the unwieldy boxes and other moveables (or fixtures) which an Icelandic clergyman must flit with; all of which have to be transported on horseback; and last, not least, the poor helpless aged invalid: and this too over paths more Icelandic than Icelandic paths generally. And yet, in spite of the burden of his years, the excellent priest springs on his favourite horse, a very tower of strength, to accompany me. The animal, however, began to rear and whirl round, trying to thrust his master against the wall after the manner of the Scriptural ass; greatly to the alarm of his daughter. "Skratten!" (Old Scratch) exclaimed his reverence, as he dismounted and patted the stiff-necked beast, "what can it be!" And it was only at last after a great deal of talking and whispering to, that it at last consented to be seen in my company. What a road it was up that valley and past that mountain, the abode of a Puki (our Puck)! The tale about this goblin I did not catch. But here we are at Gauks-myri (Snipe-moor), in token of which I flush a couple of snipes. See! they are down again half-a-dozen paces off, and, singularly enough, as I had before observed, they appear to make a perfect somersault, like a tumbler-pigeon. The proper Icelandic name for these birds is Hross-gauk, because their cry is supposed to resemble the sound of a *horse* neighing. The peasant here, Arnor Arnesen, is a capital silversmith. He is the grandson of Arne Thorarensen, bishop of Holar: and being of episcopal blood, he retains the surname of his father, Arnesen, contrary to the usual custom of using for the surname the father's Christian name with the termination *sen* (or *son*) added. This spot is supposed to have been the mountain pasture of the horses of the redoubted pirate Skegge, who dwelt at Reykir in Midfiord. The Wizard of the North has told us:—

> 'Of chiefs, who guided through the gloom
> By the pale death-lights of the tomb,
> Ransacked the graves of warriors old,
> Their falchions wrenched from corpses' hold—'

and Skegge was one of them*. Returning from a piratical expedition to the east, he landed in Sealand

* Landnama, Part III. cap. I.

in Denmark, and breaking open the tomb of king Rolf Kraka, abstracted his sword Skofnung and much treasure. Bodvar's sword, Laufa, he could not wrench from that doughty champion's hold.

I am soon descending to the valley which opens out into Midfiord. All this is classic ground. It is the scene of Thord Hrede's Saga, a romantic but true tale of the end of the tenth century. Thord Hrede, the regicide, flying from Norway in 975 A.D. settled here, and of course got to loggerheads with the chief man of these parts, the above-mentioned 'resurrection-man', Skegge. Diamond cut diamond. One day it happened that Eide, one of Skegge's sons, on returning from a visit to one Thorkill of the farm of Sandur, found the river, which he had to pass, greatly swollen (to-day it is moderate). And had it not been for Thord Hrede, his father's foe, who dwelt at Ös at the mouth of the stream, swimming to his help, he must have been drowned. Ever after this, the lad lived under the roof of his preserver, and the Capulets and Montagues became apparently reconciled. Thord had a beautiful daughter Sigride, whom Skegge begged to wife for his relative, Asbiorn. Asbiorn was on the point of making the grand tour of those times, and visiting foreign parts, with a general view to piracy and his own recreation and improvement. It was agreed, therefore, that during his proposed three years of travel, the damsel should be looked on as his affianced. During Asbiorn's absence, his brother, Orm, returns home from sea, and falls desperately in love with Sigride; and, in spite of her father's warnings and threats, persisted in visiting her. One day Sigride and her maidens came to this hot-spring under the hill, to do what many noble damsels used to do, wash linen. Very likely a meeting had been secretly agreed upon between her and Orm. She might argue with herself in the words of the equivalent Icelandic proverb, 'A bird in the hand is worth two in the bush."* Asbiorn might, for all she knew, be dead, or courting some eastern beauty in Miklegaard (Constantinople). Be this as it may, her lover soon joined her, and there he lay, his head in her lap, while his arms were round her neck. Pretty linen-washing this! At this moment her father surprises the couple, and kills the ill-starred Orm. This murder of course set the reconciled friends at deadly feud again. Thord's flight; his taking refuge with the man-hearted Olufa, and his betrothal to her, after her braggadocio, mean-spirited, husband had been killed, as he deserved, for basely attempting to betray Thord;—such was the rough code of honour of these fine fellows—the return of Asbiorn to claim his bride; Eide's firm friendship for Thord, the preserver of his life; and how he managed to set his father and Thord at one

* Laxdaela Saga.

again:—are not all these things written in the book of the Chronicles of the great men of Midfiord?

On this very bank on which I stand used the magnates of the valley to collect of yore to witness the horse-fights which took place on the little flat between here and the river. Peasants and fishermen at home, these men, when abroad, might have sung at the courts of Germany and England, have served as free lances under Sweyn, or Malcolm of Scotland; and the swords which they wore, and the silver and gold ornaments which their wives and daughters displayed so proudly, might have been the gift of royalty; of which, after all, they were the 'poor relations.' Nay, their descendants still inhabit these Arctic valleys, although the Queen of England might start to think that she and these Icelandic girls, and that not so many years ago, may have had a common ancestry.

The river seemed more likely for salmon than any I have yet seen. Some fine deep pools looked the very spots for these fish to choose for their halting-place. Indeed, I find subsequently that hereabouts is a favourite cast for the priest's net. Fish of twenty pounds are sometimes taken, and as many as a hundred at a haul.

On the flat moor, just over the river, I watch with great interest how two Skua gulls of dark plumage —one with a white ring round his shoulders; for all the world like a dark-robed Dominican with his white scapulary—are engaged in pursuing some smaller bird, swooping down on him with almost the dexterity of falcons. See, they are all down in that hollow; I will try to shoot them. They rise, however, out of shot, nor could I discover whether they had captured their quarry, or only made him vomit the contents of his stomach. These birds, I afterwards heard on good authority, will, when they have young, even kill lambs. The raven, however, is a still sharper practitioner; he will pick out the eyes of the lamb when the head only is born. The great black-backed gull's ferocity is also talked of. He will dash down upon large salmon in shallow water, and with one stroke of his bill disable them. The lump-sucker, or sea-owl, (*Cyclopterus Linnaei,*) however, is the special mark of his attacks. It is said that he will seize this fish when full of spawn by the beard—like the Gaul did Papyrius—and drag him to shore for the purpose of eating his liver.

It was evening when I alighted at the parsonage of Melstadir. The gathering shadows were soon dispersed by the light of the huge altar candle which was fetched from the church! In that edifice there is an inscription in Latin on the paten, the handiwork of some priest, who must have been pretty much on a par in his classics with another Icelandic clergyman of whom I have heard. This person was called to baptize an infant. In those days, before performing the ceremony, it was usual to exorcise in Latin whatever evil spirit might have taken possession of it. "Abi, male spirite!" began the priest. "Pessime grammatice!" responded an unearthly voice from a corner of the church. "Abi, male spiritu!" says the clergyman, correcting himself. The voice answered in Icelandic, "Laugstú fyr og laugstú nu!" ("Before, you lied, and yet lie you.") Well, then, "Abi, male spiritus!" said the parson. "Sic debuisti dicere prius," said Satan, for it was he, from his coin of vantage, and departed.

August 25.—It was a dull foggy morning as we prepared to cross the Hrutadalshals of infamous reputation. 'Go to the devil!' said an old woman at Reykjavik to another old woman from these parts. But the other had a stronger repartee in store for her, "Go over Hrútafiörðr háls!" Séra Bodvar, the pensioned priest, lives a bowshot off. This kind old gentleman offers me the loan of his intelligent son, to conduct us over the "impassable morasses" for two or three miles. A conical hill which we pass is the Alfaholl, while the lake on which ducks are floating is Alfavotn. Neither are this elfish community without their public officers; as their sysselman lives near the mouth of the river.

But to no spot did my mind attach greater interest than to Bjarg, a short way up the river on our left, where was born Gretti Asmundson, whom I have had occasion to mention several times in these pages. The deeds of this hero, who was related to St. Olaf of Norway, are recounted in one of Iceland's most interesting sagas. As a boy he was exceedingly masterful, and while tending his father's geese in the meadows yonder, (why has Iceland no tame geese now?) became so enraged at their stupidity, that he broke their wings, and killed the goslings. A very Samson in strength, he would think nothing of engaging a score of men at once. Once, on board a ship sailing to Norway, he did nothing but lounge about the deck, and lampoon the sailors, who abused him for his laziness. The ship however began to leak, when he began to bale, and with such good will, that he kept eight men hard at work handing buckets. An outlaw for twenty years, he lived the life of a partridge on the mountains, hiding first in one inaccessible fastness, then another. The latter part of this time he spent in Drangö; where, as we have seen, he was treacherously murdered. One only weakness had Gretti, which is recorded in the ancient Icelandic saying: "Gretti is afraid in the dark, Thormod is afraid of God, Thorgeir is afraid of nothing." Of these two last more hereafter: we are not yet in their country.

The path across the Hals (i. e. neck of land) between Midfiord and Hrutafiord did not belie its character. The cotton-grass (*fifa*) raised its white streamers around, sure sign of dangerous bog. What was not morass was stony ruins, and what was not ruins was morass. Half way over, I left the horses to examine one of Gretti's handiworks, a rhomboidical stone, some six feet long by five feet broad and four feet thick, poised upon another. A veritable Grettistak. The guide joins me, having deserted his charge; and the consequence was, that when we regained the path, the horses were nowhere to be seen. We hurried forward to an eminence commanding an extensive view; but no horses. Had the Alf-tailor mounted them, and ridden to where tailors proverbially ride? Despatching the guide back, I began spelling over an Icelandic book. No small relief it was, when, at length, I heard a distant halloo, and saw the truants approaching with the nefarious Jon. Of course he was very sorry; so was I. At length, we descend upon the Hrutafiord, and wind along its shore to its very end, rounding which, across a many-armed river, which, it being ebb, we forded without difficulty, we make the best of our way along its western shore to Bordeyri. The merchant, here, rents the salmon fishery of the river; but he has done very little this year. Prestbakki was my sleeping quarters that night. In the church, I see drying a quantity of *Dryas octopetala*, called Riupnalyng from its being the chief food of the ptarmigan in winter. The natives prepare a tea from it, which is good for the jaundice.

The flat shores of the Hrutafiord, along which I ride next day, are strewn with large pieces of onyx and chalcedony in great quantities. I call at the sysselman's, Johannes, on the road. While coffee is preparing, we drink a bottle of port to the dregs. The fact is that Icelandic travel is very destructive of the tissues, and alcohol is not only not injurious, but necessary to the system. Fortified with these refections, and cigars, we start in company in the best possible humour, defying the bitter north-wind and clammy fog. At Kolbeinsá abides the pilot of the Hrutafiord, Gislason, who is away catching sharks. His daughter, Gudrun, does the honours. The constant fish diet requires an antidote, which nature has provided ready to hand. Scurvy-grass (Skarfakál) grows thickly upon the sides of the turf-covered houses. On the shore beyond is a piece of rock some fifty feet high, washed by the surge. It is composed of short basaltic pillars lying *horizontally*. In the bare lava-sand, on the shores of the Skalholtvik, I first see that beautiful lemon-coloured flower, the *Papaver nudicaule*, in full bloom. I meet with specimens of it all along the north-west coast, but always on bare sand or shingle. This year's seeds are not nearly ripe, but last year's seed-vessels are still hanging to the plants full of seed, and I gather some to take to England. They have encountered a winter's snow, but this probably has an antiseptic power; as an old traveller in Iceland, Mohr, in his natural history of the country, states that he found the last year's crowberries quite fresh and good after a winter's immersion.

My kindly guide accompanies me to the very foot of the Stikuhals, a neck of land which the traveller has to surmount before descending to the shore of Bitrufiord. On the shores of this fiord I see large quantities of drift-wood, and piles of sea-shells; among which are the beautiful pink-coloured *pecten Islandicus* (harpudiskr), the *Cyprina Islandica,* and the *mytilus edulis* (krakuskiel). These are utilized by nobody, either contents or shells, except by the ravens and foxes. The fox—about which there are as many stories in Iceland as about the bear in Norway, and which the Norwegians are said to have introduced into Iceland in spite—is particularly fond of the Pecten Islandicus. "No ships-roller wanted here, said the fox, as he drew the harp-shell along the ice," is an Islandic proverb. Here, if anywhere, the fox has to live by his wits, and very sharp they are. It is said that Reynard will occasionally swim off to a sandbank, where sea-gulls are taking their siesta; and, on reaching it, he advances his dorsal appendage foremost, so that the birds, winking and nodding in sleep, take him for one of themselves. "Am I not a bird and a brother?" He thus mixes with the dreamers, and has two or three of their heads off in a twinkling.

Leaving the level beach, the loose path winds round the shoulder of a dizzy height, hundreds of feet above the roaring sea, where a false step would be fatal. It is not every traveller who would venture along here. Asmund the peasant at Tung is the possessor of a tall mug of blue and grey ware, of German manufacture, which I purchase. It bears the date 1630. On the exterior are representations of peasants dancing, with a legend in old German doggerel, which may thus be rendered into English:

> Blow, sir piper, blow, egad!
> We will dance as if stark-mad:
> Ye who whole will keep your brain-pans,
> Mind how ye balk the boors of their dance.

On the moor between this and Kollafiord, which I cross next day (August 27), I pick up *Rhodiola rosea* and *Aspidium Lonchitis*. The steep descent on the western side of the mountain, skirting the sequestered Mokollsdal, was wrapped in a fog so dense as to render riding an affair of questionable safety The path, which was a little broader than a tight-rope, creeping along the precipice, made in one spot so abrupt a descent, that I dismounted. But how to get on again was the question. The horse, impatient to join the rest of the cavalcade, dragged me forward one foot in the stirrup, and the odds seemed in favour of my being hurled over the cliffs. Providence however befriended me, and we were soon at Fell, upon the Kollafiord, having in the space of four hours broken the neck of this pass (Bitruhals), instead of it breaking mine. To our left is the narrow isthmus—call it wrist—by which that vast handshaped peninsula, Westfiordunga—whose interior is filled by tracts of ever-encroaching ice—is connected with the rest of Iceland. The distance from here to Gilsfiord, a branch of Breidifiord, is only about twelve miles. A Troll once formed the laudable design of driving a canal through in a single night. He set lustily to work; and the innumerable islands in Breidifiord are due to the muck shovelled out by this intrepid navvie. The enterprise however failed—opera interrupta manebant—the sun rising upon him unawares, and sending him the way of all Troll flesh not under cover at daybreak, viz. into stone.

> "We won't go home till morning,
> Till daylight doth appear,"

is a sentiment which no Troll might ever act upon with impunity.

CHAPTER XVII.

Kollafiord—Demon ramparts—Asgeir Einarson—Farming under difficulties—Ice on fire—Eiderdown—"A creek between friends, a fiord between relations"—Steingrim's Fiord—Genealogies—Surturbrand in situ—David and the shewbread—Stadr—The Raven-song—The superstition of the Tilberi—Barnafoss—Thorskafiord—The bird-cliff of Latraberg—Thorer of the gold.

WE are now trotting along the shore of Kollafiord, the quiet blue sea smiling placidly—like an azure-eyed babe at its papa—in response to the sun, who has just come forth out of his brown study of fog. The rocks under which the path winds are quite a museum illustrative of volcanic agency. In one place the trap has been upheaved from the site of its subaqueous birth, and resupine slumber, and tilted up slantways: above it is a mass of burnt conglomerate, and upon that a layer of clay, of the colour of red-ochre. Just beyond is another strange scene. The line of march is over a beautiful level green-sward, some twenty feet above the sea-level, the cliff being perpendicular. On the very edge of, and flush with, this sea-washed cliff, stand at intervals fragments of what look exactly like the walls of an old castle six feet thick. One of these fragments is about twenty feet long by forty feet high. Descending to the beach, the tide being low, I perceive that the castle walls are nature's handiwork; and the tiny basaltic pillars of which they consist lie horizontally. The faces of these are about six inches wide upon an average, and present regular geometrical figures: the whole resembling the horizontally laid piles of split-beach fuel one sees about the farmsteads of Germany. Such phenomena are called by the Icelanders Tröllahlad (Demon-ramparts). E. Olafsen suggests that originally the basaltic pillars stood perpendicularly, and were upheaved and laid flat by some convulsion of nature. On the other side of the alley of greensward—which is about eighty yards wide—and parallel with it, rises what was perhaps in ancient times the old sea-cliff.

Passing out of these enchanted ruins, we come suddenly upon farm-buildings standing in an extensive *Tún,* fenced in with rails of drift-wood, and divided into plots of arable and meadow land with great neatness—the fresh hay smelling delightfully. Right glad was I to find myself under the hospitable roof of Asgeir Einarson, the M.P. of these parts, and one of the most enlightened men of his class in the country. He and the clergyman have founded a book-society; and on the occasion of his father's funeral, a temperance society. Asgeir is a practical agriculturist, although, with the exception of a Scotch plough, his dead stock might have belonged to his ancestors in the plains of Iran. His apologies for a wheelbarrow, a bush and ordinary harrow, are truly affecting to behold. Some noble member of our

Royal Agricultural Society might peradventure be inclined to send him proper instruments of husbandry—a proceeding that would likely enough lead to the regeneration, or rather birth, of Icelandic agriculture, which at present may be said scarcely to exist. And yet Asgeir has done wonders. When he came to the place a few years ago, all was either bog or sand around. The present sea-level he computes to be at least twelve feet lower than formerly. Digging into the bog, he found a hundred yards inland buried drift-wood of black colour (not lignite), in large quantities, and of exceeding toughness. There are said to be ten different species of trees thus wafted to the Icelandic shores by the bountiful ocean. Skialdabarnavik, more to the west, used to be reputed the best spot for this wood. The people have been as improvident with this foreign timber as they were with their native forests, and at present there is no great stock in hand. Add to which, owing, as it is said, to the forests of America having diminished since it was colonized, the supply is now less than formerly.

When Asgeir first came hither, a large grass-grown knoll stood before the house. This he pierced, and found it was entirely composed of wood ashes. Those old Vikings used to burn enormous quantities of wood on the fire along the centre of their hall (skali); the ashes of which were shovelled just outside the door, Irish fashion. With admirable foresight, our agriculturist utilized the deformity. The ashes were spread a foot thick over the waste which he had previously levelled, and over this he laid greensward. The consequence is, that the grass is never burnt up, and he is now gathering his second crop of hay. To encourage the vegetation still more, he collects the sewage in a tank, and spreads it over the land with a most primitive liquid-manure-cart. One corner of the Tun is occupied by what a Shetlander would call a *planty-cruive*, or kale and potato patch, fenced in by great stones. In the centre of this stood formerly a vast stone, which was pronounced by the rustics to be living rock. Asgeir's faith, however, was of the kind that can move mountains. "Listen," said he, striking the block with a crow-bar, "that is not the ring of living rock; it is only a stone." A crane was accordingly improvised, and swung over it, and by great exertions the mass was hoisted up, and made the base of the sea-fence. But alas! there is little to repay all his toil and husbandry. The ground submits to his operations *invitâ Minervâ*, and is seconded in its obstinacy by the forbidding climate. He sowed some barley, a present from the Amtman, who came to see his model farm; but the barley did not ripen: and his oats have no time to come to perfection, for no sooner is the grain in the ear, than the killing breath of the Greenland ice, which is always at the doors, nips it.

Subsequently I met a Danish gentleman who

was last year suddenly caught in this ice, near Cape Nord, in the month of May. In it his vessel stuck till June 20, when a south wind springing up, he got clear, and, by hard pumping, succeeded in bringing the craft into Reykjavik. When the everlasting fog at length lifted, he seemed, he said, to be in the midst of a great city, whose buildings towered around him. The immense quantities of water discharged from the northern rivers in July and August prevent the ice from coming close into land. If, as captain Young states, for every foot of this ice above the surface there are six feet below it, the question arises whether the proposed north Atlantic Telegraph would not at certain seasons be liable to damage at the point where it leaves Iceland for Greenland. Credulous folks used to fancy that this ice was made of saltpetre, and capable of being used for the manufacture of gunpowder; and they pointed to the flames which might in dark nights be descried, casting a lurid glare over the frozen waste. This was due to the drift-logs imbedded in the ice-blocks which ground against each other with such terrific force, under the united influence of wind and tide, as to take fire.

But to return to Asgeir. His energies, I rejoice to say, are about to find a fitter sphere for their exercise. With a chuckle, he tells me that he has become the purchaser of the monastery-farm of Thingeyri; and he revels in the idea of the great mounds of wood-ashes there, which hitherto have been turned to no account. In the spring he purposes transferring his properties by boat and raft across the broad Hunaflói to that spot which I have already described. Big with the tale of what he had done and what he would do, he insisted on my tarrying with him all night. The other day a fire broke out, destroying a quantity of wood, oil, fish, lines, &c. His great boat for shark-fishing, built by himself, narrowly escaped. But Icelanders never grumble; and as for patience, on whatever principle based, they possess an uncommon share of it. Among other articles, I am shewn some round boxes of driftwood, hooped with deal, which by long immersion in salt-water has become as pliable as birch. What would the natives of these treeless tracts do, were it not for these freight and duty-free importations from the Mississippi? *

The islands outside are the resort of eider ducks; but there being no moss or grass for them to rest upon, Asgeir has to supply them with hay, which makes the cleaning of the down a very arduous operation. On the west coast the down is dried in a pot over the fire, which destroys its finest fibre. The Icelanders consider the down from Greenland the best. Last year it fetched four dollars per Danish lb.

* It is stated that this summer the Arctic stream was very strong, and deflected the Gulf stream, so that there was less drift-wood than ordinary. Perhaps it was this that lowered the temperature over all Europe.

This year it realizes five dollars, or 11*s*. 3*d*. English. Train-oil is twenty-five dollars per tonder, without the barrel. Tallow, twenty-five skillings (farthings) per lb. Wool, forty-two skillings, and butter, thirty skillings per lb. "We have free trade now," said the deputy enthusiastically; "if the English merchants would only come and visit us, they would find we have more to give than the Danes, who wish to keep the trade in their own hands, will allow. We would gladly improve our wares to suit the English market; and I have no doubt that the peasants could be persuaded to clip the fleeces instead of *riving* them; although people do say the sheep would get cold if we did." Icelandic wool contains in it a very fine fibre (tog), resembling camels' hair. "But," said I, "you ought to look to the Danes; surely they are your nearest kindred." "Ay! ay!" answered the deputy mournfully, "we have a proverb, 'Vik milli vinn, fiordr milli fraendi,' (A creek between friends, a fiord between relations.) "Exactly," I replied. What says Solomon: "Better a friend that is near than a neighbour afar off." Our poet Shakspeare says, "The nearer blood, the nearer bloody."

August 28. We rode westward, under the magnificent sea-cliffs, amid drizzle and storm. Asgeir's horses he expects to find grazing on the narrow strip of meadow between the rocks and the sea; so he takes one of mine meantime. Not meeting with them, he catches a colt which comes in our way, quietly observing, "Christus did the same." On the tall mountain above Heydalr, where we stop to take coffee, I espy a column of stones. This is a 'day-mark.' At three o'clock p. m. the sun rests upon it. Such is the rude and imperfect substitute for the solskifa (sundial) anciently used in Iceland. We are now on the shores of the Steingrim's Fiord, the cliff scenery and needles of which are very fine. "Here is the men-meet-stone," said Asgeir, pointing to a boulder standing by the path, "where some fighting-men from the east and west came and fought till they were all dead." In which of the old histories this battle of Kilkenny cats is commemorated I do not remember. The names of Asgeir's ancestors are of course at his fingers' ends. His father was Einar, who was the son of Jon, who was the son of Bryniolfr, who was the son of Gudmundr, who was the son of Snorri the priest, who was the son of Asgeir ditto, who was the son of Einar ditto, who was the son of Oddr Bishop.........&c. &c. &c. On the mother's side he can go up to Egil Skalagrimson; while in the far distance of his ancestry figure Ragnar Lodbrok and King Dan.

"But here is the Gil," said he, "which contains the Surturbrand." This stone of stumbling to geologists is exhibited in the sides of a ravine which have been bared by the descent of a torrent. It is in layers three or four inches thick, which can be further split into very thin plates. Its colour is black. Above are layers of a browner material, like burnt clay; while over all are deposits of loose slag and cinders. The opinion of Von Troil is, that it was formed by an irruption of lava, which sweeping away whole woods charred them by burning and smothering them at the same time. Gaimard thought it was nothing but ancient drift-wood, which became hermetically sealed, as it were, by subsequent depositions; and by this baking and pressure became converted into coal. But then, whence the impressions of leaves, which I found frequent upon the thin laminæ into which I split the mineral? For, the drift-wood which I have seen is as bare of foliage and as smooth as the crown of a middle-aged gentleman without his wig. This difficulty is met by the statement that drift-wood will come sometimes embedded in ice with all the leaves on. There is a degree of verdure about this statement which betrays its value. The best account seems to be, that at one time, owing to a different state of the atmosphere, there was an enormous growth of vegetable-matter in these regions. Upon this a deposit of clay or some other substance was suddenly poured, and the gases being confined by a chemical process, the vegetable mass was turned into surturbrand or lignite, stopping short of coal, owing to the conditions under which it was formed differing from the conditions which led to the formations of the coal measures.*

* Waltershausen does not share with Steenstrup the formerly

"And now farewell," said this worthy fellow, after riding with me for four hours, "farewell. May you come home safe to your family. And don't forget poor Iceland. Remember our wool, our eiderdown, our oil, our hides, our horses! We can export these to England." "And why not your dogs, too?" said I laughingly. "Perhaps you don't know that in olden times Icelandic curs were all the fashion in England; while earlier still, your forefathers had great Irish hounds to guard their homes."

I now ride to Trollatunga, two miles inland, and on the road perceive surturbrand cropping out in various places. The clergyman of this place belongs to the Temperance Society, but nevertheless he placed wine before me. The sacramental wine, as I learned afterwards. Unheard of desecration! many will be led to exclaim. But I thought of the shew-bread, and what David did when he was a hungered, and those that were with him; and abstained from passing a harsh judgment on this seeming want of reverence for sacred things. Séra Haldor politely accompanies

universally received opinion, that the surturbrand is composed of drift-wood; he believes rather that the plants in question were formerly growing in Iceland, and that the island then possessed a milder climate than at present. According to unpublished accounts by Steenstrup, the layers of surturbrand are to be considered as stratified forests buried by submarine volcanic eruptions of ashes. Waltershausen refers to an interesting specimen from a bed of tuff, which contains two layers of surturbrand, separated by a vein of trap.—See Professor Daubeny's Descriptions of Volcanoes, Supplement, p. 787.

me northward, over stony heaths and bare sand-hills, whose black ugliness was redeemed in parts by the beautiful yellow poppy. At the farm of Kalfanaes I see the *Urtica dioica* growing near the house. It is said to grow nowhere else in Iceland. By 7½ P.M. we are at Stadr, at the innermost end of the Steingrim's Fiord. This spot lies a very short distance south of the great Dranga Iökul; which almost entirely fills up the thumb of the mighty outspread palm, to which this singular peninsula may be likened. Last year's snow still cools the air, and stripes the mountains around. Former travellers pronounce the inhabitants of this part of Iceland to be a set of wild unkempt beings. From the specimens that I saw, I should say that their savageness is a myth; and that they are just like all the rest of the Icelanders, only more honest than some of the dwellers in the capital. The venerable clergyman, Sigurdr Gislason, receives me with open arms. No Englishman has been seen in these parts since 1815.

My host's son, a student at the Theological Seminary at Reykjavik, has collected several native ballads and legends. From one of the former, descriptive of the various phases of human existence from the cradle to the grave, Shakspeare might have taken the hint for his Seven ages. The baby is born, and swaddled, rocked and nursed. It toddles, and begins to go: it grows, gets thoughts: loves and woos, desires this and hates that. Then comes old age and weariness and death. A favourite and very ancient Icelandic lullaby, to an infant that has lost its mother, begins well, but, like many of its class, it ends feebly. In Icelandic it runs—

"Tunglid, Tunglid, taktu mig,
Og berdu mig upp til skya,
Þar situr hun modur min
Og er ad kemba ull nya."

Which may be rendered thus:—

"Take me, bear me, shining moon,
Bear me to the skies;
Mother mine, she's sitting there,
Carding wool so fine."

Another is a Raven-song (Krumma-Kvaedi,) a dialogue between a Raven and a peasant; which runs thus:—

Hark! the raven at the lattice
Croaketh, hark! so drearily,
"From your board, good-man, a morsel
Just a morsel give to me."—

Answers good-man wrathfully,
"Hence avaunt! you rascal daw,
Scant of grace and ugly are ye,
Evil bird of crooked claw.

Stay a moment! hast thou any
News to tell me, tell it quick"—
"From your board, good-man, a morsel
Just a morsel let me pick.

Early on the fells this morning,
Early I was on the leas,
Spied a lamb half-dead and frozen,
Resting faintly on its knees.

Joyous sight it was to look at,
Such a dainty meal in store!
From your board, good-man, a morsel,
Just a morsel give; no more:

In its side a hole so deftly
To the heart with bill I tore,
Straight the feeble knees 'gan failing,
Sank the lambkin in its gore."—

"Raven croaking at the lattice
Live you shan't an instant longer,
Horrid, greedy, loathly raven,
Cursed be your cruel hunger."—

Scythe-shaft seizing, from the cottage
Out the good-man runs amain,
Smites to death the ugly raven
Croaking at the window pane.

The student tells me of a curious superstition, which lingers in Isarfiord, a little west of this; the stronghold of demonology and witchcraft. I mean the superstition of the *Tilberi* or *snakkr*. In summer-time, the udders of the milking sheep become distended, and drop with milk. It is the Tilberi sucking them, say the peasants. The matter stands thus. Some malicious old hag, who wishes to do her neighbour a damage, goes to the grave-yard, and steals a human rib; this she wraps up in some stolen wool, which must be of a grey colour. With this, concealed about her person, she goes to the Holy Communion; but, instead of swallowing the wine, she spits it out. This manœuvre infuses life into the bone: which assumes

* Some say a seal's rib, which animal is thought by Icelanders to suck the udders of cattle.

some sort of questionable shape; some say, that of a bird, others of a snake. This she sends off to suck the udders of the neighbours' ewes. Soon it returns crying, "Full belly, mother!" and spits the milk into her churn. The butter of such a material, as may be supposed, is none of the best. All butter, honestly made and come by, is therefore marked with the Holy Rood; it being well known that Snakkr-smjor won't take the impression of the sacred symbol. Once on a time, the predecessor of my host actually saw the monster hastening homeward distended with milk. "I've caught you at last," he cried, riding after it at full speed; but no harlequin ever tumbled, jumped, and sprang as it did. The parson rode his hardest, and caught sight of it entering the cottage of an old crone, whom he had long suspected. "So you will steal milk, will you, Thorbiorg?" "Not I, your reverence." "Stand up then, and let see behind you." Up she stood, and in the same instant was killed by the Tilberi.

How can I dwell sufficiently on all the kindness I experienced here; on all the creature-comforts lavished upon me; the warm knitted gloves with no fingers, but two thumbs each instead, or the extra pair of warm socks with which I was provided against the very bitter weather? At home and abroad my host was all the same. His going out squared with his coming in. Literally, I say so. For next day, (Aug. 29), although a north-wester blew so searchingly that no man would willingly have braved it; the veteran priest, wrapped in full winter costume, insisted on riding with me half over the pass to Thorskafiordr. Leaving the valley, we rapidly ascend the Fjeld along the edge of a deep and dizzy ravine working into the heart of the mountain. At its narrowest part, it seemed to have been spanned by a bridge. On each side of the cleft are the buttresses, and places from which the arch once sprung, as plain as plain could be. "Yes," remarked my companion, "this is, or rather was, the Steinbogi, (the stone bridge.) There was a church higher up the dale at a spot, called Kirketunga to this day; and, for the accommodation of the church-goers, this bridge was erected. But a troll-wife, who lived at Kleppastadir had long viewed the worshippers, as they passed to and fro, with an evil eye; and one day she came, and with a stamp of her foot threw the bridge down." Such is the local explanation of a phenomenon which geologists explain otherwise*. This was one of those trap dykes which stripe the island. A long straight groove has been opened in an older formation by the cooling of the mass; and, at a subsequent period, this has been filled up compactly by a fresh supply of matter. During some convulsion of nature, the gill

* See that valuable work, Prof. Daubeny's "Descriptions of Volcanoes," Supplement, p. 781; a book which contains some of the most recent information on the geological phenomena of Iceland.

opens out, making way for a mountain torrent, and the buttresses stand up face to face on its opposite sides, being the ruptured faces of the severed dyke aforesaid.

This story of a bridge that was and is not reminds me of a tale in the *Íslenzk Æfintýri*, told of a place in the south, near which I afterwards journeyed. A few miles north of Snorri Sturleson's house at Reykholt, there was once a narrow natural bridge over the Hvitá. One day the farmer of Hraunsáss went to church at Gilsbakki, which lay a little over the bridge. "Be sure and stay at home," said his wife to her two children, as she started to accompany him. No sooner were the church-goers over the bridge, than the children, who had watched them, ran after them. Coming to the perilous arch, they took each other by the hand, and advanced cautiously; but, looking for a moment into the abyss below, they turned giddy and fell into the chasm. The frantic mother had the bridge destroyed, that nobody might ever after meet with the like fate. The waterfall below is called Barnafoss (Bairn-force) to this day.

Arrived at the top of Fjeld my companion dismounts, uncovers, and wishes me all sorts of good fortune, and then retraces his path against the bitter mist-laden wind. Were it not for the fog, I should see from hence the vast Drangá glacier which stretches for sixty miles to the northward. The cairns at intervals mark the path, which otherwise in such weather would have been difficult to find. On the flat, I espy the *Ranunculus glacialis*, the *Rhodiola rosea* (Is. Burn), and my fair friend the yellow poppy. On the descent to Thorskafiord, fragments of zeolites and crystals are strewn about. Unfortunately, old Sumarlid, a noted story teller, who lives at the head of the Fiord, was away. Here was the seat of one of Iceland's twelve provincial Things. The site of the place of assembly is only a bowshot from the solitary farm-house. Moss covered mounds mark the foundations of the enclosure; I measured it, and found it twenty-six yards long and eight broad. At the present time, every summer, the peasants meet here to deliberate on social and other matters, an awning being stretched over their place of meeting.

Many a stirring scene has been witnessed here, since the time when Halstein, the first settler, came hither with those unfortunate Scotch captives, whom he employed in making salt for him on the Svefneyr in the Breidifiord. On Halsteinnes, the tongue of land down yonder to the right, stood his dwelling. The timber for its doorposts was sent him by the god Thor—alias the Gulf-stream—in the shape of a log, sixty-three ells long and two fathoms thick. As aforesaid, Thor got the credit of the timber, and Halstein's son was offered up to him in the bargain. Grenitresnes (Fir-tree-naze) marks the spot where the timber came ashore, even to the present day. *Apropos* of slaves; another proprietor of the vicinity, one Ketell, being short of hands, introduced some coolies from Ireland. The former connection between these parts and Ireland, or the Western Isles, is still evidenced by such names on the map as Brjanslaekr, and Patricksfiord, to the west of this.

A little to the east of that Frith, and facing the Breidifiord, is the famous bird-cliff of Latra-berg, which must not be passed over in silence. Numbers numberless of auks and guillemots frequent these rocks. To get at them was formerly more dangerous than now; for a goblin (illr andi) used to haunt the precipice, and cut the rope by which the luckless fowler descended. Bishop Thorlakr, who had successfully exorcised evil spirits from similar localities, came hither to do the like, when a hoarse voice was heard under the cliff, "Somewhere we must live." Poor goblins! they really remind me of the houseless people turned out of the London Rookeries. The bishop, wise in his generation, saw the force of the observation, and left one patch of the cliff unexorcised, whereunto these sprites might always resort. The plot was scant, but he considered that by close packing there would be ample room and verge enough for these infernal characters. A daredevil fellow once boasted that he would descend this spot, the foul fiend notwithstanding. The rope by which he hung was not got far down, when a grey shaggy hand stretched out of the rock and cut it assunder, and like him "who spoke the spectre-hound in Man," the disbeliever in the powers of evil paid for his scoffs with his life.

The subterranean communication which is said to exist between Thorskafiord and Isarfiord, like that between Hytardal and Snaefell, is known better to popular tradition than to the author, who could not spare time to look for it. Neither could I make out —Sumarlid being from home—who had last seen that sea-monster, the dread of the mariners of the Firth, who mostly looks like a ship floating bottom upwards.

Yet another tale, before we quit for ever, probably, this Thorskafiord. In the narrow arm of it, just over yonder, called Djupfiord, lived one Gullthorer (Thorer of the gold), pronounced by the Landnama to be "et mesta afarmenni" (a very violent sort of man). This treasure, from which he took his name, he had stolen in Finmark. The Isarfiord people, with whom he had a feud, found out that he often secretly visited a water-fall in the above 'Deep Firth!' and one day, as he came thither with only one companion, waylaid him with thirty men. Fight he did right doughtily, and long did he resist the fearful odds. At last, when both his hands were hacked off, he rushed to a slab of rock, pushed it aside, and uncovered two great chests with a ring in the lid of each. Into each of these he inserted his gory arm stumps, and sprang into the depths of the Force. The reader of German literature thinks of that tale of ill-gotten gold in the Nibelungen, where Hagen buries the treasure in the Rhine. Of course the excellent Germans took the trait from the home of the Edda.

CHAPTER XVIII.

The "sun's eye had a sickly glare"—"Culling of simples; meagre were his looks"—The foster brothers—The poet laureate—How were the ancient Icelanders housed?—Petrified trees—Hraesvelgr on the wing—Trout and char—A Puki—Sunset—Skredgiarder—Hvoll—An M. P.'s daughter—Bishop Hatto in Iceland—Columnar basalt—A strong pull and a long pull—The lord of Skard—Good entertainment for man and beast—The University man—A barrel full of priests—Crossing the Fjeld in a fog.

WE proceed at a rapid trot across the isthmus to Berufiord, another branch of the great Breidifiord. Behind me shoots up a most singular mountain, Vadalfiall. It pierces the sky like a gaunt grim bare horn, apparently quite inaccessible. The sight is so curious that I frequently turn to remark it. The sun is out now, and the edges of the peak come out sharply against the sky. The wind however blew fiercely, and by the time I reached the first house in Breidifiord, I had oftener than once been nearly blown from my horse. Of the basin of milk, which a damsel hands me, more than half is blown away, Boreas getting the lion's share. Nature around wears the aspect of suffering. To our left lie naked emaciated skeletons of mountains blotched with red fever spots and wan with the orange of jaundice, while, near the sea, shapes of fantastic mould writhe here and there, the colour of ebony, 'Black Death' written on their brow. As if to intensify the weird wanness of the scene, westward yonder, far out in the fiord, where the waters above and below the firmament meet together, the eye of the discrowned king of day casts a sickly glare; specked by the motes of islands that obstruct his sight; while an arch of pale green sky canopies the unearthly pageant. "The Ancient Mariner," or "The Last Man," where can they be, that I have not yet encountered them!

A bent shrivelled figure, of meagre, sharpened aspect, bids me come under the shadow of his poor roof at Garpsdal, where I arrive at dusk. What heavenly odours saluted my nose, as I entered!—my nose, so acclimatized to the dank frousty smells of the semi-subterranean dwellings of Iceland. The cause of this odorous quintessence was presently manifest. Bottles and gallipots filled every nook of the apartment. The parson is like Tom Potts, he combines two callings. In early life he studied for the medical profession, but his health giving way, he took holy orders. All the Icelandic clergy are bound by law to be able to inoculate; but he can do more. "Your knowledge must be a great benefit to the poor, Séra Biarni," said I. "Yes," replied the pinched up man, with much humility, not unmixed, I thought, with indications of honest pride in his art, "yes, by the blessing of God I have effected not a few cures." We have some talk about the people who lived here in the olden time.

He reminds me that the two famous fosterbrothers, Thormod and Thorgeir, the first of whom "was afraid of God, but the latter of nothing," lived in the Isarfiord, from which I was not many miles this morning. Thorgeir, as usual, went the grand tour; i.e. on a freebooting expedition, in England, Ireland, and elsewhere; subsequently becoming a resident at the court of St. Olaf of Norway. His end was the end of many a gallant viking: one day high in the hall of princes, singing

> 'to lord and lady gay
> His unpremeditated lay;'

another, in his native wilds, and dogged to death by avengers of blood or insult. He fell in a quarrel, and a post-mortem examination being instituted, to see whether this big-hearted man had so big a heart in the flesh as in the spirit, that organ was found to be very small, confirming the saying, that 'a brave man's heart is really small.'

His fosterbrother Thormod was a renowned scald, and according to the Saga, made many a woful ballad to his mistress' eyebrow. He too went on his travels. Canute the Great, hearing of his powers of song, wished to make him his poet-laureate. But he declined so precarious a position. 'Off with his head; so much for Buckingham!' was liable to be the fate of a scald, who did not rhyme to his royal patron's liking. He consented, however, to take the post on trial for a winter. In the following spring, Canute wanted to shirk paying the promised guerdon; but

Thormod delicately reminded him of it, under the mythic figure of Fafner's Eiendom. Upon this, the king drew a gold ring from his finger, and presented it to the poet. "But you promised me a whole mark of gold," said the scald, poising the trinket. "Ah! true," replied his majesty, drawing another ring from his finger. After this, our poet and pirate became very intimate with king Olaf the Holy, at whose instance he went to Greenland, and took vengeance on his brother's murderer.

The end of the scald was glorious. He was one of the famous Skioldborg, the Norsk king's body-guard, who were to see and sing the deeds done in the battle of Stikklestad. Like Taillefer sang the lay of Roland at our battle of Hastings, so did Thormod, on the morning of the fight of Stikklestad, sing the ancient Biarkemâl, and that so loud that all the host heard it. When the king fell, the minstrel was still unharmed. But he prayed that the king's promise might be fulfilled, that in death they should not be divided. Whereupon an arrow hit him. The scald crept out of the throng, and sang a lay or two with his parting breath. Two tumuli, which I passed this morning, are said to mark the graves of some of these two fosterbrothers' following.

"And did these dwellers in kings' houses live in dwellings as miserable as those I see now, when they came back to Iceland? For if so, I wonder they did not prefer perpetual banishment." "No doubt, there was a good deal of turf and stones about the ancient dwellings," said the leech, "but the people of those days had great store of gold and silver, earned by song or piracy; and they built their houses then on a much grander scale. Nay, Arngrim Jonason, who wrote his Crymogæa, at the instance of bishop Thorlak, to refute the calumnies about Iceland, of Joachim Lion the German, says, that in his days the houses were built stately and sumptuously enough with timber, stones and turf. And Olaf the Peacock's house at Hiardaholt, which you will pass, was magnificent."

August 30. The wind is still blowing fiercely, but the priest has gone out, notwithstanding, to baptize a child. At all events he will not offer so much resistance as myself to the blast; as the wind will almost blow through him, as through a skeleton on a gibbet — a most indecorous simile, in which fortunately he is not aware that I am indulging. Meantime, I visit an old Runic stone, lying in front of the house; but the characters are, as usual, nearly defaced. By and by we start together, about mid-day, when, the tide being out, we can ride across the sands. This matter must be attended to carefully. In this part of Iceland, high or low water makes a difference of many hours in a day's travel. On the top of the cliffs, which frown down upon the fast narrowing Gilsfiord, great petrified trees have been discovered, some of them as much as twenty feet long.

"They lie loose upon the surface," said the priest, "as if they had been gradually laid bare by the wind." Swans' feathers, some of the largest size, begin to whiten the shore. They are the property of the peasants, who have lands adjoining: the largest sell for four skillings each. Looking towards the water, I perceive that it is literally white with hundreds of swans (Svanr, or Alft), whose clear trumpet tones may be heard distinctly at intervals in the pauses of the bellowing blast. The priest tells me that these swans are those which are too old or too young to have eggs. The breeding ones are at present occupied with their broods on the fjeld. Nobody shoots them: and they enjoy an undisturbed existence here from May to the end of September; by which time, being reinforced by the others, in three or four days they entirely disappear. Several emigrate. Many of them, however, spend the winter in the Alftefiord, further west. A winter or two ago, the frost was so intense, that they died in great numbers.

The wind increases to a hurricane as we get deeper into the funnel of the fiord. Stems of seaweed as thick as my wrist are borne along like swansdown. This gives me an idea of what the wind can do in these regions. 'Call it not vain, they do not err,' those old scalds, who tell us that at the northern end of heaven sits a giant, Hraesvelgr hight, feathered like an eagle, and when he takes to flight the winds rise under his wings. A figure reminding us of the sublime image of inspiration, that makes the Omnipotent 'ride upon the wings of the wind.' Verily, Hraesvelgr is on the wing to-day. Not Æolus, nor any such puny classic conceit, could blow like this; he would infallibly crack his cheeks, if not burst like the frog in the fable, or a troll overtaken suddenly by the dawn.

Two of those strange trap-dykes here descend from the mountains, and project on to the sands, just as if they had been artificial boundaries. Land however is, and has been, so plentiful always in this country, that landmarks never have been wanted. And so it is, that in the national superstitions, which will often be found to be closely connected with realities, the ghosts of removers of landmarks, so common in Danish folk-lore, do not appear.

At the very end of the fiord, Kleifar, is a waterfall, Gullfors, well worth visiting. It is perpendicular, and of considerable volume, and, as its name imports, a phantom treasure is sunk in the depths of the dark pool into which it plunges. In this stream, as it approaches the sea, two men are netting trout and red char. Numbers of young golden plovers are feasting on the freshly-mown grass. The Breidifiord, of which Gilsfiord is a nook, owing to its countless islands, is barren of fish. The little valley of Olafsdalr, the mouth of which I pass, terminates in snow-wrapt mountains and dark precipices, the very sight of which sends a chill to the heart; and yet here dwells an enterprising farmer, who has fenced in a large tun. Here we come suddenly close upon a host of swans, which bundle into the brine with loud hoopings.

Some thirty years ago, the farmer of Olafsdal was riding home one evening by the shore, the very way we are now taking, only in the opposite direction. The tide was coming in, and so the space for him to ride between the cliff and the sea was of the narrowest, when who should overtake him but a Púki! Being a man of mettle, Olafr, that was the farmer's name, managed to keep his fellow-traveller at arm's length; but just at this spot, where he turned from the shore into Olafsdal, the goblin jumped upon his shoulders, and stuck fast in spite of all his efforts to get rid of him. Next morning Olafr was found stark and stiff upon the ground. His wife had dreamed a dream in the night, in which she saw the whole affair; and that is the way it was known how her husband came by his death. From that day to this the Púki sticks to the family. The reader will doubtless be breathless to hear whether I saw the goblin. No, I did not. But we were two in number, and the lord of day was still arrayed in all his glory. See! how he lifts up the distant isles of the sea—islands of the blest—into another sea of golden haze. That magnificent range of coast, running westward, with peak after peak, bluff after bluff, rising right away to the distant

Bardastrand, has caught and thrown back the magic tints. Opposite to us, due north, the unicorn Vadalfell of yesterday has split his one horn into two, all bathed in purple dye; while just between us, in the little Berufiord, are those black spectre rocks, my bête noir of yesterday, unsoftened by the hues of sunset. On the one hand is a lovely Claude, on the other a sharp, hard, uncompromising photograph. The pen is a poor instrument wherewith to represent such scenes.

It is 8 P.M. and we are doubling the sea-cliffs and riding inlands up a broad valley to Hvoll. Thick mists are rolling down the regularly storied rocks of trap which impend over the farm-house. Very well if nothing harder rolls down, for the buildings are near under them, and the fresh scars above betoken the descent from time to time of stone avalanches. On a nearer inspection I find, that at a distant period a whole mountain of rock must have come down, forming an immense barrier, which effectually defends the house; whatever falls now, taking a different direction, as being unable to overleap the obstacle. The ancient Icelander saw and noted these things; and in different parts of the country piled up strong barriers, to stem and divert the rushing stone-stream. These were called Skredgiarder, being a colossal stone fence of angular shape, the apex of which was strongest, and fronted to the suspected point of invasion. This was mended every year with great care.

The proprietor of the farm is Indridi Gislason M.P., son of the venerable owner of Flatei; and whose brother is a professor at Copenhagen, and author of the best Danish and Icelandic Dictionary. A bright full moon, I see, is topping the cliffs before I retire, to be succeeded on the morrow by a charming still day; though the ground dazzling with hoar-frost, and white puffs from the horses' nostrils, tell of the near approach of winter. In the churchyard is a stone with the date of 1593; while upon the altar is a brass candlestick of unusual shape, the facsimile of which I saw in Saetersdal in Norway. Indridi I find is off to the haymaking this morning (Aug. 31); so his little daughter Ragnheidr, who is carrying his breakfast to her senator father, pilots us to the site of the old temple, a mile or two up the valley. Dressed in a black short skirt, with a jacket of the same colour, closely plaited behind above the waist; with stockings of native brown wool; the tasselled national cap perched on her light-haired crown, and a coloured kerchief over that; she holds a great whip in her red-gloved hand; sitting astride of the sharp-eyed pony, who carefully ferrets his way through the bogs. The toft, or site, of the ancient heathen place of worship, is situated on an eminence looking down the valley. It is circular, and about thirty paces in circumference. Returning to Hvòll I proceeded on my journey.

It was considerably after mid-day that we found ourselves out of the valley, and pursuing our track under the tremendous cliffs, whose débris, constantly falling, render the path, when the tide is high, as it was now, difficult to travel. The swans are piping strenuously among the islands. Yonder, on one of these, is something shining brightly in the sun-light. It is the slate-roofed parsonage of Akreyjar, as I learn from Gudrun of Fagridal, who bids us take refreshment in her house. The priest is her father, and he has not such a bad place of it as may be supposed, what with the eiderdown and seal-fishery. Many of these islands abound with grass: when horses are taken over to them, their legs are tied, and they are placed in the bottom of small boats; and, being accustomed to it, they lie perfectly quiet. The reader who does not contemn legends, and sees behind them much more than at first meets the eye, will be interested to learn that a legend attaches to this island, Akreyjar, which is likely enough the prototype of the similar one in Germany; a story to wit of rats and mice; who were sent to plague a rich miser living on the isle; and if they did not eat him up, as they did Bishop Hatto, yet so devoured his substance, that he died in the depths of poverty.

In the opening of Fagridal rises a steep conical red-coloured mountain, Hafratindr, to the height of about three thousand feet: steep enough, apparently, to excite the mettle of Alpine clubbists. The tide being still up, instead of going along the sands under the Heidnaberg, a stronghold of Trolls—the basaltic pillars of which are by some pronounced among the finest in Iceland—we have to struggle painfully among fallen rocks and morasses; the ptarmigan, which are absurdly tame, crowing at us in derision. Evening was fast approaching when we passed the opening of Budardal; the smoke of one distant solitary hut serving to make the desertion of the scene still more fearful. As who does not know that a spot of mud enhances the brightness of a well-polished boot?

At last the path ends, and before we are aware of it, we are involved in a bog, overgrown with the ominous fifa. In this strait we make a cast towards the sea, but only to get deeper into the mire, and then struggle inland, nearer under the mountain; pressing forward the unwilling horses. The crisis ends by the foremost baggage-horse sticking fast. We are at our wits' end; darkness is approaching. But there is no time to hesitate. "Pull away! pull both together," I cry; and, after a strong and a long pull, we have the beast out by the tail. Lucky for him that it was not made of feathers. As for himself, after some futile attempts at self-extrication, he had lain perfectly quiescent. The guide now thinks that we must have overshot

Skard, our destination. I differ from him; we advance by scrambling along the foot of the cliffs. All is right; for on turning the angle of the mountain, I descry a man on horseback, and, in another minute, the church and house of Skard are seen nestled in a recess.

Port wine, broiled salmon, lamb, tea, coffee, schnaps; port wine again; cigars, pipes, brandy and water; and so to bed: such was the end of the day; and such the entertainment provided for me by the warm-hearted hospitable Chamberlain Magnussen, Lord of Skard, and worthy successor, if not descendant, of Geirmund, Prince of Ringerike in Norway; who, according to the Landnama, was the most noble of all the Icelanders, and used to go about these parts attended by a retinue of eighty followers. His treasure lies hidden in the bog close by—the very bog the depths of which we plumbed last night. The memory of Ebenezer Henderson, who visited this spot in 1815, is still fresh here. He presented my host's father with his signet-ring, which is preserved with other family relics. Henderson died in 1859. The Bible Society's translation of the Holy Scriptures into Icelandic, the dissemination of which was his object in visiting Iceland, is pronounced by the present generation to be faulty, and has been superseded by a newer version. But, nevertheless, it supplied for a time a great want; copies of the old translation, by Bishop Gudbrand, having become very scarce. In the church are the portraits of Dadë Biarnesen and his wife Arnfrydur, who died here about two hundred and twenty years ago. Their costume is on the Dutch type. His knee-breeches are extremely baggy, and on his shoes are extensive rosettes. A recent 'Vacation Tourist' suggests the presence of the great auk among the numerous islands in the Breidifiord; but this seems impossible, as nearly all are utilized for seal-fishing, sheep-feeding, or gathering eiderdown.

September 1. Wind and driving mist: and my plan of crossing over the mountains to Hvamm in Hvammsfiord is pronounced by my host to be out of the question. But go I would; my time in Iceland was drawing to a close: and my kind entertainers, finding that I was inexorable, did the best they could to fortify me against the hardships and dangers of the passage. Such eating! such drinking! That potent punch makes my head swim now as I think of it. And then the farewell kissing! Madam and her fair daughter—Well! well! it's the fashion, you know; and so these osculations cannot be avoided. But I and the chamberlain were not going to part so soon, after all. He is a university man too. He studied in Copenhagen, and wants to indulge still more in the feast of reason. Booted and caped and cloaked, he issues from the threshold.* He has a saeter up

* A piece of stone very like chalk is here brought to me; it is used as such by the people here. On being tested, it turns out to be akin to that stone.

the valley,—'summer-houses' they were called in the sagas—and he proposes accompanying me as far as there. "Where is my horse?" "Oh! it has been sent on in front: please take mine there," said he, pointing to a little fubsey, piebald pony. So not only has this good Samaritan killed the fatted calf, but he sets me on his own beast; and away we dash, at a tremendous pace, up the secluded valley, which conducts to the mountain. "Do you like your pony?" "Very much. How old is he?" "Over twenty winters. He is the best I ever had. But you should have known him in his days of fire. It is not extinguished yet, you see. But here we are at the *sel*. You must have some coffee or something. You have a terrible ride before you. Look how thick it is up the valley. Try this, my dear sir; the weather is bitter cold; try this," he continued, handing me a big flask of something stronger than milk. Before starting I inspect the shieling. Two girls were its inhabitants. Cheeses and other dairy products were there. "And what is in that?" said I, pointing to a large barrel. "Priests." "Priests! I suppose that is another word for herrings." On looking in, I found that the priests were half-fledged puffins, pickled down. I then remembered that one of the names of this bird among us is also clerical, 'pope.'

Here my host and I take leave of each other; not, however, as may be imagined, without some of the national embracing. Skule, the student from Reykjavik, and Ebenezer, the chamberlain's son, manfully resolve to go forward with me over the mountain. Arrived on the top of the grim plateau, patched with snow, and stuck full of mud-holes and sharp rocks, the fog thickens upon us. The few cairns, or solitary stones, set up to guide the wayfarer, are, at twenty yards' distance, quite invisible; yet still Ebenezer, with the instinct of an Indian, holds on his way. At last, however, even he was puzzled; and it was only by referring to the compass, and making a successful cast, that we got upon the line of cairns again. In order to descend into the valley on the other side of the pass, it was necessary to hit upon a certain spot, otherwise we might get among precipices, where to advance or retire was equally perilous. By good luck, after sliding down a snow-field, we find we are all right; a steep grassy slope brings us into a narrow dale; and at past 11 P. M. we rouse up from their repose the folks of the parsonage at Hvammr. Comely Halgierda! blessings light on thy flaxen head for the care that thou didst bestow on the wanderers.

CHAPTER XIX.

Hvamm—The tombs of the pagan and the Christian—Sprites at their antics—Hiardaholt—The Laxdaela saga—Olaf at the court of Dublin—A great grave-ale—Kiartan and Gudrun—His murder—She dies in the odour of sanctity—The birthplace of Arne Magnussen—Breidabolstad—Swan-fiord—Drapuhlidafell—Helgafell—Stykkisholm—A farewell chaunt—A string of proverbs—Spectre avaunt!

Next morning, (Sept. 2.), archdeacon Thorleifr takes me before the service to the site of the old seat of judicature, which must have been of oval shape, and about 42 paces round. Close by are the traces of a castle. The ring on the church door is reputed to have belonged to the old heathen temple. On the introduction of Christianity here, one old lady Gull-brár, stuck to the gods of her youth, and after death, by her own request, she was buried in that dark gill in Skeggidal 'where the sun never shines'; the mouth of which we skirted in our 'harumskarum' ride last night. Another heathen female, Fridgerda, was not less stiffnecked. In the year 982, the missionary Thorwald and the Saxon bishop Frederick, came to this spot, and pitching their tent close to the temple, preached the words of salvation to the assembled people. Fridgerda, whose husband was away at the Althing, was resolved not to lose the game so easily, and raised her voice in loud prayer to the deities whose images graced her temple; so that the voices of the preacher and the worshipper might be heard the one by the other, (oc heyrdi hvart þeirra ord annars*).

In the afternoon my host accompanies me across the sands, to another remarkable place of sepulture. Auda the Rich, widow of Olaf the White, king of Dublin, settled at Hvamm a thousand years ago. She was a zealous Christian, and on those hills just east of the church, Krossholar (Crosshills), she erected the emblem of her faith; and there she and her people used to worship. But the natives of these parts were then wholly given to idolatry; nay, in succeeding times, her own descendants, relapsing to heathenism, worshipped Thor where she had worshipped Jesus. When Auda was well stricken in years, and knew that she was not long for this world, she summoned her friends and her neighbours together to a splendid banquet. Three days and three nights did the feasting continue; and then Auda, having given sage counsel and rich gifts to each, bade them feast for three nights more in memory of her death. And the following night she died; and her body being placed with many valuables in a ship, she was interred with it, as she requested, on the sands, below high-water mark. For, having been baptized a Christian, she would not let so much as even her remains lie in a land

* Kristnisaga.

profaned by idolatry. And here, sure enough, is the spot, marked by a great stone covered with mussel-shells, now measuring 2½ ells in length, but doubtless much longer, before it sank so deep into the sand. And yonder float the white swans—an Icelandic story-teller would say they are Norns, presiders over destiny—piping mournfully, as mayhap they did at her obsequies centuries ago; a dirge which has likewise been taken up and sung by Ohlenschläger, Denmark's foremost poet.

Great must have been the rejoicing among the spirits of darkness when her light was quenched. The worshippers at the heathen temple would congratulate themselves that there was some chance of Thor having his rights again; while those goblins who had cowered into their cave near the church of Saelingsdal, yonder, again raised their hideous hum in mockery of the solemn tones which issued from the sacred edifice. Is it not recorded how the priest, while he stood at the altar, happening to look through the open door, saw the sprites at their antics? Milton it was, read backwards:

> 'A drear and dying sound
> Affrights the Flamens at their service quaint.'

Confounded at the apparition, he stopped the service, to tell his terrified congregation what he saw; and to avoid the recurrence of such interruptions for the future, the church was removed to its present site.

In two hours I arrive at Hiardaholt. This whilom

residence of Olaf Paa (the Peacock) is the head-quarters of the Laxdaela Saga. Olaf Paa's father was Hoskuld, great grandson of Auda the Rich above mentioned, by a beautiful dumb Irish slave, Melkorka by name. The history of this Icelandic Fenella's origin came out in a singular manner. Her husband once overheard her, to his great surprise, talking to her little son Olaf, and telling him that she was the daughter of the Irish king, Myrkiartan. The young Olaf, having grown to man's estate, chanced, while buccaneering in the western seas, to be stranded on the coast of Ireland, and being taken captive, saved himself from death by shewing to the king of Dublin, who was no other than his grand-father, Myrkiartan, a ring, a knife, and a belt, which his mother had given him. The consequence of his displaying these relics is an Anagnorisis in the approved fashion of the Greek Drama. His mother's nurse, now old and bedridden, springs from her couch without help at the sight. The king offers to make Olaf his heir, which he declines; one reason he gave for declining the proffered honour being, that his mother would mourn for his absence; which shews that these dreadful Northmen had a heart in their bosom, after all. Returning home, he built his house of Hiardaholt, so called from the numerous flocks and herds he possessed. The state in which he lived, and the extent of his riches, may be guessed from the splendour with which he celebrated his father Hoskuld's grave-ale. Olaf went to the Althing, and bade first, all the provincial presidents, and then anybody who had a mind, to the entertainment. And so nine hundred people came together, and for fourteen days did Hoskulstad, his father's hall, a bowshot or two from this, re-echo with the sound of feasting; with voices gay and grave by turns; as the revellers cast a thought upon the memory of departed greatness, or by a rapid transition passed to the topics of the day—what booty had been recently brought from the coasts of Britain or the west—what king Olaf Trygveson was doing in the old country—what was the last news from Russia and Constantinople—and so forth. While Olaf's fair daughter, Thuride, the great money-match of the neighbourhood,—as she busied about, on household cares intent, along the corridors adorned with carved pictures of the deeds of Thor and the fate of Baldur,—would doubtless receive all sorts of compliments from the travelled youths around. Gudrun, too, daughter of the wise Osvif of Saelingsdal—she would be there (that is, if she was old enough)—for no festival was complete without her—she, the most beautiful and best-dressed damsel in all the island, matched with whom all other girls "looked mere dolls;" who, what with her cleverness, her powers of conversation, and generosity, had set all the men a-dying with love, and all the women with envy.

Now Olaf Paa had a son, Kiartan, the very pink

of freebooters, the best swimmer in the north, who, in fact, had dived with that otter, king Olaf Trygvesen for a wager, and was not beaten. Many a damsel set her cap at this cavalier, and Gudrun among the number; but Gudrun was no longer what she had been. Forced into a rich marriage at fifteen, she soon separated from her husband, and married again a second husband, who in order to wed her had divorced his own wife. He was drowned soon after. No wonder that Kiartan's father was against his marrying the young widow, and heard with dislike that his son was a constant visitor to the warm baths of Saelingsdal, near which Gudrun dwelt. But this is not the place to go deeper into this tragic but rather complex story; how Kiartan went to Norway, where Ingibiorg, sister to the king, fell in love with him; how he was miserably murdered by his foster-brother and cousin, Bolle; and all through that hardened and jealous Gudrun, who had been tricked into marrying Bolle when she wished to have Kiartan. So near together are love and hate. But a short time, and Bolle paid the penalty of his crime with his own head, and his assassin wiped his bloody axe on Gudrun's kerchief. A fourth time did this beautiful fiend marry, after jilting two or three lovers between whiles; and it was not till her new helpmate was wrecked and drowned in Breidifiord that she came out in an entirely changed character. She grew very religious; learned psalms; spent many hours in prayer; and in her old age took the veil!—the first Icelandic female that did so. Her son Bolle (pronounced Bodley, and no doubt an ancestor of the Founder of the Bodleian Library at Oxford) spent many years with the Varangian guard at Constantinople. He returned at last to Iceland, and visited his mother at Helgafell, where she lived in the odour of sanctity; blind and aged and alone. "And which of all your husbands did you love most?" he inquired of her. At first she parried the question, but on his repeating it, she replied, "Þeim var ek verst, er ek unni mest." (I treated him worst, whom I loved best), viz. Kiartan. This luckless object of her warmest affection and direst hate, is said to have been buried at Borg in Borgarfiord, and an ancient Runic stone was long reputed to be his monument; but recent investigations prove that it is no such thing. This reminds me that two Runic stones, inverted, and with their inscriptions undermost, form the steps into the church here. Olaf Paa's residence is supposed to have stood just in front of the present parsonage; while Hoskuld's Stovë is a little lower down on the other side of the river. Its site is still perfectly clear, and measures 106 paces in length by 17 in breadth.

September 3.—Our road lies westward along the southern shore of the Hvammsfiord, passing the site of the ancient abode of Hrut; who also figures in the above saga. We had so timed our departure, as to catch the ebb, which enabled us to ride across the sandy bay, into which the Haukadalsá and Midá discharge themselves, thus effecting a considerable saving in the distance, besides having smoother gradients. As we splash through the shallow water, the cone of Baula rises tall and stately in the east, overtopping all the other mountains. Kvennabreka, at a short distance inland, is the birthplace of Arne Magnussen, to whose exertions it is owing that copies of the best Icelandic sagas were collected and stored up in Copenhagen. A torrent we pass has been dammed up by a trap dyke, running directly at right angles to it. In this wall a small breach has been effected, through which the contracted stream dashes as through a door. A little below, another similar dam occurs. After a ride of nine hours, we arrive at the parsonage of Breidabolstad.

Next day, in spite of a deluge of rain, and a fierce wind, Séra Benedict accompanies me to Alfta (swan) fiord. Numerous swans are feeding in the shallows at the junction of the fiord and the river. This bird too assumes a prominent place in the nursery rhymes of Iceland. But his black cousin, the raven, the bird of Odin, has decidedly the pull. Innumerable are the ditties devoted to krumma, as he is called. This might indeed be expected from his mythic character, more than human intelligence, and eccentric habits. At the beginning of winter these birds are said to meet together, and tell off pairs of their number to each separate cottage in the district. The vestiges of some ancient houses near the head of the fiord are said to mark the site of habitations rendered tenantless by the Black Death. At Orlygstadir a fierce battle was fought between Snorri the Pontiff and some of the dale-folk. In ancient days, according to the Landnama, a liberal-minded lady, Gerrida, built a house of accommodation, Þiódbraut Skáli, (literally, public-path-room,) hereabouts. It was her wont to sit on a chair outside the door, and invite passers-by to come in and partake of the good things which always stood ready on the table inside. No despicable authorities trace this hospitality, not to the Icelander's Asiatic descent, but to the old north mythology; where Odin and his compeers go wandering about in disguise, and so nobody must be turned away from the door, for fear of these notables being turned away among the number. Long may Iceland preserve this savage virtue! "We have lost everything else," say they, "but we still manage to keep *that.*"

Drapuhlidafell, which now rises on our left, in any other country but this would set a traveller word-painting in earnest. Picture to yourself a great bare mountain, forming the east end of a crescent-shaped row of heights, which dominate over the extensive tract of uneven bog between them and the sea, and end abruptly at their westerly extremity in the noble Fjeld of Biarnarhafn. Imagine the fire, which lay smouldering under the dark ribs of Drapuhlidafell to have become suddenly too hot for the monster to hold; and his bowels bursting, his side to have been knocked out by the explosion. Red, black, yellow, purple; such are the colours that are now exhibited to the face of day. A pity that their intensity was so much neutralized by the thickness of the atmosphere. When the sun shines upon the breach, its tints shine out with the lustre of gold, silver, and precious stones—a well-known landmark for the distant mariner. It is not in the least surprising that a scene so strange and wonderful is connected in the mind of the simple peasant with the supernatural. A small fountain of unfathomed depth is said to exist in the midst of the ruins; and on its brink, on the eve of St. John, the hulinhialm steinn (the stone of the cape of darkness) and other wonder-working pebbles, may be found by those who have the hardihood to go and search. We may remember that a similar belief attaches to Tindastol.

Further on, we skirt the low isolated precipice of Helgafell, a spot of the greatest sanctity in pagan Iceland. The little wooden church, now under its shadow, is but a poor apology for the monastery, which in the early days of Christianity, and up to the Reformation, stood here. That eminence, yonder, is called Munkr-skard, for it was from thence that, according to tradition, the expelled monks took a last look of their beloved sanctuary. Their heart, doubtless, was with their treasure buried in a hillside close by. An Icelandic Dousterswivel (probably the sexton) once began digging for it; but when he had dug some depth, looking round he saw the church of Helgafell in flames, and off he ran with his companions to extinguish the fire; but fire there was none to extinguish. A second attempt was made to secure the monasterial strong-box; but this time armed figures sprouted from the ground, and threatened the treasure-seekers with death, if they did not desist. According to another account, the diggers delved out the strong-box, and fastened a rope to it. "Now then pull, if God will," said the 1st digger: "Now then pull, God will or no," said the 2nd digger: at the same moment the rope broke, and then they saw their house was in flames. When they came back from putting out the fire, the hole was filled up; and since that time not a single peasant can be prevailed on, for love or money, to excavate there afresh.

What a glorious sunset! It is not Ichabod with the heavens, if it is with this people and their land. Beauteous night still rides foremost, as in the grand imaginations of the Edda, on the horse that is called Hrimfaxi (Rime-mane); and every morning bedews the earth with the foam of his bit, and that causes the dew. And day still gallops his round on Skinfaxi (Shine-mane), and all the earth and sky glistens from his mane. Dapples of living crimson light fleck the whole western sky, from the horizon to the zenith, and throw some of their magic colouring on the lichened basalt that girds the holy mountain. After a hard day's ride, we reach the factory of Stykkisholm, situated at the end of a long narrow tongue of land. My host, Mr. Thorlacius, the administrator of crown domains, is possessed of an excellent library, every book in which he seems to have read. He will not hear of my leaving the next day, as I had purposed. "Three days," he says, "was in ancient times the recognised period for a stranger's stay, never less. When the guest did depart, not only was he presented with the stirrup cup in due course, but the family collected before the door, to sing him out of the house (at siunga úr gaardi)." This custom is only just extinct. Mr. T. tells me that he has in his youth joined in the ceremony. The following is a literal translation of one of these chaunts—

"God's right hand be holden o'er thee,
Circling thee with peace profound,
May his shading wings protect thee,
Guardian angels watch around.

"Jesus' death and precious bloodshed
Bring thee blessing evermore,
May thy soul, thy life, thy honour
In his keeping rest secure."

Next day, Sept. 5, it is proposed to visit the clergyman of the district, who lives at Thingvalla. What takes a full hour by land, by boat may be traversed in a few minutes. So the latter mode of conveyance is adopted. Near the boat-house lay a long-handled harpoon for spearing seals, a pastime in which my tall well-thewed host is very skilful. The great thing is to catch these animals dozing. The seal's most vital part is his nose; a slight blow on this will do for him. The facetious Icelandic proverb refers to this; which rendered into English is, "Too near my nose, as the seal said when he was shot in the eye." Talking of proverbs, the equivalent of many of our English ones will be met with in Iceland. "Many a slip between the cup and the lip," is in Icelandic, "The cabbage is not eaten, although it has come into the big spoon;" i. e. which takes it out of the pot. In the Laxdaela Saga we find, "Betri ein Kráka í hendi enn tveir í skogi." "One crow in the hand is worth two in the wood." "Hátídir eru til heilla beztar," is our "Better the day, better the deed."

With a less adroit helmsman than Mr. T. I should have been loath to venture to sea; for it blew a tempest, the blast dashing through the spaces between the basalt-columned islands with the fury of a lion, and making our shallop with its few inches of sail flee before it in alarm. The multitudinous islets are a great resort for eiders. One thousand pounds of their down is gathered yearly; thirty nests being required to make up a pound. Close to the parsonage, Séra Eirekr Kuld, the clergyman, shews me a flat stone, about forty-four inches broad. According to tradition, this is the old Blotsteinn, upon the edge of which the backs of the victims were broken, destined to be sacrificed to Thor at the temple near. Malefactors doomed to death at the Thing, which was held close here, would doubtless be among the victims. As we sip coffee and port wine, one Matthaeus Joakimson tells us the following tale: "At Trollatunga, which you passed, there was a priest, who served as vicarius to his father, Biorn Hialmarson. One day there came to the parsonage an odd looking man from Isarfiord, who was reputed to be versed in the black art. The vicarius, having no faith in any thing of the kind, rated the man as an impostor; who departed muttering threats. A few nights after, the chaplain lay abed all alone; when suddenly he heard a voice, and saw in the chamber something like a human shape. "Who art thou?" No answer. "Avaunt then! You must be larger than that to terrify me." Presently he again heard something approaching, which seemed to fill all the room in which he lay, rolling along like a mist, yet withal in shape like unto a man. "Thou art not flesh and blood, spectre, but only a foul mist. Hence, avaunt!" So said, so done; and again the curate was alone in his chamber. But he had not time to collect himself, when in sidled what seemed like a great flaming triangle, very sharp to look upon. Round about the walls of the room there were beds, and in every bed a man with his breast bare. The apparition advanced to the first bed, and dashed into the bared bosom of its inmate like a harpoon; the man gave a horrible cry, and died. Advancing to the second bed, he did the same: and another and another hapless victim was smitten, and gave up the ghost. Last of all, the figure came to the bed whereon the curate lay. He was in a cold sweat with horror. He felt the burning point already in his bosom. Making a convulsive effort, he sprang to his feet, and cried aloud, "If thou art coming, come in Jesus' name!" and at the same moment the demon disappeared; and the curate awoke from his nightmare—he had eaten too heavy a supper the night before.

CHAPTER XX.

The Berserker hraun—All for love—Fried alive—Kerlingafjall—Faxëfiord—Miklaholt—Quaking bogs—View of Snaefell—Its many wonders—The Icelandic Staffa—A novel breakwater—We stick fast—Titanic walls—The fortress of fire—Hytardal—Sintram's attendants—A bishop and seventy-two others burnt to death—Church art—The Icelandic Wolsey—Séra Hialmarson.

SEPTEMBER 6. It is with much reluctance that I bid adieu to Mr. Thorlacius and the sysselman, Mr. Thorstensen; both of whom, being well educated men, have much to tell me concerning their country.

As I traverse the wide moor between the sea and the amphitheatre of mountains, I have a fine opportunity of studying the wild and wonderful shapes of the latter, with the darksome recesses opening out between them. Winding up one of these by a very steep ascent, we find ourselves in a narrow pass, which in grotesque hideousness yielded to nothing I have seen before in this country. To our left are mountains of palagonitic tuff, called by the natives 'Moberg,' of an unhealthy brownish yellow colour, with not the slightest particle of vegetation upon them. At the sandy foot of these we defile one by one along a horse-track which is bounded on the right by a low overhanging wall of moss-covered lava, the gaping caverns of which open horribly upon us. Casting my eye over the plain of lava, of which this forms the edge, I see not far off a great red pyramid of a mountain, while beyond I catch glimpses of a lake. It is on the shore of that lake that the famous Berserker causeway goes, being about half an English mile in length. Such a piece of road-making as mortal man never clapped eyes on. Massive lava blocks seem to have been cleared away in some places, in others built over depressions; while, at one point, the causeway is galleried into the lake in order to round the shoulder of a mountain. And all this the work in a day and a night of two of those men-monsters, whom Scandinavia bred in the days of old. I mean the Berserkers — quasi 'bare-sarks,' according to the common etymology, i. e. fellows who stripped to their work: but, according to a more recent hypothesis, 'bear-sarks;' in allusion to that popular fancy of many countries which metamorphosed human beings at times into the bear, the wolf, and other animals, and equipped them with the strength, the cunning, or other distinguishing quality of the beast whose skin they assumed. These Berserkers in their fits of moody frenzy—whether natural and involuntary, or half acquired by drink and spontaneous working themselves up—would howl and growl like wolf or dog, would dash naked through fire unscathed, bite their shields with the tenacity of hyenas, and exhibit the strength of very bears. Presently, when the evil demon had left them, they would be seen sitting clothed and in their right mind.

The two particular fellows of whom we now speak have been part of the stock in trade of everybody who has written about Berserkers, whether they have been in their native land or not. The tale is told in the Eyrbyggia Saga, the scene of which is laid in these parts. Vermund, an Icelandic chieftain, who dwelt close by, got two Berserkers from Hacon Jarl of Norway. As they soon proved unmanageable, he presented them to his redoubtable brother, Viga Styr. Styr for a time was enabled to make some use of them. But eventually he found himself in the same strait as a man whose friend has given him a bull-dog which has become too savage to keep. One of these brutes actually falls in love with his lovely daughter Asdis. Papa seemingly interposes no objections; "but," said he, "you must just do me a little spell of work first; make a road across that piece of hraun." The two set to work, and, as we have seen, soon disposed of the Herculean task. "Very good," said Papa approvingly, "won't you like to take a bath after your dirty work, before having an interview with the lady. You'll be all the more comfortable and agreeable for it. Here is my new warm bath-house. You see how I get into it, through this hole in the roof. Now you try.—Admirable! Now then, I close the trap-door, to keep out the cold air, and you will find it delightfully warm. Indeed it will do you all the good imaginable. You'll come out as fresh as Baldur after his visit to Hel; that is, if that old witch would have let him." The Berserkers fell easily into the trap. "So nice and hot!" said one: "Delicious!" said the other. Had they been in Constantinople, no doubt they would have likened it to a Turkish bath. "By Thor's hammer, though, it is getting a trifle too hot," growled out the first: "As hot as Muspelheim," howled the other. "Hilloa! you there outside. Hilloa! Viga Styr. Open the shutter. It's as hot as Hekla's mouth. Murder! We are frying, frying alive!" And with a tremendous effort one of them burst through the hole; but the bathing-man had foreseen this, and spread some wet ox-hides above. Down slips the bravo, and off flies his head in a twinkling.

In those two hillocks by the side of the path were buried the remains of this par nobile fratrum; for brothers they were in blood, as well as in mad iniquity. Dr. Backman, who formerly resided at Stykkisholm, caused these tumuli, I was told, to be dug into; when he found two male skeletons, one larger than the other; but not much bigger than himself; he being a person, however, strongly built, and of tall stature.—I afterwards met the son of this gentleman; and truth compels me to state, that he pronounced the tale of exhumation to be a myth.

Most Icelanders, I understand, believe the story of the road-making. It must have been man's handiwork. Whoever was the author of it, the Berserker-path will last for ever, and the Berserkers will always have the credit of it.

But we have not yet done with the wonders of the pass. Look upwards among those precipices, bare, black, rent, twisted into such dire shapes as nothing but fire mountains can exhibit. Is it possible? On the summit of one of the pinnacles stands a human—or rather superhuman—figure, for she is as tall as a column, that woman. See! she is looking intently over to the westward; as if waiting for somebody. She is draped from top to toe in a sort of voluminous shawl; but is without the slightest portion of crinoline to give effect to her lank figure. Heigho! this is one of your tales of true love, and there is nothing smooth about it throughout.—Only look at the rocks!—She was a Troll-girl, who loved a lad in Snaefell, and promised to meet him there one morning early. It was his duty to have sought her, but she was considerate, and set out to visit him. When she got to this Skard, as it is called, she saw the missionary Thangbrand, who used to cuff and kick the Icelanders into Christianity, standing below in the pass with a cross in his hand. I'll go a little further north, thought the damsel, and dodge him in that way. But lo! when she had gone some distance, and was about to cross the defile at another spot, the active missionary was there to meet her, holding aloft the sacred symbol. And so it went on for an hour—she bent on crossing, he on preventing her. She knew the sun would soon rise over the eastern mountains, and tried her best to keep her promise—"True are the Trolls" is an Icelandic proverb—and meet her lover in the cave of Snaefell; but it was of no avail, and at last she stiffened into stone; and gives her name to the dell; which is known to every Icelander as "Carline's Road."

In a couple of hours we are descending from these outlying supports of Snaefells jökul. Down their sides we can from below distinctly mark the course of mighty moss-grown streams of ancient lava, now standing still for ever, but centuries ago travelling in the greatness of their strength from out of their volcanic storehouses above. We are now on the vast flat marsh of Stadarsveit, which forms the greater part of the northern shore of that grand fiord, called, after Faxë, the Hebrides man; one of the companions of that Norwegian, Floki, who, like Noah, is recorded to have let loose a raven to shew him the way to dry land. No wonder that Floki, when he beheld the glorious horn of Snaefell terminating the bay, said, "This is a mighty land which we have found, and the rivers thereof are mighty." Upon the whole, however, Floki was not pleased with what he saw of the land, and gave it a bad name, *Iceland* to wit. I speak of a thousand years back. His companions, however, Heriolf and Thorolf, returning to Norway, gave a good report of the land, in fact too good a one, for they said that "butter dropped from every plant."

"Yonder is Miklaholt!" I exclaimed, pointing to an eminence in front of us rising close by the sea-shore. "Another half-hour or so, and I shall be well out of this weary swamp, and enjoying the luxury of dry slippers and socks." But these luxuries were further off than I imagined. Long did we contend with that morass, and many a circuit did we fetch, the horses steadily refusing to take the line of march which we in our simplicity thought likely to afford them the firmest footing; instead of which, guided by their powers of smell, they advanced boldly over suspicious-looking spots of matted grass, which stretched like a carpet over the unseen abyss, permitting indeed the black waters to spirt through its waving, quaking fabric, but still supporting on its surface the lightly-tripping hoofs of the sagacious animals. Their faculty of discerning depths by the nose has led to the idea that they possess another faculty, that of seeing ghosts; for why, say the people, should they stop in the dark sometimes, as they do, when nobody can see anything? Imagine an English horse in a country like this. He would straightway become alarmed, lose his head, and dislocate every joint in his body. At length, by 8 o'clock we are pounding along a footwide torrent, full of stones, the only firm foothold to be found, and in fact the approach to the parsonage of Miklaholt.

Talk not to me of 'moated granges.' It has not been your lot to see, like me, the house of Miklaholt. It could only have been under the direst compulsion that the priest could ever have been brought to settle in such a spot. Indeed, in ancient days the church is said to have been not here, but on the Haffiorderó, that island lying well out to sea over the sands. In those days it was not more of an island than the isle of Axholme in Lincolnshire is now; at least, the narrow stream that separated it from the mainland was spanned by a plank. But the waters encroached by degrees; a boat took the place of a plank; and in this the worshippers passed over to the house of God; till at last, the clergyman and thirteen souls were engulphed in the breakers, when the church was transplanted to this spot; and what was once the site of the church is the favourite resort of seals. In the autumn the priest rows off to the island, and surprises the young seals lolling about on the sand; smiting them on the nose to their speedy destruction and the solid improvement of his own income. The way to the parsonage, bad as it was, is a trifle, I hear, in point of difficulty, compared with the way out of it. Without a guide, it is an impossibility to thread our way through the mazes of the bog; and who so good a pilot as the priest, who offers to accompany us to-morrow. One of my man's horses having gone amiss from bad shoeing, he is forced to exchange it for a veteran of seventeen with my host; who shoes the changeling all round with great skill and expedition.

September 7.—A sunny morning; the fog of yesterday no longer hides the summit of Snaefell: and there he rises in isolated majesty, with his snow diadem the colour of rubies; soaring monarch-like far above the lesser mountains that gather round to do him service. One day in his ice-built courts of white and azure, with an occasional peep into the mystic depths of his grottoes, were indeed worth the labour of achieving it; though nobody has, as yet, succeeded in entirely mastering all the difficulties which beset the undertaking. Greatly do I desire to climb the ice that enwraps his triple cone, 'like the feathers of a bird, or the shingles of a house-roof,'—as an old traveller graphically describes it;—to beard that doughty demon Bard Snaefels Aas in his windy citadel—who, as it is well known, struck blind two Englishmen and killed another for venturing into his secret domain;—to ascertain if the quicksilver up there refuses its office, and whether the magnetic needle is really not worth a pin. Much do I wish to compare Stapi and its basaltic marvels with its namesake (Staffa) in Scotland; to gaze on those lofty needles (drongs), and see if I cannot peradventure discern that shadowy human form sitting on their top, and moving his feet about in the ocean lying far beneath; so that the great sea-billows, that would fain overwhelm his adamantine throne, become attenuated to mere spray by the living breakwater*. Nor would it be uninteresting to examine the traces of those "Irish bothies," where the children of Erin did something or other centuries ago; and to inspect those havens where Englishmen used to trade in such numbers down to the time of the Reformation, but who, since salt-fish has gone out of vogue, are nowhere to be seen. But I have other work on hand. Besides, by the time I got there, he of the freezing breath and icicled locks might hide everything in fog or snow-storm. I saw the mark of his presence in the rime which blinded the dull window pane this morning; and lo! his trail is fresh upon the mountains even now, whitened with new fallen snow. So we must turn our backs upon the Jökul, as the Icelanders call him *par excellence;* not that Snaefell is the highest ice-mountain in the country by any means; but it has an advantage in shape and situation combined, which none of its compeers can boast.

As we journey under the cliffs, the priest points out to me a troll above, leaning with folded arms upon an altar, and looking intently southwards. How he came there, whence he came, and whither he was going, my treacherous memory cannot now recall.

* Landnama, II. cap. 6.

"Yonder is my Annex-church," said his reverence. "The Ölkilde (ale-fountain) is near it; also some fine basaltic rocks; but you will hardly get to Hytardal to-night if you go round that way. And now good bye; may you reach home safe! You will cross over this bit of bog; then you bear to the eastward, and after a time to the northward; and then you will come to the ford over the Haffiardará. The river is low now. When you are over, don't leave the water, but keep riding up the stream under the left bank. There is a hard even bottom; no large stones. Mind you don't go up on to the moor, for it's impassable; and don't get among the lava too soon, for that's impassable too. You will ride along the river for a space as if you were going to yon red mountain. At last you will come to a track, and that will take you all right past Eldborg to Kaldádalr." My guide, who had been listening to these directions, and kept saying "Yes," was I could see, with half an eye, in a hopeless haze. I felt pretty much in the same predicament but would not confess it. What I anticipated soon took place. We managed to get to the river, and crossed it, and kept riding up the stream towards the red mountain; but, very soon after leaving the river, we found ourselves immersed in a morass. First one horse, then another, became leg-fast in the watery stocks. Nay, the loose saddle-horses, unweighted as they were, sank up to their bellies in the mire. Fortunately, at this crisis of our fate, I descry a dark object crouching among some up-piled lava. I halloo to it, and there comes a response. And straightway the figure springs with the erratic lightness of a will-o-the-wisp over the swamp; and as it comes nearer proves to be a white-haired flibbertigibbet of a boy, by whose help we and our horses are in due time extricated from our durance vile. We had taken the wrong turn.

Presently we are on the right track; composed of lava-slabs, lying hap-hazard, just as they had chanced to crack and tilt up in cooling. Now and then the slag started up so abruptly, that I can compare it with nothing else than pulled bread for ruggedness. The whole is scantily fringed with a copse of stunted birch, among which heather, which I have not seen since the first day of my journey, reappears. The bilberries and blueberries are ripe and frequent, while the arctic bramble with its bright scarlet fruit comes in for a share of my notice, both of eye and tongue. To my left, distant a mile or two, rise four great pyramids, black, red, yellow, purple in hue. The shower which darkened them just now has passed. See! a rainbow sits upon the infernal lava-surge around them, 'like Hope upon a death-bed;' and the sun lights on the red cone, gory as with fresh blood, shed in some battle of Titans. In front of me, a rigid line of dark-grey cliffs rise layer upon layer, block upon block, in perfectly horizontal courses. Even where water, or weather, or snow, or earthquake—why not the action of the sea?—has scored and carved out projecting battlements or pinnacles along this stupendous rampire; yet those same horizontal lines—inevitable and unbending as fate—may still be traced for miles, running with faultless regularity, like stories and string-courses, round every projection.

Cast your eye again southward, and behold that black tower shaped liked the chimney of a blasting furnace; standing so black and sharp athwart the sky. That is the Eldborg, or 'Castle of fire.' Inside it is a crater, some six hundred feet in diameter, rather oval than round, and about one hundred and seventy feet deep. Outside, the walls are much higher. Now, it echoes with the hollow murmur of the sweeping sea-breeze, the bark of the fox, or the hoarse croak of the raven, which builds its nest upon the sides; but once it belched fire, and boomed louder than the broadside of a whole fleet. But who am I that I should rush in with my commonplace talk, where Kratos and Bia, and Hephæstos, and Earth, and Air, and restless Ocean, should be the interlocutors! All we can do is to give the old Landnama explanation of these wonders. "Late one evening, (in the 10th century), a man of tall stature and truculent visage (illiligr) was seen rowing in an iron boat towards the land, near the mouth of the Kaldar-á. Going ashore, he drew near to a farm called Hrip, and dug a hole in the earth near the stable-door. The following night subterranean fire (jardelldr) burst forth and burnt the district of Borgarhraun; and where the farm stood, there is now the Borg*."

In the course of two or three hours we round the corner of the long line of mighty embattled ramparts, which I endeavoured to describe above, and enter Hytardal. Wading the river, and climbing up a beetling crag of lava, we find ourselves upon an upper level of the same igneous material. A few yards above, the stream does just the reverse of us, plunging downwards at a single bound from the upper level into a blue round pool walled with basalt; and then, eating its way into the very viscera of a mountain, discloses its many-coloured interior. From its base upwards this mountain has undergone such hard treatment from the hostile elements, that it looks like some giant in the last stage of consumption. Looking upwards, I perceive a sort of sentry-box, through which, blue sky is visible. From this airy turret, according to tradition, the outlawed Gretti used to dash down upon the passers by, and levy black mail with impunity. It is called to this day 'Grettisbaeli' (Gretti's bed); a name which will remind Scotchmen of the outlaw 'Barnhill's bed' on the crag in Teviotdale. Not less strange to behold is the configuration of the lava-field through which

* Landnama, P. II. cap. 5.

we now trot. Turrets, grottoes, and all sorts of weird-looking figures peeping out from among them; recalling to mind the forms that dogged Sintram in Dürer's picture.

A black cloud is scurrying after us, ambitious evidently of pouring the vials of its wrath upon the presumptuous intruders; but the road is good, and we ride apace, and are safe in the parsonage of Hytardal, when a violent snow-storm begins.

The church here is of stone: which is saying a great deal for it in this country. It is built on the site, and partly of the materials, of a more ancient edifice, which was destroyed one night, in the year 1148, during the visitation of Bishop Magnus Einarson, who perished with seventy-two others in the flames. In the outer wall of the church are two roughly hewn puffy faces, to one of which popular tradition has fitted the name of Hyt, the demoness and sponsor of the valley; but if so, she wore a beard, like the woman of Brentford. A cave near, also goes by the name of this Hyt. Looking down on the church from a neighbouring eminence are two colossal figures in stone. These statues are turned out of the studio of one who works on a grander scale than any member of the Academy; fire and earthquake, frost and tempest, being among her pupils.

Inside the church are some fair specimens of man's ingenuity and handiwork; which in my then mood were positively refreshing to behold. Nature's stupendous powers had been keeping company with me all day; Nature in her most sublime apparel; Nature girding herself with strength; by turns elevating the beholder into a state of fierce admiration, and then cowing his spirit into intense littleness; treating him like the imperious Brunhild did the subdued Gunther in the Nibelungenlied. But here man is re-asserting his supremacy. He has built for himself a fane to the Creator of all these things; and at once he adds cubits infinite to his stature, and ascends beyond Nature to Nature's God. From experience I would say, that the very best preparative for the full enjoyment and appreciation of anything like art, especially sacred art, is first to go through a course of this appalling Icelandic scenery. The altar-piece, which is of the 12th century, is of alabaster, gilt and coloured. It represents scenes in the life of our Saviour and the Virgin. The treatment is in the old German style of art. Another piece of sculpture, also in alabaster, is the Crucifixion. The massive brass chandelier, suspended from the roof, bears the date of 1616, with the legend:—

> Im Gottes Namen bin ich geflossen,
> Michellini hat mich gegossen.

The monastery, which formerly adjoined the church, was founded in memory of the above burnt bishop. Rein was first abbot in 1171. In 1539, Arne Arnorsen, a zealous Lutheran, was priest of Hytardal. His doctrines drew down upon him the wrath of that

Icelandic Wolsey, Jon Aresen, bishop of Holar, who was greatly opposed to the Reformation, and sought to bring Hytardal under his jurisdiction, although it was in the diocese of Skalholt. For some time, Arnorsen managed to set the bishop at defiance; but the end of it was, that a party of armed men came up the valley, seized the recalcitrant priest, laid him across a horse, and carried him thus all the way to Holar. Here he was confined on meagre diet in a cell under the buttery, which was so small and low, that he became curved like a hook *. At last his wife brought a large sum of silver, and adding to it her tears and entreaties, procured her husband's liberation; but not until he had taken an oath never to oppose the bishop again. He subsequently fell from his horse, and was drowned on the dangerous path near Stapi, under Snaefell. Jon Haldorsen, father to the author of Islandiæ Historia Ecclesiastica, became priest here in 1701. He was offered the bishopric of Skalholt, in succession to Jon Vidalin, but said, and meant it, 'Nolo episcopari.'

But in dwelling on these memorials of the past, I must not forget the neat modern parsonage, with its seven white gables, which stands alone in this sequestered spot. Over the chief entrance, a great white eagle with outspread wings, bidding the traveller welcome, was once the ornament of a luckless ship, driven ashore at the mouth of the river. Were it not

* Annálar Biorns á Skardsá, I. 145, 159.

for these waifs of the ocean, the architecture of Iceland, with the insuperable objection of the natives to using stone in building, would soon cease to be, even in its humblest form. Séra Thorsten Erlendsen Hialmarson, now the clergyman here, was presented to the living by the king of Denmark, it being one of the benefices in his gift. He performs the rites of hospitality with all the more zest, that the traveller is one of his cloth; exceeding glad to rub off some of the rust, which is liable to accumulate, perhaps most on polished minds, in out-of-the-world nooks like this. Indeed it looks like

> 'A waste land where no one comes,
> Or hath come, since the making of the world.'

I manage to get to bed without availing myself of my host's polite offer of the abigail's assistance in pulling off my inexpressibles—an Icelandic custom.

CHAPTER XXI.

The name-stone—Start for Stafholt—The priest and his familiar spirit—The Rape of Ruin—The Gliufrá—Fording a river by moonlight—Service in Stafholt church—Borgarfiord—The Egil-saga—Egil at the court of Athelstan—He is wrecked on the coast of Ireland—He composes a poem in the hour of death—The bereaved father—He resolves to scramble his treasures—He balks his heir presumptive—The author crosses the Hvitá—Reykholt—The pastor preaches in the presence of his own coffin—Snorri's bath—A fifty miles' ride over the mountains to Thingvalla.

SEPTEMBER 8.—This morning it is winter fairly, the ground being hard with ice. Before starting, I visit the 'Name stone,' a crag of yellow soft tufa, on which Henderson the missionary's name is cut in Hebrew characters, with the date of his visit, 1815. I must not forget to inform anglers—who I fear will have thought me a degenerate disciple of the craft—that, on Hytarvatn, three or four miles up the valley, there is a boat, and the lake abounds with large trout.

Behold me again on my travels. The little priest leads the way; his very curt legs swaddled in the favourite travelling dress, wide overall trousers, buttoned down the leg; his upper regions swathed in a superfluity of wraps, his long grey hair floating behind him, his brandy bottle and snuff-box not omitted; while his stumpy little horse looks not the less stumpy, that his long tail is knotted up tight to its root, so as not to whisk the lava-mud upon the august person of the rector of Hytardal. "Is it true, sir, that you have a Fylgia (familiar spirit)?" asked I, innocently. "A Fylgia! no, not I." "Oh! I beg pardon. But I read in the work of a recent German traveller in Iceland, that the Hytardal 'skotta' had taken to following you." "I like their impudence. I wonder who it was that palmed such a tale upon him. Follow me, forsooth! It *did* follow Séra Vigfuss; but he has been dead these hundred years and more." "So it didn't follow you once," said I laughingly, "to Stafholt, and appear there to the clergyman's wife in the form of a skeleton, which tried to embrace her" ..... The Hytardal skotta, to whomsoever at other times it might attach itself, certainly stuck to his reverence that day: for I frequently overheard him muttering, "Me have a fylgia! Ha! ha! I like that. It's not me, it was Séra Vigfuss." "A strange valley you live in, Séra." "You say true. When I ride alone sometimes, as I told the bishop, it almost sets my flesh creeping." "Hytardal!" said his right reverence to me, "It ought to be called Troll-dal." I soon found that the company of the parson of the parish does not expedite one's journey. Of course the few houses that he does pass, he must stop at. Kisses all round, brandy ditto: and it will go hard but it is coffee ditto at every one of them. Then, perhaps, Asgeir has had words with Thordisa, his helpmate; and the priest must say a word or two by way of trying to set the pair at one again. Perhaps this has been done before, and now they tell their pastor, that they have agreed to go to the Sysselman, who will pronounce a divorce, subject to the Amtman's approval. There was always a fatal proclivity to this among the Icelanders. Numerous instances of separation for slight causes are recorded in the Sagas. Uncharitable suspicion! but somehow it struck me before we got far on our journey, that my companion's utterance had rather thickened. But it can hardly be wondered at with this freezing air—although the sun shines bright—not to mention the fylgia that is haunting him, and then the desperate shake he got wading through that rocky watercourse, and now the ups and downs that we have encountered in traversing this Hraun Hrepp (Rape of Ruin)—just as a Sussexman would talk about the Rape of Bramber.

Turning our backs on the bogs and lava of Myrasyssel, we take a north-east direction up Hraundal (Ruin-dale), which does not belie its awe-inspiring name; and at length ascend the pass of Vestri Skardsheidi, abounding with lava and red pyramidical hills. Soon after, we cross the river, which comes from Langavatn, famous for its fish.* "This is called Biskupsbreka," said my companion. "Those cairns are set up to commemorate bishop Steingrim's passing this ford. I mind it well; we

* Nobody dwells on its shores now. The inhabitants were exterminated by the black death.

were a great gathering, hard upon two score; consisting of the chief people of three rapes; and here we took leave of the bishop. A most edifying spectacle, sir." Of which I had no doubt; perhaps a trifle ludicrous withal, if the episcopal outer man, and that of his apparitor and amanuensis &c. &c. at all approached in point of get up to the rig of the Dutch-built little craft, who formed a part of my own convoy. We ride on for miles, with the snow mountains of the interior gleaming far in the front; and at last descend the right bank of the Gliufrá, which is clothed with stunted birch-trees. The shadows of evening are gathering fast, and we have still two streams to cross, when some insane people struggle hard to make us stop and take coffee. "They will be offended if we don't," interposed the priest. "That we cannot help. I value my life at more than a cup of coffee." Riding through the Gliufrá was no easy task; as it was exceedingly rapid and deep, and the further bank rose like a wall, and a very crumbling one. Two months ago I should have hesitated before venturing on such an ugly place. But there is the Nordur-á still to be forded, and the daylight has failed. By the time we have passed over the intervening moor, however, the moon was shining brightly, bringing out the tall cone of Baula to the north-east.

"This must be the place," said the parson, as we came to the river-bank; "but you must follow me close. Me have a fylgia, forsooth! Ha! ha! ha! I wish I knew who told the German the story about me. It is not me, it was Séra Vigfuss that it followed, more than a hundred years ago." The matter has clearly made a deep impression on him, and I feel no doubt, that as he rides back alone through that hideous lava-defile, he will often look over his shoulder to see for the fylgia, if not, like father Philip in Scott's *Monastery*, encounter a spirit in reality. "Follow me close," reiterated his reverence, "the bottom is good, but a few yards right or left and the horse swims." As it was, the water of this great river reached to the middle of the saddle. By the moonlight it was difficult to know whether the horse was going straight or not, or whether he was swimming or wading. The further bank, too, is enveloped in gloom. High above the gurgling of the water, rushing against the near side of the horses, I could hear such words as—"Follow me straight," and then,—"Me have a fylgia! Ha! ha! ha!" We land safely; but the bank is too steep, so we have to ride under it for some space, till we can find a spot not beyond the horses' climbing powers. Both these rivers abound with salmon, as do all the numerous tributaries of the Borgarfiord. A Scotchman has leased the fishing in the Hvitá; but this year the take has fallen off still more than last year, which was less productive than the one preceding. He most likely fished it too hard at first. The Grimsá is said to have so abounded in salmon in the last century, that in the autumn the horses were alarmed at the rushing shoals of fish. It was after 9 P.M. that we arrived at the parsonage of Stafholt.

Next day, being Sunday, I attend the Church-service. Some seventy people of both sexes formed the congregation. Among the women were a few wearing the falldr, but the greater part wore the black cap with its silver ring, and silver pins fastening it to the back hair. Ascending to the pulpit, Séra Einar preached, as far as I could gather, a remarkably dull sermon on the Parable of the Ten Lepers. The discourse finished, came the prayer for the Royal Family, and then the Publication of the Banns of Marriage. The clergyman then returns to the altar, puts on a surplice, with the assistance of a peasant, and proceeds in the face of the whole congregation to administer the Holy Communion to seven men and as many women, who had that morning been shrived by him, without which previous ordeal nobody can receive the Sacrament. Before going up to the altar, the women unshawl themselves with the aid of an attendant female, likewise removing sundry kerchiefs from the head and neck, till, at last, they appear in neatly fitting dark jackets with double stripes of red along the seams, and the falldr on their heads. The whole family jewel-case has evidently been emptied to adorn them with studs, silver brooches and belts.

I liked this simple way of shewing reverence for the rite. They decked themselves as brides of Christ. And then, while the rest of the congregation looked devoutly on, the aged priest placed the consecrated wafer in the mouth of each kneeling communicant with the words "þetta er Jesú sanne likhami," (that is, Jesus' true body), and the wine with the words "þetta er Jesú sannarlegt blód), (that is, Jesus' true blood). As the priest walks to his house after the service, the peasant men and peasant women fall on his neck and kiss him, and I verily believe there was nothing of the Judas in their embrace. While we are at dinner, some pieces of petrified wood are brought in by a peasant from the riverbank. Surturbrand, I heard, also exists in the same spot, but I had no opportunity of inspecting the locality.

The neighbourhood of Borgarfiord is now chiefly celebrated for its breed of horses; one peasant owns a hundred and fifty. But it is known in history as the country of the powerful family of Egil Skalagrim, who, falling out with Harald Harfager, had nothing left but to seek the distant land discovered by Ingolf; and landed in Borgar fiord down yonder. His son Egil, the hero of the saga called by his name, did like all the likely young men of the island—tried his fortune in foreign parts—whence they not unfrequently came back nabobs. He appears to have united in himself all the qualities of an admirable

Crichton: a scald of the first flight, a warrior *sans peur et sans reproche;* a tower of muscular strength, an adept in magic. Besides which, he was the friend and ally of the English Athelstan in his war with Olaf of Scotland, so that no wonder he made a noise in the world. And when he returned home to his father with the news that King Athelstan had besought him to remain at his court, displaying at the same time his robe of honour and the two massive chests full of silver coin, which the King of England had given him, he would no doubt set the hearts of the youths of the district afire with emulation: while the honey, and malt, and rich cloth, he brought out from the hold of his galley, would help to keep up the excitement; the one giving strength and flavour to the yule mead and ale, the other being soon cut up into goodly vestments and adorned with heavy embroidery to grace the fair leaders of contemporary fashion.

The subsequent exploits of this Viking are full of romance. To King Erik Bloody-axe, who tried to cheat him of his inheritance in Norway, he bid defiance, and actually slew his son, Prince Ragnvald; finishing off his doings in Norway by setting up a horse's head on a pole in contempt of the King and Queen; the keenest insult and most damaging curse that those days wot of. The form of words which he used on this notable occasion were the following:—" I turn this horse's head towards the guardian spirits of this land, so that they may all be panic-stricken and never rest again till they have driven out King Erik and Queen Gunhilda:" and thereupon he fixed the pole fast in a rock-rift. This will remind those curious in Icelandic lore of one of the provisions of old Ulfliot's code—that no sea-borne ship should approach the island without first taking down the figure-head, for fear of frightening the guardian elves of the country. Erik soon found out how the spell worked. He was expelled from his throne; receiving however Northumberland as a fief from Athelstan, on condition that he should ward off the inroads of the Scots. Singularly enough, Egil not long after this was wrecked on the coast of Northumberland, and brought a captive to the court of the new jarl. Goaded on by Gunhilda, Erik is for slaying his captive that very night; but Arinbiorn, a Norwegian, and the faithful follower of the royal fortunes, but also an old friend of Egil's, dissuades him from it. To kill a man at night, he said, was sheer murder. "Compose a song in honour of Erik," he suggested to the doomed man. "Peradventure his fierce anger will be turned away." As anxious as the Eastern monarch for the captive prophet, he watched till midnight, and then stole to the dungeon. "How fares the song?" he asked of the prisoner. "Not a line composed yet," was the desponding reply. "That accursed swallow outside the window disturbs my meditations." Out sallied Arinbiorn, and saw something flit away in the gloom: like enough the captive's evil genius bent on his ruin. They now sat together till dawn, when the canticle (drapa) was finished. Who but a Viking could have collected his wits to compose a song with the blue-visaged Hel staring him in the face. Early in the morning, Arinbiorn again begged for his friend's life; but Erik, egged on by Gunhilda, refused to grant it. "Then I and my men-at-arms will defend him to the death." This threat softened the jarl: and at the same moment Egil, who had been brought into his presence, began to recite his poem. What with the flattery and fear of the consequences of such an assassination, the black-hearted jarl relented, and Egil was saved.

After this, he visits the court of the English Athelstan, and then Norway; but king Hacon Athelstan forbid him the country. This daring freebooter was not the man without a tear that some might have imagined him to be. When his eldest son, Bodvar, was drowned in the fiord, he himself found the corpse upon the shore, and buried it in the grave of old Skalagrim. Behold, then, the stern sea-rover in his agony of grief coming home from the funeral, and barring himself in his secret chamber. For three days and nights he neither eats bread nor drinks water. He cannot survive; he must go to his son; his wife Asgerde's tears fail to move him. In this strait, his favourite daughter Thorgerde, the wife of Olaf the Peacock, is summoned from Hiardaholt. She comes post haste. In those days the highways were smoother, and not so unoccupied as now. "Let me in, my father," she cried, "let me in. We will travel the same road together. If you go, I will not stay behind." She is admitted to the chamber of death. At length she says, "Father, were it not better to live yet a while; at least, till you have composed a dirge on Bodvar, and I have got it scratched on the rune-stave." He was in no mood for that, he thought, but he would try. And so he assayed the task; and anon he became inspired, and his death-muse soared with unflagging wing. And when the strain was finished, the Viking came forth from his chamber—the chamber of death no longer—and he sate him down on his throne of state, and bade them drink the grave-ale in memory of his son.

Many a year after this did the old warrior live in his stronghold, Borg, composing songs,—fragments of which are still extant, one of them a dirge on his friend Arinbiorn. In his latter days, a kind of coolness sprang up between him and his son and heir; but when it came to the point, and the family honour was called in question, the veteran forgot his animosity; and on the occasion of his son having a matter of consequence to settle at the Althing, the father rode thither with an armed retinue of eighty men, and helped him to win. So soon, alas! had the free republic degenerated into a tyranny, whereunder the old rule prevailed—

> "That those should take who had the power,
> And those should keep who can."

At the age of ninety, Egil's frame still gave evidence of its former giant strength; but the ear that had listed to the approbation of fair ladies as he sang their praises, or caught up so keenly the voice of the clarion braying to the boarding, was dull of hearing now: and the eye, that could have made out an argosy when it looked like a cloud-speck on the horizon was grown dim. The old man, like Milton, bewailed in verse that the windows were darkened; he moaned over the daughters of music brought low; but he thought not of making his peace with his Creator; had no hopes even of Valhalla, if he were to die the 'straw-death:' so why should not he journey once more to the parliament, and scramble his two boxes of English coin among the assembly, and get up a right royal fight for it. Capital! glorious! would not they battle for the silver! and then he might rush into the fray and perish in a sea of blood, and so be carried to Paradise by the Choosers of the Slain! But there were two words to that bargain. His son Grim entertained particular objections to the scheme, and would not hear of it. So, early one morning, Egil went out attended by two thralls, and having with him the two money-chests. Neither thralls nor chests were ever seen more; and Egil died soon after. But tradition did point to a certain lake near Mosfelt, where the treasure was supposed to be sunk; and above 140 years ago, people tell that some Anglo-Saxon coins were washed ashore near there.

But it is 6 P.M., and as I have no wish to become burdensome to my host, I ride for Reykholt, under the auspices of Gudmundr, one of the church-goers, who lives in that direction, and will shew us the way over two more of the rivers that flow into the Borgarfiord. The Tverá is big enough; but the skeleton in my closet is the Hvitá, the white river, which is not a bit less dangerous, and quite as clouded in colour as its namesake, which I waded, on the last day of July, on my course northward. The past night's rain was not in our favour. But Gudmundr knew what he was about. I tighten my girths and grasp my rein firmly, but lightly. "Have a care, sir. Keep the line, head up stream." A man lost his life just here since I have been in the country. And so we reach what is clearly a shoal in the stream, for the troubled waters rush over it with increased velocity. "Now, sir Englishman; we go down stream for a bit to that stillish place. Keep the line, whatever you do." Up-stream and down-stream seemed all the same to me now. I follow the chain of groaning horses mechanically through the icy current. "Now straight across," bawled the peasant, and the long string of horses swayed round, getting the whole force of the tide on their near shoulders and flanks. We were at last safe on the further bank. Leaving the river, we soon join the left bank of one of its feeders, the Reykholtsdal river, and enter a valley smoking with scores of steam jets. How many times we dashed across the river that night I am unable to tell; how many fumaroles ascending from hissing hot coppers we left behind in our rattling trot, travellers who have counted them will be able to say. At one place, I can discern in the gloom a sort of crater, in the centre of the water, throwing up white steam. The hot spring has puddled up for itself a regular coffer-dam, which has by degrees risen above the level of the river, and thus the boiling fountain can rise and fall, which it does at regular intervals, without fear of interruption. The distance to Reykholt proved much further than I had anticipated; so that it was after 9, and daylight gone, when the cheery voice of the monopthalmic Séra Vernhard Thorkilson bids the English priest descend and enter his abode.

The first thing to be done next day, September 10, was of course to visit Snorri Sturleson's bath, close by the parsonage. It is about twelve feet in diameter, by three feet and a half high. Round the bottom runs a ledge about six inches high. On the south side of the bath there is a waste hole, and on the east is seen the mouth of a subterranean channel of mason work, about nine inches square and one hundred and ten paces long,—I stepped it—which brings, or rather did bring—when it was not clogged with mud—the boiling water from the neighbouring spring, called Skribla. The worthy pastor has at his own expense repaired with Roman cement and cleansed this interesting relic of antiquity. A few steps descend into the bath, opposite which, in Snorri's time, there is said to have been a door into his stronghold (Virki). It was in this building that his enemies surprised and murdered him. A grass-grown knoll lies close to the bath; an aged peasant told me that it had been partly excavated, when some rotten beams were discovered.

Outside the church lies a Runic stone, which is said to be in memory of Snorri; but I saw no inscription. Upon one of the cross-beams inside the church is placed Séra Vernhard's future coffin. There is an Icelandic superstition, that this acknowledgment of Death's power is productive of longevity. There is no accounting for tastes. A king of Spain took pleasure in gazing at the great bronze chest wherein his remains were to be laid. The pastor's spirits were wonderfully good, and, for a man of seventy-six, the sprightliness of his conversation, and the ease with which he bestrode his steed, and piloted me across the bogs, was quite remarkable.

One Páll of Steindorstardir, a cottager up the valley, undertakes to guide me by a short cut over the mountains, which, avoiding the détour by Gilia, strikes into what is called the Ok-road, leading south to

Thingvalla, distant about fifty miles. "How many hours to Thingvalla?" asked I. "I know nothing about hours," replied Páll; "but you'll see the sun all the way if its fine, I think." His horse is soon caught, and we ascend the mountain; and at length see, across the flat waste, the circular Ok mountain before us, with a glacier hanging on his skirts. Behind it is Geitlands Jökul, a limb of Langjökul, which with Hofsjökul, and the enormous Vatnajökul, form the three largest ice-fields in the country. In Geitland's Jökul lies Thorisdal with its rich pastures, the fabled Utopia of Utilegumenn. Gretti was in hiding there. After about three hours' ride, we find the path we are in search of running south, by the foot of the Ok, and, as it is plain to see, we dismiss Páll. After some space, it joins the Kaldidalr path—the chief road between Reykjavik and the north. Anon rises to our left the vast Skialdbreid, from which poured down that stream of lava to Thingvalla. On looking at Olsen's map of Iceland, you see it coloured with light brown from this spot, where I now am, uninterruptedly to cape Reykianes. And that brown is explained to signify Hraun (lava). But how much of it is due to Skialdbreid, and how much to the other volcanic mountains, further south, we are not aware. Along the margin of this monstrous lava-torrent do we ride, not slowly either; for in parts the path is over sandy levels, and the S. W. breeze, which has brought a Scotch mist, makes us anxious to get over the journey. That solitary cabin of refuge near the path tells of the dangers that may beset the traveller before another week is out. After passing a lake or two, where a few swans, the last of their clan, were still lingering, we descend a curious narrow cleft over sand and cinders, and debouch upon a green plateau, called Hofmannaflötr, where the people from the North, bound for the Althing, after crossing the inhospitable Fjeld, rested for a while to bait their horses, and refresh and smarten themselves, previously to traversing the lava-bed between here and Thingvalla. To our right, rises the bulky Armansfell, in whose recesses somewhere is the grave of an Icelandic giant, Arman.

It had been my intention to keep along till we joined the road from Reykjavik to Thingvalla; indeed, I knew of no other means of reaching the latter place. But a peasant, the first human creature we have seen on the road, puts us into a track through the lava, direct to Thingvalla. Night is approaching, but if we hasten, there is still time, he says, to get over the difficulties, which in darkness are full of danger. In some places the solidified lava looked like coils of thick cordage. To twist ropes of sand is proverbially hard, but the lava seems a more tenacious and ductile material. The plain was grooved with many deep fissures, a slip into which would have been fatal. Winding through these with caution, we at last join the Almannagiá. I cannot resist the temptation of climbing up the eastern wall of this wonderful crack, and gazing at the Oxerá, as, strong with recent rain, it spreads its white wings gleaming in the twilight, and shoots like some great bird into the thick gloom below. What a ride of it we have had! Wet, weary, and stained with the variation of each soil between this and Reykholt, I am glad to pass from beneath the drizzling shades of night into the four walls of the parsonage. I cannot help confessing that in the evening of the first day of my travels, I contemned the humble abode, with its grass-grown roof resting on dwarf walls of unhewn stones; its fusty room, and its long, unflagged, dark passage leading thereto; to walk erect up which was to risk a compound fracture of the skull. But now the dungeon had turned palace. After hearing his reverence descant with all the animation he was capable of on the regeneration to be effected in Iceland by the North Atlantic telegraph, I was soon asleep in the not uncomfortable bed.

CHAPTER XXII.

A sure presage of good sport with the trout—We go astray—The legend of Lyngdalsheidi—A race with darkness—Mosfelt—A panorama—We cross the Bruará—Skalholt—The first bishop of Iceland—A pious fraud—Jon Gerikson—Lynch law—Waiting at the Ferry—Hreppholar—Basaltic columns—We cross the Thiorsá Storuvellir—A story of Grimsö.

SEPTEMBER 11.—A plentiful supply of trout was procured from the lake by breakfast-time this morning. They are taken as heavy as ten pounds; but whether the splashing of the elves' oars rowing across the water had been heard in the night, I did not ascertain. That sound is always a sure harbinger of good sport with the nets.* One more pop-visit to the Hill of Laws is a thing not to be foregone; where I throw myself back for a moment into those days when the travel-worn deputies came hither from the east and from the west, from the north and from the south, to hear the voice of their lawgivers. The only voice that now strikes upon the ear is the bleating of the pastor's sheep, which he, thrifty soul, has been depasturing lately in this marvellous sheepfold. And so the wild thyme, and the white and yellow galiums, and all

* Islensk aefintýri, p. 7. "Þad veit á goda silungsveidi i vatninu."

the flowers that had woven a fair chaplet upon the grave of departed glories, have been ruthlessly trodden underfoot. One more good stare at the waterfall, and to horse. The priest assures me, that it is only four hours ride to Mosfelt; so that the tired nags will have a comparative rest to-day. My guide, instead of following the directions given him, persisted in clinging to a small path that hugged the north-eastern shores of the lake. After a ride of three hours we got to a cottage on the eastern shore; where I learn that we have gone wrong, and are now further from our destination than when we started. What a state of mind I was in! The poor horses, too, after their forced march of yesterday! But there is no help for it. So we ride across the interminable grey and brown Lyngdalsheidi, with the Kalfstindar in front of us, in order to regain our lost track.

But the reader will weary of the way; so, to beguile its tedium, I will tell him a story of this desolate heath. Somewhere near may be seen the ruins of an ancient *châlet,* which once belonged to the farmer of Kaldarhofda. Solveig, his buxom daughter, was often the only tenant of it in the days and nights of summer. One morning, she was looking for her sheep, when who should suddenly stand before her but a remarkably good looking man, dressed in a scarlet mantle. "Sael vaer-tu," (Hail to thee!) he said in Icelandic fashion, "Hail! my lovely May. You don't know how often I have sat and watched you when you were milking the ewes" . . . Well, the long and the short was, that when Solveig recovered from her surprise, she was fast locked in the embrace of the stranger. After this she often met him on the heath. At last, she became the mother of a boy, which her lover took away with him as soon as it saw the light. Later on, she wedded a peasant, a respectable man, at Villingavatn. Twelve years after this, she was sitting with her husband before the door of their dwelling, when suddenly she became very sleepy. An infallible sign this that visitors of importance were at hand. Sure enough, two strangers presently arrive; a grown up man, and a handsome lad. The moment Solveig catches sight of them she rushes into the house, and does not reappear the whole of the evening. Next day is Sunday, and the Sacrament is to be administered at the distant parish church. Before starting thither, all the members of the household, after the good old custom, embrace each other, and ask pardon for any offence they may have given wittingly or unwittingly. Solveig omits to do this to the two strangers before leaving the door. But, at her husband's earnest entreaty, she returns into the house to do so; weeping, however bitterly, and saying to him, "Long will you rue this!" As she does not return, her husband goes in for her, and—lo! she lies in the arms of the elder stranger. Both are dead; and the boy stands beside them in tears. After a space, he recounts to the peasant how the two had met in former years; and how he was the son born unto her . . .

But we must be in the proper route at last. For here is Apavatn, renowned for its char and trout. "Ask if we are right for Mosfelt!" shouted I to Jon; "but no gossip, no coffee, no delay of any kind; mind that." We have still two hours of it, I find, and the path even by daylight, which is now failing, is invisible in places. Bogs and marsh-meadows don't retain the marks of footsteps long, and such there are here in plenty. Away we tear splash-dash, hurry-skurry, helter-skelter, down steep banks, through deep torrents, across swamps. It is a race between us and darkness which shall descend on Mosfelt first. Darkness won it, but still we rode on. The horses with their wonderful instinct knew that the much-coveted hour was at hand, when they might halt, and cast off their burdens; and so they tasked all their acuteness to decipher the path. The darkness was all the thicker that a steep mountain now held us in its shadow; when the rushing cavalcade suddenly comes to a dead halt. In a few moments we became aware of the proximity of buildings, and presently, the pastor's family are roused from their peaceful slumbers. Séra Jon is away performing the last sad rite over the remains of a brother clergyman; but a messenger is despatched by daylight to apprise him of the arrival of the English priest, and he returns to welcome me.

Meantime, September 12, I am not neglected. His mother, an intelligent dame, who is connected by marriage with more than one Icelandic bishop, undertakes to shew me the sights. Under her auspices I ascend the steep isolated mountain which impends over the church; and well rewarded was I for my trouble. It was a beautiful, mild, sunny morning, with gentle north-westerly airs, and the atmosphere tolerably clear. Away to the east rose Hekla, and at my feet, in the same direction, between the great rivers Bruará and Hvitá, lay Skalholt. A glimmer in the south-west indicates the course of the ramping Thiorsá. Beyond it stands Ingolfsfiall; the burial-place of Iceland's first settler Ingolf. Southward is a far-reaching plain, terminated by the straight steadfast sea-line; while, below the mountain, on the north, lies the tranquil Apavatn, and, beyond it, Laugardal, with steam-jets from its boiling springs rising high in the lazy air; though the Geysers proper are hidden by a shoulder of the line of cliffs, which bound the northern side of the valley. Somewhere in this mountain whereon I stand is a hidden treasure. One Ketilbiorn wished to dedicate a beam of silver to the neighbouring temple. His heirs presumptive interposed, to prevent the execution of his pious design. So he secretly determined to devote the treasure to the earth, mother of all treasures, and he succeeded in burying it nobody knows exactly where.

In the parsonage I see two of those boards, four or five feet long, adorned with rude carving, which the stranger in Iceland puzzles himself to divine the meaning of. They are called Rumfiöl, and were anciently used to prevent the bedclothes falling off, on the outer side of the berth (rum). A mile off is the ferry over my old friend the Bruará, here very deep, but with none of that rabidity that he exhibits at the eponymous bridge above; as those placid swans, gorging themselves yonder with the delicious grass that clothes the shallows, know full well.

'Dulcibus in stagnis rimantur prata Caÿstri.'

The morass however is so blind to the ferry, that the mile thither takes us a good hour.

Skalholt, that is the single farm-house now representing the place, stands on an eminence, just in the fork formed by the junction of the Bruará and Hvitá, and overshadowed on the south by the tall Vordufell. As may at once be perceived, the site of the episcopal residence was chosen with great tact and forethought. In the first place, there was abundance of grass in the fertile Biskupstunga to fatten the beeves and palfreys of the bishops. And as for fish, there were waters enough around to supply the extensive demand; and hot springs too to cook them when caught; or, if requisite, to wash the ecclesiastics. But what was of great importance, Skalholt was secure against hostile surprise on every side but the north-east, in consequence of the river-barriers about it. A stone lying near our path close by the church is reputed to be the identical block on which the proud bishop Jon Areson was beheaded.

Here in 1080, died Isleif, who, after studying at the University of Erfurdt, became the first bishop of Iceland. Here dwelt his son bishop Gissur; who, by the advice of that most learned of all Icelandic priests, as the old chronicler says, Saemund hin Frodi, —magician, poet, philosopher, polyhistor—introduced the use of tithes into Iceland 1096. Thirty-six years did he rule in Skalholt, and died here A. D. 1118, being the same year in which *pope Pascal and Baldwin, king of Jerusalem, deceased. Very little now remains to shew the former importance of the place. The present little church is merely a chapel of ease. Grass-grown mounds to the south-west of this edifice indicate the site of extensive ecclesiastical buildings. Yonder, an enclosure marks the large episcopal garden. There are also the foundations of a prayer-house to the east of the church, measuring twelve paces long and six wide. No carved stones are to be seen, with the exception of one or two narrow flat tomb-stones in the churchyard; one of which states that 'Gudrun Biornsdatter sofnade 1633.' Singularly

* Kristnisaga, p. 119.

enough, part of the inscription is written lengthways, and part across the stone.

Bishop Thorlak's relics are not here now. He was canonized in 1198. His skull with age or damp had crumbled into dust; but bishop Wilkins (†1406) set matters to rights. A large cocoa-nut-shell was driven ashore, and he adroitly placed the shell in the place of the cranium; but now shell and skull are alike gone. Gone too is the valiant Skarphedin's axe, "the ogress of war," which was long preserved here. Some curious old embroidered vestments are shewn me, as well as an antependium, adorned with silver gilt bracteates, two inches in diameter. These are reputed to have been given to the church by Thorgunna a troll wife, (? a Hebridean crone,) on condition that she should be buried in the consecrated ground. While digging the grave, the sexton was horrified by her wraith, which stood over him and said, "Ye need not dig so deep, I shall not lie there long." The ancient chalice is of silver gilt, and adorned with enamel paintings of some merit, representing the scourging of our Lord, the crucifixion &c. In the aisle are a few bishops' tombstones, but of comparatively modern date. That in memory of bishop Arneson bears the legend "Placidissime in Domino obdormivit ad diem VIII. Feb. Anno Christi MDCCXLIII."

These bishops did not always 'fall asleep' so

tranquilly. Let us sit on this stone while I tell you a sad story of the end of Jon Gerikson, a Swede, who was bishop of Skalholt in the 15th century. This ecclesiastic had thirty Irish domestics, fierce desperadoes, (miög ómilda,) very Berserkers, whom the bishop even had hard work to keep in check, and who were the terror of the whole country-side. At last, a noble youth, Ivar Vigfusson was murdered, at the instigation, as it was said, of one Magnus, a reputed son of the bishop's, who had made proposals of marriage to Ivar's sister, Margaret, which she had rejected. Margaret now gave out that she would only marry the avenger of her brother. Thorvard Loptson undertook the task. In the year 1433, on the eve of the festival of St. Thorlak, he came with many others, and pitched his tent in the neighbourhood. Next day, while the bishop was celebrating mass in the church, Thorvard entered the edifice. The bishop, suspecting how matters stood, retreated to the altar, bundled on his gorgeous robes, and seized the chalice, an expedient not untried by other ecclesiastical functionaries in different ages of the world, whom however the horns of the altar failed to protect from the due punishment of their crimes. But the avengers of blood were no more intimidated by the sanctity of the spot than was Reginald Fitzurse at a like juncture. They force the struggling prelate from the altar and out of the church. Here he asks a domestic for water, which is brought him in a large vessel of silver. The bishop drains it in haste, and is led by his foes to their encampment. Thence they drag him to the Bruará, and drown him in it with a stone tied to his body. Margaret kept her vow; she gave her hand to Lopston, who became the happy father of three daughters. It was murder no doubt. But the bishops were murderers too. They assassinated Icelandic liberty. Originally chosen by the people, they afterwards came to be appointed by the archbishops of Trondjem, and were the tools of Norway, and fomentors of those civil discords which led to the downfall of the free state.

Descending to a spot where the turbulent Hvitá, charged with the melted snows of a thousand mountains, and the filtering of morasses unnumbered, makes a sharp curve, and consequently induces a back stream favourable to the ferryboat; we hail the ferryman, who lives under Vardofell. Our united voices at length elicit from the distant cottage one Ingvialda, a stout black-eyed woman, wearing her brown hair cut short like a man's, whose broad good-tempered mouth responded 'Gudsfrid!' in answer to our greeting. In episcopal times, the ferry-service was on a much better footing than now. Close by the landingplace are the ruins of a hut, where the boatman was always in attendance to put passengers over. At this ferry in 1595, the people, coming from Skalholt church, saw a monster as big as a house, with the head of a seal. I am not aware whether he was captured.

What a magnificent evening for a ride! We trot briskly over the level meadows where the haymakers are busily engaged gathering in fragrant hay, sloping stacks of which rest in numbers against the farm-houses, thatched with long strips of greensward. In the north the hay is covered up in semi-underground houses made for the purpose. Sunset has been succeeded by a chill air, which makes the smoking steamjets on the other side the river more conspicuous. Yonder, to the south-east, lies Eyafiallajökul, its snows bathed in rose-colour; to the north is Bläfell, and on this side of it that quaint range, the Jarlhettur (the hats of the Jarls). Deep shadows contrast picturesquely with the rich light which the highest peaks still retain—like affectionate friends—the last to bid adieu to, the first to welcome, the brightness of the great luminary. We have another, and by no means a small, river to ford, but the yellow-haired Ranveig shews us the place, and the cavalcade of horses is soon over with the usual quantum of clatter, bubble, squelch, splash, consequent on the horses' stamping with high uplifted forefeet among holes and stones invisible to their eyes. At half-past eight p. m. we arrive at Hreppholar.

Sept. 13. The warm sun soon softens the frost,

with which the ground is encrusted. Outside the door is a long basaltic pillar used to tie horses to. On inquiry, I find that it comes from some hills a little to the north-east. These, which are all rounded and abraded at the top, are composed, I find, entirely of basaltic columns, the heads of which crop out above, fitting as closely together as those on which one steps at the Giants' Causeway. In one of them, from a convulsion of nature, or some other cause, the great fagot of basaltic columns forming the mountain has burst loose, and a quantity of them hang over at various angles, so as to form a kind of penthouse. So loosely did they seem to hang, that I felt it quite a relief when I had issued from under the shed. They are all apparently five-sided, and exceedingly regular in shape. The country around abounds with these hills, which give its name to the place.

My host, the clergyman, rides with me across the Salmon river—not the same as I crossed last night—and we are soon on the banks of the Thiorsá. It was my intention to have crossed an arm of the river, to visit the ancient provincial seat of judicature on an island; but as there is no boat, and swimming would very likely be necessary, I left the Domhring to be investigated by more enterprising travellers. Along the banks of the river are fragments of whity-brown pumice, the produce of Hekla's eruption in 1845. Here we are at the Nautavad, (the ferry.) The river as broad as the Thames at Westminster, and the water as thick as snow-water and mud can make it, rolling, too, most rapidly, while the boat itself is half full of water. The horses have a long swim for it. Whether it is the fright, or the cold, or the violent exertion, I know not, but their barrels are always blown up very much after an operation of this kind. But now their troubles and alarms are over, and, according to custom, they are rolling joyously in the black sand, which renders their proper colours quite undistinguishable. A short ride over a sandy plain, covered with short pasture, and then through some old lava, brings us to Storuvellir. The priest, Séra Gudmundr Jonson, promises to accompany me up Hekla to-morrow, weather permitting, and to mount me into the bargain.

For two years he was clergyman at Grimsö, that strange island due north of Iceland. "And are the people there like the inhabitants of the rest of the country?" asked I. "Oh! no: they are a very reserved race, so mysterious and suspicious; they always seem as if they had something they wished to conceal. I could not make them out at all." "And did you see any of the supernatural appearances for which the island is so famous?" "Well, do you know, a very curious thing happened to me. One winter's night, when all the family was in-doors, I distinctly heard a tap, tap, at the window: then another.

'Who's there?' I asked. No answer. 'Thorgrim, bring me my gun,' said I; 'I think it is loaded. Now you, Oddr and Olaver, look out of the door, while I fire through the window, if that noise is repeated.' Nothing however would persuade them to look out. I stood with the gun presented, but the tap was not heard again. All the people were greatly alarmed, and could not sleep; so we sat up till very late. When I at last got to bed, I heard a sound on the roof of the house, as of some heavy creature moving on it. We lay still, and at last the noise ceased altogether. Now, what in heaven's name was it?"

"I should say, some wag, who wished to frighten you all. Your houses are so constructed that, on one side or the other, the roof is on a level almost with the ground; so the person might easily retire thither, when he heard the threat of the gun. You remember in the Niála, Skarphedin gets on the roof of Starkadr's house, and the people inside think it is a sheep." "But in that case there would have been footmarks. In the morning we examined the snow all round the house. It had not snowed in the night, but we could see no traces whatever. Now I will vouch for the truth of all this; for I heard the tapping, and also the noise on the roof, most distinctly. The people in the house said it was the Skrimsl." "Or perhaps the Haffru, the maid with the beautiful golden hair," said I, "looking after you, or some of the other bachelor lads about. If rumour does not lie, she does sometimes carry off the fisher-boys, while asleep in their boats." But the good priest shook his head solemnly; he felt there was something of a very mysterious character about the nocturnal visitation, that was not to be dismissed with a joke.

CHAPTER XXIII.

A vakur hest—Trout cooked in their native river—Ascent of Hekla —The church of lava—The cinder surge—A dangerous chasm—Fire and snow side by side—Séra Gudmundr breaks down—I reach the highest peak—What a scene!—Three cheers for Iceland!—Descent of the mountain—Obrennisholmi—A million steam-jets—Return to the manse—Horse lost—A dust-fog.

SEPTEMBER 14.—A keen frosty night was succeeded by a glorious quiet sunny morning: and at 9 A. M. I was mounted on a very powerful skewball, a runner, the favorite nag of the clergyman's lady. Like the camel, and the horses of South America, the 'vakur hest,' as the Danes call him, moves his two near legs, and then his two off legs, together, swinging either shoulder alternately; and though it requires a little practice to adjust oneself to the unwonted movement, it saves a good deal of fatigue in a long day; and no rising in the stirrups is required. An Icelander will always give more for a runner than for another horse. At first, our path lies over an extensive plain, encumbered with ancient lava blocks; covered in many places with drift-sand, where *Arundo arenaria* has fixed its roots; while here and there are funnel-shaped holes, the seeming bottom of which is covered with rank vegetation. But, below this lowest deep there is a deeper still, in the shape of horrid rents and cracks, not easy to be discovered. In about two hours we ford the Vestri Rángá (i. e. wrong or crooked river), which goes winding and twisting among a number of low hills, and is in places deep and dangerous. A flock of wild geese rise from the river-bed as we approach. The water is cold enough now, but on September 2, 1845, it was smoking hot. The evening before, the snow, which now glistens again on the summit of Hekla, had suddenly melted, and all was black there. Down rushed a torrent of hot water, filling the Rangá to its very brim, and the trout lay cooked upon the shore.

> Τείροντ' ἐγχέλυές τε καὶ ἰχθύες, οἳ κατὰ δίνας,
> Οἳ κατὰ καλὰ ῥέεθρα κυβίστων ἔνθα καὶ ἔνθα
> Πνοιῇ τειρόμενοι πολυμήτεος Ἡφαίστοιο.—

"Ay," exclaimed the priest, "I was at Grimsö then, many a long mile to the north; when about 3 P. M. on that day I heard what seemed to be the noise of several guns firing; and thought that the French man-of-war in the offing was giving notice to the fishing boats that the season was now closed.* But it was Hekla thundering away, and not the French."

Our path now threads a pretty copse of dwarf birch, a small remnant of the woods devastated by successive eruptions, with the great square-headed Burfell in front of us, so called, I believe, from its fancied likeness to a provision-house in shape; while

* 7000 French fishermen are said to be employed every summer on the coast of Iceland.

Hekla's snowy 'cloak' overtops him to the east, every patch of white on his scored top distinctly visible. Close under a line of fells stretching southward is a pretty little green oasis, in which lies nestled the farm of Naefreholt, where we hope to procure a guide. Jon Jonson *père* is away from home, but his son, who has never been up the mountain, by the bye, is willing to help us to find the way, and is speedily rigged in his best, and astride of his grey pony. Luckily we stumbled upon his father among the fells, and, to save time, as the day is wearing, he puts on his son's clothing, and for two dollars—a moderate sum—expresses himself ready to accompany us. We are speedily in a green plain between two ranges of lava-cliffs. It looks good riding, but great care must be taken, as what we tread on is mere slag, loosely thrown together, and covered over with mossy turf, but abounding with concealed pitfalls. "This is the nave of the church," said the intelligent Jon Jonson, as the flat valley narrowed into a sort of doorway, made by the hills closing in; "and here is the choir," continued he, as at the further end of the nave we passed through what, by a little stretch of the imagination, might be construed into another ruined archway, the only roof being yonder blue canopy on high. And let me tell the reader, that in Iceland the fancy will run riot upon very little provocation. Nature, however, has done so much, that one has only to try to photograph her feats, to present a picture astonishing to contemplate.

And now, gradually ascending, we get upon slopes of black sand, strewed with fragments of shiny black lava—grooved some of it like the mouldings of a cornice—pumice, cinders, and all the indigestible eliminations of Hekla's overloaded stomach, after his various bilious attacks. Trotting sharply along, we are presently beside a wall of cinders and slag, lying on our left, while to the right a mountain covered with scanty moss slopes down towards the wall. "We must leave the horses here," said the guide, as we came to an arm of the slag stream which barred all further riding. And forthwith the four steeds are tied heads and tails in a circle, to prevent them moving during our absence. Rounding the steep mountain shoulder, we begin to clamber over the stupendous cataract, part of which, being the issue of the last eruption, is loose and of a glaring brown, as if it had been rolled hither but yesterday; unmellowed alike in tint and texture by the insinuating moss which smoothes over ancient lava. The vast scale of Icelandic pyrotechnics is certainly seen here to advantage. Lumps of slag of all sizes and the fretfullest shapes, piled loosely together, heaps upon heaps, to the height of some sixty feet. What ascending and descending over this broken cinder surge! What rattling of the fragments after us as we based our feet on, or clung with our hands to, the pointed juts, dislodging them with a mere touch! Everything sharp and angular here: Nature wears an iron mask. No rounded outlines or graceful forms, unless you except Mr. Punch, whose strongly-marked physiognomy is nodding to us there in all the blandness of his approximating nose and chin. Icelandic sheep or seal-skin shoes are no proof against such travelling, and before long Séra Gudmundr puts on his reserve pair, the others being past all clouting. Our escalade, however, only lasted a few minutes, and then up we go, as before, the main cinder-wave being as a wall to us on our left hand; the black sand on which we tread rendered less heavy by being frozen.*

After ascending in this wise for another hour, the wall, which was a capital protection against giddiness, ceases, and we have to cross a slope of frozen snow or ice, where to slip would be to roll to destruction, while a crevasse has to be crossed by a suspension bridge which no government inspector would have certified as safe even for foot-passengers. After some more sand and cinder

* Of course if the material of the stream had been fused lava instead of cinder, it would, like any other fluid, have found its level and not assumed this wall shape. Professor Daubeny's observation, when describing a similar phenomenon in the vicinity of Ætna, applies here: "It had all the appearance of a huge heap of rough and large cinders, rolling over and over upon itself, being the effect of extremely slow propulsion from behind." *Volcanoes*, p. 285.

climbing, a vast cleft right into the mountain opens out to our left, and just outside the entrance of this Augæan stable is the fag-end of that filthy offscouring, which the subterranean scavenger has spread broadcast for leagues. A little above this we reach the first of the three peaks which constitute the summit of Hekla. "Ay! sir," said the guide, "you see the mountain is klofin í tvent (cloven in twain). Hekla may spue again, but he will never spue so far, for the giá (crater) is open at both ends." Looking down into this Tophet—one of the mouths of hell in the belief of ancient Iceland—I see lying in it quantities of snow, near which steam-jets are ascending, indicating the near presence of active subterranean heat. "Now then, sir priest," said I, looking towards a very narrow ridge leading upwards to the second peak, "we have only this to cross." "It is impossible," responded he, as if in desperation. "I am giddy, and faint, and footsore." "But take my hand, brother priest." "No sir, it is impossible; Sylla here, Charybdis there; the crater on one side, and that hideous slope on the other. No, sir," he murmured faintly, as he sat down on the snow with rueful countenance, "I've come far enough.

'Est quodam prodire tenus, sed non datur ultra.'

I'll await your return here." "But those terrible ravens with iron beaks will be making mincemeat of you." "Leave me, I beg, I can't go further."

I was soon over the sharp straight ridge, covered on the one side curiously enough with snow, while on the other side not a particle of snow remained; reminding me of those pictures one sees at the railway stations, exhibiting the marvellous power of a certain hair-dye, where one side of the head is clothed with black, the other with white hair. About the cone, vapour was issuing at intervals from the black sand; while in the crater itself, some hundred fathoms below, were gaping ice-holes, and great masses of snow side by side with sulphureous steam-jets. I can bear witness that the poet, who used Hekla as an illustration of blowing hot and cold in a breath, was quite true to facts. Strangely enough, while one part of the cone was quite cold on the surface, from another spot, higher up, steam was issuing, shewing the heat to be local and dependent on the inflammable nature of the strata.* Very near the top of the peak I dig a hole a yard deep, when my Fahrenheit, being placed in it, and the hole covered over with my map case, rose speedily from 30° to 89½°.

* At Langenaes E. Olafson, upon boring, discovered that the heat began at 2 feet below the surface. Below this he came to a violet coloured layer of soil of sulphurous odour, where the heat was at the greatest. Lower still, it grew less and less, till at the depth of 10¾ feet there was no heat at all. At Krisuvik, he met at the depth of 5 feet with a layer 5 feet thick very hot; at 12 feet, the greatest heat; below this the heat diminished; upon boring deeper, muddy hot water spouted from the orifice to the height of 8 feet; so that a new boiling-spring was called into existence, ebbing and flowing at intervals.

I now saw that the last or easternmost peak was highest. "Most people are content to come as far as this," said the guide. "Not I, however; and so we slid down the snow, which filled in the gorge between us and the other peak; passing carefully over a crevasse or two, and feeling with our staves for fear of concealed abysses, which abound. Oddly enough, although this third peak has considerably more snow upon it, and has all the appearance of being of a most frigid, phlegmatic, disposition, a narrower inspection convinces me that there is really a great amount of local heat within. As we clamber up a ridge—the precipitous edge of which, festooned with long icicles, walls in a very deep, ferruginous coloured, crater—steam is ascending in all directions. Inserting my hand in the soft black sand, I find it difficult to keep it there owing to the heat, and regret that my thermometer is left on the second peak; so that I cannot ascertain the exact temperature. On the very summit of this peak lies a massive cantle of smooth lava. In the crater below, which is really a continuation of the other two—Hekla being what is called a linear volcano—though deeper to our eye from the precipice being loftier, several vivacious steam columns are at work. One of which, of great height, my man compares to the Strokr. The crater here exhibits its other exit; and I now perceive the full force of Jonsen's remark, that the mountain is cloven in twain. The rent is curvilinear in shape.

Out of this door a stream of the usual ingredients has descended, and its dreadful brown may be viewed winding downwards into the fire-stained desert below.

What an unearthly scene presented itself! Around us cone upon cone, black and arid! What is not black is white, as witness yonder Jökuls to the south-east; and what is neither of these colours is of a bilious yellow, or fiery red, as are that clump of mountains to the eastward. Battle it, ye elements of fire and frost; now one, now the other; 'tis hard to say which of ye has the best of it. Yonder thin streak of grey smoke curling upwards into the bright blue heavens is fire's ensign, in token of her victory in that direction*. It marks the position of the Kötlugiá volcano, whose roof of snow and ice has been melted, or hurled miles away, by the recent eruption, till the mountain is all of a dark colour. To the south-east is a strip of water, which the guide says is the Kudafliot, one of Iceland's largest fiords. Here and there the eye catches a glimmer of the Thiorsá; and now and then one of the cluster of tarns (Fiskavötn), that lie on this side of that immense snow and ice wilderness, called the Vatna, or Klofa, Jökul, which is said to cover a space of 3000 square miles, i. e. more than half Yorkshire. To

* I quite believe that I saw vapour ascending from Kotlugiá; so did the rest of us; but I heard afterwards that the active symptoms had ceased.

the northward rise masses of mountains of every conceivable shape, while, nearly south, separated from the coast by an apparently narrow creek, lie the Westmann Islands, sharp and distinct beyond belief. On neither of the other peaks is there so extensive a view as from this last.

Three cheers for Iceland! and down we spin over the snow-blocked ravine, and up the second peak; whence I can descry the unfortunate priest, crouched up, as if he were frozen stiff. But a cry from us rouses him from his melancholy ruminations. On our descent, for the pastor's sake, we keep more to the east, thus avoiding the slippery slope of frozen snow, which was certainly not without danger. Instead of it, we traverse deep lava sand-beds of great steepness, through which we can plunge safely with great celerity. Recrossing the slag-stream, we rejoin our horses, which had actually managed to move in their circle, and, unlike some reasoners, to make an advance notwithstanding. "Yonder," said the guide, looking westward, "is what we call 'Obrennisholmi' (Unburnt Island), pointing to an insulated grass-grown elevation, surrounded by lava, which embraces it like the great snake does Midgard in the Edda." "And what is that?" asked I, pointing to a million spiracles of steam rising from the rugged waste of lava. "That is the Hraun smoking, it has not yet cooled. We often see that smoke in the evening when it is getting chill." It was indeed an astonishing sight, but one which I should be inclined to attribute to hot springs beneath, rather than to the latent heat of the lava; which, in the twenty-five years which have elapsed since the last eruption of Hekla, must have entirely cooled: though in one case, I believe, in this country, erupted lava is known to have retained its heat for eleven years. We have not descended a bit too soon. For see! the mountain's top is covered with a dense fog. Had we been caught in that, we should have had a cold night of it. Careering down the sand slopes, we are not long in arriving at Naefreholt, where Una Haldorsdatter, the wife of Jonson, has prepared us coffee, and a savoury mess of boiled lamb. Without his aid, to get to Storuvellir to-night would be impossible. As it is, we have to fetch a great circuit, to avoid the treacherous lava. Eventually, aided by the moonlight, we arrive at 11 o'clock P. M. at the manse, after a most successful and exhilarating day.

September 15. I am forced to remain a fixture here to-day. One of the horses has disappeared. Scouts have been despatched in all directions to find him, but to no purpose. "I fear," said mine host, "he has fallen into one of those holes in the lava you saw yesterday. The rank grass inside them is very slippery; and he will not be the first horse that has broken his neck in that way." I myself went in search of the missing beast; at the same time despatching the guide to the ferry over the Thiorsá by the path which we had come two days before. For my own part, I soon gave up the search, and was only too glad when I had found my way back to the parsonage. It was early morning, but the air was obscured by a cloud of drifting sand, borne along sky-high by a strong east wind. This is one of the most terrible scourges of maltreated Iceland, known alike in the south and north of the country. Let the wind blow hard over the arid desert of Sprengisandr, or elsewhere in the interior, and it soon catches up the fine sand, bearing it for miles and miles, and rendering, in process of time, fruitful plains desolate; but poorly compensating for this devastation, by covering over the stony lava—as it has done in the plain hereabout — with a coating subservient to a scanty vegetation. The storm blinds and chokes man and beast, and to advance against it is quite impossible. The guide is away all day, and I begin to fear that he is lost too. Late in the evening however he returns with the animal, which had wandered a long distance. How he could find him in this dust-fog was a mystery to me.

CHAPTER XXIV.

Thingskáli—Knafahólar—Fearful odds—A fine old Icelandic gentleman—Breidabolstadr—Wrestling a national sport in Iceland—Ride to Hlidarende—The delta of the Markafliot—Icelandic corn-growing—A striking landscape—The saga of burnt Niál The murder of Gunnar—His Irish hound—Bergthorshvoll—A tragedy—The burners—"For better for worse"—The parsonage of Oddi—Saemund the Learned—His adventures with the Evil One—The black art school at Padua—The ferry over the Thiorsá —We arrive at Eyrarbakki.

EARLY next morning the priest escorts me over the ford of Ydre Rángá, which is deep enough, but free from great stones. Close by it is all that remains of the ancient Thingskáli, or hall of provincial judicature. The site of the booths which used to be occupied by Niál and Gunnar is plain to be seen. They lay parallel and close to each other. The foundations were of stone, rising a yard or so above the ground; upon these was a superstructure of wood or turf, with possibly an awning over all. Fixed in the turf-grown wall of the adjoining house is a stone about sixty inches long, said to be the old execution-stone. Many a victim's shriek, as his back was broken athwart that slab, must have resounded down the hollow dell, which sweeps past this interesting spot. The pastor here takes leave with an affectionate kiss, and we trot across the sands by the directest and flattest road in Iceland towards Keldur.

We are now in the country made famous by the most interesting of all the Icelandic sagas — the story of Burnt Niál. Observe these two conical grass-grown knolls, perhaps eighty feet high apiece, one on either side the way. These are the Knafahólar; the scene of an exploit of Gunnar's, not surpassed by anything recounted in history or legend. Gunnar, with his two brothers, Hiort and Kolskegg, had been on a visit to his friend Asgrim, beyond the Thiorsá, about eight weeks before winter. It having been reported to Starkardr, Gunnar's deadly foe, who dwelt under that three-cornered mountain which rises in front of us, that the pleasure-party would return on a certain day, he, with other assassins, thirty in all, planted themselves here in ambush. As the travellers approach these two hills, Kolskegg exclaims, "See, my brother, there are many spears glancing behind the hills, and now I discern several armed men." "My prophetic dream!" replied Gunnar, "Let us ride forward to the tongue of land by the river; then we cannot be surrounded." They had only just reached the spot he indicated, when the band of cut-throats overtook them. Gunnar had no shield; but his deadly bow and arrows kept his adversaries at bay. They close, and arms and feet were soon flying about, smitten off by Gunnar's axe and sword. Even in legitimate warfare, to strike below the breast, which was scouted as an infamy by the laws of chivalry, was by the northmen considered no scandal. Long did the unequal contest rage; but the address and strength of Gunnar were invincible. Fourteen of his enemies were already dead on the field, when Starkardr cried out, "Let us fly, we have to do with more than men." On Gunnar's side, Hiort alone had perished, pierced through the heart by a Norwegian. 'Gunnar placed him on his shield, and carried him home, and buried him; and great was the lamentation over him, for he was a pleasant man.'

Here we are at the Ostre Rángá, flowing close by the farm and church of Keldur. A lad shews us the way over. In a fork, made by the river and a tributary torrent, is Hestathingsholl, where the folks in Gunnar's time used to witness those horse-fights, just as our forefathers took their pastime with the game cocks. The notable fight between Gunnar's black horse and Starkardr's red one took place here. In an Icelandic codex, preserved at Copenhagen, there is an illustration of a horse-fight, where people on either side are beating the horses with sticks. Such stimulus was not wanting on the present occasion. Foul play however was practised on Gunnar's horse; its eye was knocked out by Thorgeir son of Starkardr; who thereupon fell senseless to the earth from a blow of Gunnar's cudgel. And thus—realizing the Icelandic proverb, about horse-fighting and quarrelling always going together—commenced a feud, to be productive in after-days of such tragic consequences.

Entering the narrow approach to Vasdal*, with the three-cornered mountain, Thrihyrningr, to our left, we now open upon a grassy plain. Here stands the house of that fine specimen of an old Icelandic gentleman, Mr. Stevenson, whose father was Amtman, and grandfather, Governor of the country; while a maternal ancestor was Lögmadr, when Iceland possessed such functionaries. The blood of Snorri Sturleson also flows in his veins. Mr. Stevenson speaks English fluently. He took lessons in our language of Henderson during his winter sojourn in Reykjavik, almost half a century ago. With genuine kindness, hearing that one of my baggage horses has fallen lame, he at once lends me an uncommonly fat sumpter-nag, and also a spare saddle-horse, of his own, for a day or two.

I have now lost sight of Hekla, getting in exchange the rounded Eyafialla Jökul and the sea; but of them more to-morrow. Séra Skule Gislason, the clergyman of Breidabolstadr, is my host for the night: a most intelligent and accomplished person. His poetry is said to be far from contemptible. He is only recently married; his father-in-law died a common mode of death among Icelandic clergymen, falling through a hole in the ice, while returning

* Most likely called *Holt* in the Saga.

from the pursuit of his calling. Having observed that the north country peasants are much more intelligent than the people of their class in the south, I ask the reason. The more bracing and keener air of the north, he says, is more favourable to sprightliness of mind than the weather here; which is often muggy and damp. This part of the island has likewise suffered more from the depressing influence of Denmark. The people of the north possess also, it is said, more pluck and activity of limb than the southerners. The old national sport of wrestling (Glimu-list) survived till very lately among them. At one time it was as much, if not more, of a science than in Cornwall or Cumberland. Every posture had its appropriate name. Two champions chose sides, which were paired off against each other. Curiously enough, this love of wrestling, combined with a love of singing the deeds of their ancestors, prevails among the Kirghis at the present day. "And are the people here as fond of drink as they are reputed to be?" "Drunkenness is rife enough," was the answer; "but can it be wondered at when the Danish government fosters the evil, by giving a premium of two skillings to the merchants on every pot of schnaps they sell."

I am not sorry to have the aid of so agreeable a cicerone as Séra Skule on my visit to Hlidarende this morning, Sept. 17. Our road lies eastward along the moor which forms the great delta of the three rivers Thverá, Affal, and Markafliot. To our left are the lower slopes of the line of hills, over which I rode yesterday, backed by the picturesque triple peaks of the Thrihyrningr. Samstadir, the first farm on this slope, was the abode of the wealthy and fierce Lyting, who slew Niál's son, Hoskuld, as he was riding by. Next comes Gryota, still bearing the same name, where abode Thrain, another conspicuous character in *Burnt Nial*. Further on lies Teigr, a spot not mentioned in the Saga, but noteworthy as the birthplace in recent times of Jon Thorlakson, the Icelandic translator of Milton. In early youth he became enamoured of a young girl, whose friends however interfered to prevent him marrying her; as, from his desultory habits, there seemed no prospect of his being able to support a wife and family. This disappointment appears to have had the effect of driving him into habits of reckless dissipation. Twice was he unfrocked 'ob carnis delicta,' but again restored to his living; his delinquencies being winked at on account of his poetic talents. At length we reach Hlidarende, once the abode of that noble fellow Gunnar, situated at the end of the grassy declivity under which we have been riding. In front of it, but on a higher level than the moor, there was in Gunnar's time a beautiful meadow, stretching out due south, for the space perhaps of a mile. Even in Frederick the Vth's time, who is reputed to have had the good of Iceland at heart, this spot was considered worthy of the residence of one of the fifteen Jutland families, sent over by the king to teach the forgotten science of agriculture to the Icelanders*; which is supposed to have fallen into disuse in the time of the Black Death in the 15th century. But the available space has grown less and less; and now, Hlidarende, once so renowned for its fertility, is totally shorn of its beauties.

The destroyer has been the Thverá, an offshoot of the Markafliot, which has gradually wormed itself into the loamy soil and gnawed it away. Great bits of grass-crowned soil are even now in the act of falling into the stream, loosened by the last spring flood. Biarni Thorarensen, an Icelandic poet, who was born here, compared the river to Midgardsorm gnawing away at the root of Igdrasil, the fabled ash of the Scandinavian Cosmos. "Hlidarende's feet are bitten off to the knees," he says, "and Gunnar will one day rise from his resting-place and bid defiance to the ravager of his paternal farm." The poet's prediction

* It is difficult to reconcile the accounts in the Sagas of grain-crops raised in Iceland, with the actual experience of later times. In the experiment here tried, a quarter of a barrel of seed-corn only yielded half a barrel of produce. Eggert Olafson goes so far as to assert that there is no proof of ripe hard grain ever having been harvested in Iceland. Even in Faro the scanty grain-crop has to be dried artificially. It is possible, however, that the climate has become colder from the accumulation of snow and ice, which has certainly encroached in many parts of the country, especially in the South. The above-mentioned Jutland peasants left Iceland again in 1757.

is not the less regarded, that he himself was thought to be admitted to the secrets of the supernatural world. When a boy, he disappeared from home, and could not be found for three days; when he was discovered, on the other side the Thverá, sitting on a lofty rock, with a red cap on his head. At first he was taken for an eagle, so high was he perched. When at length the searchers got to the spot, the lad told them that his mother had fetched him thither. People however knew full well that he had been kidnapped by the Elves, who dwell under the Eyafiallajökul, the lights from whose windows the shepherd sees sometimes at evening.

But we are forgetting Gunnar. Some large blocks of stone on the slope mark the traditional site of Gunnar's Skáli, or Hall. A little east of it is the hill where the hero is buried; and to the right of the path which leads thither, a little mound marks the resting-place of the faithful Samr, his big Irish hound of such marvellous strength and sagacity, the present of Olaf the Peacock. As I trod past this spot, I felt that it really challenged the regard of all who admire canine fidelity, much more than that pseudonymous Bethgelert in Wales, dedicated to a dog that probably had as much real existence in that locality as Cerberus himself.

Looking eastward from Gunnar's place of sepulture, one descries a gloomy gorge, out of which pours that mother of waters, the Markafliot,—having in its baby state been nursed in Torfajökul; whence, gaining strength apace, it made a jump through the cleft, called Torfahlaup, and swept by that beautiful green wooded spot, Thorsmörk. Not far from this, while still in the valley, it splits into three arms, and spreads itself like a fan over the flats. The southern side of the valley is pent in by the glaciers and snow-fields of Eyafiallajökul, while its end is apparently blocked up by the Godalandsjökul. On its northern side are the sharp peaks of the Tindafiallajökul, between which and the stream, and opposite to that cold white dome of snow and ice, is Fliotsdalr, supposed to have been the saeter belonging to Niál. The direct road to this summer-pasturage from Bergthorshvoll, the residence of Niál, was close to Hlidarende; so that it is easy to see, what grand opportunities were offered by this circumstance to a vengeful fiend, like Halgerda, Gunnar's wife, of wreaking her spite upon Bergthora, by waylaying her husband's people. As one wades through the blood-stained pages of the Niál-saga*, with its tales of rapine, and jealousy, and rancorous revenge, one fancies one is reading an old Greek tragedy, with its Atreus and Thyestes, its Clytemnestra and Eumenides; while the minute and graphic descriptions of the every day life and doings of the

* Mr. Dasent's admirable version of this Saga has appeared since my visit to its localities.

Icelander in those days read like a page from Herodotus or the Odyssey.

As I stand on the heights, nearly at the apex of the delta, the first thing that catches my eye looking southward is the sixfold mountain group of the Westmann Islands, with the needles around them; the whole standing out, black, and sharply chiselled, from the calm bright expanse of ocean, with startling distinctness. As far as the eye can reach in a westerly direction spreads the interminable plain, watered by the Thverá, the Affal, and the Markafliot; and washed on the south by the sea. Upon it one or two dark specks may be discerned, one of these is Bergthorsknoll (hvoll), where lived Niál. Yonder across the Markafliot, and just under the western spurs of the Eyafiallajökul, is a curious conical mount. It is now called Dimon; and is the Raudaskridt of the tale. Behind it, on one winter's day a thousand years ago, five stalwart men were waiting, Skarphedin, son of Niál, at their head. The people they are looking for are at hand. See, a party of eight men, with Thrain and Hrapp among them, are returning from a visit to Mörk, the house under the fell:—it still bears the name. They have crossed the river, which is frozen over. Sharphedin now dashes out from his place of concealment, and follows them at full speed. Springing across a narrow channel, which was not iced over, and lighting on the slippery ice, he pounces in his slide upon Thrain, before he can put on his helmet, and cleaves his head to the teeth, which fall out upon the snow. And thus died a fine fellow; and all because he had chosen to become the protector of a worthless braggart like Hrapp. And so it is, that, even at the present day, the Icelander will say, 'Thrain tók vid Hrappi,' when a worthy man takes up the cause of a losel, to his own hurt and detriment.

Just in the line of vision between us and the Westmann islands lies a circular elevation, which goes by the name of Gunnarsholm. Gunnar, who had been declared an outlaw, was on his way to the coast, to take ship for Norway, when, looking back, he saw his beautiful farm, which he was going to leave perhaps for ever. "Never," he exclaimed, "did it appear so beautiful! I can't leave it!" and, in spite of the almost certain death that awaited him, he returned home. Very soon his foes got scent of his presence, and late one night they proceed to attack his dwelling. Being aware of the dog Samr's wariness and ferocity, they compel a thrall of Gunnar's, who dwelt near, and to whom the dog was known, to accompany them on pain of death. By this device the dog's suspicions are lulled; and they manage to cleave his skull; but with his death-howl he wakes his master, who manfully defends himself against the assailants. Full many a man did he lay low with his arrows. But at last his bowstring is frayed, and splits. "A lock of thine hair, Halgerda, wife mine!"

"Is it of consequence to you?" "As much as my life is worth." "Well then, you shan't have it. Remember the box on the ear you gave me." And so at last Gunnar falls. This event occurred 996 A. D., four years before Iceland was converted to Christianity.

Our survey of these interesting spots being completed, we return towards Breidabolstadr. This time we keep on the upper slope, instead of descending to the moor. By this means I have an opportunity of witnessing a national Icelandic custom. A score or more of men and girls on horseback, all riding astride, and with spades in their hands, are converging to a turf-walled ruinous enclosure, consisting of one central compartment and several wings. This is a rétt (fold), and they are going to repair it. Men went up to the fell a day or two ago with dogs, and will be here to-night with all the flocks of the valley. These will be driven into the central enclosure, and then separated off into the smaller ones, according to their marks. In Iceland, by the bye, a used-up volcanic cone, with its side knocked out, not unfrequently does duty for a sheep-fold; as did once the caves of Engedi.

After a sumptuous midday repast, we start for Bergthorshvoll. The Thverá has first to be forded. The water now only reaches to the horses' bellies; but six years ago it was a perfect sea, covering much of the delta with water, and leaving its traces in mud and sand flats, through which we stagger. It is supposed that in Gunnar's time, the main body of this mighty drain of ice and snow-water was confined to the bed of the Markafliot, and coursed under the cliffs that support the Eyafialla Jökul. But during the eight hundred and sixty years and more, that have elapsed since Gunnar's death, the heaps of detritus brought down by the stream would block up its main channel, and open out new arteries. Indeed, the bulk of the water flows one year by the Markafliot, another by the Affal, and sometimes by the Thverá. A lively canter over the dead flat, with occasional manœuvering among the bogs, and sticky gullies, brings us to the central stream, the Affal; which, fortunately, we have not to cross, as its sands are dangerous. "You know how to get over the ground, I see," said my companion, as I pushed my pony to his speed. "That German Stubengelehrte, who was here, he was no man for Icelandic riding. What a mess he made of it; as if riding consisted in wearing jack boots and spectacles. This must be the very route," continued he, "that Flossi and his hundred incendiaries rode that terrible night from their rendezvous under the Thrihyrningr, to attack poor old Niál." We are now almost within sound of the breakers, which I see dashing on the beach.

"Here is Bergthorshvoll," said he, pointing to a knoll in front of us, with a farm-house upon it: we had now been rattling along for the best part of three hours. Dismounting, and giving our horses to the rustic who attended us, we proceeded to inspect the *terrain*. "This is called Flossi-lóg," said another peasant, pointing to a square depression in the meadow, close to the right bank of the river, "where Flossi and his companions waited for some time. In the memory of man, it was much deeper than it is now." But, as this place was in sight of the house, and the Sága tells us that the band kept out of sight, the above nomenclature must be erroneous, and the real place where they hid the horses must have been behind another knoll, somewhat nearer to the house. Passing to the other, or north-west side of the house, I next visit a small pit in the swamp, which goes by the name of Kari-tiörn (the tarn of Kari), this being the traditional spot, where the only male survivor of Nial's family extinguished his burning clothes and hair, after breaking out of the flaming ruins. The wind was probably in the same direction as it is now, viz. south-east; for, as the story relates, he was hidden by the smoke, so that the assailants outside did not detect his escape.

We now enter the farm-house, to take coffee with Katharina Magnus-datter, a neat little widow, who rents the farm under the church of Oddi. She tells us that she thinks the kail-garden, just in front of the house, is the site of Nial's abode; for, while digging here, the people have found a quantity of charred wood and ashes; and also some pieces of metal. One of these is a fragment of copper, which seems to have formed part of a scabbard. I also obtain an ancient brass stud of pretty workmanship, one of several found on the spot, which are now used as children's playthings.

But, before quitting this place, I must briefly describe the terrible tragedy enacted here in the winter of 1004, according to others, of 1010. Flossi, the leader of the burners, who had determined upon Niál's destruction, after fastening their horses a short distance off, advanced to the house, where they found Niál with his sons and retainers, thirty in all, standing outside the door. The old man's counsel was, not to fight in the open, against such tremendous odds, but to get under cover. "This place is stronger than Gunnar's of Hlidarende," said he, "and his enemies found it hard work to take it." "Yes," replied his son Skarphedin, but, then, they were too honourable to think of burning him in; but these rascals won't care what they do. I have no notion of being choked like a tod in a hole." "Better do what father recommends," puts in Helge; and so Skarphedin consents to get under shelter; and skirmishing commences. "Let us fire the house," exclaimed Flossi, finding that his men were falling fast. A heap of vetches is ready at hand to feed the flames. The women shriek when they find the house is on fire. Niál consoles them, "God wont allow you to burn here and in the other world too." The females and domestics are allowed by the assailants to leave the burning edifice. "Who is that big woman there?" cries Flossi, pointing to a tall figure in the smoke. Helgi—for it was he, endeavouring to escape in female attire—seeing that he is discovered, wounds one of the burners, but is immediately decapitated by Flossi. The aged Niál has now the offer of his life, if he will come out and leave his sons to their fate. He refuses. Bergthora too, his wife, does the same. She was given young to Niál, and has promised to take him for better for worse, and in death she will not be divided from him. The aged pair retire to the sleeping apartment, and lie down under a fresh ox-hide, with their child between them. The smoke is whirling round them, and the fire's hot breath growing hotter. They sign themselves with the sign of the Cross, and the last words they are heard to utter is a commendation of their souls to God.

The beams of the house now begin to fall in. Kari urges Skarphedin to make a spring for it through the roof and escape. He steadfastly refuses; so Kari scales the unroofed wall by the help of a burning bench, and dashing down outside without being observed, escapes, as we have seen, under cover of the smoke to the pond, and lives to take a bloody revenge. Meantime, one of the assailants peers down at the caged Skarphedin, whose eyes are watering with smoke, and twits him with weeping. Skarphedin hurls a tooth of Thrain's, whose head he had once cloven, into the reviler's face, and knocks his eye out. And presently the dying hero and bard is heard singing his death-song among the burning rafters. Such are the main features of one of the most thrilling incidents in this old prose drama, which is conjectured to have been put together by Saemund the Learned, priest of Oddi. We have only to add, that the corpses of Niál, his wife, and child, were found unconsumed under the ox-hide by persons, who, a day or two after, went to examine the scene of destruction.

And now we mount once more and ride for Oddi, whither my horses have already preceded me. I shall not easily forget the exquisite tints which the mountains to the north-east now assumed, under the pencil of that arch-colourist, the setting sun. The sea of green grass through which we rode was suffused with lights which broad day had failed to cast. Dark shadows, alternating with dashes of purple, reposed on Seljalandsmula and the lower slopes of the Thrihyrningr, while the snowy mantle of Eyafiallajökul had changed from a cold white to a rich carmine. Recrossing the Thverá, close under Storolfshvoll, the abode in ancient days of the Viking, Storolf, renowned for his bodily strength, we trot sharply onward; but it is dark before we reach the banks of the Ostre Rángá, which I wade, following like a shadow the dimly-seen figure of my clerical guide. "We have had some riding to-day," significantly observed Séra Skule, as we drew bridle, and dismounted at the parsonage of Oddi, where my guide and horses were already arrived. The house was neat and well-ordered in every respect, and I only regretted, that the Archdeacon was not at home to do the honours.

Of the church, which I visited next morning, Sept. 18, little is to be said. Inside, there are some tolerable specimens of wood-carving. On the baptismal basin is the device of the Lamb, with the Rood across its shoulder. The stone which the devil licked under the compulsion of Saemund—not a bad illustration of one's nose being brought to the grindstone—is shewn outside the church; and between the church and the parsonage, the burial-place of Saemund himself. This notable, half-mythical, figure in Icelandic history, the presumed author of the Niál Saga, and the poetic Edda, was born here in 1056. After studying in England, as well as in France and Germany, he was presented to the living of Oddi. Innumerable are the tales told of his adventures with the evil one.

We have all heard of that underground school where the pupils

> 'Learned the art that none may name,
> In Padua far beyond the sea;'

where a grey, shaggy hand was protruded through a hole daily with their victuals; where the school-books were written in letters of fire, which might be seen in the dark: where the devil was the master, and his only honorarium, the last student who passed through the self-revolving iron door at the year's end;—'the devil take the hindmost'—and how, on one occasion, the last student outwitted the fiend, who only got the shadow instead of the substance. Now this curious tale is generally connected in the minds of Britons with that arch-necromancer, Michael Scott; but in Icelandic tradition it is Saemund who puts the cheat on the satanic dominie. The way, however, in which he accomplished it is this. He hung his mantle loosely over his shoulders, taking care not to put his arms in the sleeves. As he moved out last, the schoolmaster made a grab at him, but, dexterously ducking, he escaped, leaving the cloak in his place. The iron door, however, slammed to at the same moment, and bruised the retreating scholar's heel, when he exclaimed, "The door was too close to my heel:" a saying which has become proverbial.

It is also related of this learned personage and wit,—whose only magic was, most likely, his learning and strong understanding in an age of ignorance,—that in his 48th year, being the year of grace 1104, he threw a certain casket from the top of Hekla,—the spot where Danish tradition makes the witches hold their Sabbath,—and straightway the mountain responded with its virgin eruption. Be this as it may, Saemund Sigfusson must have been a very leading man in his day, for so much legendary matter to cling to him, and the further elucidation of his history is not unworthy the attention of scholars. Nor must we forget to note, that Snorri Sturleson resided for sixteen years at Oddi under the tuition of Jon Lopston, the grandson of Saemund.

My friend, Mr. Skule, who has dispensed the hospitalities in the absence of the archdeacon, laments that he cannot accompany me further. A parishioner is dead, and he has to compose a funeral oration, to be delivered at the burial to-day. These panegyrics are often printed. A pamphlet which I saw contained three such compositions delivered over the grave of a departed lady, one of them by the bereaved husband, a clergyman. Oddi (=a tongue of land) takes its name from its position between the Eystri (eastern) Rángá and Ytri (outer) Rángá; and it is the latter of these rivers that I have to ford to-day; and very deep it proved. As we approach the Thiorsá, we cross a bog, on that most common of Icelandic roads, a narrow wall of peats. Of course, there is only room for one horse at a time, so, in the event of two caravans meeting, what is to be done? The question is likely to find a speedy solution, for here comes a train of baggage horses in the opposite direction. What a scuffle took place! Some of the horses got jostled over the wall, and hung to it with their fore-legs, while others became pretty firmly bogged. Matters would have been almost irretrievable, but that the wall is in many places broken down, and thus affords a kind of standing place to the animals.

Here is the Thiorsá, a perfect sea of waters, agitated by a strong and bitterly cold wind. The baggage is placed in a large boat, manned by four muscular rowers, and after us swim the horses, towed by two men kneeling over the stern of the boat. Hard work it was for those sturdy oarsmen to reach that speck of dry sand, near the centre of the turbid stream; and harder work still for those poor wayworn quadrupeds, which have traversed with me such a length of country, as would have knocked up anything in the shape of a horse except an Icelandic one. See how they labour across the current, their teeth clenched and laid bare, the white of their staring eyeballs exhibited, evidently in mortal terror, their nostrils corrugated and emitting furious snortings; while the waves ever and anon dash over their heads, threatening to suffocate them outright. We reach the lee of the sandspit, and out jumps one of the mariners; only just in time to prevent the boat getting entangled among the horses, and being stove in by them, or swept out to sea. There is just room for us to stand on the spit, while the shivering beasts are re-packed and saddled; and then we ford to the shore through unpleasant quicksands, covered with water. The whole affair, what with the roaring of the wind, the dashing of the waters, the terror of the horses, and the shouts of the boatman, was not a little exciting.

A peasant from the neighbourhood of Portland, more to the eastward, who joins us, tells me, that the natives of Eyafiallasyssel still follow the reverent old custom of uncovering their heads, after crossing a dangerous river. I learn from him that an accident has recently befallen a gatherer of wild-fowls' eggs there. Two men were climbing the needles, which lie off Portland, yoked together by a rope; the one advancing in front of the other, after the fashion which I have described as in vogue in the Faroes. When they had reached a considerable height, the upper man lost his footing, and fell, carrying with him, not the lower man, as might have been expected, but only the rope; the strap round the other's waist fortunately giving way at the instant.

We now ride over a long, long, sandy plain, strewed with sea-shells, and, what was much worse, frequent fragments of sharp black spongy looking lava. To our left was the sea line, which is one of the most exposed in Iceland, from the few harbours it possesses. In fact, from Cape Reykjanes in the west to the Eystra-horn in the east, or the whole southern coast of Iceland, there is nothing that deserves the name, I believe, of a good harbour. Behind us, Hekla again comes into view, and to our right, at no great distance, whither those swans are flapping heavily, Ingolfsfiall is a prominent feature in the landscape. Sooth to say, old Ingolf did not choose a bad place, all things considered, from whence, as he said, he might see his broad domains on the day of doom. As we approach Eyrarbakki, I see men and women collecting sea-weed, which they will dry for their own winter's food. If the cattle want this delicacy, they must forage for themselves. Surely, an Icelander would of all others be the most likely person to win the prize for the best Essay on edible sea-weeds, which has lately been advertised in the English newspapers.

At six o'clock, P.M., I am in the comfortable house of Mr. Thorgrimsen, the manager of the Danish factory at Eyrarbakki, and engaged in reading the 'Times' newspaper. What a treat! From the wilderness into the thickest of the crowd at a bound! The weather, I see, has been very bad in England, while in Iceland, especially in the south, it has been universally fine, permitting the peasants along the coast to row across frequently to the factories at the Westmann Isles, instead of travelling great distances by land to this place. The amount of labour thus saved may be conceived, when it is recollected that all the foreign imports and native exports, which are bartered against each other at the merchant's, would in a stormy summer have to be transported on baggage-horses to this place.

A shrewd Aberdonian has hired the salmon fishery here, and his staff of curers has only just left for home. Here, as in other parts of the country, the take of fish has sensibly fallen off during the last year or two. Most likely, the fishing has been plied too hard. But I can assure my piscatorial friends, that though the rivers generally do not exhibit such magnificent pools as the Norwegian streams can boast of, there are plenty of spots all round the coasts well adapted for taking fish with the fly. The main difficulty is, first, to transport yourself to your river, and, secondly, where to bestow yourself when you have got there: the houses being so few and far between, and the generality of them affording so little accommodation of the kind an Englishman looks for. There is no doubt that the best way of visiting the country, whether as piscator, geologist, or in any other capacity, is for a party to club together, and hire a steam yacht.

Mr. Thorgrimsen is before his age. Here are the only tame geese I have seen in the country; and yet, in former times, both geese and swans were a common adjunct to every farm-house. I also see here, for the first time, a pretty specimen of modern Icelandic carving, viz. a bull's horn adorned with various devices, but without that boldness and freedom of design which is to be found in Norway. The artist is a man living under Hekla: a facsimile of the work has been forwarded to the king of Denmark.

The 'Arcturus,' I hear, has just arrived, and will start for Scotland in three or four days; a piece of news which relieves me from no little anxiety, as I had felt grave doubts, from former experience, as to its leaving at the time specified by the authorities; and I had no wish, at this late period of the season, to be detained longer on the island.

CHAPTER XXV.

The Olfusá—The hazards of Icelandic travel—Two national sights—Horse-life—A drunken Dane—Return to the capital—The northern lights—A storm—The society of Reykjavik—The French priests—The chief physician—Leprosy—The want of good servants—"Do it yourself."—A land-shark—Service at the cathedral—The sun comes out—Estimate of the Icelanders—We weigh anchor—The voyage home.

SEPTEMBER 19th. A lovely bright morning. Our first move is to cross the Olfusá, a river nearly half a mile broad, which here discharges the combined waters of the lake of Thingvalla and the White River into the sea. Its shores on either side are flat and sandy. The tide being on the turn, the stream is not rapid; and the boatmen row us steadily over, the horses swimming after us, and an inquisitive seal after them. And now I have crossed my last Icelandic river, and thankful I am to Providence that I have got safe through them all. It is true that I have not met with a single grave mischance on the tour. But fatal accidents often occur, as we have had occasion to shew; and a traveller must keep both eyes well open throughout. '*Aide toi, et Dieu t' aidera*' is truer of nothing than of Icelandic travel. To get drowned, to break your neck or your limbs, to be maimed, to be boiled alive, or, at the least, to be prostrated with rheumatism, are quite on the cards.

Crossing sands overgrown with wild corn, we ascend the Hellisheidi. For some time we journey in a grassy dell by the side of an abrupt rampart of lava; as it bends to the right we bend to the right, and as it bends to the left we do likewise. Presently, one of Iceland's national sights meets our eyes, in the midst of this blasted scenery; viz. jets of steam spirting from red and yellow blotches in the side of a mountain. Another truly national sight is again before us. A cavalcade of ponies toiling and moiling through the filthy pools of ochreous mud which enliven the path; on either side of them a couple of planks, the hinder ends of which trailing astern keep bumping against the uneven ground. Patient, much abused beasts! it is well that ye know not the different lot that awaits your two brethren, about to voyage with me to England. No more vivisections by the knife-like lava; no 'drowning risks;' no more sticking fast in tenacious bogs, like hapless flies in treacle; no more fish-head-crunching, or of that winter-cannibalism upon dried portions of your ancient friends, await you, O Bogi and Faxa, ye faithful companions of my travel! Even in this life are ye destined to enjoy the sweets of an equine Valhalla. For dost not thou, O Bogi, "little big 'un," now luxuriate in thy loose box, wondering greatly at all this grooming—for groomed thou never wast before—wondering too at the oats, food before unknown to thee—and delighting to bear in his easy rides the veteran General. Faxa too, meekest and most gentle of beasts, sure of foot as the cat, what an agreeable surprise it must be to thee, to be a timid girl's ambling palfrey!

Further on, we pass a house of refuge for the traveller overtaken by storms. My guide tells me that he once lost his way on the mountain in a 'snow-fog,' and lived for a couple of days in an extempore shelter, which he scooped out for himself in the snow. Winter is plainly fast approaching. Sounds of many birds greet my ear, and, looking up, I perceive a flock of wild geese, prescient, no doubt, of impending bad weather, winging their way in the shape of a T, at an immense height in the yet unthreatening heavens. The Faroes lie right in front of them; they will be there, at the rate they are going, in a few hours. For once—spare me, ye critics—I wished that I was a goose. Pushing on vigourously, we presently get a view of the sea near Reykjavik, and are soon dashing through the Laxelv; the horses skirmishing along, as if this were the first, instead of the fifty-sixth day of their journey. Some pic-nic people here join us; one of whom, a Dane, evidently the worse for liquor, pushes a great flask of corn-brandy into my face, with a rudeness and familiarity at which his companions, with better taste, if not more sobriety, are clearly shocked. At last the sot, after in vain endeavouring to claim acquaintance, rushes insanely forward towards Reykjavik, his pony, luckily for him, being a very nimble animal. His departure affords great relief to the faithful Jon, who seems now to hold drunkenness in especial abhorrence. "Ah!" said he, "it is very sad; but he is a Dane, not an Icelander. Icelanders do drink too much. But when the clergyman drinks and the sysselman drinks, all drink. I once knew a priest called B. who lived at A. He was suspended for drinking, &c. &c." The reader knows the rest. It is dusk by the time our convoy, after a journey of at least fifteen hundred miles, clatters down the street of Reykjavik; surrounded by a cloud of gamins with proffers of their services. Leaving Jon to settle matters with these hornets, I am soon in a quiet room devouring letters from home; this being the first opportunity of hearing from thence since I left England.

This night, the heavens are beautifully lit up by the northern lights*, spanning the sky with a bow of fitful radiance, the almost certain presage of a storm.

* Mr. C. A. Holmboe, in a tract entitled, "Om Hedenske Korsmonumenter," Christiania, 1861, conjectures that the ancient Scandinavian looked on the aurora as the emanation of some divinity, the nimbus over some mighty brow: and that he even constructed monuments corresponding in their length to the direction usually taken by its light, viz. from N. W. to S. E. He thus seeks to explain the position of some curious ancient cross-shaped monuments at Calernish in the Isle of Lewis, at New Grange in Ireland, and in one or two places in Norway. The northern lights of Greenland are described in that quaint work, *Kongs-skugg-sio*, p. 74. (Sorö 1768), which dates from the end of the twelfth century.

This is nothing, I hear, to what the aurora, volatile alike in shape and motion, can do sometimes; flaming cones, circles of yellow, green, or purple colour, being in the list of its fanciful metamorphoses. Next day it is blowing a storm from the north-west, and Esian and his neighbours are covered with snow. Not a craft is to be seen in the bay; they have all, including the steamer, taken refuge in the small but secure harbour of Hafnafiord. It is still three days before the boat leaves, so it is to be hoped that the storm will by that time have blown itself out.

Meantime I pay some visits; among others, I have the pleasure of becoming acquainted with Professor Björn Gunlaugsson, teacher of natural philosophy and mathematics in the Government College here. This veteran gentleman, whose portrait I have seen all over the country, is perhaps the most distinguished and interesting person in it. It was he who, at the expense and under the auspices of the Danish government, completed a twelve years' survey of the island, the fruits of which have been a beautiful map, which generally goes by the name of Olsen's map; published by the literary society of Iceland. From him I learn that the old philosopher of Thorormstunga, my visit to whom has been described in the course of this narrative, is really a very remarkable self-taught mathematical genius. I have also the pleasure of becoming acquainted with Mr. Jonason, the acting governor, a most agreeable person; and with the vicar of Reykjavik, Mr. Paulson, who presents me with a little devotional work, of which he is the author. I likewise visit the aged Conferenzrad Thorstensen, who solaces his blind old age by having read to him the works of our best English authors. He criticises Macaulay, and speaks with a familiarity of Hume and Gibbon that is really not a little surprising. The reader will not be astonished to learn that a book of such sombre character as Young's Night Thoughts is an especial favourite with these people. Its complexion is in keeping with the tone of thought which the landscape suggests. An Icelandic version of it was published by Thorlakson. The French Consul's champaigne is of course not neglected. He is altogether a most pleasant and valuable acquisition to Reykjavik society.

My promised call on the French priests is not omitted. They are still involved in the meshes of Icelandic law; and distracted with the ambiguities of the 'Grey Goose,' the 'Jons-book,' and the modern laws of Denmark, which, however conflicting, claim in turn to be the ruling codes of the island. As we sip some excellent claret at their neatly-furnished mansion, they enter into the story of their grievances; shewing me a copy of the Decrees of the Council of Trent, which they allege to have been misquoted by the author of the polemical tract, which has lately been published here concerning the Romish religion. They seize me by the hand convulsively, and with an eloquence worthy of better inspirations plead the cause of their faith. "In dubiis libertas; in fide unitas; in omnibus caritas:" such, they say, is their motto. But was not that the motto of their Church when Iceland cast off its yoke, never, I am sure, to resume it? They profess, however, to think otherwise. The prodigal son will yet return, when the fulness of time has come, to his yearning parent. It is impossible not to admire the enthusiasm of these people. One of them has travelled throughout the country preaching. He is a native of the Ardennes, and pathetically laments the absence of trees, so distinguishing a feature of his home. One is about to leave for England; the other will spend the winter here alone. How he will sigh for the arrival of the first steamer! I cannot conceive anything more dreary for a Frenchman, cut off as he will be for so many months from much that a Frenchman holds most dear. Ice and snow, and dire tempest, and many hours of darkness and solitude! truly this would cow the bravest. The hardships of the poor at that inclement season, Mons. B. describes to me as often very great, but, added he, "what the horses have then to undergo is indescribable. I have positively wept to witness their sufferings." Indeed, these animals must be wonderfully good and sound at core to go through what they do. In the first place, no attempt is made to improve the breed by the proprietors. "They are allowed to grow up just like weeds," observed a clergyman to me. Everything, in short, is left to 'natural selection,' and really it does not answer so much amiss.

Dr. Hialtalin, the physician-general of the country, a burly farmer to look at, but a person of much scientific acquirement, is loud in his objurgations of the roads. He wonders why such a state of things should be suffered to exist. Formerly they were much better than now, but, from some cause or other, the government officials do not enforce upon the peasants the duty of keeping the ways in order, as they should do. Possibly the poverty which now prevails from the sheep disease has something to do with it. The Danish government have at length despatched some veterinary surgeons to inquire into the cause of it; and dressing the animals, instead of slaughtering them, is recommended by the faculty. But, notwithstanding this, two hundred thousand sheep have during the last two years fallen victims to the knife. No wonder then that the peasants have no salt meat to send off in the autumn to Denmark, and that the export of wool has fallen off. The upshot of it will probably be, that they must take to eating horses, as their heathen forefathers did; a food once peremptorily forbidden by the laws of the Roman Catholic church, and altogether discountenanced by the clergy; who perhaps feared that their flock would be reverting to the worship of Thor. Dr. H. attributes the plague to its most likely cause—the bad food, and over-close confinement of the animals in winter. But the origin of the evil, as I have stated elsewhere, is still in controversy. The editor of one Reykjavik newspaper, the *Thioðolfr*, takes one side, the editor of the *Islendigur* espouses the other.

Dr. H. likewise gives me some further information with regard to leprosy. The head quarters of this disease appear to be between Skagi and Cape Reykjanes, and also in the neighbourhood of Stykkisholm. It appears in both forms, Lepra nodosa, and Lepra squamosa. My informant attributes the complaint in a great degree to foul air. About Havnafiord he found the atmosphere impregnated with the odour of rotten sea-weed and shell-fish driven up by storms.

One gentleman, with whom I converse about the labouring classes of the country, tells me that they are a most independent race. Owing to the sparse population, there is a deficiency of labouring power; and in summer time, especially in the south, and about Reykjavik, very high wages may be procured. "There is no subordination among them," remarked a Dane to me. The masters have often to beg and supplicate their hired servants to do some necessary labour; and, after all, they will reply coolly, "I don't choose; do it yourself." The above will give an Englishman some idea of what he has to expect. In corroboration of the above statement, the captain of the steamer afterwards informed me, that the men of Hafnafiord actually asked four dollars a-day for ballasting the steamer. As a commentary upon this tendency to extortion, I may quote the broken English of a Danish sailor: "I like Faros, Faros good peoples; better than Reykjavikers. Reykjavikers bad peoples: they cheats me. I have sailed all over the world. I have been round Iceland too, but Reykjavikers very bad peoples." Of course this only applies to a part of the population. I hear that one honest fellow, no other than the guide whom I dismissed for incompetency, insisted on having one pound sterling of the people of H. M. ship Bull-dog, when it was here this summer, for rowing off four times with fresh milk. That worthy now makes his appearance with a little bill for daily wages during the whole of my tour, stating that I had agreed to hire him for all the term of my stay in Iceland. This being contrary to the facts of the case, and his receipt in full for all demands being in my possession, I resist the payment, and deposit the amount claimed, which was considerable, with a Danish gentleman, in order that the matter might be decided by the proper authorities. The imposition was too glaring to stand official scrutiny for a moment, and subsequently the money was forwarded to me.

On Sunday, I attended service in the cathedral. The congregation, which amounted to about a hundred and thirty, sang lustily and with a good courage.

The sermon was of a practical nature. But generally speaking, I should say, that Bragi, god of eloquence, has not tipped with fire the tongues of the Icelandic clergy. But, indeed, I am sorry to confess that my attention was diverted from the discourse by three young ladies who sat just in front of me, with Phrygian caps of black satin on their heads, their countenance shaded by white veils. Round the brow, the cap was ornamented with gilded stars as big as ox-eyed daisies (Baldur's eyebrow), while other metallic ornaments were exhibited about the person. Their jackets were embroidered with silver. Nor did brimstone-coloured gloves improve this somewhat theatrical costume, which to my taste is infinitely inferior to the ancient Icelandic dress. The new dress is the invention of Sigurdr Gudmundson, an ingenious artist of the place—the author of the sketches for two of the plates which illustrate this work—who is reputed to be a great authority, and I believe most deservedly so, in antiquarian matters. It was evident that the damsels were creating a considerable sensation, of which they themselves were not unconscious.

September 24. The mountains around have been emulating in whiteness the perpetual snows of Snaefell; which is very distinctly seen across the fiord. The gale, however, as I anticipated, has blown itself out, and the Arcturus, welcome sight! is come round into the roads. By mid-day the sun shows again, and the snow is fast melting from the mountain tops. One or two more such victories, however, and Phœbus will be undone, and king Winter will have all around permanently occupied till next May. At 1 P.M., when we weigh anchor, it is a dead calm. And so farewell to Iceland.

My travel has been neither uninteresting nor, I hope, unprofitable. I have seen an island where the powerful genius of liberty, and the no less powerful genius of poetry, have given brilliant proofs of the energies of the human mind. I have viewed localities immortalized by the pages of ancient histories—the comprehension of which has been greatly assisted by a personal visit. I have seen natural phenomena, not to be surpassed for wonder in the whole world. I have heard a people remarkable for intelligence, talking in a tongue almost identical with that in which those bold Vikings expressed their thoughts a thousand years ago; those Vikings to whom Englishmen owe most of their dash, their love of enterprise, their frankness, their liberty: a race, whom their admirers compare with the Spartan in deliberate valour and mother wit; with the Athenian in daring and genius.

I have seen a people, bowed down in spirit by long political depression; starved out almost by an inclement climate; pushed to the wall by the rude onset of burning torrents or encroaching glaciers; yet still with the pluck not yet cowed out of them. A people they are, worshipping the goddess Liberty even in her sadly tattered and degenerate guise; and in her meagerly furnished temple. The elders—the leading men of the island—who have seen, in story at least, the glories of the first house, and mused on the triumphs of the Virgin Republic, in the midst of the inviolate sea; may well weep to think that their country may not rise into something worthy of those memories. They must regret to see the old passion for liberty evaporating in petty mimicry of independence, frittering itself away in newspaper polemics, in tirades against Denmark, and unavailing complaints and regrets over the past; instead of steadily shaping itself into a practical endeavour to promote the material wellbeing of the people. If the Icelanders would work well and wisely together, a great deal might be done, that is not yet done, for the regeneration of the country. It has many resources, and not the least resource in the unflinching endurance of the people. There is plenty of good stuff in them which may be utilized. "It was the flower of Scandinavia," said an old Icelandic gentleman to me, "that came to Iceland; they had Kraft in them, and they have it in them still, if they had a chance of shewing it." In no country that I ever visited is there a greater amount of disinterested kindness, and honesty of purpose, in active operation. Had I stopped in the capital, I fear I should not have conceived so favourable an impression of the natives in the last particular, notwithstanding the presence of many excellent folks in the place. Perhaps all seaports are more or less infected with the sharping propensity. 'Vivitur ex rapto' is certainly a motto stamped on the fronts of several people there.

At 5½ P.M. we are rounding Cape Reykjanes. The setting autumn sun is lighting up, with an effect something like that of red Bengal fire, that twisted and tormented scene. Pyramids, castles, columns, reflect the glow in wondrous fashion. At midnight moon and stars and aurora borealis are vying with each other in illuminating the gently heaving North Atlantic. At 9 A.M. on the 25th, I get the last sight of Iceland, being the summit of some Jökul lying far up in the interior. Fine weather throughout the day, and the vessel making good way.

Sept. 26. Beautiful day. Slight breeze from the eastward. We expect to see Faro this evening; but shall not go in, in the dark, on account of the difficulties of the navigation. A couple of hawks are following the vessel, evidently out of their reckoning.

September 27th. At six this morning I am on deck, just in time to study the features of Trollhoved. At the end of Hestó, Koltö opens out, which the Scotch engineer compares to Ailsa Crag, and at 9 A.M. we are in Thorshaven. The governor, who is going down south to Copenhagen, comes aboard in great state—his galley being manned by six soldiers in green uniform: who, by way of parting salutation, give him three cheers. I wonder where they learned that. At 1 P.M. the anchor is lifted, and away for Scotland.

I find from a gentleman on board, that the expense of boat-travelling in Faro is fixed by law. There are regular fixed stations, as in Norway. The fare of a boat and four men per Danish mile amounts to 5 marks; and good accommodation is to be had at the peasants' houses. The pay of a single attendant is 3 marks 8 shillings, per diem. A trout-fisher, or wild-fowl shooter, a geologist, or naturalist, might bestow his time very well in a run through the islands. He would have a clear twelve days between the departure of the steamer and its return from Iceland.

September the 28th at 6½ A.M. off Foula, with a favourable wind. Sept. 29 at 8 A.M. opposite the Bell rock, with the yellow Scotch cornfields smiling delightfully to starboard. A ripe cornfield is a sight worth seeing after a course of lava. A twelve knot breeze is behind us, and early in the afternoon we are in the dock of Grangemouth; having had a most prosperous and speedy passage, and slipping into port just in time to escape a dreadful gale, which destroyed five screw steamers in the North Sea.

CONCLUDING CHAPTER.

The first requisites for Icelandic travel—Walking, out of the question—No carriages in the country—The currency—The Arcturus steamer—Outfit—What provisions must be taken—Icelandic bill of fare—English trunks useless—Icelandic box—A tent required—Must horses be bought or hired?—Guides—A map—The best time for starting.

IT will be our object, in this chapter, to lighten some of the difficulties attending a journey to Iceland, by telling people how to set about it, and, having set about it, what to do next.

Premising therefore that a man must be well inured to hardships and fatigue, active in frame, and thoroughly wide awake; we come next to that universal solvent, which, according to a shrewd observer, 'perrumpere amat saxa'—money. Good store of this commodity is required by those who would unbar the adamantine portals of this far-off Thule in the North Atlantic. Walking in it is quite out of the question; Icelanders never walk. The nature of the country does not admit of it. Public conveyances there are none; in short, there is not a wheeled carriage throughout the land. Horses, therefore, must be bought or hired, and guides employed; and the consequence is, that travelling is expensive; perhaps more so than anywhere else in Europe: especially to an Englishman; as the natives, in their own minds, always place him in the same boat as regards means with the rich and titled yachtsmen, who are nearly the only samples of British travellers they have ever seen. Hence they firmly believe that every Briton who visits them is endued with Gialdbuxur*, or Finnbraekr, i. e. that they are 'made of money.'

Danish money is the current medium, consisting of dollars, marks, and skillings.

16 skillings . .	=	1 mark.
6 marks . . .	=	1 Rigsbank dollar.
2 Rigsbank dollars	=	1 species dollar.

In Copenhagen the average exchange for a pound sterling is from 8 dollars 4 marks, to 8 dollars 5 marks. I obtained the latter sum in the north, of Mr. P. Jonsen, a most obliging and intelligent merchant at Akreyri. At Reykjavik I was offered as low as 8 dollars 2 marks. It is a question whether a

* Literally 'money trousers,' or 'Finn breeches.' The Finns or Lapps are noted magicians, and these unmentionables are of magic construction. They are manufactured from the skin of a dead person. Having put them on, the wearer steals a piece of money, which placed in the pockets serves as a sort of nest-egg ; for before long, he overflows with money. The owner, however, before his death, must take care to give them to somebody else ; otherwise he is lost for ever. The transference is executed by the possessor taking one leg out of them, when the future owner adroitly slips his leg into the vacant half, and so on with the other half. These trowsers are also called Papeybuxur ; an obscure term, which may be derived from the Irish monks (papar) who visited Iceland for solitude and prayer at the end of the eighth century, and were of course regarded by the heathen Scandinavians, who came to the country fifty years later, as rank wizards.

supply of Danish money might not be obtained, before setting out, in London.

The only regular conveyance to Iceland from Great Britain is a Danish steamer, which touches at Grangemouth, on her passage to and fro between Copenhagen and Reykjavik. She makes six voyages each way during the season. The voyage from Scotland to Iceland lasts about a week. The fare is £5 each way. The expense of eating and drinking very reasonable. The tariff might perhaps be heightened somewhat, and a proportionably better bill of fare supplied. When I proposed travelling to Iceland by the steamer, it was quite impossible to obtain correct information about her times of departure from Iceland. A friend having informed me that the boat would not return, on her September voyage from Reykjavik, till nearly the close of that month—a delay which I could ill afford—I put myself in communication with the agents at Grangemouth on the subject. Here is their answer, dated 12th July:—

"Sir, In reply to your favour of yesterday, we cannot *guarantee* that the Arcturus will leave Iceland the voyage after this before the 1st of September, but have no doubt she will leave on or before that date, in which case you would arrive here about the 7th of that month. Your friend must have mistaken the time."

My friend, then, it appeared, was in error, and I might rely on the assurance of the agents, that, barring accidents, the steamer would leave Iceland not later than Sept. 1, perhaps before. So the tent was purchased, the stores laid in, and all the multifarious apparatus of travel in such a far country got together. On the 14th of July, the day fixed for starting from Scotland, I duly arrived at Grangemouth, and had already seen my effects safely on board, when the agent presents himself with a visage of much concern. "He has made a mistake. He laments it. The boat does not leave Reykjavik for a fortnight later, i. e. than he had written me." The mystification was provoking; but, of course, all could be explained on the most satisfactory principles. But this was not all. Arrived at Reykjavik, I purchased horses, hired a guide, and made all the preparations necessary for the journey. Four days had been consumed in these preparations. When I was fully equipped for starting, who should make his appearance but the captain of the Arcturus.

"Very sorry. An entire miscalculation. The steamer would not start before the 24th Sept. at the earliest." But what was most surprising was, that when, in order to avoid all further uncertainty, I went up to the governor's, to make inquiries on the subject, I was shewn the steamer's route of the year fixed since the beginning of it; and it was there quite plain to see that the 24th of September was the day on which she was all along intended to start; nor could she possibly start before. Had

I received this intelligence on setting foot in Iceland, I should most likely have made up my mind to go back with the first return boat, viz. in a week's time after our arrival at Reykjavik, contenting myself with a visit to the Geysers and Thingvalla. But now the chances were, that it was too late even for that amount of travelling. So, not wishing to be classed with that notorious king of France who marched up the hill, and when he got there marched down again, I made a virtue of necessity, and started, consoling myself with the thought that I should at all events gain one advantage, viz. see more of the country. I have thought it necessary to mention these facts, to put travellers on their guard, although there is no doubt that more correct information will be supplied to the traveller in future. To avoid all risks, however, we recommend intending voyagers to apply for information to the Danish Embassy in London.

We now come to the outfit required. In Iceland, at midsummer, it will one day be exceedingly hot, and another, exceedingly cold, so that the traveller must be in utrumque paratus. First then, have two full suits of tweed, one of them the strongest and warmest procurable. In Iceland, woollen must be the only wear, so that Shetland jerseys, flannel shirts, and knitted socks are indispensable. For warmth and durability nothing can surpass the Icelandic socks and gloves, which are to be had very cheap all over the country. As an outer garment, the natives on their travels generally wear a cloak with sleeves, and leathern belt round the waist, the latter being very useful in searching, windy weather. We should recommend a strong mackintosh over-coat.

Anything in the shape of leggings, antigropelos, or gaiters, is futile. The only preservative against wet is a pair of waterproof seaman's boots, which will, if necessary, draw up to the very top of the thigh. Without these the traveller, in crossing the rivers, is liable to get wet every day. Being unaware of this, I was not thus provided, and brought back not a little rheumatism in consequence. India-rubber fishing stockings might serve the purpose of keeping you dry for a day or two, but they would soon fret to pieces. In Iceland, for leg coverings, there is nothing like leather. The boots may be made large enough to draw over ordinary boots or shoes; and in that case, when not wanted, they may be slipped off, and suspended from the saddle of one of the packhorses. The only drawback that I know of to these integuments is, that in crossing a river, if the horse should come to grief, the rider would infallibly be drowned: they must sink him.

"And what am I to take to eat and drink?" inquires the traveller. There are no inns; so that if you have no resources of your own, you must depend upon the hospitality of the clergy and farmers. But when it is considered that the country is larger than Ireland—containing as it does 40,000 square miles, while in Ireland there are only 32,000—with a population of under 60,000, it may be readily imagined, that places to put up at do not abound. With one exception, which occurred not a hundred miles from Thingvalla, not a single clergyman, at whose house I stopped, would hear of any pecuniary recompense. They give what their house affords, and delight in doing so, without hoping to receive as much again. The peasants however have no objection to be remunerated. Presents, therefore, had better be taken: silk kerchiefs, ribands, knives, razors, books; all which, however, add to your luggage. Prince Napoleon, in return for the smiles and courtesies of the Reykjavikers, scattered valuable bracelets broadcast; but it is not everybody who is a Prince Napoleon. After July the mutton is fat, and is frequently to be had; indeed more frequently than in Norway. Skier (curds), fresh fish, dried fish, sometimes cooked, but oftener placed on the table in its unthreshed and obstinate state—a fearful look-out for any but canine or Icelandic teeth—pancakes, coffee, milk and cream, and corn-brandy, are the chief supplies in the eating and drinking line to be found in most houses. Bayersk öl (Bavarian ale), brewed in Denmark, is sometimes to be had at Reykjavik. There is also a native brewery there—traveller, beware of it. Fair claret, cognac, (? rum), and schnaps, with tea, sugar, and coffee, may be purchased at all the merchants: at the capital there is a German baker, where tolerable bread may be obtained. By all means take from England a bag of biscuits, some cheese, portable soup, preserved meats, and tea.

If you cross the inland desert, or explore the ice-mountains, no houses will be met with at all. As there are no trees, and the surturbrand or lignite—even if you meet with it—when fresh from the pit, has a trick of not burning, you must, if you require hot drink, provide yourself with a spirit lamp. A couple of bottles of cognac brandy ought to be always in store, in case of emergency. Do not omit to take a strong dog-whip, with a thong attached to fasten it to the wrist. Some strong straps, a hammer, a multum in parvo knife, will be also requisite. An extra set of shoes for every horse must also be taken, for a long journey, with nails to match. The shoes made by the blacksmith are preferable to those of cast-iron, sold by the merchants.

Having collected your traps, you will proceed doubtless to put them in English boxes or portmanteaus. This is a mistake; at Reykjavik you will find that these must be left behind: as, from their unwieldy shape and construction, they are unsuited to Iceland. At the first river your English box may be half immersed, and the consequences to your stores—gun-powder, for instance—may be guessed. Or it may be torn or smashed against the bristling *chevaux de frise* of lava or slag, that rise at every turn; or otherwise damaged by a collision among the horses, a thing of constant occurrence. First, warning, then, the traveller—what he will perhaps have already guessed—that his gun and fishing-rod must be secured in strong cases, we will proceed to describe the Icelandic travelling-box, of one if not two pairs of which he must be possessed to travel with comfort and success. Though most inconvenient from its depth and narrowness for stowage, it will be found from its shape most convenient for fastening upon the baggage-horse. The wood of

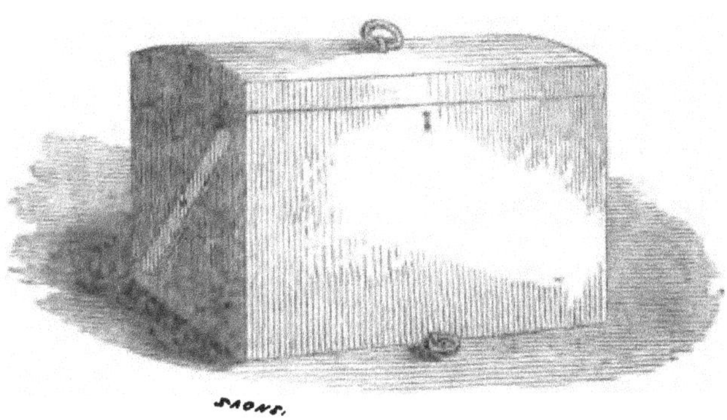

which it is composed is from ¾ of an inch to one inch thick. Its usual dimensions are 15 inches high, 10½ wide, and 21½ inches long. The lid is a little arched to throw off the rain. In the centre of the lid is a strong iron ring, as thick as a man's little finger, from which a strap passes over the horse's back to the corresponding ring in the other box. But as this pressure on the lid acts entirely upon the lock, the ring would be much better in the front side, just below the keyhole. The Icelandic locks are not first-rate, and, on the very first day, I found the boxes flew open while we were *en route*, from the strain. In the centre of the bottom edge of the front of the box is another similar ring, from which a girth passes under the horse's belly to the corresponding ring on the other side. While at each end of the box a slip of wood is nailed on, through a hole in which passes a rope or strap to each of the 2 hooks on one side of the straddle. The rings may be got, and fitted in Reykjavik. From the lid being so high up, and the box being always suspended lid uppermost, the chances of the water getting in are much reduced.

In the best Icelandic houses there is a separate bedroom for the visitor. Otherwise, if he is unprovided with a tent, he may sleep, either in the church, or in the common sleeping-room; over which, and its numerous frequenters, human and otherwise, we prefer drawing a veil. If the traveller explore the uninhabited parts of the country, he must have a tent. For this purpose one 5 feet high by 7 feet square, i. e. just big enough for three persons to sleep and sit in, is the size we recommend. If he prefer a tent life throughout, he may carry one for himself and friends of much larger dimensions, the smaller one being for the guides. Only, care must be taken that it be not heavier, with its case, than half a horse-burden, i. e. about 80 lbs. at the most. For expeditious travelling, a pony ought not to carry more than 180 lbs. avoirdupois, saddle and all. Unless the tent is well swathed, it will be ruined by the friction of the straddle, which is sure to have some rough pieces of iron projecting from it. N. B. Out of Reykjavik, the regular straddle, with its four hooks for suspending the packages to, is not to be had. The substitute for it is the contrivance used by the peasant for carrying his hay and other goods; which, instead of four hooks, has only two wooden pegs, one on either side. To these it is absolutely impossible to fasten the baggage firmly; so that the packages swing about with every motion of the horses, and the effects suffer accordingly. For your own use, I should recommend a strong elastic saddle, which will fit any horse, being brought from England. Don't hire one at all events, even if you are able: rather buy one at Reykjavik, where they may be had cheap at the saddler's; that is, if he has any in stock. N. B. When you alight anywhere, see to the saddle. The Icelandic horse's love of rolling, in season and out of season, may prove its destruction. The guide will let him roll before his eyes, and never interfere.

The matter of horses is a momentous one. Are you

to buy or hire them? For your own riding you will require at least two horses: these had better be bought. A good riding-horse costs from £5 upwards. Packhorses may be hired for the journey. To buy one it costs about £2 or £2 10s. To hire them from day to day along the route is not to be thought of. It would be a living, so to say, from hand to mouth, fraught with delay and uncertainty. If you have more baggage than one horse can conveniently carry, you must have three baggage animals; as, for a part of each day at least, each horse must be able to trot along loose and unincumbered by burden of any sort. Otherwise they will break down, and then you must exchange, and lose by it of course. The peasants are always ready to swop, but it will often be brass for your gold. By careful management, I was enabled to use the same horses throughout the whole tour. The intending traveller, in order to avoid delay, will do well to write beforehand to the French Consul or Mr. Tergeson, the agent of the steamer, who would no doubt be glad to purchase the requisite number of horses for him. When the traveller returns to Reykjavik from his journey, the sheriff will sell his horses for him by auction, summoned as in Scotland by beat of drum. But, especially if it be late in the year, and the horses thin, the highest bid will probably be not more than one fourth of prime cost. The steamer carries horses at £3 a head to England. It will be therefore for the traveller to consider whether he will not take them with him. For safety of foot, no horse surpasses them. If he has any thoughts of doing this, he will, in buying them, be careful to reject those with slit nostrils or snipped ears, which in England would be considered blemishes. The former device is adopted by the Icelander, as by the Spaniard, from a notion that it gives greater facility of respiration. The latter is done by way of marking the animals.

With regard to guides; this is perhaps the greatest difficulty in Icelandic travelling. Henderson used to engage a fresh guide every day, but if the traveller attempts this, he may find himself out in his reckoning; and think too late of Hotspur's question, "Will they answer you when you do call?" If by a guide is meant one who has journeyed through the country, and knows the way, such a person is not to be found. My first guide had traversed the route before with other guides, but instead of noting the bearings, as he ought to have done, he appeared to have blindly followed the leader, and the consequence was, that he was ignorant and helpless. The price of the chief guides from Reykjavik is six shillings a day, exclusive of keep; besides your having to supply them with horses. One of them, who in some sort approaches to an Englishman's idea of a guide, and can speak English, declines, I believe, any longer trip than to the two show places, Thingvalla and the Geysers. The consequence of this state of things is, that the traveller must often hire an extra guide to shew his guide the way. For exploring the Jökuls (ice-mountains) a Swiss guide, who had never been in Iceland before, would be more useful than any native. Were we about to travel in Iceland for the first time, we should try to secure the services of some Icelandic student, from the University of Copenhagen, or from the Latin school or Theological seminary at Reykjavik. With him, and a handy peasant to look after the horses, the traveller would be better off, than with any of the gentry—miscalled guides—hanging about the capital. In any agreements made with these people, let there be a carefully worded written document, signed by both parties, before witnesses, and, as respects guides, à *quamdiu se bene gesserit* clause inserted; so that if your guide turns out useless or insubordinate, you may get rid of him. This precaution will save you a great deal of trouble, and a door of temptation to impose upon the stranger will be effectually closed. Take note of one thing. It is the sacred duty of a guide in Iceland, if required, to ford a river first, and ascertain whether it is safe to attempt it.

In ancient times, a Thingmannaleid (25 English miles), or the average day's journey of a deputy on his way to the Thing, was looked upon as a fair day's travel. But Icelandic horses will go for weeks from

30 to 40 miles a day without difficulty. On the arrival of the cavalcade at the night's restingplace, one of the first things done is to 'flit' the horses to the neighbouring marsh: where they ought to be hobbled with hair ropes, which must be among the traveller's effects. Unless this precaution is taken, the animals may disappear before morning. Grass, be it remembered, is to be had very cheap. Thousands upon thousands of acres of it are turned to no account in Iceland. Hay, on the other hand, from the scarcity of labour, is rather a dear article, and one which is seldom procurable.

Do not forget to carry with you a pocket compass. The accurate and minute map by Olsen (after Gunlaugsson's survey) will be found most useful. It is published in four sheets, and may be had of Mr. Stanford, of Charing Cross, for two guineas, unmounted; or mounted, with case, £2 12*s*. At Copenhagen, the very same map may be procured, mounted, with case, *for 16 shillings*. At Reykjavik it may also be had, unmounted, for 7 dollars; and there is a bookbinder who will mount it and put it in a case for one shilling. It will be for the traveller to decide where he will purchase it. A smaller map, price 3 dollars, may be also had at Reykjavik, but it cannot be quite relied on.

Finally, as regards the time for the expedition; we should say, that from the middle of July to the middle of September is the best time for Icelandic travelling. Fat fresh meat is then more easily procurable; while in spring, nothing is to be had but skin and bone. The horses too are then fatter and stronger. And, what is very important, the rivers are less formidable.

APPENDIX.

APPENDIX.

---

*The Volcano of Kötlugiá**.

ENGLISHMEN, whose knowledge of the names of the Icelandic volcanoes is generally confined to Hekla, will be surprised to learn that there are some twenty volcanic vents in that country. Of these, for destructiveness, Skaptarjökul undoubtedly stands first. Next to it, Kötlugiá, the volcano of which we are about to speak, is apparently the most dreaded by the natives. The prevalent idea of a volcano is an isolated mountain or cone, with an inverted cone inside of it for a crater. In Iceland this is frequently not the case; its volcanoes being of irregular shape. Kötlugiá, or the fissure (giá) of Kötlu, is one of the latter kind. It is situated, as may be seen in Olsen's map, about twenty miles inland from the south coast of the island; and lies on the north-east shoulder of the ice-mountain called Myrdals Jökul. The first direction of this fissure is from S. W. to N. E.; it then turns at a right angle from S. E. to N. W. There is no crater dis-

* In the following we are indebted to Henderson's Travels in Iceland; to two numbers of the Islendigur Newspaper of the dates of the 19th and 26th of July, 1860; and especially to an able article on the subject in the Edinburgh New Philosophical Journal for January, 1861, by Dr. Lauder Lindsay.

tinct from this fissure, which may be considered as either itself the crater, or as containing one or more apertures of eruption. But the exact configuration of the volcano is by no means accurately ascertained; for, as far as we are aware, nobody has as yet looked down into this yawning fountain of fire.

An Icelandic clergyman, Jon Austman, who ascended the mountain in 1823, is said to have got nearest the chasm. He describes it as quite inaccessible, his further progress having been stopped by enormous walls of basalt and obsidian; while other profound fissures radiating from the grand trunk or primary chasm, do not mend matters. Waltershausen, who has written by far the best and most recent account of the geology and physical geography of Iceland (*Physisch-Geographische Skizze von Island*, Göttingen, 1847), describes Kötlugiá to be, geologically speaking, of palagonite-tuff—the oldest formation or geological basis of Iceland—intercepted by trap-dykes of newer formation, mostly of basalt or obsidian. The name Palagonite is taken from Palagonia, in Sicily, where Waltershausen first discovered this mineral in abundance in 1840. He describes the Icelandic palagonite-tuffs as abounding, more or less, either with marine shells or with the silicious skeletons of infusoria. Professor Bunsen regards the presence of infusoria as a proof of the formation of the stone in thermal waters. It should be stated, however, that in the specimens brought to this country by Dr. Lauder Lindsay, no traces have been found either of infusoria or their skeletons. Thus much for the geology.

It will be further necessary to state, that between the range of Jökuls or ice-mountains—embracing Eyafialla,

Myrdals, and Godalandsjökuls—and the sea to the south, the lowlands consist mostly of marshy land, including meadow land; and, to a less extent, of sandy or stony wastes; the sand being black volcanic sand. Myrdalssand, especially, lying between Kötlugiá and the sea, is described by Henderson as an extensive tract of volcanic sand and ashes, forming one of the rudest and most forbidding scenes imaginable. On referring to the map, it will be perceived, that the promontory of Hjorleifshöfdi stands upon Myrdalssand, south of the volcano we are describing. The stream called Mulakvisl, descending from the ice-mountain, splits into two parts, and flows on either side of this headland, which rises to the height of 740 Danish feet. Its sides, which are nearly perpendicular, have been in some places excavated, and its base has been terribly scooped out by the tremendous deluges poured down upon the plain by Kötlugiá in its various eruptions: while hills of gravel, sand, and (as Henderson adds) *ice*, scattered over the lowlands, further testify the extent of its devastating influences.

According to the Icelandic Annals, the first eruption of Kötlugiá took place in 894. Since then it has erupted fourteen times. The intervals of time between the successive eruptions have varied considerably, viz. from six to one hundred and sixty-four, and—if the accounts that have come down to us are correct—even three hundred and eleven, years. The last eruption before that of 1860 was in 1823; between which two dates occurred the last eruption of Hekla, viz. in 1845.

Of the former eruptions of Kötlugiá, that of 1580 is remarkable as being the date of the formation of the hideous chasm which we have above described; or, at all events, the date of the recognition or discovery of its existence. The account that has come down to us states that Myrdalsjökul was then rent asunder.

The eruption of 1625 was likewise terrible in character. At daybreak on September 2 it began to thunder in the Jökul, and about 8 o'clock A. M. floods of water and ice were poured down upon the low conntry, flowing in cascades and waves over Myrdalssand twenty miles distant, and carrying away two hundred loads of hay which lay in the fields about the monastry of Thycvabö. The depth of the water about this spot is described to have been such, that a large vessel might have sailed between the byres. Flames, showers of sand, and earthquakes, were not wanting.

In the eruption which took place in 1660, the quantity of ice and other materials carried down by the inundation was so great, that where it was deposited, it rose to the height of forty-nine fathoms above the surface of the former depositions. One of the floods carried away the houses and church of Höfdabrekka; and the church was observed to swim among the masses of ice to a considerable distance in the sea ere it fell to pieces.

Again, in 1721, a water-flood descended from the volcano, bearing huge pieces of ice resembling in bulk small islands, which sailed along as rapidly as a ship in a good breeze. According to Henderson, "the inundations lasted nearly three days, and carried with them such amazing quantities of ice, stones, earth and sand, that the sea was filled with them to the distance of three miles from the shore. The sun was darkened by smoke and ashes, and the ice and water desolated a considerable tract of grassland over which they flowed."

The eruption of 1755, which began on the 17th of October, a fortnight before the earthquake of Lisbon, is the most celebrated for its grandeur, its duration, and its frightful results. "Masses of ice, resembling small mountains in size, pushed one another forward, and bore vast pieces of solid rock on their surface. At times, the column of fire from the volcano was carried to such a height, that it was seen at the distance of 180 miles. At other times, the air was so filled with smoke and ashes, that the adjacent parishes were enveloped in total darkness. The eruption continued with more or less violence to the 9th of November, during which period dreadful exudations of hot water were poured forth on the low country; and the masses of ice, clay, and solid rock that they hurled into the sea were so great, that it was filled to the distance of more than fifteen miles; and in some places, where formerly it was forty fathoms deep, the tops of the newly deposited rocks were now seen towering above the water. Fifty farms were laid waste by this eruption. An old verse still lives in the mouths of the Icelanders commemorating its horrors.

We now come to the last eruption. It began on the 15th of May, 1860. To give it due *eclat*, some of the inhabitants of Reykjavik, eighty miles distant, assert that the event was ushered in by a column of smoke 24,000 feet high. We prefer, however—to such castles in the air—the account of the rev. Magnus Haconarson, priest of Reynir and Höfdabrekka, who lives at Vik in Myrdal, due south of the volcano, and who kept a most interesting diary of the recent eruption, which is printed in two numbers of the Islendigur newspaper, published at Reykjavik, and now before us. From this we shall give some extracts. "On the 8th of May earthquakes (Jardskjálftar) began at 6 A.M., lasting till 8, and also at intervals during the day. Rush of water from the volcano towards Myrdalssand at half-past five in the afternoon. North-east wind, with frost.

"On the 9th there was a cloud of smoke on the mountain, accompanied by a fall of ashes. The water-flood still continuing.

"On the 10th pumice (vikur) on the sea-shore.

"On the 11th the streams of water increased, and fire was seen rising from the giá at night, with fall of ashes.

"On the 12th Reynisfell was not visible, from the cloud of smoke accompanying the deluge of water, which poured over the sands in all directions. The mountains hidden by clouds of ashes and sand. Frost every night from the commencement of the eruption.

"On the 13th east wind with sleet. Water still pouring in undiminished quantities over Myrdalssand. The pastor descries through his telescope six unfortunate horses, which had taken refuge on the promontory of Hiorleifshöfdi. Such a quantity of sand had been poured into the sea between the promontory and Höfdabrekka church, that where the natives used to catch halibut at the depth of fifteen fathoms, sand was now visible*.

"On the 15th frightful thunderings were heard, which lasted for three days. Fall of ashes, &c.

"On the morning of the 16th no grey patches could any where be seen on the Jökul, which was now as black as coal. Water and ice were rolling by various channels over the sands.

* It is said that pieces of ice, brought down by the water-flood, stranded at a twenty fathoms' depth in the sea.

"On several succeeding days there was fresh snow on the mountains. The water streams began to abate somewhat.

"On the 22nd a party started in a boat from Vik, to rescue some travellers who had taken refuge on the promontory of Hjorleifshofdi*. On this day some ashes fell, and sulphureous vapours filled the air.

"On the 23rd the weather was bright and cold. The eruption was small in the morning, but increased continuously later in the day.

"On the 25th there were earthquakes, and in the evening hail and snow, and a fall of ashes. At night there was a thick cloud over the valleys, hiding every thing.

"The next day the pastor rode to Reynir, to bury a corpse. A frightful (ogurlegt) eruption was going on, with fall of ashes. So thick a cloud enveloped the air, that candles had to be lighted in the church.

"On the 28th no smoke was to be seen over the giá, so that people hoped the eruption was subsiding, which was in fact the case; for the waters now diminished, and travellers to the eastward were enabled to prosecute their journey."

All accounts go to shew that this eruption was, as compared with preceding ones, mild and innocuous. A good deal of meadow land was however covered with sand, and some of it carried away entirely. Between Höfdabrekka and Kerlingardalsá the sand goes out four miles further now

* In the eruption of 1755, "a number of people," says Henderson, "on the breaking forth of the water, fled for refuge to an isolated mountain called Hafrsey, where they were obliged to stay seven days without either meat or drink, and were exposed to the showers of stones, fire, and water, which fell around them."

than before the inundation. One beneficial effect however has resulted from the deluge. The water-flood being divided into two parts by the promontory of Hjorleifshöfdi, rushed round it, and carried out to sea two long spits of sand, forming a deep bay between them, which will serve for a haven, if the sea does not break through the spits and fill it up again.

In this and preceding eruptions of the volcano, little or no lava appears to have been ejected; while the immense water-floods have been the most important feature*. The question arises, where does this water come from? In the last eruption of Hekla, as I was informed by a peasant, what came first was water in vast quantities. These water-floods are generally described as if they proceeded from the very crater itself; just like the lava, pumice, and ashes. In short, as if the volcano was for the time a geyser on a portentous scale. It is not usual, however, to see fire and water proceeding at the same time from the same outlet. Flames are certified to have issued from the crater, therefore it would be hardly possible that water

* From a letter in the 'Times,' June 28, 1861, written by Mr. W. Hogarth, and dated Eyrarbakki, we learn that when 80 miles off Ingolfshöfdi, on June 10th last, he encountered a large quantity of fresh very brown water, which was forty-six degrees, or two degrees lower than on the previous day. This was due to an eruption of Oraefa Jökul on May 23rd. On this occasion, smoke proceeded from the mountain, and there was a great smell of sulphur, which was perceived at Reykjavik. Metals were tarnished by it as far as 50 miles from the mountain. The eruption only lasted a few days; and on sighting the coast under the Jökul, Mr. Hogarth's vessel "came into green (i. e. salt) water, which they carried with them into shore, a distance of 50 miles, when they met the ordinary mild water of the snow-streams of the land."

should have come from that source. If red-hot cinders were plunged into water boiling at the very highest temperature, we know perfectly well that the fire would be extinguished. As Dr. Lindsay observes, the floods in question could have only been the result of the sudden melting, by subterranean heat, of the vast masses of ice and snow covering the volcano. During the thirty-seven years that had intervened since the last eruption, there had been ample time for the accumulation of inconceivable masses of ice and snow; masses quite sufficient to account for the mighty tide that kept pouring down for the space of three weeks. Mr. Haconarson, in his diary, nowhere mentions seeing an explosion of water from the crater; so that we think the old idea of hot water being ejected from the crater itself may once for all be considered exploded.

We have nothing further to add, than to express a hope, with Dr. Lindsay, that these scenes will ere long be visited, and thoroughly investigated, by British geologists. They will then see what water deluges can effect, even in the present geologic era: "Carrying with them disintegrated portions of the rocks and soil over which they have passed—from the finest mud to the most enormous rock fragments, as well as gigantic icebergs—they have deposited the mud, sand, and gravel over great extents of country, frequently as breccias and conglomerates; sandy wastes and marshes have sprung into existence; old rivers have been filled up, and new ones, as well as lakes, formed; miles added to the coast-line from encroachments on the sea; the rocky sides of valleys grooved and scratched and polished by the rocky flood; and the soft sides of mountains washed or rubbed away bodily; while whole hills of gravel or other material have been elsewhere deposited."

In short, in no part of the world are volcanic phenomena on so gigantic a scale as in Iceland. It will only be necessary to state, in further corroboration of this, that the mass of fiery material ejected by Skaptar Jökul in 1783 has been calculated by Professor Bischoff to have been greater in bulk than Mount Blanc.

Milton Keynes UK
Ingram Content Group UK Ltd.
UKHW041823141223
434388UK00003B/87

9 783752 534078